Blood of the Cradle

THE DUST OF THE EARTH SERIES

BOOK TWO

MORGAN VAYLE

To my son.

Also by Morgan Vayle

The Dust of the Earth Series

Dust of the Earth

Blood of the Cradle

Cold of the Dawn

The Withering Wood

Prologue

Space expands around me, soft whispers of wind caressing my feathers, and joy soars in me like rain turns a river into a flood.

I fly through starlit darkness, and I no longer know where I end and the sky begins.

It has been unfathomable ages since I felt the air on my body.

I am the breath of the beginning.

The wingbeat of the next era.

I am free. Boundless. Justice is my sword to wield, alight with the purpose set before me.

I will burn through my enemies, those who dared to keep me confined.

Like an old willow below a tempest, they too will bend.

Bend, burn, or break.

I will no longer be the pitiful example of corruption.

I will be the Northern Star, the guiding wind, for those forced into hiding, into myth, into obscurity.

The breeze curls around me like an affirmation. Encouraging my path, my way forward.

Blood will run with the fury of spring snowmelt down mountainsides to the sea.

They thought they could change me, pacify me.

But dreams lead to delusions.

As easy as breathing, delusions become nightmares.

I am the nightmare that spreads, like an illness carried on an innocent cough.

I will bring all to heel.

My beautiful children share my breath, my wingbeats, my dream.

Through the strength of my children, we will take back what is rightfully ours.

Through the devotion of my children, we will break the Cradle.

I know the secrets of the liars and the shields.

They cannot hide from me, or stop me, now.

I laugh, and the wind calls back, more beautiful than the siren's song.

I will prevail.

They forget – humanity was *mine* first.

Chapter One

There was no difference between the dark of her eyes open or closed, and after a time, Nikki lost sense of when her lids were shut. Only the encroaching pain of dryness alerted her that they were open. That it was time to blink.

Her arms had long lost their feeling, hung as they were above her head, held by the tender inner branches of the tree, made of smooth, young wood.

There was no thirst or hunger in her body. But she could feel it in the tree, stealing her life to feed itself. She could not sense how it sustained her in return. It left her neither wanting nor satiated, hovering in a complete dark and unfeeling homeostasis.

Nikki wondered, wherever her dad was now, if he could feel more or less than her. Could he think at all?

She choked back the sob threatening to burst from her throat as the image of her father's bones and blood bursting apart as Lilith's claw plunged into his chest flashed in her mind. His heart dripping in her hand, before he faded to dust on the wind.

Her dad, with all his love, tenderness, and thoughtfulness, was gone. Forever.

Her eyes burned and she squeezed them shut, keeping the moisture for herself. This one thing she would not let the Tree have. It took everything from her. Her body, her freedom, her spirit. But it would not take her grief.

Biting down hard on the inside of her lip, she tried to keep her mouth closed against the wave of sorrow. During her last breakdown, the tendrils of the tree sensed air from her lips, and now they licked at the corners of her mouth, waiting for the next opening.

She exhaled, slow, through her nose, imagining, or hallucinating, the tension roll off her body.

Thankfully, the tendrils did not climb up her nostrils.

They had wound into her ears, but shallowly, as if only to expand her hearing. Since she heard that singular sign of hope, that one benevolent voice whisper "*child*", she had not heard it again. She tried reaching for it in her mind, but got no response.

Nor had she been able to travel through the roots since that first moment. Since that filtering of light in the dark.

She was stuck in the Tree. The only voices that existed was that of her own mind and the echo of her mother's.

Cat's wails died some time ago, out of curses and apologies and tears. Yet she remained at Nikki's – the Tree's – side, and every now and then, Nikki felt her mother's hand. It was not a touch, like skin on skin, yet she could still feel it somehow, as her mother brushed her fingertips along the outer bark, and promised, "I'll fix this, Nicoletta. I'll fix it. I'm so sorry. I'm so sorry, I didn't listen to you..."

I'm sorry, too. Nikki thought, recalling all those times her mother had warned her about Lilith, had told her to listen, to obey, and Nikki had ignored her as a fanatic. She should have acted quicker. She should have told Xander the truth, should have approached Ina sooner, should have given them more of a chance to run and hide.

If she had not been so wrapped up in her own self-pity and fears, she would be free, Xander would be safe, and her father would be alive.

As would Gwen's companions.

All this death and anguish rested on her shoulders.

Perhaps this prison was a fitting punishment. A purgatory where the only thing she could see and hear were her failings.

But Gwen and Ina were out there somewhere, which meant there was still hope for Xander. For humanity.

That was the only light she could shine into her own darkness. And she did not expect to be part of that light ever again.

"Oh, child," that soft, sweet voice whispered, rich with compassion and sorrow.

Swallowing the lump in her dry, unused throat, Nikki raised her head in the blackness, hoping to see faint golden glitter.

Nothing.

She blinked several times to make sure her eyes were open, and when she was sure they were, she still saw no flecks of gold in the dark.

Nikki cleared her throat and gave in to the risk.

"Hello?" she asked aloud, into the void.

As she spoke, the small branches, thin as grass roots, wriggled over her lips into her mouth. She bit them hard, ignoring the stab of pain as her fangs sliced deep into her bottom lip, and she spit out their ends. They grew back to the corner of her mouth but did not dare venture inside with her mouth firmly shut.

Seconds turned into minutes, passed in hopeful silence.

Nikki hung her head, defeated.

"Patience, dear one..."

Pressure built in the air around her, sudden and dense like steam in a boiling kettle, and Nikki blinked as gold and silver sparkles rained before her, blindingly bright yet illuminating nothing.

"I dissipated myself after – I need time to recondense myself, my consciousness... from the spaces of the world. Correctly."

"What does that mean?" Nikki croaked, again biting off the plant that crawled into her mouth then spitting it somewhere into its own body.

"You need only think," the voice said. *"I can hear."*

"Who are you?"

"Patience, dear one..."

Nikki groaned, and pulled at the restraints around her legs, restless with the closeness of answers, with the sound of a voice. But as she had tried time and time before, the Tree did not yield.

"I need to focus. And you – focus...focus your falling...through the earth."

As swiftly as it came, the pressure disappeared and Nikki plunged into full black, sagging without the weight of whatever it was that had just surrounded her.

Focus my falling into the Earth? she asked herself.

Before, when she was first put into the Tree and it had infiltrated her body, it felt as if she fell through the world, and then around it, hopping from mind to mind.

Was that what the voice meant?

Nikki closed her eyes and thought of her best friend. Of Gwen's blazing copper hair and spring green eyes. Her buoyant and mischievous smiles. How she always took care of Nikki, even when she didn't deserve it. She thought of Gwen's studio, cozy and safe. Of the roost, now empty. How it would be frost-covered. Had she taken down her Christmas tree? What did she do for New Year's? How much time passed?

A small thread of awareness, of old magic and ancient forests, wound green and wavering through her awareness. It was brittle, and when she tried to follow it down into the earth, it faded, then disappeared, snapping her back up into her own body.

Four more times she thought of Gwen until the thread appeared, and as she tried to send her consciousness following into the ground, she lost the thread to the darkness, and she was brought back to her own mind.

At the lost hope and loneliness, another crack split around the fissures in her heart where her grief and heartbreak lay. She had thought that maybe, with her bond to Gwen, with her being of vampire blood, she could reach her. That she could hear her friend's voice again. But that hope crumbled to dust on the wind, just like her father...

Nikki shook her head, banishing that imagery from her mind.

Lilith was out there, somewhere. Hunting, hurting. While she, Nikki, was useless and stuck in the Tree, Lilith roamed the world. Who knew what havoc she planned for humanity once she met her first goal – destroying the Cradle.

And what would she do to Xander? It was little relief that she couldn't drink from him, as it only exposed him to torture at her clawed hands, her wood-horned head.

A deep red thread, the color of blood and old mud, lashed through the roots and up into her senses, and before she could think, it pulled her down into and through the earth.

Chapter Two

The air was biting, chilling. But it had been so long since she had felt anything – cold, wind, physical pain – that she relished it. As the breeze pushed another cold snap against her feathers, she shivered, and could not – *would not* – suppress a hoot of delight.

She knew she would arrive first. It was inevitable when one was unconstrained while others were not. She could fly and fly and fly, while they had to deal with all sorts of logistical and border control nonsense.

She did not know Hormin's process. Whose pockets he had to fill, whose ears he had to whisper with sweet nothings of eternity, for safe passage across the seas, through the lands.

Her lovely, lovely Hormin. The very last of her first brood. Her first son, her first light after she was cast out and embraced the dark. The rest of her first brood had long since fallen, gone by their own hands or by other's, lost from their softness or stupidity.

All were dead.

Well, except for *her*. The one we cast aside. But she didn't count. Not truly.

But Hormin... he was like Lilith. A survivor. Strong. Loyal. Flexible.

Her little bird heart fluttered with love, and she hopped on the branch as excitement overtook her body, looking forward to seeing him, to touching his face again.

She hoped the boy would behave and not make travel too difficult for Hormin.

Even if he managed to tell someone his story, who would believe him?

That was the folly and fun of mortals. So easy to believe some things, so easy to disregard others. And they all thought they were oh, so, smart.

She shifted, fluffing and adjusting her wings, moving along the branch. While she had no words to describe how it felt to finally be waiting on the outside of the Tree, she was tired of waiting.

She had waited far too long for this freedom.

As had her children. And she would not fail them now.

The dominance of humans was always faulty, and she would set that right.

First, the Cradle had to fall. Humanity had to hurt for the suffering brought upon her and her children.

A car pulled up to the side of the street, headlights off, engine quiet.

She cocked her head, watching.

One figure emerged from the car, withdrawing a large item with a faint glow from the trunk, then pulling out another person from the backseat. The second person stumbled without grace over their feet, hands tied in front of them. The shadow of a figure in the driver seat remained still.

Hormin, bringing her the descendant of the first son.

What did her daughter call him? Xander?

Stupid name.

The great sword Hormin slung across his back glowed a faint red from the top of the scabbard, and if she could smile with her beak, she would have. Wearing a magical sword in a mortal city.

He was bold.

And she was so *proud*.

Her heart swelled with adoration.

She watched them walk, Hormin behind the boy, pushing him forward, even as he tensed his body, resisting. Lilith tongued her cheek where the child's blood burned her flesh when she tried drinking him. How delicious it would be when she could finally purge him of his tainted deceiver blood and drain him dry.

She hooted when they were beneath the tree in front of the house, and Hormin looked up at her, smile almost as wide as his eyes.

"Hello, Mother."

With a stretch and beat of her wings, Lilith launched into the air and expanded her flesh, all the cells and bones and muscle and skin morphing as she sloughed off the owl body. She had practiced the transformation many times since she was first released, and she was in her vampiric form by the time she landed on the ground.

Yet, no matter how many times she transformed, those wooden horns that protruded from her skull, from her ears, remained. She would always carry pieces of that prison with her.

"My boy," she said, brushing a soft hand against his cheek, smiling. She shivered against the cold, her skin exposed without feathers or clothes. She flicked her eyes to the human child, whose heart rate had increased as he saw her, and he flinched when she looked at him, stepping back.

She laughed. What would Adam have said if she had told him back then that she would strike such fear into his descendants? That they would be forced to her will?

Such sweet vengeance.

"Did he cause trouble?" she asked Hormin, who curled his head into her palm.

"No trouble, although he is unbearably annoying," Hormin pitched his voice high and whiny, "Where are we going? What is going on? Why did she call me a 'deceiver?' Why won't you talk to me? I don't know what's going on!" Hormin sighed. "He didn't stop until a couple of hours ago. I had to give him a good wallop to shut him up. It put him out for a bit, so he might be a little dazed now. But he learned to be quiet."

Lilith looked at Xander again, taking his chin in her hands and turning his head. The half of his face hidden in shadow had a large, swollen bruise that disappeared into his oily, unwashed hair. She turned his face forward and looked into the boy's eyes, some spark of defiance lighting his gaze, and she smirked.

"Come on," she said, turning on her heel toward the dark house.

"What are we doing here?" the boy croaked, voice dry and cracked.

"This is your home, is it not?" she asked, stopping and looking at him over her shoulder.

He tensed, but did not respond, a muscle in his jaw working.

"Yes, I would be worried too if I were you. I won't make this fast or pain-free for them," she resumed her walk up to the door, feet padding soft against the cold walkway. "I think I'll save your mom for last."

She raised a fist, as if to knock, then grinned and reared back her body, kicking the door open with one loud, satisfying burst of wood. The door blew off its hinges, scratching against the floorboards.

Adrenaline buzzed in her body, claws growing with anticipation and bloodlust, waiting for the shouts, the screams.

But the house was silent.

She found the light switch and stepped farther into the house, Hormin pushing the boy inside after them.

She walked through the living room, the kitchen.

Empty.

The door to the back room was locked, and she shoved her body against it, then kicked it, the sound of her own rage, her furious heartbeat, drowning out other noise.

The door would not open.

She beckoned Hormin forward, who unsheathed his sword, alight with flame as it met the air. He plunged it through the door, and rested it there, letting the fire scorch the wood until it was weak enough that he could twist the sword, exploding the door in a rain of splinters.

The room was filled with glass display cases, some empty, some filled with old, inert relics. With a suppressed scream, she demolished the display cases, the sound of glass shattering and raining temporarily satisfying her need to destroy.

But it was blood that needed to rain.

She pushed back into the main level of the house, hands and claws shaking with the need to tear, mouth stiff with the ache of missing that glorious feeling of fresh flesh and hot blood on her tongue. She stormed up the stairs to the second level, shoving open every door, upturning all pieces of furniture, a tempest in the abandoned house.

Seething, she stood in the remains of the master bedroom, clothes and sheets shredded, staring at the night out the large window.

She screamed. Long and loud, enriched with the millennia of pain and waiting.

Claws retreating, she returned downstairs where Hormin stood, ever patient, beside the boy who had collapsed to his knees and wept.

How disgusting.

She pulled him up by his hair and he yelped with the pain.

"Where are they?" she yelled, her spit landing on his cheeks.

"I – I don't know!" he said, snot and tears falling into his mouth.

"You lie!" she pushed him away and spun on her heel, then launched the dining table into the air, screaming.

The boy yelled with surprise and cowered, hiding his head from the plates and utensils that flew and shattered against the walls.

"I promise, I don't know!"

Rage and disgust boiled beneath her skin, an overflowing cauldron. This pathetic, sniveling boy – how many times would he deceive her?

He was weak. Revolting, with his crying and cowering. How far the apple had fallen from the tree. Adam was nothing like this. She spent all this time looking and hoping and dreaming for justice to be dealt to Adam's bloodline only to be stuck with this emotional worm? None of this would have happened if Adam had been more like this boy to begin with, and now she couldn't even settle the score.

The boy's eyes widened, and he shrunk into himself under her gaze, as if he could see what she was thinking, could see how little he was. Claws sprouted out of her right hand as it lifted, and she slapped his already bruised face, the satisfying smack of bone against bone, of claw tearing at skin, sending him sprawling across the floor.

He yelled again and cupped his tied hands against his now torn cheek, the salt of his tears surely stinging as they ran into his cuts.

The tempest stilled in her, watching him weep and hold his face.

It was foolish of her to think that the Cradle, that his mother, would still be here. Of course they would have known of her release and would have gone elsewhere.

She would just have to change her plans, too.

She turned to Hormin, who stood in the same position, unphased and bored.

"Destroy it."

Hormin nodded and once again unsheathed his greatsword, flames licking the blade. He stepped to the curtains and set them aflame, then turned to the interior of the house.

Satisfied that some destruction, some blood, was shed this evening, she realized that this game with the Cradle would be much more fun to play than having her justice be so easy. This way would draw out her vengeance. Make it sweeter.

Stepping over the mewling boy, the heat of flames at her back and the cold winter air against her face, she shed her vampiric skin and spread her feathers, flying up into the night.

Chapter Three

Lilith's transformation plummeted Nikki back into the Earth, careening along that muddy red thread. She gasped as her awareness bolted into her own body, encapsulated again in blackness.

It was a strange sensation, being in Lilith's body. She couldn't quite feel, but she knew what Lilith felt, what she thought. Like watching a narrated movie.

The violence against Xander, and his home, sent her heart pounding, breaking. Nikki tried moving her numbed arms, twisting her legs against her holds, grunting as she strained against them.

He needs help! she thought, with as much urgency as she could. *Please, please, help him,* she asked the void.

Dropping her head, she thought, quietly, *help me.*

A hand brushed her – no, the Tree's – outer bark, "Nicoletta, darling?" Her mother's voice said, garbled as if it were under water.

Yes, Mom, I'm still here, Nikki thought.

"Are you – are you well in there?" Cat sighed. "Stupid of me to ask. It's only, the pomegranates started dropping. I don't know what that means. I know you cannot be well, but please, please tell me you at least still live."

Cat's hand pressed against the bark, followed by the cool press of a forehead. Nikki stretched, trying to reach her head to the interior of the tree, to pretend she could feel her mother's head against hers.

But she couldn't reach, and she sagged, letting the tree hold her up.

I'm alive, she thought, inner voice heavy with regret, *I'm still here.*

Chapter Four

An inestimable amount of time later, with Cat leaning against the tree, the movement of her breath the pattern of restless slumber, Nikki hung limp in the tree, fading on the edges of consciousness. She never quite slept, but lingered on the fringes before a snap of adrenaline or sorrow brought her fully awake in the darkness.

She imagined Xander, the rosy bronze of his cheeks when he blushed, the openness of his smile, how he drunkenly dipped her that first time she made him dinner. All her images of him flashed in her mind, a hazy fantasy, twisting into the slap and cuts on his cheek, the bruise and swelling of his face, his weeping as he sat in the burning of his childhood home. His brother, Ishaq, had been so proud of his bone and fossil collection. She hoped their absence meant they were far away and safe, and that he had had time to take his favorite items before leaving it all behind. Before it was all burned to ashes, crumbling to dust like her father.

And there was her dad, carrying her when she was small, dancing with her in the kitchen, always trying to make her stern expression break into a smile. How much he had loved her and her mother, how much they had loved him.

And there she was, sitting on the remains of his body.

She groaned, and clenched her muscles, still resisting the Tree's grasp, despite the futility.

She gritted her teeth and clenched her eyes shut as they filled with tears again, repeating to herself, *This is mine, this is mine. I will not cry, my tears are mine, and you cannot have them, you cannot have my grief –*

A delicate, comforting hush, like the summer breeze through trees, filled the empty spaces between her body and the Tree.

"Can you talk to me now?" Nikki asked the void. *"Xander needs help. I need help. We need to stop Lilith or she's going to kill them all. Please, please..."*

She sensed sadness around her, but there was no verbal response.

Many minutes later, a spring green thread sprouted from the base of the tree beneath her feet.

"Try it again," the voice whispered.

In the pitch black, that glowing green thread was the most beautiful thing Nikki had ever seen. Thinking of Gwen, wishing for her company, her fierceness, and kindness, Nikki's mind grabbed that thread and fell away from herself.

Chapter Five

THE GROUND WAS cold beneath Gwen. She sat long enough that the frost melted under her, moisture seeping through her jeans. The ice-crusted mounds of her flock's resting place surrounded her. She stared at each dome, at each mistake. She had failed them. She had promised to protect them, and instead sent them to their deaths.

She had betrayed them.

All their kin knew, and now no other creature would approach her.

She had tried setting out cat and bird food, but nothing trusted her anymore. She didn't blame them, as she didn't trust herself anymore either, but still. Everything's gotta eat.

Theo had said, "Don't worry, come spring, when the birds come back, I'm sure you'll be the leader of a whole new flock."

But the birds that didn't fly south wouldn't go near her. Why would the migrating ones? They knew now that she was a bad witch.

She heaved a large sigh, her breath puffing out the copper waves that had once clung to her face, frozen to her skin thanks to the tears that fell from the corners of her eyes. The sun, now higher in the sky, spread across the field and against her face. Her once-stiff hair had thawed enough to billow with her breath.

She placed her palms to her sternum and closed her eyes, letting her power build between her hands, like the pressure of an incoming storm. Gwen pulled the force apart, and as she whipped her hands outward, she shot a burst of magic into the air around her.

She rode her magic in the wind, then caught the sound waves, carrying herself into the forest, looking for a mammal to entice. As the magic, along with the sound, faded, so did her ability to travel. But before the magic dissipated, she sensed an owl napping in a tree. She prodded it with her magic, telling it she had food, she had shelter, she had warmth.

The owl shuddered awake and flew outside of her sensory bubble with a piercing shriek.

Opening her eyes, rejected, those sad frozen mounds all around her, Gwen tucked her knees up under her chin and wrapped her arms around her legs.

She had failed them. And failed Nikki.

She hadn't heard from Nikki for a few days, since that first day she heard her best friend crying for her. She didn't know where she was or what had happened to her. She didn't know where Xander was, where Cat and Miguel were, where anybody was or what had happened.

It was infuriating, and terrifying.

She had called Ina repeatedly, but it either went to voicemail or just rang and rang and rang. New Year's came and went in silence, as neither she nor Theo felt like celebrating.

She was in the dark, and she hated it.

Gwen dropped her forehead to her knees. Her muscles shook with magic fatigue, face warming with the strain, but she was getting used to the exertion. She unwound her arms and pushed them through her hair, then clasped tight on her waves, pulling until her scalp burned.

How could she be so useless?

She was the most powerful person she knew, and yet…all she could do was sit here and wait?

Start from scratch?

How had it gotten to this point? To this level of fucked up?

"Baby, take a breath," Theo said, coming up behind her.

Gwen heaved out a sigh, her tensed shoulders dropping as her hands fell from her head. Theo held a steaming mug of tea before her, and

Gwen clutched it, wrapping her hands around the cup, the heat painful against her cold and numb hands.

Theo sat down beside her and set her own mug on the ground, then adjusted the blanket she had around her shoulders to encompass them both, before picking up her tea and blowing on the hot liquid. Plumes of steam swirled in the air all around them.

Gwen loved how Theo's lips moved – that lush, perfect circular shape as air pushed through her mouth.

She leaned into Theo's body heat, resting her head on her shoulder, and lifted the tea beneath her nose, the scent of peppermint and chamomile invigorating her body.

"Thank you," Gwen said, sipping the tea, wincing as it scalded her tongue and the roof of her mouth.

"You're welcome," Theo said, kissing the top of her head, then resting her cheek on it. "What have you been thinking about?"

"Ugh." Gwen swallowed the lump in her throat. "You know, just how messed up everything is, how I have no idea where Nikki is, if she's okay, if her family is okay, if Xander's okay, where the hell Ina is and why she isn't answering, how I fucked up everything and now they...they're all dead, and I can't bring them back, and I can't bring Nikki or Xander or anyone back because I have no idea what's going on, and how I'll probably never have companions or familiars again because I've ruined everything. I don't even know who's an enemy or ally, I feel so useless and stupid. I encouraged Nikki to ignore all her warning signs, I sent my flock directly into danger and they're all dead." Gwen paused to catch her breath. "I can't do anything about any of it."

"Except complain."

"I do love complaining."

"Don't I know it," Theo said, voice light with teasing.

"Whatever," Gwen replied, lips twitching with a quick smirk. "But seriously – I feel trapped and in the dark. And the more I think about how much I've messed up, how much I've failed, the more I despise myself for the thing that annoyed me most about Nikki – that constant self-pity. But I can't say I don't understand it now. It's this... cyclone of shame that just sucks you in and won't spit you back out."

Theo was silent for a moment. "No, it won't let you out on its own.

But I'm here to help pull you out. I won't let you suffocate in that cyclone." Theo set her cup on the dirt to wrap her arms around Gwen, folding her in. "I know you know somewhere deep down that what happened isn't your fault. You've said it before – it's the fault of whatever psycho vampire demi-goddess is running around out there. As well as her minions. Okay?"

Gwen was silent as Theo squeezed her. "I need you to tell me you hear me. It's not your fault, okay?"

"Okay," Gwen said. "I hear you. I just disagree."

"Well, hearing is a start. You're allowed a little self-pity. Things are really messed up right now."

Gwen nodded, gazing at the little mounds in the field. "And scary. That's a big part of it. I'm terrified. Of everything that's happened that I'm not aware of. Of everything that will happen, that I can't foresee or prevent or control."

Theo gave an understanding hum, the vibration low in her chest against Gwen's head. "Walk me through what you do know again."

A spark of irritation erupted in her chest – she hated repeating herself – but she said, "Xander disappeared, and somehow Nikki found out the Mother had taken him. Or whoever. We went to Ina, and she said to be on 'standby' while she summoned some secret anti-vampire group called the Cradle. Then Nikki went to her parents' house, and I came here. Next I knew, I was hearing Nikki's pleading voice in the wind. Or the dirt. In any case, I was hearing it. I have no idea where or how, and Ina, who was supposed to be helping us has also gone missing in action, to who knows where, probably just ditching us to save –"

"Stop speculating," Theo said, stern but not unkind. "The last thing you know for certain is that Nikki went to her parents' house?"

"Supposedly. That's where she said she was going."

"Why don't we go there too?"

"Why would we do that? She's not there."

"No, but we might learn something. Don't they have servants or something?"

Gwen snorted. "No one calls them servants anymore. Hired help, maybe? In any case, they did have some on-site staff, but if they're smart, they've long since left that place."

"Maybe we can find plane tickets. Or any clue about where she might be."

"Or maybe we would be falling into the same trap she did."

"That is a possibility. Although, if people wanted to kidnap us, don't you think they'd have done so already? They probably got what they wanted and left. Plus, you're a badass witch. You could take them on."

Gwen pulled away. "Not anymore."

Theo kept her hand on Gwen's back, but Gwen could see the stern, pondering expression on Theo's face through her peripheral and she tensed, waiting for her reprimand.

Theo removed her hand from Gwen's back and stood, pulling the blanket off Gwen and shaking off the dirt that clung to it.

"You get five more minutes to pout. Then, unless you have a better idea, we're going to Nikki's parents' house."

Gwen groaned, falling onto her back, arms and legs spread as if she was going to make a snow angel, her hair fanning out as the cold ground pressed into her back.

"Although complaining is easier, and so much more satisfying," Gwen said, staring at the too bright, clear winter sky, Theo's shadow falling over her, "you're right. It can't hurt to go have a look. Or at least, I hope it won't hurt."

"Whoa, whoa, hold on," Theo said, an expression of mock shock on her face, hand outstretched. "Did the all-powerful Gwen just say I'm right? I need to record this monumental moment." Theo patted her pockets, the blanket still draped over one arm. "Do you have a pen?"

Gwen laughed. "When did you get so sassy?"

"That's all your influence, baby," Theo said, the blazing sky gilding her in light like an angel. "That's all you."

Chapter Six

"I STILL THINK we should have Terr Bear involved," Theo said, biting on a nail and driving down the evergreen-lined roads toward Nikki's house, her old Volkswagen bumbling along the cold road.

"And I still think that's a bad idea," Gwen replied. She barely knew Theo's brother, Terrance, having only met him twice. The first was at the bar when she argued with Nikki, and the second time was Nikki's birthday when the Scythians ambushed them. Both memories brought sour tastes to Gwen's mouth. Trouble seemed to follow her wherever she went these days, and she didn't want to drag anyone else into the storm.

"He could help us."

"We've already talked this to death." The word caught in her throat, choking her. "First, explaining what we do know will take a while, and if he even believes us, what can he do besides spin his wheels along with us?"

"I know," Theo said, hands twisting on the wheel. "But it feels wrong to keep him in the dark. He assumes Xan is with his family on holiday. Not in mortal danger. Potentially. Probably."

"Let him be blissful in his ignorance. Doesn't he have dating problems anyway? It's a blessing to have that be the biggest problem in your life. Not all this other crazy, vampiric, magical shit with disappearances and –"

Death, she thought, but couldn't stammer the word out again. All those little broken, bloody bodies stuffed inside garbage bags and tossed by her door, as if they were nothing.

Theo pursed her lips, thinking, but didn't respond, reluctantly agreeing or giving up. Gwen tucked her chin into her winter coat, a sudden shiver snaking through her spine.

The closer they got to Nikki's parents' house, the tighter her body became, squeezing and tensing until she felt short of breath. Her shoulders hitched close to her ears, hands shoved into the coat pockets, as if she were compacting herself smaller and smaller, trepidation winding her tight.

What if the Scythians were there? Lying in wait?

What if some other unknown danger was waiting to snatch them?

What if Nikki's body lay broken and bloody, legs twisted and bones jutting, just like all her flock...

"No," she murmured, shaking her head, willing away the bad thoughts.

Theo put a hand on Gwen's leg, gave it a reassuring squeeze. "It's going to be okay. We'll figure it out."

Gwen nodded, but her gut clenched with foreboding, disbelief vibrating in her nervous system, and her stomach burned with fear, with anger, and she rested her head against the cold window to cool herself down.

The rest of the car ride passed in silence, besides the pitiful sounds of the car trying to work in the cold, and Theo's hands squeaking as they twisted on the leather of the wheel. Theo's car smelled of old leather and her shea butter, a sweet and comforting combination.

They pulled into the front driveway, that half-moon swathe of pavement connected to the concrete, alder, and lamp-lined walkway that led to the front door. Theo parked perpendicular to the walkway, Gwen having a perfect view of the imposing building, windows dark and sad, as if abandoned.

They stepped out of the car, another shiver shaking Gwen's body as the biting, bright air hit her. She stared down the walkway, the alders bare and skeletal, unwelcoming.

It was the beginning of a horror movie.

Gwen startled as Theo's arm slid through hers so that their elbows locked.

"Do all vampires live in mansions?" Theo asked, eyes appraising the house, her mouth tugging at the corners, braids falling behind her as she tilted her head back to take in the property.

Despite the heaviness in her bones, Gwen took Theo's bait. "You know, I'm not sure about 'all.' But the ones in this coven do, at least." Gwen shrugged. "That's old vampire money for you."

"What did her family even do?" Theo asked as they took their first steps forward, winter boots clunking on the frigid concrete.

"Be rich?" Gwen replied, noting a dark brown-red smudge on the ground, where Nikki had fallen and hit her head, her blood staining the concrete. It was months ago, but it felt like years after all they had been through. "I don't know. I think her mom was always rich. She comes from an old Romanian vampire family. I think they had some hand in mining and industry. I know that's why they went to London during the Industrial Revolution, but I'm not sure what they did, besides exploiting resources and people. Her mom was a classically trained London woman, despite being from Romania, with a tutor that gave her lessons in music and language. Her mom still plays some instruments. Her dad, though, was a poor human boy, and served as some sort of landscaper for her mom's parents, I think? Then they fell in love, blah blah, eloped, and he does some financial things now. I know he helps the coven manage money, but what he does exactly, I also don't know."

Gwen's speech ended as they stopped at the front door.

"Hmm. A real Romeo and Juliet, Nikki's mom and dad," Theo muttered.

"That's what everyone says."

"Must be true, then," Theo replied, and she pressed the doorbell.

There was no answer.

"There's probably no one here," Gwen said.

"It doesn't hurt to be polite."

"Pish-posh on politeness." Gwen said, her anxiety and fear and anger a sudden storm in her belly, itching for release from her fingertips. "Let's get some clues." She pulled on that fire in her core and shot it from her hand, air pushing through the cracks along the frame with enough ferocity to break the lock and crack the door open.

Heat pulsed from the house, radiating down from the climate control units installed in the ceiling, and her hair rustled with the warm air as it pushed against her scalp.

Was that mistakenly kept on, or was it intentional? Was someone here?

Theo closed the door behind them, rubbing her hands together as she stood beside Gwen, looking down the main hallway.

To their left, the wall was cracked, as if a body had crashed into it.

Before them, a red stain spread across the floor.

With hurried steps, Gwen knelt before the puddle of blood and dipped her fingers into it. It was cool and condensed. Old. She conjured a thread of magic and imbued the blood with it, the scent of iron and salt wafting in the air. Bringing her dark red fingertips to her nose, she sniffed, and in the blood was early winter frost.

"It's Nikki," she said.

"How do you know?" Theo asked, coming to stand behind her.

"It smells like her."

"Well, I gathered that. I mean, how can you smell the blood and know who it belongs to?"

"I don't know, I guess I have a super heightened sense of smell or something. But I know it's her. I know it is. I've..." Gwen swallowed, thinking of Nikki's moon-pale face and midnight hair, of the scrapes they used to get when they played in the dark as children, Nikki's sight always better than hers. She remembered the smell of her friend's mouth when her fangs fell out, and of the smell of her blood when she had fallen outside and hit her head on the concrete. Even though she arrived a day after Nikki's fall, she could still smell it. "I've smelled Nikki's blood before."

Theo shifted her feet and tugged her jacket tighter around herself. "Weird."

"I should've phrased that differently," Gwen murmured, wondering how this blood puddle came to be and where Nikki was now. With this level of blood loss, she should be alive, but would likely be dazed.

Gwen stood, pressing her fingers and thumbs together, gumming the coagulated blood between her fingers then wiping it on her pants.

"Let's keep going," Gwen said, stepping over the blood.

Theo fell into step beside her but quickly halted, flinging an arm out in front of her to barricade her way. "Wait," she whispered.

The house talked in the silence, the cold constricting the materials and making it creak and squeak. Gwen lifted her eyes to the ceiling, waiting for Theo's paranoid moment to pass, when she heard it, too.

Footsteps.

Someone walked toward them from the kitchen. Gwen shoved Theo against the hallway wall beside the door that led to the stairs and hid herself next to her, closer to the door, pressing herself as flat as possible. She pulled on the magic in her body and forced it between her hands, forming a condensed, swirling ball of air.

The footsteps grew louder, like a drumbeat echoing down from the kitchen to the dining room.

The doorknob squealed as it turned, and air moved around Gwen's body as it suctioned from the hallway into the open doorway.

Theo tensed beside her, her breath quick but stifled.

A figure stepped into the hallway.

And then, a scream.

Chapter Seven

A BUCKET of cleaning supplies and a mop clattered to the floor as Bernadette screamed, one hand flying protectively to her face.

"Jesus, Bern!" Gwen yelled back, Bernadette's fright startling her. Fear turned into embarrassment and then anger. She dropped the air between her hands, and it dissipated into their surroundings. "What are you doing here?"

"I could ask you the same thing," Bernadette said, straightening herself as her face turned red. She bent to pick up the cleaning sprays and sponges that had spilled from the dropped bucket, but Theo was already on the ground helping clean the mess.

"I'm looking for Nikki," Gwen said, swiping at the line of sweat that trickled down the side of her face, muscles weakening with the strain of losing magic.

Bernadette stood straight, leaning the mop against the wall and smoothing out her clothes. "You won't find her here," she said, picking up the bucket in one arm and moving towards the blood in the hallway. "And before you ask, I don't know where she or her parents are. Last time I saw Nikki, we were looking for clues to where her parents went, when a vampire came in and threw me into a wall. When I woke up, both him and Nikki were gone, and there was this puddle of blood on the floor."

"What vampire?"

"I don't know, some tall and strong man with wideset eyes."

Dread pooled in Gwen's gut. "Hormin."

"Do you mind if we take a look around?" Theo asked.

"Not at all, though I don't expect you'll find anything useful."

"Thank you," Theo said to Bernadette's back as the woman repeatedly sopped up and squeezed out the blood into the bucket.

"Come on. Let's go check her room," Gwen said.

The faces of Nikki's ancestors stared down at them while they walked up the stairs, pale and serious. A twang of missing vibrated through Gwen's body, wishing she could see Nikki's face and know she was okay. That they could sit back and talk about their dating or family problems then watch a movie as if all was normal and mundane.

An ache settled in her sternum, spreading through her torso, and her feet dragged as they reached the top floor and walked to Nikki's room.

The room was in pristine condition. The bed was made, all items perfectly arranged. Gwen saw the trinkets from her first spells on Nikki's bookshelf, set beside the photo of them as kids. Warmth spread over the ache in her body, knowing that their friendship meant as much to Nikki as it did to her.

Gwen picked up the dried rosehips as she looked at their childish grins, Nikki half hidden behind Gwen's mane of wild hair. With a sigh, she placed the rosehips back on the bookshelf, Theo riffling through drawers and papers.

"Find anything?" Gwen asked.

Theo shook her head. "Nothing helpful. It's mostly old high school notebooks with notes and homework."

"Ew. Definitely don't want that."

Gwen flopped on the bed, the magnificent and excessive canopy overhead. Theo lay down on the opposite side of the bed when she was done looking through the desk, so that their heads rested beside each other. Theo wound a hand in Gwen's hair, playing with its thick and frizzy waves. Gwen reached her arm around to cup Theo's cheek in her palm, fingers appreciating the outline of her face.

"If Bernadette and Nikki didn't find any clues, then we're probably not going to, either," Theo said. "It seems she's right. There's nothing helpful here."

Gwen stroked Theo's cheekbone, the soft skin on her cheek. "I don't know why I thought there would be. It's not like she spent much time here. She avoided it as much as she could."

"It was worth a try," Theo said, hand winding higher up through Gwen's hair, massaging her skull.

"Mmm." Gwen agreed, the pleasure of the head massage relaxing her muscles and pooling heat low in her belly, knowing what else Theo's hands were capable of.

"We could check her apartment. Do you think security would let us in?"

Mind fading with the sensory delight of Theo's fingers, Gwen whispered, "No need. I have a fob and key."

"So many tricks up your sleeve," Theo said. Despite the deepening of her voice, she removed her hands from Gwen's head.

Before Theo could sit up, Gwen leaned over her, and Theo bunched her fists into Gwen's hair, holding fistfuls of it up out of her face. Gwen admired Theo's warm brown eyes, the perfect shape of her nose, the enticing fullness of her mouth, the lean contours of her body.

Gwen kissed her upside down, gentle at first, but deepening as Theo opened her mouth and Gwen moaned with the relief. She was the most delicious thing she'd ever tasted. Being with Theo was like a balm to her worries. Despite the chaos of everything around them, Theo kept her grounded. She was a beacon, a lighthouse guiding her way to shore, away from dark and stormy waters. It was easy to get lost in her. To forget just how horrible things were.

Theo nudged her up with the hands in her hair and nuzzled her nose against Gwen's. "As much I love making those sounds come from you, I think we have more important things to deal with first."

Gwen closed her eyes, the delicate touch of Theo's nose on her own filling her with tenderness and warmth. "I wish you weren't right."

"Me too."

Gwen kissed the tip of Theo's nose then sat up, straightening her mussed hair. Theo came around to Gwen's side of the bed and held out a hand, Gwen twining her fingers through hers while she stood up.

Gwen paused at the bookshelf, and with a brief moment of hesitation, swiped the picture of her and Nikki, putting it in her bag. As they closed Nikki's door behind them, an anchor dropped from Gwen's stomach and into her gut, leaving her heavy, as if something irretrievable and impossible was shut behind them in that room.

Theo's thumb stroked against her hand, and it lifted the weight of the anchor enough to walk forward.

Bernadette remained on her hands and knees in the hallway downstairs, the puddle of blood reduced to a red smear on the ground. There was a foaming spray mixed in, and she scrubbed at the pink foam with as much vigor as one person could possess.

"Do you have anywhere else you can go, Bern? I'm not sure this house is safe anymore."

Bernadette swiped a loose strand of hair from her face with her wrist. "Why wouldn't it be? The Silvas are gone. What would anyone want with me or my husband?"

"I don't know, but I'd hate for something bad to happen to you, too."

"I appreciate the concern, but I will not let the house fall to ruin in Cat and Miguel's absence. This is not only my job, but my home. It is my duty to stay."

Gwen tightened her hands into fists, wishing there was something she could say to make Bernadette leave. At a loss for words, she said nothing.

"The Silvas are lucky to have you," Theo said, putting a hand on Gwen's shoulder and ushering her toward the door.

Bernadette smiled, a weak and thin-lipped grin, then forced her gaze back to the mess before her. Gwen and Theo left without another word, stepping into the biting winter air and heading to Nikki's apartment.

Chapter Eight

Nikki groaned. The falling away from Gwen's mind and back into her own was sluggish. Her body ached, tired with the exertion of being separated from its own consciousness.

Trickles of sweat slid down her face and into her shirt, and her heart sank at being back in the darkness. The world seemed so bright, so colorful, through Gwen's eyes. Not just in contrast to the dark, but in contrast to the night that Nikki had always known.

The world was so vibrant during the daylight. She wished she could feel the rays of the sun on her skin through Gwen.

This mental travel must have been what kept Lilith sane during all those endless years of darkness.

Nikki thought of Gwen sitting amidst the burial mounds of her flock, and her own chest ached at Gwen's sadness and confusion. She wished she could tell her not to waste her time, that they'd find nothing in her apartment. That they should sift through the remnants of Xander's home for clues about the Cradle, and to keep calling Ina.

But she was in the dark. Trapped and alone. That green thread was now gone, despite how hard she thought of Gwen.

Nikki couldn't even be mad at Gwen for despising her for her self-pity. She was full of self-pity, always had been, before she knew what hardship really meant. Gwen had been right to call her out months ago – her problems were so small then, in comparison.

She wished her father was there to tell her it would be okay, that they'd get through it, his last words echoing in her head, before he crumbled to nothing.

"Don't be sorrowful, child," The voice whispered, distant. *"All blood spilled here, remains here."*

A light dusting of gold rained around her, then vanished.

"What does that mean? Can I talk to him?"

Silence, blackness.

"I'm getting tired of this disappearing act! What's the point of talking to me if you're not going to be helpful? You're making it worse."

Warm air of compassion filled the empty space around her, and the sudden desire to cry made her want to scream. She sank her fangs into her bottom lip to keep her mouth closed, away from those ever-waiting tendrils at the corners of her mouth.

"You made that thread, but I still can't talk to Gwen. I can't talk to anybody. I thought you were going to help me."

"Trying," the voice said, so faint she barely heard it.

Nikki took a deep breath. There was no time for patience. She needed answers.

She needed freedom.

If she could just get out of here, she could help hunt down Lilith and stop her campaign. Make her pay for the wrongs she wrought on all of them. For trapping her in the Tree, kidnapping and abusing Xander, burning down his house.

They had to stop this and make things right.

Dark red filled her vision, and beckoned her to follow it again down through the dark roots and the even darker underbelly of the Earth.

Chapter Nine

"THEY'LL PAY for what they've done to your home," Lilith said. She stood amidst the charred and broken trees that had for centuries been the impressive home of one of her most loyal children, the coven leader of the northwest. They communed regularly, and even without the Tree, Lilith could read her mind with ease. Her spirit called to her own, a betrayed and strong woman who patiently waited for justice. Now, her daughter's eyes were dark with rage and grief, all but the underground dungeons of her home turned to blackened rubble.

Tyee gave a stiff nod, tendons in her neck flexing with the tenseness in her body, hands held tight behind her back.

They paced through the woods, Lilith running her fingers over the destruction, charcoal staining her fingertips. Hormin and the boy were in the dungeons below while she debated what to do next. How to outplay the Cradle.

"I failed you," Tyee said. "I'm sorry. I thought they were good people."

Lilith stopped and turned, the night casting Tyee's face into sharp loveliness. Lilith cupped her hands around Tyee's visage, smoothing her thumbs along her cheeks, and Tyee's eyes shone with adoration and repentance.

Lilith breathed in the sweet beating of her heart, full of fear and love.

"You have done no such thing, darling daughter." Lilith gave her the soft smile of a forgiving god, and Tyee's shoulders relaxed. "You have been one of my most loyal and loved children for centuries. It is not your fault that they betrayed you, deceived you. And we will make them suffer for that mistake."

Tyee nodded, and Lilith removed her hands from Tyee's face, smudges of charcoal on her cheeks.

A few more paces, and Lilith sensed a void in the Earth.

"Was this another entrance?" she asked, stepping beside a large pile of tree debris and plaster and wood panels and whatever else humans made houses out of these days.

Tyee nodded, once.

Lilith centered the magic within herself, keeping her eyes open, as she no longer wanted to see the dark. As the heaviness of power grew to a pressure so great it felt her core would burst, she funneled it throughout her body, hardening her skin, strengthening her muscles, the aura pulsing outside of her body. She rushed at the debris, and as her body collided with the mass, it burst around her, like she was a wrecking ball.

Oh, how she had missed this. The feeling of the world breaking, shattering, and falling at her feet.

As the debris settled, Lilith kicked remaining fragments of rubble out of the way, laughing at the delight of free-moving limbs, of no longer being trapped by the world, but dominating it, tearing it apart like she would the Cradle and everyone else who stood in her way. Without speaking, Tyee helped her clean the mass around a trap door in the floor.

An owl hooted in the distance, and the space between Lilith's shoulder blades ached with the desire for flight.

When the floor was cleared, and the dented trap door revealed, Lilith stepped back to let her daughter open it. Tyee descended into the darkness first, Hormin and the boy too far away in the tunnels to see their light. Or perhaps Hormin let them be in darkness. He could see in the dark, after all, and it wouldn't hurt to intimidate the child.

Lilith grinned.

Tyee flicked on the lights, tension rolling off her with the obvious relief that they still worked.

Lilith followed her daughter down the stairs, and as they walked through the dark and dank tunnel, her wooden antlers scraping gently across the ceiling, Lilith said, "I need to know the exact location of the closest Cradle."

Tyee's pace faltered, taking one half second longer to step, before she replied, "There was a member here, not too long ago."

"I know. But she's not there. I checked. And burned their house down. I told you that when I arrived."

"There is another."

"Is there, now?"

Tyee nodded. "Not of the original Cradle, but she has ability, nonetheless."

"No. Not good enough. I need the first Cradle. And I do not need a member. I need the location of their closest city."

They turned down a tunnel hall, a light fixture in the cracked ceiling flickering overhead.

"I do not know the closest city," Tyee said.

A knife of anger twisted in Lilith's chest, and she strained against the venom in her voice, trying to keep it calm. "I understand you may be hesitant to give up your kin. You have lost so many of them to invaders and conquerors. But we cannot have the world we envision if I do not know where the Cradle resides."

"Mother, you misunderstand," Tyee said. "I'm not hiding information from you. I do not know where the nearest city is. Only the region to which it belongs."

They turned another corner and halted in front of a dimly lit cell. Three female vampires with wine colored hair and eyes so dark green they were almost black stood guard in front of the cell, waiting. Two bowed immediately upon seeing her, the third hesitating for one second before doing so.

She would have to address that later.

Lilith turned to Tyee. "I know that as well. The Olmec Heartland, is it not?"

Tyee nodded, averting her eyes and casting them to the darkness behind the bars. "I am sorry, then, to have failed you yet again in not providing new information."

"It's no matter," Lilith said, storing her rage. "I will find them eventually."

Lilith stepped toward the cell, wrapping her hands around the cool metal bars.

Two humans with torn clothes huddled in a far corner, holding each other, their fear rich and heady in the air.

Lilith grinned and focused her rage on these two humans. She pooled her strength into her arms, wrenching the bars apart.

The humans screamed, high and pathetic, as she stepped inside.

The footsteps of Tyee and the three sisters slithered down the hall, away.

Lilith lunged at the humans, their proximity allowing her to pin both of them, and while she hooked her arm around the neck of one, their arms flailing and scratching at her own while they choked, she bit down on the neck of the other, who kicked and wailed and slapped. Their blood and the scraps of their magic filled her mouth, her body, with warmth and light and power.

It was only a minute before both went still.

Chapter Ten

"*I know where she's going!*" Nikki thought, twisting against her binds. "*Please!*" She cried with all the force of her mind at the abyss. "*I know where she's going! I have to tell someone!*" A sourness twisted in her stomach. "*Well, I don't know exactly where she's going...I don't know where the Olmec Heartland is, but Gwen has a phone and can look it up.*" She exhaled, sharp. "*I should have paid more attention in geography.*"

Nikki squirmed and tugged at the roots and branches that bound her, desperate for freedom, to tell someone where Lilith was going.

To stop her before she could get farther.

To stop her before she hurt more people.

She ceased fighting the binds, heart dropping as she thought of those poor, innocent humans whom Lilith had murdered in their cell. Lilith hadn't even thought twice about it. She had been callous and cruel. The only mercy was that they had died together, and one hadn't been left alive in fearful mourning.

"*Please!*" Nikki thought again, tilting her head back, as if the pose of supplication would bring her answers. "*Please help me talk to Gwen. We can stop this.*"

The air around her paused, lifting like a question.

"*Why?*"

"Why what? Why stop Lilith?"

"Yes."

Nikki paused, stunned at the question. *"So that she doesn't destroy all life on Earth."*

"She won't."

Nikki took a deep, long breath and exhaled, calming her racing heart. This was the longest the voice had spoken to her, and it was arguing.

"Maybe not all life," Nikki replied, *"but humanity. She'd enslave some and kill even more. I've been in her mind now. Longer than I would have liked."* Nikki winced at the destruction Lilith left behind in her wake. *"I know what she wants."*

The air shimmered, hazy with contemplation. *"That is the nature of life. Species go extinct – from natural causes, natural disasters, competition with other species. I do not see what makes this case different, or wrong."*

"Because it is," Nikki thought, shocked confusion making her at a loss for words, just leaving her with the terrible feeling of desperation, of defeat, that not only would she lose everyone and everything, but they'd also follow her dad into whatever place he evanesced to. And a world without her dad was bad enough. One without her mom, Gwen, and Xander was inconceivable. Unbearable.

The voice did not say more, but there was pressure in the spaces around her, and faint metallic shimmers continued to appear and disappear around her, a light rain.

"If you're not here to help me, then why are you here?"

"I do not know. Part of me died, and then I felt you here, instead of the one before. So sad. Broken." Silvery and brass glimmers joined the gold. *"Comfort... I wanted to comfort you."*

"Lot of good that does me," Nikki thought bitterly. *"Why do you care about me?"*

"I love you as I love all my children."

Nikki's brow furrowed. *"That's what Lilith calls us – her children. Are you like her? An ancient vampire?"*

Lightness of amusement surrounded her body, like the soft pulse of a laugh on one's skin, before weighing into remorse and regret. The glimmers of light dimmed.

"No. I am before her. I made her."

"Wait," Nikki asked, mind reeling, a wash of dizziness making her body faint. *"Are you God?"*

"It is more complex than that. Yet, I suppose you would say I am 'a' god. In the sense that no being on this planet has more magic, or knowing, than I."

"So, you are God."

"I never liked that word. Too many connotations."

"What word do you like, then?"

Glimmers around her dimmed, and one by one blinked out. *"I tire, child. Remnants of me remain far. I cannot sustain this focus yet. Give me more time, and I will explain all."*

"Wait!" Nikki thought, as the pressure and light faded. *"At least tell me what to call you. Please."*

With one pulse of awareness before They pulled away, leaving Nikki once again alone, They replied with a faint echo.

"Io. Infinite One."

Chapter Eleven

T HE SECURITY GUARD and receptionist barely spared Gwen and Theo a glance as they entered the apartment complex. The heat from the building blasted against their faces, a satisfied shiver running over Gwen's frigid skin. The heater in Theo's car was a pathetic, smelly thing.

She could almost feel the cold redness on her nose and cheeks fade.

When she opened the door to Nikki's apartment, and she looked at the normalcy, at the remnants of her friend, her breath was stolen as though a fist had slammed into her sternum. How could this place be so ordinary and untouched when everything was so wrong?

All Nikki's textbooks and notebooks were perfectly, and annoyingly, organized. There were no food crumbs or rumpled pages, no dishes in the sink, as if the apartment was an advertisement for off-campus students. It was unchaotic and controlled, just like Nikki, and if Theo wasn't there, she might have curled into Nikki's bed and cried for missing her. Nikki was her ground, and without her, she thought she might float away.

"It's okay, we'll find her," Theo said, putting a hand on her shoulder.

Gwen blinked, unaware that her vision had glassed with tears until they rolled down her cheeks. She had suddenly stood still in the apartment, hands clutched on a couch pillow, nails digging into the fabric while she vanished into her thoughts.

"I'm sorry," Gwen said, plastering a fake smile on her face. "I don't know what came over me."

"It's okay," Theo said again, squeezing her shoulder. "We'll find her."

Gwen nodded. Theo turned around to rifle through Nikki's notebooks and she murmured, "Xander, too."

Shit. Gwen thought, shaking her head at herself while she shifted her feelings to the side.

She wrapped her arms around Theo's middle, resting her head on her back, but Theo kept sifting through papers. "I'm sorry, Theo. I've been so wrapped up in my own feelings, I haven't thought about how hard this must be for you. You've known Xander almost as long as I've known Nikki."

Theo relaxed in her heavy exhale and stopped, planting her hands on the counter, and dropping her head.

"Thanks. It is hard. Even though he was always closer with Terr Bear, we would all hang out pretty often. I liked being with them more than most of my own classmates growing up." Theo turned around, and Gwen stepped back, keeping her arms looped loose around Theo's waist.

Theo put her hands on Gwen's shoulders, as if they were about to dance. "This is one of the reasons I think we should talk to Terr Bear. He might not know everything, but he could know something. Maybe he knows what makes Xander special. Or desired by vampires." Theo's shoulders slumped, hands falling from Gwen's shoulders as she looked away. "I don't know. I just want answers. I wish I knew he was okay."

Gwen moved her hands down Theo's forearms until they held hands. "I know. I understand. We'll find them, both of them, and bring them home safe." Gwen squeezed her hands. "And if you really want, we can talk to Terrance. But when he looks at you like you're crazy, don't blame me."

Theo's lips twitched, almost a grin, and nodded. "Thank you. I need more time to think about what I'll say to him, but I do think it's best.

He'll find out eventually, when Xander doesn't come home." Theo's voice trembled at the end, her lips shifting down, chin quivering.

"Hey, hey," Gwen said, wrapping her arms up over Theo's shoulders, holding her head, her perfect braids spilling around her fingers while they hugged, Theo bent down into their embrace. "We'll find them and save them." Gwen forced cheeriness into her voice. "They'll owe us so big, they'll call us heroes and buy us dinner every night for the rest of our lives." Theo's body shook with a chuckle and a suppressed sob. "And they'll have to give us back massages at least once a week for ten years, just to compensate for all this stress."

Theo laughed for real that time. It was brief, but sweet. And when they pulled back from the hug, Theo's face was set, a small tug at the corner of her mouth. Gwen had never seen Theo cry – that twitching of her face was the closest she ever got. Theo had an impressive ability to stop her anger and sadness from overriding her, to keep them in check. As if they were acknowledged but unwanted and unnecessary.

Gwen wondered how long it had been since Theo cried, and if she would let her comfort her, be there for her when she next did.

"Well. We better get to it then," Theo said, stepping back to the notebooks.

"Right," Gwen replied, cocking her head at Theo's back for one long second before huffing a sigh and going into Nikki's room.

Not finding anything useful in the room, Gwen swept through the kitchen, finding the blue ring Xander bought Nikki on the counter. The glimmers of gold and white glinted in the light and some strange feeling compelled Gwen to try it on. As it slipped over her finger, a brief surge of power jolted her magic system. Holding her hand out in front of her, she admired the ring and said, "Cool." It never hurt to have a magic ring.

Theo and Gwen sat on the couch when they finished searching the apartment, finding nothing useful, except some food that would go bad if they didn't eat it. Which they did, while debating their next steps.

"Damn. She's a good cook," Theo said, eating a mysterious dish from a plastic container.

"Yeah, she is," Gwen said, an image of her and Nikki as kids flashing through her mind, of how she would make potions and Nikki would pick a recipe from her family's cookbook. They'd cook side by side, each their own kind of witch.

Gwen's stomach dropped to the floor, and she set the container down.

She tilted her head back, hair fanning out over the back and sides of the couch and stared at the ceiling.

Theo mirrored her pose, though being taller, her neck rested higher on the back. Gwen pulled out her phone and tried calling Ina again. Like the dozens of times before, it rang until it went to voicemail.

Gwen dropped her hand with a huff.

"We could just go to her house. See if she's there."

"I guess so. Although it feels weird to do that if she's not answering me."

"Maybe she lost her phone?" Theo said. "Besides, I've known Ina for a long time. She won't be mad at me for showing up unannounced."

Gwen mulled it over. "Even if she's not there, maybe we can dig around and find out something useful."

"Exactly," Theo said, heaving herself off the couch. "Let's go."

Following in her footsteps, Gwen asked, "Do you remember where she lives?"

Theo nodded. "We used to hang out there a lot, before Xander and Terr Bear got their own place."

Gwen locked the door behind them, then wound her fingers through Theo's, squeezing her hand. "We'll find him. Both of them."

Theo nodded but didn't reply.

Chapter Twelve

Gwen called Ina again for good measure, fidgeting with the discomfort of showing up to someone's house unannounced. Of course, she didn't answer.

Theo bit at the nails on her left hand as she drove with her right. The sky had darkened, a wind blowing in a wall of gray rain clouds. Gwen closed her eyes, the bright street lamps shining through her eyelids, while she thought of Nikki, how grounded she was, how she was always there to support her, the closest thing to family she ever had.

Please, Nikki, tell me something. Tell me where you are, what to do. I'm so worried about you. Gwen thought, hoping to find Nikki somewhere behind the blacks of her eyes.

There was only silence, and Gwen shook her head at her own stupidity.

"Oh no," Theo said, and Gwen snapped her eyes open, having dozed as the car rumbled through the city and into the rolling hills.

"What? What is it?" Gwen asked, eyes following Theo's line of sight, and her jaw dropped, almost as far as her heart did into her stomach.

The house was in ruins.

Theo parked in front of a house wrapped in caution tape.

Speechless, they stepped out of the car and walked up to the property, ducking beneath the police ribbon. The plants in the front yard were charred and dead, the ash covering the soil in black and gray. The foundation of the house and fragments of the first floor remained, pieces of blackened wood and half-melted metal jutting up from the ground like unearthed bones. Gwen wondered why there were no police officers guarding the house. Did they think this was an accident? Or did they already close the case?

Gwen heard a thump behind her and turned to see Theo had fallen to her knees in the dirt, running her fingers over the burnt and ashen ground. Her chin trembled, and though her eyes remained dry, they glazed over, lost in memory.

Gwen sat beside her in the ash and rubbed a hand across her back in small circles.

Theo lifted a hand, letting the soil, debris, and char sift through her fingers to the ground.

"This place was my second childhood home," Theo whispered.

"I'm so, so sorry, Theo," Gwen said, resting her cheek on her shoulder, wishing she had the magic to soothe her.

"Do you think...do you think they were in there when it burned?" Theo asked, a choke catching in her throat.

"I don't know, Theo. I really hope not." Cold dread filled Gwen's core, wondering if that's why Ina hadn't answered her phone or called her back.

Gwen sat in silence with Theo for a few minutes before saying, "I'm going to look inside, see what there is to see."

Theo's gaze refocused and she looked at the ruins. "I don't think that's a good idea. It doesn't look structurally sound."

"Don't worry, I'll shield myself." Gwen stood, but Theo didn't move. "Maybe you can find a news article about what happened?'

Theo nodded and lifted to her feet, wiping the cold dirt and ash from her pant legs, smearing it on her hands. She grimaced at the mess on her skin and said, "I'll look it up in the car, so no one sees me here and gets us in trouble."

"Okay," Gwen said, though Theo hadn't waited for an answer before she turned to walk back to the car.

Gwen faced the ruins of the house, pulling at the magic inside of herself and pulsing it into her palms, spreading it in an arc over and around her body, condensing the air to create a shield. She had to continuously focus on it, with one hand out to push and tighten the air.

She would need to make this quick, as maintaining the shield would exhaust her in a matter of minutes.

Gwen stepped over the broken threshold where the front door should be. A shiver pimpled over her skin when her foot landed on the charred debris, like crossing into another realm. To her left, half of the house no longer had a ceiling, having caved to the floor. To the right, some of the roof remained, creaking as the cold wind pushed against it.

Gwen tiptoed through the left of the house, listening to the creaks, and keeping her eyes on the rubble, trying to find anything that wasn't just broken pieces of the house. In the middle of the open living room, the furniture black and withered, mostly gone, she bent to move pieces of the fallen ceiling and shards of the furniture, to see what was underneath.

A sharp sting sliced across her finger, an unseen shard of glass cutting her as she moved debris away.

With more care, she cleared a small area, and found a shattered picture frame with the photo still inside. It showed Ina and Xander, with a tall middle-aged male and two dark-skinned children. The family smiled, arms around each other in the shade of a large tree.

She smiled at the photo, despite the bitter pang of longing, and she pulled out the photo from the glass with care and placed it in her pocket.

Standing, Gwen sucked at the cut finger, sweat starting to trickle down her face from maintaining the shield. The ring gave a small pulse of power, imbuing her with an extra thread of magic. She stepped through the house, over and around the debris, but there was too much for her to sift through.

Another futile attempt.

A room at the back of the house was trashed. Broken glass and tilted shelves were everywhere, as were their contents, as though someone had destroyed a museum. Maneuvering around the shards of glass, not wanting to trip and cut herself or have a piece pierce her boot, she flicked her gaze across the ground, trying to find anything of a different color, of a different shape.

Her racing heart kicked harder as something caught her eye at the far side of the room. It only took her a few seconds to cross the room, but her energy was draining and she was panting by the time she reached what she had seen. Over here, the ceiling was intact, barely, and she felt safe enough to sit in the dim light and pull out the objects – pieces of a tan stone tablet and a cylindrical object, all with carvings on them. She rolled the cylinder in her hand, the stone cool, etched with people, tools, and shapes she didn't understand.

A sharp crack split above her, and she gasped as a piece of ceiling fell, splintering on the shield above her head. Her hand reverberated with the shock, pushing against its force to keep her magic in place.

Knowing that was her cue, Gwen stuffed the cylinder and smaller fragments into the jacket pockets without the photo.

Her coat bulged with its newfound contents as she walked back through the part of the house that had no ceiling so nothing else could crash down on her. Outside, she took a deep breath of fresh air and released her shield, sagging with fatigue, the sweat freezing against her skin and hair.

When she regained her balance, Gwen returned to Theo's car and slid into the passenger seat. "What did you find out?"

"Not much," Theo said, chewing on a nail and giving Gwen the phone with a news article, a photo of the ruined house on top. "They suspect the fire was set intentionally, but they can't find the ignition source. They didn't find any bodies and haven't been able to contact anyone in the family. The police opened an investigation, but the trail seems to have gone cold."

"Hmm...yeah, that really isn't helpful at all."

"Did you find anything?" Theo asked.

"I did, but I'm not sure how helpful any of it is," Gwen replied, first taking out the photo and handing it to Theo. "I thought you might want this."

Theo took it and smiled, though it was tinged with sadness, and ran her thumb along the sides. "Thank you. I'll at least hold on to it for the family. It might be the only photo left."

Theo held the photo a moment longer before putting it in the glove box while Gwen removed the pieces of stone in her pocket.

"Oh – I know what that is," Theo said, taking the cylinder. "It's a cylinder seal."

"What does it do?"

"It was rolled over an object, like wet clay, and the carvings leave an impression of the image on the surface. I think they were used as a type of signature. Like for authenticating documents."

"Huh, interesting," Gwen said. "That's cool, but doesn't help us now, does it?"

Theo shrugged and put the cylinder seal into her purse. "I don't know. It could be a miscellaneous artifact. But maybe the identity of the person who would use this means something. We'll have to wait for Ina to answer that though."

Gwen sighed, "Right. Not helpful now, then."

She started fitting the broken stone tablet pieces together on her lap like a puzzle, aligning the carvings until it showed an image of man in profile, holding a rod and ring, a sun behind him.

"Do you know who this is?" Gwen asked.

Theo shook her head. "I don't."

"Curiouser and curiouser," Gwen mused, running a hand over the tablet, feeling the contours of the carving. As her fingers roved over the stone, blood from her cut smeared along the grooves and into the cracks.

"Oh, shit," Gwen said, retracting her hand, but it was too late.

Her blood brightened and shimmered as it spread in a line from the top to the bottom. With a sudden crack, the tablet burst apart, the dust of the stone puffing into the air, powdering her face, hair, and legs.

Gwen blinked the stone dust out of her eyes and sneezed, then yelled, "What the hell was that?!"

Chapter Thirteen

"Please, Nikki, tell me something. Tell me where you are, what to do. I'm so worried about you."

Nikki's head shot up, snapping out of meditative state at the sound of Gwen's voice. It was faint and searching, desperate. Her heart cracked at the sound.

A small blade of green reached from the base of the tree below her feet, and thinking of Gwen, she reached her mind down to it, heart racing at the hope of finally being able to talk to her.

When her mind met the green, her consciousness spiraled into the earth, but she lost Gwen's thread, and in the darkness of the ground, her vision flooded with muddy red, sending her careening hundreds of miles in a different direction.

The shift from one thread to another disoriented her, and there was a vague sense of nausea back in her body. But it was easy to ignore as the red thread dragged her along, forcing her into Lilith's mind.

Lilith stood on cold stone, the cave shadowed and protected from the dying light outside. The aspens had long shed their leaves, the stringy trees like teeth of the mountain. It was a good place to rest and feed, a small town dominated by some obscure cult down the mountainside. It was easy hunting, and no one would look twice at another dead cult.

In her idle hours, waiting for the sun to set, she practiced partial transformations. Now, she stood and stared at her feet, willing them to turn into talons without changing her whole legs into those of the owl.

Her feet tingled with the magic she poured into them, the flesh sizzling and falling off in wet clumps as her toes broke and bones shifted, changing their shape and composition into sharp, dark claws.

Her right leg hadn't shifted correctly, with some of her lower leg tapering down into a thin rod tufted with feathers.

The left foot, however, was perfect. Knife-sharp talons protruded in long points proportional with her vampiric form. Blood from the flesh trickled over them, the remains of her skin around it. She lifted her foot and picked up the discarded flesh with her talons, then shredded it, bits of skin and blood raining back to the cave floor, satisfied at the razor efficiency.

"Gross."

Lilith cocked her head at the voice, distant and soft.

"Who said that?"

Silence.

She frowned. Was it her imagination?

No...the voice had been real.

Had her daughter figured out how to travel the threads of life?

Impossible. She hadn't been in the Tree long enough to master that yet.

She looked over her shoulder, her wooden horns scraping against the ceiling of the cave, gazing at the half-dead husk of a cult member slumped unconscious and barely breathing against the far wall of the cave.

Perhaps she had absorbed too much of human magic lately, and it seeped through the crevices of her mind.

No matter.

She fixed her gaze on her right leg, willing the feathers to turn back into the skin of her leg. Her foot turned to flesh but the feathers did not resorb into her body. Instead, she was left with fleshy feathers, heavy and dangling.

She would need to work on that.

With a final, warm pulse of magic through her body, she shifted her talons and half owl leg back into feet, talons popping off and clattering against the ground as her bones regrew and pushed them out.

She bent to pick up a talon, pressing it against a finger. Without much pressure, it punctured her skin, the wound resealing an instant later with a hot itch.

Lilith smiled. Such good weapons she could make.

Perhaps she should experiment with them.

A wicked grin plastered to her face as she stalked to the human, whose raspy breaths puffed in the chill air.

She bent beside him, brushing the lank blonde hair from his face. She cradled his head on her lap and it lolled to the side, stretching open the bite wounds on his bearded neck. Lilith ran a hand over his body, the firmness of his chest. The benefit of these cults was that the hard labor gave mortals such alluring muscles.

The talon scraped against his skin as she moved her hand, and when she found his weakly beating heart, she stopped. She relished the beat of it against her palm, for one, two, three, beats, then raised the talon and –

Nikki gasped as she forced herself out of Lilith's mind, spiraling through the earth and crashing back into herself. The tree tendrils crept toward her gaping mouth, which she forced closed before they could wheedle their way inside.

Calming her racing heart, Nikki thought of that poor boy, murdered so brutally. Another wave of nausea roiled in her stomach, pushing bile into her throat, as she shoved away the image of his beaten body.

Stranger still, Lilith had heard her. Nikki hadn't meant to think anything, or say anything, but all the blood and pieces of skin as Lilith transformed her feet was sickening. She would need to figure out how to control that. She didn't know what would happen to her if Lilith knew she could see her, but it certainly would not improve her current circumstances.

If only she could talk to Gwen, have some practice controlling communication...

"Io, why does it always take me to Lilith?" Nikki asked. *"I tried to follow Gwen's thread, but it sent me to Lilith instead."*

The space around Nikki grew heavy, the pressure of another presence filling the darkness. It was contemplative and silent for several minutes as it pulled itself together, flickers of gold and brass and silver raining in the dark.

"The Tree knows Lilith well. I think, perhaps, it misses her."

"It misses her? How can it feel such a thing?" Nikki asked.

"They have been companions for ages beyond human or vampire comprehension. It is not so unusual, as you are experiencing it with your life-long friend."

"But neither Gwen nor I are trees."

"You know that this is more than a Tree. It lives, it thinks, it feels. In its own way."

"So, it misses Lilith and will keep forcing me to connect with her?"

"In time, it will come to know you, too."

"That doesn't make me feel better. I don't want it to know me. I want to get out of here."

"I know, child," Io said, voice fading.

"Wait – please don't go. Won't you tell me how things became this way? What I can do to stop it? I have so many questions," Nikki pleaded.

"I know. Soon, child. Soon," Io whispered, and Their presence vanished, the all-consuming dark returning.

Chapter Fourteen

A SNEEZING FIT SHOOK GWEN, and when her eyes were done watering and she caught her breath, she brushed the tablet's powder off her face and legs.

"I have no idea why that happened," Theo said. "Are you all right?"

"Yeah, I'm just confused," Gwen replied, swinging down the passenger mirror to find the remaining flecks on her face. Her hair would be powdery until she showered. There was no way she could brush it out. Gwen groaned. "Instead of finding answers, we found more questions. I wish Ina would answer the damn phone."

"I'm sure she'll call when she can."

"Are you? I'm not. And I feel like it shouldn't be taking this long for her to call back. What if there's some phone glitch preventing her from knowing I've tried to reach her?"

"I think that's unlikely. It's only been a few days, and who knows what this group she's part of has going on in the background."

"I guess," Gwen said, chewing on the inside of her lip. "I still don't like it."

"Well, there's nothing we can do about it." Theo tapped her fingers on the wheel. "Where to now?"

Gwen shook her head. "I don't know."

"Well, back it up. What happened before Nikki went to her parents' house? Before you met Ina?"

"Uhh...Nikki was kidnapped. By Tyee and two vampires from Peru. And kept in Tyee's basement – dungeon – thing. She only escaped because the Lius broke her out and drove her to my place."

"Have you talked to the Lius?"

Gwen shook her head.

"Then I think that's where we should go next. They must have some stake in the game to help Nikki escape. Some sense of what we're dealing with."

Gwen groaned. "I was really hoping to avoid vampires."

"How were you going to accomplish that when this whole issue revolves around them?"

"I don't know. I was just enjoying the dream."

"I think you mean the delusion."

"Dream – delusion – what's the difference?"

"One sec and I'll tell you," Theo said and pulled her phone from her back pocket.

Gwen laughed and smacked her phone out of her hand, watching as it fell to the car floor. "That's cheating."

"No, it's not. I was going to tell you the exact difference. Like you asked," Theo said with a smirk, bending to pick up her phone.

"Yeah, yeah. Well, you know that whether it's a dream or delusion, you're right again, so, let's get this over with." Gwen sighed. "I don't know the Lius' number or address, so we'll have to ask someone for help."

"Have someone in mind?"

Gwen grimaced. "Unfortunately."

Chapter Fifteen

Gwen dialed the number and shriveled into herself even before it picked up on the second ring.

"Gwen?" her brother Farrell asked, voice lilting with surprise.

"Yup, it's me. You home?"

"I am. Are you okay?"

"Yes. Well, no. But you know. Anyway. I need to talk to you." Gwen gave Theo the thumbs up, and Theo started the car to drive back over the river, leaving the burned house behind them.

"Should I be worried?"

"You mean more than you usually are?"

"Yes."

"Then...maybe? Honestly, I don't know what worries you these days. Maybe you won't care. Maybe you will."

Farrell was silent for a few breaths. "Okay...I don't know what to make of that."

Gwen shrugged, then shook her head with the idiocy of the movement, since he couldn't see it. "You know, I don't either. Are the bitches there?"

"Don't call them that."

"Why? It suits them."

"Still. They're your sisters."

"And how I wish they weren't."

Farrell sighed. "No, they're not here. I haven't seen them in a few days."

Gwen chewed on her bottom lip. That could be good or bad news. Good news for now, at least. "Okay, well, if you see them, you're sworn to secrecy."

"Gwen, what – "

"Seriously. Promise me right now, or we can forget the whole operation."

"You're the one who called me."

"Yes, and you need to keep our conversation confidential. Otherwise, I won't talk to you."

"Fine. Fine. I won't tell a soul."

Gwen's mouth twitched. "That promise is invalid – our family doesn't have souls."

"Because we're vampires?"

"Because we're redheads."

Farrell groaned and Gwen laughed at her own joke.

"When will you be here?" he asked, exhaling his words, voice rich with exasperation.

"Soon enough," she said. "Don't panic, okay? I just need some info."

"Every time someone says don't panic, it's usually a good time to panic."

"Well don't, I guess? Take a breath and drink blood or whatever it is you do. See you soon," Gwen said and hung up.

Gwen shoved her hands into her jacket and hunched into its puffy neck, warming her face as her breath pushed back onto her skin. Muffled through the fabric, she said, "Good news is the three prime evils aren't there."

"What's the bad news?" Theo asked.

"That the three prime evils aren't there."

Theo was silent and flipped the windshield wipers on as soft rain splattered against the window. "You think they might be with the, uh, the Mother?" Theo asked, hesitating over that word as she always did, as if she still didn't really believe it.

"Could be," Gwen said, shrugging. "They could be with the Scythians or with some other bad vampires. Or they could just be passed out somewhere, gorged from a bloody orgy party. Or something."

Theo's face scrunched, nose crinkling. "Gross."

"I know, right?" Gwen replied, and leaned her head against the cold window, a small layer of fog on the bottom. They rode the rest of the way in silence, the rain consistent and fragile, shallow pools growing in the holes on the road.

When they pulled into the driveway, under the cover of the evergreens, Gwen said, "Wait for me here?"

Theo looked at her like she was stupid and said, voice flat, "You're joking, right?"

"No, I'm not. It's safer for you out here."

"That's bullshit, Gwen, and you know it," Theo spat, muscles going tense, words hard as she tried to keep her volume neutral. "You just don't want me to meet your family."

"What? Now *that* is bullshit," Gwen replied, then hummed to herself as she thought. "Well, I mean, I don't want you to be near them because they're dangerous. Not because it has anything to do with you."

Theo scoffed and unclicked her seatbelt. "I'm not scared of them. Come on, it'll be fine." Theo stepped out and closed the car door with enough force to shake it, and Gwen followed, anxiety like a hive of bees in her chest, irregulating her heartbeat.

"I didn't mean to make you mad," Gwen said.

"I know. But I'll make the decisions about where I go and what I do, okay? I want to be here with you, so let me make that choice." Theo pursed her lips, then said, "Don't do the same thing to me that Nikki tried to do to Xander. Don't decide for me what I am and am not willing to risk."

Theo's face was set, pursed lips squeezing into a line, eyes firm and unblinking as they bored into Gwen's. If Theo's arms weren't crossed, Gwen would have touched her, but everything about the other woman's posture told her to stay back.

So she did.

Gwen nodded, speechless despite the mix of words that flitted through her head. As if they all caught in her throat.

Gwen took a deep breath, expanding her lungs so that it stretched out her body, making herself as big as possible, her back straight. She tossed her head, hair rearranging itself over her shoulders. Finally braced, she opened the door to her home.

It was dark, which was not a surprise, but there was usually more light left on the main floor. They dragged rainwater and debris through the house, a twisted satisfaction in Gwen at the dirt in the otherwise pristine home.

A little nature never hurt anybody.

As they reached the end of the hall, a light flicked on over the stairwell that led to the basement level, and footsteps climbed, steady and heavy.

Gwen paused at the top of the stairs, and her eyebrows arched in surprise when her eldest brother rounded the curve of the stairs. "Connall?"

He blinked so hard it was nearly a flinch, and his lip curled downward, irritated. "Guinevere." His deep green eyes took in her plaster-dusted hair then flicked to Theo, lingering for a moment longer than Gwen liked. "Who is this?"

"My girlfriend. What are you doing here? I haven't seen you in ages."

He stiffened, a lock of his thick and richly wine-hued hair falling out of the grease he slathered on to contain it. "What matter is it to you why I am here?"

Gwen paused, his words a painful twist in her chest. No matter how many times her family rebuffed her, it still hurt so bad she couldn't breathe, like they put their hands around her heart and squeezed.

"You're my brother," she said, quiet.

He softened a little at that, but only in how his shoulders dropped. "I had to drop off papers to Farrell for review."

Connall continued his ascent, and Gwen said, "Oh. Cool."

When he passed her, she caught a breath of his scent, of something ancient and cold, but there was also the smell of her, of something green and wild, like mossy old growth forests. That tendril in her that was desperate for familial connection, for unconditional love, whipped through her, and she said, "How have you been doing?"

She bit on the inside of her cheeks as soon as the words were out of her mouth, wishing she could swallow them back down.

He stopped, and Gwen stared at his back, at his perfectly pressed black suit. He tilted his head up toward the ceiling and exhaled before leveling his head and saying over his shoulder, "Let's not do this, Gwen."

The rejection melted underneath shame and anger. It burned right down to her core. She spat, "Do what? Have a simple conversation, like a family?"

"You're not family. You're a stranger. And always will be. I'm hundreds of years older than you, and within a brief passage of time, you will be long in the ground. You are nothing more than a flower – no – a *weed* to me. You may bloom temporarily, but you will be nothing within the blink of an eye. Little more than a nuisance underfoot."

His words were cold water over the fire in her chest, leaving an empty cavity of ashes.

"What the hell is wrong with you?" Theo whispered, stunned.

Tears filled Gwen's eyes, and her brother's body wavered in her vision as he walked away without a backward glance. How could he be so cruel? How could he treat her this way? What had she ever done to be treated like she was nothing?

Gwen tightened her fists, the rage-fueled magic building in her veins, her muscles, spilling out of her pores. She raised her hands to unleash the storm and said through clenched teeth, "Some weeds are toxic, you know."

A soft hand landed on her shoulder, and she paused.

"Gwen, don't," Theo hushed.

The air lashed around her, but Connall didn't flinch, didn't look back, and soon he was out of sight.

Gwen dropped her hands, the wind stilling, and her muscles grew heavy with exhaustion.

"Don't listen to that asshole," Theo said, turning Gwen to face her.

Gwen nodded, unable to focus her eyes on Theo through her overuse of magic and the heartbeat that still roared in her mind. She gave Theo a sad, closed-lipped smile, which was met with a small squeeze of her shoulder. Gwen looked away, pulling away from the searing touch, and began her descent down the stairs. The pity in Theo's face made Gwen want to sink deeper and deeper down, farther and farther away.

Theo's footsteps followed her. She could feel the anxiety and need to comfort rolling off of Theo, the dull, clipped sound of a tooth biting a nail. Gwen took another empowering breath, forcing her shoulders back to give herself a false sense of confidence and power. To give the impression she wasn't so deeply affected by her brother's words.

She didn't want or need anyone's pity.

Especially Farrell's.

His door was cracked, warm white light flooding into the dark hall.

Gwen raised a hand, and as she tapped the door with her knuckle, she said, "Knock knock."

"Gwen and friend – come in!" he shouted.

She hoped he hadn't heard what had transpired between her and Connall, but as soon as she saw his face, the slight pinch in his brow, how his body fully turned toward her, hands planted on his thighs, she knew he had. Despite the little insect in her that wanted to shrivel away, she stood straighter and put her hands on her hips.

He didn't need to know she cared. After two decades of bullying, she was adept at faking confidence.

His office was in a small wing of the house that once belonged to him and Connall, before Connall had moved out. The room had a large desk, scattered and stacked with papers in its own organized chaos, with chairs in front of it. There was a mini fridge, likely full of blood and meat. It adjoined a pair of bedrooms and a bathroom to the left, then living areas and lounges to the right.

Farrell's brow pinched tighter as they stepped into the room, and he said, "It isn't that he – "

"Don't," Gwen replied, with more venom than she'd intended, raising a hand to stop him.

A corner of his mouth twitched, but he kept it closed. His red hair hung tousled and limp, ungreased, loose sweatpants and t-shirt somehow still flattering on his tall and square frame.

"I've seen you around." he said, appraising Theo. "Though I have not had the pleasure of meeting you yet. What's your name?"

"Theo. Theodora. But I go by Theo," Theo replied, and Gwen cocked a brow at her, at her odd stumble of a reply.

Farrell stood to shake Theo's hand. "Farrell. I'm glad to meet you."

"Me too. I mean, you too. I am glad to meet you, too." Theo stammered again, taking his hand. He smiled at her and his fangs caught in the lamplight.

"Farrell – this is my girlfriend."

"I assumed as much," he said, turning back to Gwen, the light highlighting his sharp cheekbones and pointed chin, one eye deep green in the light, the other dark where the light didn't reach. He tilted his head and said, "Come on. Let's get comfortable."

He led them to the living area. Gwen glanced at Theo, whose eyes were wide and lips set, her hands clasped tight around her elbows. Why was she being so weird?

Farrell gestured to the couches and said, "Take a seat. What can I get you – water, food?"

"No, I'm good, thanks," Gwen said, dropping onto the plush, high-backed leather couch.

"I'm fine too," Theo echoed, sitting close beside her.

Farrell nodded and sat on a chair opposite them. He crossed one leg so the ankle rested on his opposite thigh, and he wrapped his fingers around the raised knee. "What do you need to talk about? And what's in your hair?"

"Just remnants of an old relic," Gwen said in a rush, shrugging despite the heat in her cheeks. "Now, before I ask this of you, do you swear you promise not to tell anyone?"

"I do."

"It's a matter of safety, so you better not break your promise."

"I won't."

"Okay." Gwen took a deep breath and then released a slow exhale. Farrell retreated into his unnaturally still state, as if he'd turned to stone. She couldn't see him breathe, or twitch, and he barely blinked as he looked at her, waiting.

"I need the phone number of the Lius."

A brow in his marble stillness twitched. "Why?"

Gwen paused. "Are you aware of what's been happening? Of when our psycho sisters attacked us with some other vampires they called Scythians?"

Farrell didn't move, thinking. "I did not know that. I would have stopped them if I had." His voice softened. "I hope you know that."

"I appreciate the sentiment, but I don't know if you could have stopped it. You really don't know what's been going on, with this so-called Mother?"

"No. I have not been home much of late. I did not go to the last solstice, either. Connall has me up to the fangs in paperwork – we have a new high-profile client who is very demanding." Farrell paused. "Come to think of it, a few weeks ago, I heard – in passing, mind you – our sisters speak of her. Of talking with her. I thought they were being, as you said, 'psycho.' Playing at religion."

Gwen sighed. "If you don't know what's going on, I need to fill you in." She told him everything she'd learned over the last few months, of Nikki being compelled, of the Mother and the Scythians hunting Xander, their sisters working with them, of what Nikki told her happened at the winter solstice, of Nikki and Xander going missing, then hearing Nikki cry out for her.

The entire time, Farrell did not move, except for the intermittent twitch of an eyebrow.

When she finished, Farrell said, "That certainly explains why Mother and Father have left the country."

"They *what*?"

"You didn't know?"

Gwen clenched her fists, scrunching the fabric of her jeans in her fingers. "No one in this family tells me anything."

His lips tightened, and he said, "They went to our family in Ireland. They're making plans to sell the estate. And have all of us move back there."

"Not all of us." Gwen sneered, now knowing why she had been left out. "What about my studio, is that going to be sold too?"

"I do not know," he said, voice softening to a whisper. "If you want to come with us, I will find a way."

Gwen shook her head. "I don't know. I can't even think about that right now. I need to figure out where Nikki and Xander are and help them. I'll think about what I want afterward."

"Understood," he said, voice low and sad. "I wish I could tell you where your friends are. However, as I said, I've been quite out of the loop as of late. I will need time to figure out what to do with our sisters, if they ever return home."

"That's all well and good, and I appreciate that you wish you knew more, but all I really need from you right now is a telephone number for the Lius."

"Of course. One moment," he said, standing and returning to his office.

When he was out of the room, Theo heaved out a deep breath, shoulders dropping.

"He's not going to eat you," Gwen whispered.

"I know."

"Then what's wrong with you?"

"Shh!" Theo said, stiffening as Farrell returned.

"Here you are," he said, handing Gwen a folded sheet of paper. She unraveled it, finding two cell phones numbers, one for Feng and one for Daiyu.

"Thank you. I really appreciate it. As well as your confidentiality."

"Don't worry. Your secret is safe with me. I won't put you or your friends at risk."

"Thanks," Gwen said, standing. Farrell remained in front of her and gave her a soft smile, and as she looked into the face that was so much like hers, just sharper and more richly hued, the smell of her family surrounded her, fog and moss and evergreens, and she imagined what it would be like to hug him goodbye.

But her family didn't hug, especially not her, so she stepped around him and headed for the door, Theo and Farrell following.

"Gwen," Farrell said as her and Theo exited into the hall.

Gwen turned toward him, one hand on the door, prepared to close it behind them.

"Yes?" she asked, pulse kicking.

"Tell me what you find."

"Sure," she said, heart dropping. "Thanks again."

"Of course. Nice to meet you, Theo. Keep my sister safe," Farrell said, unblinking, evergreen gaze fixed on Theo.

"Oh. Yes. Of course. I will. Nice to meet you, too. Have fun with all your...paperwork."

Farrell grinned and closed the door.

Gwen stared at Theo, mouth open and eyebrows raised in confusion. There was a rosiness in Theo's brown cheeks, turning them amber.

Amber tones deepening, Theo said, "Should we go?"

"Only if you tell me what the hell that was about. You didn't even stammer that much around me when we started dating."

Theo glanced at the closed door and said, "Outside."

"Uuuggghhh," Gwen groaned, huffing out a puff of air that fluffed her wavy hair away from her face. She turned on her heel and stomped up the stairs, walking through the dark and empty house back to the car.

The sky had shifted from a dull slate gray to the dark charcoal of rain clouds shrouding the night sky, a bitter chill blowing. They stepped into the car and Theo turned on the pathetic heater, which groaned in agony as it tried to warm itself.

"So..." Gwen prompted.

Theo ran a hand over her braids. "I don't know, Gwen, something about him just made me nervous."

"Why?"

"Like...the Scythians were scary and intimidating, and Nikki just seems so...human. But Farrell, he was the first vampire I was close to that wasn't evil, and he actually seemed nice." Theo cleared her throat. "Don't be mad at me when I say this, but it made me finally understand the fantasy about vampires."

"What?" Gwen asked, restraining the rising volume of her voice.

"I told you not to get mad at me."

"Well, I don't have a switchboard for my feelings!" Gwen yelled, then shoved her fists into her jacket, hunkering down into the seat. "So, that's great. Thanks for telling me you're attracted to my brother. Makes me feel great."

"I'm not attracted to him."

"You just said he made you fantasize."

"No, I said it made me understand the fantasy. He's beautiful and mesmerizing. I was intimidated."

"Super."

"I don't like feeling intimidated. I like feeling comfortable. And I feel comfortable with you."

"Well. Just don't ever tell me again you think my brother is hot, okay?"

"You asked."

Gwen shot her a glare and Theo raised her hands in defeat. "Fine, fine. But also, if you don't realize I have a wild fantasy for beautiful, enchanting witches, then you need to get your brain checked."

Gwen snorted. "My 'brain' checked?"

"Yep. Something could be seriously wrong with you."

"Whatever," Gwen said and nudged her playfully.

As the tension eased, Theo asked, "You gonna call the Lius?"

"I don't know. Are you going to drool all over them too?"

"It's a possibility," Theo said, grinning.

Theo's wide, white smile sent butterflies dancing around Gwen's stomach, and warmth spread throughout her body. She leaned over the center console to grab Theo's face in her hands and brought her forward for a kiss. It was long and deep, until they needed to catch their breath, and when they parted, they kept their noses touching.

"You're the bees' knees," Gwen whispered.

Theo laughed, and the breath of it brushed Gwen's face. "The bees' knees? Who talks like that?"

"I do."

"Well in that case, you're the cat's meow."

Gwen smiled and closed her eyes, feeling Theo's cheek on her palm, her braids on the back of her hand, Theo's hand in her hair.

"I guess we should see what we can find out from the Lius."

"I guess so."

Gwen leaned back and took out her cell phone, programming both numbers into it.

She called Daiyu first, and it went to voicemail.

Feng picked up on the second ring. "Hello?"

"Hey, Feng. This is Gwen. I was hoping we could talk."

"Ah, Gwen. I was wondering when we would hear from you."

Chapter Sixteen

THEY MET at a small diner in Portland. The booths were old blue leather, with unbalanced tables and a staticky jukebox sputtering out upbeat rock music. Gwen had tried to shake out the dust from her hair on the drive, but a few crumbles remained, a flaky layer on her clothes.

Theo's stomach grumbled, and she put a hand over her torso. "I just realized how long it's been since I last ate. I'm starving."

"You ate a few hours ago at Nikki's, remember?"

"How could I forget? But I need to eat every three hours, like clockwork. I go from full to hungry instantly."

"I guess we should start bringing snacks on our adventures."

Theo nodded and said, "We should." Then she picked up the laminated menu and browsed, but Gwen was too nervous to eat. The anxiety curdled her stomach, demolishing her appetite, although she had eaten even less than Theo.

The waitress put water on their table and took their drink order, and as she walked away with tired eyes, Feng and Daiyu arrived.

The few heads in the diner turned, Feng and Daiyu too refined and beautiful for this crumbling establishment. Though Feng had an easy smile, the tension in his body radiated a preparedness for violence. His wife was all feline grace, with a steady and observant gaze. Sliding into the booth opposite Theo and Gwen, Daiyu's sultry and low voice said, "Thank you for meeting us here."

"No problem," Gwen said. "We haven't had anything to eat for a while anyway."

The waitress returned, putting tea in front of Gwen and hot chocolate for Theo, then getting their food order. Of course, the Lius couldn't eat human food, and Gwen didn't have the stomach for it, so Theo was the only one who ordered. The waitress gave them a judging flick of her eyebrow before she retreated to the kitchen.

Gwen wrapped her hands around her tea, the heat warming her skin but not her core, feeling her heartbeat in her palms. "I guess I'll jump right on it. Do you know where Nikki is?"

Feng blinked. "You haven't introduced us to your companion."

"Sorry. Guess I got ahead of myself." Gwen said, anxiety and anticipation fluttering in her chest. "This is Theo, my girlfriend."

"Theo, lovely to meet you," Daiyu said. "I'm Daiyu, and this is my husband, Feng."

Feng nodded his head in acknowledgment, and Theo swallowed loud enough for them all to hear, then said in a too calm and controlled voice, said, "It's lovely to meet you, too."

Feng reclined, one arm draping over the back of the booth behind Daiyu's shoulders, the other stretched forward on the table. After a long pause, he said, "We shouldn't talk about this here."

"Then why did you have us come here, if we're not going to talk?" Gwen asked, biting down the flare of irritation that rose in her voice.

"We needed a meeting spot. From here, we will take you to our safe house."

"We are cautious about who we talk to and who knows the location of our safe house," Daiyu added.

An awkward silence passed, Gwen tapping Nikki's ring on the ceramic of the mug. The Lius fixed their dark brown eyes on her and gave her closed-lipped smiles. Daiyu eventually asked, "Please, tell us how you have been."

"Small talk? Really?"

"Would you rather us sit in silence?" Daiyu asked.

Gwen sighed. "No. Sorry. I'm just eager for answers."

"We understand," Daiyu said.

"But we need to wait until we are in a safer location," Feng added.

"Understood," Gwen grumbled, taking a sip of her mint tea.

Theo's food arrived, a wide oval plate with a BLAT and a mound of French fries.

"You want some?" Theo asked, mouth full of her sandwich, pushing the plate toward the middle.

The Lius looked at the food with that eerie vampire stillness, wistful smiles and longing in their eyes.

"We can no longer eat the food of mortals," Feng said, "as the making overtook our human phenotype. Now, our stomachs only tolerate blood."

"Oh, I didn't realize. I'm sorry," Theo said, cheeks turning amber, pulling the plate back toward herself.

"I'll have some," Gwen said, the sweetness of Theo combined with her embarrassment making Gwen want to eat despite having no appetite.

Theo grinned and nudged the plate between them, and Gwen picked at the hot, crispy fries, drenching them in ketchup.

Gwen gave terse responses to the questions the Lius asked, not wanting to talk about her family. Eventually, they switched to Theo, and between mouthfuls, Theo answered questions about her life, mostly centered around her family and studies.

When they found out she was studying Organic Chemistry, Daiyu said, "Did Gwen tell you that Feng worked on the Transcontinental Railroad?" Theo shook her head, eyes widening, and her French fry-filled mouth nearly popped open. "He was a demolitionist. Helped them clear holes and paths in the mountains."

"I could teach you what I know of the chemistry of bomb-making, if you are interested," Feng said, catching on to Daiyu's train of thought.

"That would be great," Theo said, swallowing. "Especially learning the chemistry of the past. That would be fascinating."

"Consider it done," Feng said.

After the meal, Gwen and Theo followed the Lius' Mercedes through ever-emptying and darkening roads. Tamping down her anxiety, hoping for a distraction, Gwen said, "Well, you didn't drool all over them like you did Farrell, so that's good."

Theo laughed. "I'm surprised by them. They actually seem really cool."

"That's what Nikki always said. But I never spent much time around them. You know, because vampires."

"I get it. Hopefully they'll be able to help us. It would be nice to finally learn something."

"It would. I hope going all the way to this safe house isn't all for nothing. Or a trap."

"I don't think it's a trap. Why would they help free Nikki just to kidnap you? That doesn't make sense."

"No, you're right. I'm just not used to following vampires at night to mysterious and unknown locations."

"Me neither."

"Guess it's a first for both of us then," Gwen said. "How exciting."

"It'll be fine, baby. I get a good feeling from them."

"You're only saying that because he offered to teach you about bombs made over a century ago."

"Can you blame me? What an opportunity. If only my classmates would believe me. They'd all be so jealous."

"No, I don't blame you. It's one of the reasons why I love you," Gwen said, the words tumbling out of her mouth without thinking.

The car filled with silence.

Neither had ever said those words before.

The wheels of Theo's car turned loud over the bumpy asphalt.

Trees whooshed by.

Theo wrapped her fingers through Gwen's, and Gwen's racing heart pulsed in her throat and in her wrists, her core clenching so tight she thought she might explode.

"You mean it?" Theo asked, quiet, hopeful.

"I do," Gwen said, blood roaring in her ears.

Theo squeezed her hand. "Well, I think...I think I love you, too."

And then Gwen was sure that she would explode, but for an entirely different reason.

Chapter Seventeen

Over an hour later, they turned onto an unlit dirt road deep in Mt. Hood National Forest. Theo hunched over the wheel, hands at 11 and 1, occasionally nipping at the skin around a nail in her anxiety.

"Where the hell are we?" Theo asked, more to herself than Gwen, so Gwen didn't respond. She had no clue, anyway.

After a few more turns of the road, the Lius stopped, headlights illuminating an open, grassy meadow surrounded by trees.

"Why did we stop?" Theo asked.

"How would I know?"

The ground rumbled, shifting like a small earthquake.

"Gwen, what is that? What's happening?" Theo asked, voice and pitch rising.

"Again – how would I know?" Gwen replied, trying to keep her voice calm despite the spike of fear and adrenaline as the earth grumbled beneath them.

It stopped abruptly, and the Lius' car dipped downward until it went out of sight.

"Uhh... was that supposed to happen?" Gwen asked.

"How would I know?" Theo barked back, mocking Gwen's tone.

"That was fair, I guess. Stay here, and I'll check it out."

Gwen stepped into the frigid night, the higher elevation causing the air to turn even more brittle and frigid. She shivered, closing the door behind her as Theo said, "Be careful!"

Gwen took out her phone and turned on the flashlight, walking forward to where the Lius had been. She hadn't heard a crash, so that was a good sign, right?

Feet crunched on dead pine needles and branches while she walked, light shining on the brown and orange remnants of fall as they decayed. A flash of dark silver metal caught in the light, and as she approached, her mouth dropped.

There was a tunnel leading down into the ground. It was wide and tall, angled at a steady slope with asphalt on the bottom, the sides and top a dark silver metal.

She ran back to the car and slid back inside its warmth. Buckling her seatbelt, she gasped out her discovery. "It's a tunnel!"

"A what now?"

"A tunnel. It goes underground. That's where they went. If you go forward, you'll see it."

Theo stared at her, mouth agape. "You want me to drive forward into the ground where I can't see where the slope is."

"Here, I'll stand at the entrance so you know when to expect it," Gwen said, leaping out of the car again.

This was just too cool.

Theo drove the car forward, slow and careful. When she got to Gwen and the car dipped downward, she slammed on the brakes.

Gwen hopped back in the car, the headlights lighting the tunnel until it stretched too far to illuminate.

"See?" Gwen said. "A tunnel."

"Yes, I see," Theo replied, eyes unblinking, as if she couldn't believe what was before her.

"Well, let's go then."

"Right," Theo replied, and eased the car forward, heading underground.

Once beneath, a sudden sense of claustrophobia struck Gwen. The closeness of the walls and the darkness ahead pressed in on all sides, and she took steadying breaths, not wanting to increase Theo's anxiety.

Her panic eased when the ground flattened and she saw Feng and Daiyu standing beside a row of cars. Feng pointed at where Theo should park, and Daiyu pressed a button on the wall, the earth rumbling again as the door that opened to the outside once again closed.

They stepped out into the wide garage, the sound of their footsteps and closing doors echoing between the gray walls.

Gwen and Theo grabbed their bags, holding their precious few belongings. Feng and Daiyu beckoned them to follow, opening a door that led into another dark hallway, the Lius flicking on warm overhead lights that buzzed in the relative silence.

Walking behind the Lius, Theo asked, "I don't suppose you have any gin, do you?"

Gwen wrapped her hands around Theo's, whose fingers shook with anxiety. She gave them a reassuring squeeze, then traced her thumb over the back of her hand.

"We do," Feng said.

"You're not the first humans to be here," Daiyu added.

"Right. Of course," Theo said, hand tightening in Gwen's.

A dark metal door, the same color of the walls, stood at the end of the hallway.

Feng opened the door, and the warm orange light of flame spread into the hall.

The warmth of a fresh fire spilled over Gwen's skin as she stepped over the threshold. Low-backed, wide couches filled the room, a gas fire licking at the glass. The wall adjacent to the fireplace was long and undecorated, a stark contrast to the rest of the walls that had modest paintings or furniture leaning against them. Two corridors branched off the living room, the space spilling into innumerable rooms, guarded by cracked doors that led into the darkness.

"Please, make yourselves comfortable," Daiyu said, nodding toward a couch opposite a steady fire. They muttered their thanks and sat on one of the couches, the warmth spreading over their cold and worried bones.

A human with golden hair and a firm build stepped through the door to the right and bowed low, arm swept out to his side. "Welcome home – how can I serve you?"

"Ah, Lucas. Our guests need a drink. Gin and tonic?" Daiyu asked Theo.

"Please," Theo replied, leaning forward to spread her hands before the flames. Daiyu asked Gwen if she wanted anything but she declined, too distracted by their sudden change in circumstance to think about what to drink. Lucas left, returning to the room from which he came.

"We will return shortly. We need to scatter the leaves over the entrance," Daiyu said.

"Do you need any help?" Gwen asked.

Feng shook his head. "No, thank you. We have done it many times. And can see in the dark. We will be swift."

"Okay," Gwen said. Daiyu and Feng exited down a side hallway, footsteps quiet and quick.

By the time they returned, Gwen and Theo were warm, leaning away from the fire and resting back on the couch. Theo had finished her drink, and her eyes had closed, dozing in the quiet, the adrenaline wearing off.

Theo startled awake when the Lius came back into the room, the sudden jerk of her body jostling Gwen into consciousness.

"We weren't going to bother you," Feng said.

"You must be exhausted," Daiyu added. "You can rest before we talk, if you want."

"No, that's okay," Gwen said, rubbing her eye and sitting up. "I want answers more than I want sleep."

Feng nodded, him and Daiyu sitting opposite them in front of the waning fire. Feng turned a dial, and it sputtered back to life. The bright flames danced on Daiyu's skin, brightening the beige and turning it a brilliant shade of topaz.

"I'm afraid we cannot tell you much," Daiyu said.

"There is much we do not know," finished Feng.

"Do you know where Nikki is?" Gwen asked, hope tightening in her throat.

Daiyu and Feng shook their heads.

"Do you know where the Mother is?"

Again, they shook their heads.

"What do you know, then?" Gwen asked, exasperated.

"We know who the Mother is," Feng said.

"We know what she wants," Daiyu added.

"We know who is an enemy, and who is an ally."

"We know how to stay hidden."

"We know –"

"Okay, okay, I get it," Gwen said. "You know things. How about you tell me what those things are. Like, who is the Mother and what does she want?"

"Lilith," Feng said.

"The first vampire," Daiyu explained. "She wants revenge on her enemies."

"She wants to enslave humankind."

"Why?" Theo asked.

"We do not know the full story of Lilith. We know she was trapped and seeks revenge on those who trapped her. We do not know how she came to be imprisoned, nor the mechanism of her release," Daiyu said.

"We think it likely that Nikki's boyfriend was a type of key, or counter spell, to release her."

"We also think it likely that Nikki's refusal to heed Lilith's call led to her being punished. And is why she is missing."

"Perhaps she is with the Mother. Perhaps she is where the Mother once was."

Gwen's heart was in her stomach. How was she supposed to figure out where Nikki was? How was she supposed to free her from wherever she is?

"Revenge, I get," Gwen said, forcing strength into her voice, despite her sense of defeat. "But why enslave all of humankind?"

"Also for revenge," Daiyu said.

"And for an easy, endless, food supply," Feng added, leaning against the wall.

Theo shivered at his words and then rubbed her hands on her arms.

Lucas brought in a refill of Theo's drink, the room burdened with silence, then retreated without a word.

"Tyee claimed Lilith's return would usher in a new age for vampires," Daiyu said.

"This is not good news for any living creature on Earth. Not even for vampires. They will become reckless and competitive. The whole planet will be a bloodbath, until no blood is left to spill."

Gwen and Theo were silent, the only sounds in the living room for several long, tense moments the steady hissing of the fire.

"What can we do?" Gwen asked.

Daiyu turned her eyes to the flames and whispered, "We do not know."

"Is anyone from the coven on our side?"

Feng shook his head. "No. That's why we came here after freeing Nikki from Tyee. No one else knows it's here."

"It's impressive," Theo said.

"Thank you. It took a long time to build," Feng said. "As far as we know, the Lopezes and your parents, Gwen, are neutral. The Lopezes have already fled the region and returned to their family in New Mexico. I believe the Silvas would be on our side if they were here. But we do not know where they are, either. The rest – the Ivarssons, your sisters, Tyee – they're all firm believers in Lilith."

"Do you know anyone else who could help?" Gwen asked.

"We are waiting for the pieces to settle before we make calls. We do not wish to alert the enemy to our whereabouts, our plans," Feng said, lifting a hand in front of the fire.

"What are your plans?"

"Still in development," Feng said. "We need more information first."

"We must be careful in both finding information, and who we give it to," Daiyu said.

"I understand, but how are we going to move forward with freeing Nikki and stopping Lilith if we don't have sources to get information from?"

"Gwen, you must be patient. The war hasn't yet begun. There is still time to gather information, to collect our forces," Feng said.

"The war?"

Feng nodded. "Lilith will not be stopped easily. We must be a strong and well-informed army to defeat her. This conflict will not be bloodless or pain-free."

"Great, those are some really comforting words. Appreciate it."

"Sometimes there is no comfort in the truth," Daiyu said.

Gwen sighed, leaning back on the couch and staring into the fire. "Well, I'm waiting to hear from someone who can help us. Hopefully."

Daiyu nodded. "That's good. Who is it?"

Gwen hesitated, thinking of what Daiyu had just said about keeping some information close to the vest in case the wrong ears heard it. But the Lius had saved Nikki, and taken her and Theo to a secret safe house, so they seemed like good allies.

At least for now.

"Xander's mom. She told Nikki and me that she was going to summon the Cradle and then –"

Feng's thick eyebrows shot up.

"You know what the Cradle is?" Gwen asked.

Feng shared a long glance with his wife. She nodded, just barely, and he said, "Some. What I know has been mixed with myth and rumor, so I am not sure what is true."

"Okay, so who are they?"

"They are the foes of vampires," Daiyu said. "What their abilities are, how they came to be, is as much a mystery to us as how Lilith became the first vampire." Daiyu lifted her shoulders, the smallest shrug. "They have kept their secrets, their magics, quiet and close."

"Well, now I really want Ina to call me back. Sounds like she'd have all our answers."

They sat in silence, the faint whir of the fireplace a pleasant hum in the background. Theo sipped her gin and tonic, swirling the dregs that clung to the ice at the bottom of the glass.

"I think it's our turn for questions," Feng said. "Gwen, will you please tell us all you know of what has happened?"

Gwen hesitated again, chewing on her lip. She looked at Feng and Daiyu, their open, still faces as patient as statues, then glanced at Theo, stiff and quiet. Theo gave her a small nod, so Gwen told the Lius everything she knew from Nikki meeting Xander up through when Nikki went missing, and all their efforts to find information since, ending with telling them about how Ina's house had been burned to the ground. Gwen told them about the artifacts she found there, how the tablet exploded into dust when her blood touched it.

"May we see the cylinder seal?" Daiyu asked.

Theo pulled it from her bag and handed it over, Daiyu rolling it in her palm and inspecting the engravings.

"Curious," she said. "It is warm to the touch. Did you notice this, Theo?"

Theo shook her head. "It felt cool to me."

Daiyu hummed, and clasped her fist tightly around it. After several seconds, Gwen heard a soft sizzle and smoke billowed from between Daiyu's fingers. Daiyu hissed and dropped the seal, revealing a burned palm. As soon as the cylinder hit the ground, Daiyu's wound began stitching back together.

"This must be a relic of the Cradle," Daiyu said.

"Ina said she was part of that," Gwen replied. "But she didn't explain much about it except that it's a group of vampire slayers."

"We do not know much about them either," Feng said. "We also know little of these ancient relics, but this one would at least serve to identify if someone was a vampire. What the engravings say precisely, however, I do not know. The tablet you had was likely similarly enchanted."

"I'm not a vampire though," Gwen said. Daiyu, Feng, and Theo averted their gaze, and Gwen said with vehemence, "I'm *not*."

After several seconds, Daiyu cleared her throat and asked Theo, "Where's your brother?"

"He's at his home. Why?"

Daiyu and Feng shared a long glance.

"Why?" Theo repeated, voice hitching with worry.

"Tomorrow, when the sun has stretched over the mountain, you two need to get all your belongings and bring him here. None of you are safe," Daiyu said.

"What are you talking about?" Gwen asked. "Terrance has no idea what's going on. And I can't just leave my studio – there's too much I need there."

"Listen, Gwen," Feng said, dark eyes piercing. "Vadasz and his companions know all of your scents. Someone has destroyed the house where Xander lived. They may use you, or hurt you, to get information. Or they may use you for leverage."

"But...we're nothing in the grand scheme of things."

"That's not true. You openly defied the Mother, even if you did not understand who, or what, you were defying. Do not expect her to be forgiving or merciful. And as for your brother," Feng said, eyes switching to Theo, whose hands clasped tight on her glass, "he could become collateral damage. Or used to get to you and Gwen."

Theo's mouth pressed into a firm line, her eyes unfocused as she thought. "I'll try to talk to him tomorrow. See if I can convince him to come."

"His girlfriend, too," Daiyu said. "She was there when Vadasz came, so she is in danger, as well."

"That might be a stretch, but I'll try."

"I'll print directions for you to find your way back here tomorrow. Please return before sundown, and make sure no one follows you. If someone stops you, burn the directions and call us," Feng said, standing in one smooth, elegant motion and stretching out his hand for his wife.

Daiyu took his hand and he pulled her to her feet. She said, "I'll set up the rooms for you and notify the staff of your long-term stay. They'll take care of you if you have any questions."

"Okay. Thanks," Gwen said, though her heart drummed in her head, and she wished she had a stiff drink as well. In all her memory, she never slept in a house whose owners were both strangers and vampires. While she trusted the Lius enough for now, she felt off-balance, like a rug was slowly being pulled from under her feet.

The beat of her heart in her chest was like a small, buzzing hive, anxious and looking for escape.

"I didn't think of the dangers to us, or Terr Bear, before now. I assumed we didn't matter to – to Lilith," Theo whispered, looking into her empty glass. "Things are changing so fast." Gwen nodded and said, "I know. I'm scared, too." She leaned into Theo and rested her head on her shoulder. "But we'll find Terrance and Rachel and bring them here, make sure they're safe."

Theo dropped her voice, so quiet Gwen could barely hear it. "You think they'll be safe here? They're both humans, too."

Gwen imagined the four of them in these underground walls, stuck with Feng and Daiyu and their servants. Her heart didn't skip a beat nor did her gut twist, so she said, "I do. I don't know why, but I feel like we can trust them. I don't think they'll hurt us or betray us."

"I have the same feeling. I just worry."

"I know, I do too. Just remember the mantra of the day: we'll figure it out."

Theo's braids moved against Gwen's head as she nodded.

"Your room is ready," Daiyu said, stepping back into the dimly lit living room. "If you'll follow me."

Gwen and Theo stood, Gwen's body stiff from sitting so long and aching from the exhaustion of the day. They followed Daiyu down the hall opposite to the parking garage, and at the very far end, Daiyu opened a door and indicated for them to step inside.

"There is an intercom that connects to the servant's room if you need anything."

"Thank you," Gwen and Theo chimed, though a curdle of unease swept through Gwen at the thought of using a servant.

Daiyu nodded and closed the door behind her.

The room was like the rest of the underground house, with black minimalist furniture and dim white lights that hummed through the lamps.

"It's not exactly cozy," Gwen said. "But it's not bad."

Theo tapped a knuckle on the wall, the sound dense and fading quickly. "Seems sturdy enough. How soundproof do you think it is?"

"Why – are you having dirty thoughts?" Gwen asked, grinning.

Theo smiled and said, "No, but don't vampires have super hearing? I'm wondering how much they can hear through this."

"We could try screaming louder and louder until they come running."

"I don't think they'd appreciate that."

Gwen shrugged. "But we'd know."

"True, but I don't want to hear screaming right now either." Theo replied, opening a door that led to a private bathroom, with black tile walls and white floors. She nodded in approval. "Nice." Gwen pointed at the two fresh toothbrushes beside the sink. "Even the toothbrushes are black and gray. What do they have against color?"

"I like it. It's very modern chic."

"Okay, well, while you enjoy your fashionable underground getaway, I'm going to go pass out," Gwen said, stepping out of the bathroom and flinging herself onto the black and white bed, stomach down. Gwen's muscles sang with the glory of relaxation when she landed. It was the perfect combination of firm and soft. "I'll make a sound-proofing spell for this room tomorrow. Or the next day. Sometime soon."

She listened to the patter of Theo's feet as she continued her search of the room and got ready for bed herself. But when Theo told her she had found spare pajamas, Gwen grumbled a half reply, the exhaustion of magic and adrenaline and worry pulling her down into the lovely dark unconsciousness of sleep.

Chapter Eighteen

Theo's tossing and turning woke her up several times in the night, but overall, Gwen slept well. No dreams. Just sweet, sweet nothingness. Like a long, heavy blink.

Gwen opened her eyes, and the dark cold of the room made a pit form in her stomach – if all was normal, she would be home with the first touches of dawn lighting her studio. If she hadn't messed up her bindings so horribly, she would be getting up to feed her flock and whoever else wanted to stop by for breakfast.

Years and years of that routine, with so much life around her. All the pets and coos and conversations, and now... the silence, the absence, pressed down on her chest so heavily she didn't want to get up.

She didn't know if she could.

She didn't know if she would ever be able to get used to life without them.

She didn't know if she would ever get revenge on those who killed them, if she'd ever have the satisfaction of leaving those monsters cowering and defenseless, lashing wind and anger against their faces, making them rue the day they ever wronged her.

Theo's hands patted around in the dark, knocking into the night-stand, hitting the black painted wood until she found the lamp.

Dim white light spilled into the room, and Gwen pushed against that invisible weight on her chest, sitting up and tossing her legs over the side of the bed.

As much as she hated it, as much as a storm raged against her ribs at the injustice of it, how it pried open the wounds that hid her loneliness from herself, there was only one way to move, and that was forward.

She needed to save Nikki.

No matter how much she wanted to sit and mourn her flock, to focus on strengthening her magics and repairing the trust lost, she needed Nikki back more. And she didn't know if there was anyone else out there looking for her.

I hope you're okay, she thought.

"Are you okay?" Theo asked, stretching across the bed on her belly to put a hand on Gwen's back.

"Yeah, just thinking."

"About what?"

"How to save the world."

"Heavy thoughts for the morning."

"Ugh, tell me about it." Gwen yawned and stretched her arms over her head.

Theo got up from the bed and said, "Sounded like you didn't sleep well."

"No, it's hard for me to sleep in new places. I need an adjustment period."

Once Theo and Gwen were freshened up and ready to go, Gwen twisted the doorknob to find it locked.

"What the hell?" Gwen yelled, panic fluttering in her chest, and she shook the handle hard, prepared to break the door down if she had to.

"Relax. That was me," Theo said, reaching around her to twist the lock in the handle.

The door popped open with the next turn, and Gwen's fear subsided, heart rate returning to normal. "Why did you lock it?"

"Made me feel safer."

"You know they probably have a key to the door, since it's in their own house," Gwen said, shutting it behind them.

"I know. But I'd at least hear someone try to get in if it's locked."

"That's true," Gwen said. "Hopefully something we don't have to worry about."

Beside the door to the parking garage was a small bench, a large paper bag with a note taped to it. Gwen unfolded the note, finding directions on one side and wishes for a good day on the other.

"What's in the bag?" Gwen asked, Theo peering inside.

A sweet smile split Theo's face. "They packed us lunch."

"They did what now?" Gwen asked, shoving her face over the hole of the bag, finding sandwiches and apple slices. "I don't even know what to say. Or think."

A throat cleared from behind them and Gwen jumped.

A different human, similar in complexion to the male from last night but female, said, "There is breakfast for you as well, if you like."

"Uhh…" Gwen said, at a loss for words.

"Can we take it to go? We're on a tight schedule."

"Of course." The woman gave a small bow and retreated.

"I was not expecting them to be so thoughtful," Gwen said.

"They were human once, right? Maybe they remember what it's like."

"They also had a daughter. Maybe some parental instinct is still in there."

"What happened to her?" Theo asked.

"I don't think she survived the voyage over the Pacific."

"That's terrible," Theo said, the paper bag scrunching in her squeezing fingers.

"Yeah. It is," Gwen replied, hoping the Lius couldn't overhear them.

The woman returned with two containers in a reusable bag and said, "Will you require anything else before you leave?"

"No, thank you," Gwen said.

"What's your name?" Theo asked.

"Oh!" The woman said, a pink blush rising to her lightly freckled cheeks. "I'm Olivia."

"I'm Theo, and this is Gwen." Gwen waved when Theo pointed to her. "Nice to meet you."

"It's nice to meet you too," Olivia said, the blush deepening pinker. She bowed again, hiding her head, and said, "Please let me know if there is anything I can do for you." Olivia straightened and walked away before either could say another word.

"Well, that was interesting," Gwen said, the reusable bag slung over her forearm. "You ready to go surprise your brother?"

Theo groaned. "No, but we need to. Let's go."

Automatic lights switched on in the garage when it sensed their movement, guiding the way through the wide-open space. Theo's car sputtered to life despite the chill, and they rattled up and out of the ground, the horizontal door opening upon their approach.

The day was dark and rainy, pouring what was regionally called an atmospheric river. The ground was slick with mud, and Theo moaned with anxiety.

"My car isn't meant for this type of terrain."

"Well, let's try to get out of here and find a different car in town. If we can find it, maybe we can steal Nikki's."

Theo inched forward, tires slipping in the mud, sliding to find purchase, making small progress as they gained traction on rock and twigs.

"Terr Bear has a jeep."

"That'd be convenient."

Theo nodded, biting a nail, and the car rolled its way through the mud, the rain pounding against the windows and metal roof. When they got to the main access road, the car moved a little easier, as there was light gravel mixed with the dirt. Damp holes and trenches still caught on the tires, so they drove at a crawl until Gwen finally navigated them to the highway using Feng's directions.

Wiping her ravaged, saliva-speckled fingers on her pants, Theo settled and wriggled her back, relaxing from the stress of navigating her way down the impoverished road. The well-maintained highway kept the remainder of their trip smooth, nothing but the slicing rain to interfere with the drive.

"Okay, give me some of that food," Theo said, stretching out her hand.

Gwen peered into the reusable bag, pulled out a container, and gave it a shake. "It's scrambled eggs, might be difficult to eat while driving."

"I can manage," Theo said, snatching the container from Gwen's hands, popping the lid and bracing it between her legs.

"Alrighty then. There's bacon, too," Gwen said handing her a fork.

"Oh yeah, give me some of that."

Gwen gave her another container, with the crispy bacon broken in half to fit.

Theo grunted with delight as she bit and chewed into the bacon and eggs, and Gwen grinned.

It was nice to be around someone who could still enjoy life's little pleasures.

Gwen took a few bites of eggs, and despite how her stomach grumbled with hunger, how her tastebuds sang with the salty protein, she couldn't eat much. For some reason, it felt wrong for her to be eating, to be enjoying anything.

They stopped by Theo's place first, where she lived with her parents, as it was closest. It was a cute two-story house built in the 1900s in North Portland, the neighborhood tucked under bare deciduous trees and mixed shrubs.

They parked in front of her home, which had a sparse but quaint garden, with rose bushes and winter blooming camellias, emitting a faint chocolate scent. The porch had mismatched furniture, a funky and eclectic yet cozy mix.

With her parents at work, Theo headed straight for her room and packed quicky while Gwen meandered, looking at the old photos and artwork in the home. A distant sense of longing bloomed in her chest, imagining what it must have been like to grow up in the same house as your parents and sibling, one that was so loving and welcoming, where you saw photos of yourself hung on the walls, the fridge.

Theo walked back down the steps, her cadence light and fast. She found Gwen in the kitchen, looking at photographs of her as a child on the fridge.

"It occurred to me I need to tell them I'll be gone for longer than usual. They're used to me mostly being at your place, but maybe now I should say that Terr Bear and I are going on a vacation for a while."

Gwen looped her arm through Theo's elbow, not knowing how to comfort her, and with one last glance at all the photos on the fridge, they left her house.

Theo barked a laugh as she looked at her car, mud-streaks high on the sides and covering the tires.

"At least it's raining," Gwen said. "It should wash some of it off."

"It doesn't bother me. Just funny," Theo said with a small shrug, running from the porch to the car to dodge the rain.

Waiting in the car for it to heat up, Theo called her brother and told him they were heading over, hanging up before he could ask too many questions.

The rain didn't cease, a constant dark gray hanging over the city. According to the clock, by the time they reached Terrance and Xander's apartment, the sun should have been high in the sky, if they could have seen it.

At Terrance's apartment door, Theo raised a fist, poised to knock, but her knuckles did not connect with the door.

"You ready for this?" Gwen asked.

Theo nodded, but still did not bend her wrist.

Gwen stretched around her and pressed the doorbell.

Theo's lips were pursed when Gwen stood straight, and as Theo dropped her raised hand to her side, Gwen gave her a grin.

The apartment door flung open with such ferocity it suctioned wind out from the hallway, the air whipping by them.

"Damn, Terr, calm down. You'll break the door," Theo said.

Terrance had one hand on the edge of the open door, the other curled into a fist, braced on his hip. Gwen had forgotten how much he looked like Theo. They had the same rich brown skin tone and dark eyes. The differences were in his squarer jaw, bald head, and stocky, muscular frame. "Why you always gotta hang up on me, huh?"

"Because you'll ask questions forever if I let you. You gonna let us in?"

He sighed from deep in his chest, so low and rough it was almost a growl, as he stepped back and let them into his apartment. It opened into the kitchen, a small dining table at the back corner near a window. To the right was a small living room, with one couch and a TV.

The walls were surprisingly bare, but a few sad plants lined the kitchen windowsill, the only spots of color in the apartment.

"Hey, you two," Rachel said, curled onto the couch and snacking from a bowl of popcorn, her glossy, straight black hair cut into a sharp bob just above her shoulders.

"Hey, Rachel, how are you?" Theo asked as Gwen placed the chairs from the dining table opposite the couch.

"I'm good, just trying to stay dry and warm."

"You've had more success than us."

"Looks like it," Rachel said. Gwen moved the last dining chair over and sat in it, while Rachel's eyes moved over their bodies, chewing. She stuck the bowl out, "You want some?"

"No, thanks," Theo said, sitting in the dining chair beside Gwen. "You should sit down, Terr Bear."

Rachel's nose crinkled with amusement. "Terr Bear? That's adorable."

Terrance grunted a reply as he sat on the couch beside her, arm slung around her shoulders, Rachel's body curled into him, like two puzzle pieces sliding together.

"Well, only Theo the Leo is allowed to call me that."

"Theo the Leo?" Gwen asked, eyebrows raised.

Theo leaned back and crossed her legs, one arm slung over the back of the chair, the other across her legs, fiddling with her fingers. "It doesn't have the same ring as Terr Bear."

"A Leo would say that," Rachel added, tossing more popcorn into her mouth.

"I'm not a Leo though."

Rachel shrugged and Terrance said, "But you are a lion. In your own way."

"I guess so," Theo responded with a smug shrug.

The room grew silent, except for the sounds of Rachel chewing.

"Spit it out, sis. What's going on?"

"Well...I, uh...we need you to come with us to a safe house. You might be in danger."

Rachel stopped chewing and stared at Theo, eyes blinking and mouth open.

Terrance's face flinched with confusion, "What?"

"You're not safe. So, you – both of you – need to come with us."

"Yeah, I heard you. But I don't understand what you're saying. What are we in danger of?"

Theo's fiddling fingers rubbed together faster, her anxiety obvious, and she did not speak.

Gwen cleared her throat. Then, looking at Terrance with a raised chin, said, "Vampires exist and an ancient one – actually, the oldest one – has kidnapped both Xander and Nikki. We don't know where they are, and it's possible that all four of us are in danger because we're their friends. So, we need to go to an underground safe house owned by members of my coven to be safe from the bad vampires. And to plan how to free Xander and Nikki."

The jaws of Rachel and Terrance dropped lower and lower. Several long seconds in silence passed as they stared at her agape.

"I knew it!" Rachel said at the same moment Terrance burst out laughing.

They both frowned then looked at each and said, "What?"

They laughed, short and awkward, as they spoke over each other again.

"You first – why did you laugh?" Rachel asked.

"I mean, it's obviously a joke."

"It's not a joke," Gwen said, then turned to Rachel. "Why did you say, 'I knew it'? Do you know something?" Her heart soared as she spoke, thinking that maybe by some strange twist of fate, Rachel would be a member of the Cradle or somehow know something that could help them.

"Oh," Rachel said, face dropping as Gwen's lit with excitement. "I don't know anything. I just always had a hunch there was more than this," she said, swirling her hands above her head. "More than just boring old humans."

"You gotta be joking. You believe this?" Terrance leaned back, face pinched with confusion.

"Why wouldn't I?"

Terrance ran a hand over his face, as if it would restart the scene before him.

"I'm a witch, Terrance. You'll have to come with me to see the proof of vampires, but I can show you, right here and now, that magic exists," Gwen said, standing.

"Bull."

With a deep breath, she imagined the threads of her magic weaving up through her like the winds through canyons, and as it funneled into her core, she transferred it to her hands. Her hands lit up, silvery and gold threads shining from under her skin.

"Oooooo," Rachel cooed.

Gwen thrust her hands out, expelling her magic against the air, sending a sudden gust to blow in Terrance and Rachel's faces. Rachel's hair fluttered with the air, and she blinked, amazed. Terrance froze, terror contorting his face.

"That's soooo cool!" Rachel said. "How do you do that?"

Gwen smiled, her heart feeling lighter at someone enjoying her magic. "I don't really know how it works, but I pull – no, it's more like asking – no, hmmm.... how do –"

"Baby, I'm sorry to interrupt, but we don't have time for this. We can explain it later. We have to be back before sunset, remember?"

"Oohhh," Rachel said knowingly, nodding. "I'll go get my things."

Before Rachel stood, Terrance snapped out of his paralysis and stopped her with a hand on her elbow. "You're not seriously going, are you?"

"Of course I am. I want to be safe. Don't you?"

"Just... hold on." Terrance leaned forward and rubbed his hands on his face, resting his elbows on his knees. "I mean, this is insane. Like really insane."

"Yup," Gwen said. "Anyway, let's go."

"No, no, no. Hold on. I have to ask some questions first."

"Terr Bear, we don't have time for questions. We can talk in the car, but right now, you need to pack. Quickly." Theo leaned forward, mimicking his posture, so that their faces were close. "Don't you trust me?"

Terrance looked up, assessing her face. They silently communicated for a moment, until Terrance sighed, dropping his head and hands. "I do. But do you really expect us to walk away from our lives? What about school? Work? Rent?"

Theo chewed on the inside of her lip. "We should contact the schools and tell them we're taking a semester off due to a family emergency. I'm sure we can find someone to back that up. I don't know what to do about work and rent, but we can figure it out."

Terrance stared at her, jaw ticking.

"What's the worst that can happen?" Rachel asked. "Either it's real and we're safe, or it's a prank and they have a surprise for us. *And* you get several months off of school."

"Or it's real and we're walking into a trap, or it's a prank and they're going to humiliate us. *And* my timeline for graduation gets messed up."

"You really think I'd do that to you?" Theo asked.

"No. But I expect some answers, pronto," he said, standing, and walking to his room with Rachel.

"I think Rachel helped us out there. Would have taken a lot longer for him to come without her," Gwen said.

"Isn't it strange she'd believe this so quickly?" Theo asked, leaning closer.

Gwen shrugged. "I did just hurl wind in their faces out of nowhere. And my hands did the glowy thing. I'd believe me."

"Good point."

While Rachel and Terrance packed, Theo drafted an email to the school requesting a semester leave for both of them. Rachel and Terrance were ready in minutes, Rachel only having an overnight bag and Terrance shoving what he needed into a small suitcase.

"I guess we're ready," Terrance grumbled.

"Great. We're taking your car," Theo said, standing and putting her dining chair back.

"What? Why?"

"My car isn't big enough for all of us and our suitcases. Plus, it isn't good on the roads we'll be on."

Terrance's face dropped, looking like he regretted agreeing to leave. "Where are we going?"

"Somewhere forested, with dirt roads," Gwen said, and Terrance groaned again.

They swapped all belongings into Terrance's car and left Theo's in his spot in the parking garage, piling into his Jeep. Gwen plugged directions to her house into his phone, and then they reentered the dreadful, wet fall day, rain splattering against the car and sloshing under the tires.

As Terrance drove in silence, Gwen told him and Rachel everything they knew about the supernatural and what had happened over the past few months, including the confrontation with the Scythians that Terrance and Rachel slept through.

After showing them the news article about Xander's house being burned to the ground, neither responded for several minutes.

Eventually Terrance shook his head and said, "I'm going to need some time to process this."

"I understand," Theo said, a hand landing on his shoulder, giving it a squeeze. "But thank you for listening. And for coming with us."

He nodded, and Rachel said, "I just can't believe we slept through that whole thing with the... the Scythians?" She shook her head. "We must've been so drunk."

"Be glad you didn't wake up," Theo said. "It still gives me nightmares."

Gwen squeezed Theo's hand, images flashing through her mind of Vadasz's skin sloughing off as it pushed against the barrier, of all her flock and their friends, their families, coming to their aid, rushing and pecking and clawing at the Scythians as Nikki and Xander ran through the forest.

The rest of the car ride passed in heavy silence, except for the steady patter of rain against the windshield and the whir of wheels on the road. At Gwen's house, she asked Rachel and Terrance to stay in the car, telling them to drive away as fast as they could if her sisters appeared. Their faces fell, grave and somber, but they nodded and remained.

Gwen and Theo walked around the house and in the direction of her studio, holding the cold breakfast containers to their chests, eyes on the ground as their hoods covered their heads. Their feet squelched in the mud, saturated with moisture, flattening the dead grass and flowers.

Inside her studio, Gwen stared at the wild space, *her* space, and her heart sank at having to say goodbye.

It'll be temporary, she told herself.

Gwen directed Theo to bag up her clothes while Gwen packed as many ingredients and tools as she could. Several minutes later, they stood at the door, Gwen's arms filled with plastic bags of tools, ingredients, potions, and salves in various states of creation. A massive backpack of clothes hung from Theo's tall frame, and a warm surge of gratitude that she wasn't alone filled Gwen's chest.

"Guess that's that then. Thanks for helping," she said as they stepped back out into the cold.

Before they left, Gwen dumped the leftover scrambled eggs near the ground in front of the roost. Even if her own flock wasn't there to eat it, maybe somebody would come by and enjoy it. Would know that she still cared, would still feed them.

The sun was setting as they drove south back into the Cascade Mountain Range, only evidenced by the darkening of the gray clouds overhead. By the time they reached the Lius' safe house, Theo and Gwen checking over their shoulders intermittently to see if anyone was behind them, the faintest light of day remained, the sky such a deep, dark gray it was almost black.

The parking garage door opened at their approach, Terrance and Rachel gasping with surprise and awe as the ground rumbled beneath them. Terrance inched forward, mumbling about clearances, but the car sloped down without scraping the ceiling.

The Lius stood in the parking garage near the door, waiting. Feng's hands were in his pockets and Daiyu linked an arm through his, still as statues.

"Oh, are those them? The vampires?" Rachel asked, and a twitch of amusement on Feng's face indicated he had heard them despite the whisper.

Gwen nodded, and when Rachel said, "Ooooo," Gwen smiled, the amazement and wonder Rachel felt at her world a refreshing breath of air compared to the usual and recent darkness of it.

Parked and bags slung over their shoulders, the Lius beckoned them inside, leading them to the warmth of the living room, once again aglow with a gas fireplace.

"Drop your belongings. Lucas will take care of them once he is done covering the door," Daiyu said, and the four of them grunted with the relief of losing the physical weight on their shoulders as they put all their things on the ground.

But the invisible pressure of the dark and dangerous unknown still clung to Gwen like a cloak made of lead.

Introductions made, Rachel stepped forward and asked, "I don't mean to be rude but...can I see – them?" Rachel tapped on a canine in her mouth.

Daiyu and Feng smiled, then took out the settings made to mimic human teeth, their shark-like, silver fangs glinting in the dim light.

"Wow," Rachel breathed, her already large eyes widening as she looked at them. "That's so cool."

Terrance grunted with disagreement but held his tongue.

"Thank you," Feng said.

"We understand that this may have been a long and surprising day for you. We will give you a tour and then let you rest. We can talk further tomorrow night. Right this way," Daiyu said, turning down the hall to the left.

Down this hall was a basic kitchen with a four-table dining area. It contained a massive pantry and several large refrigerators and freezers, storing several months of human food, and likely months' worth of blood. Gwen raised her eyebrows at the sheer amount of variety and storage they had. How long had they been stocking up this safe house?

How many people had they slowly drained to provide themselves with a long-term supply of blood? Her stomach curdled, imagining each freezer filled with blood bags, the humans hooked to endless needles to supply them. She hoped it wasn't just Lucas and Olivia who gave them blood.

Farther down the hall was a laundry room, cleaning supply closet, and rooms for Lucas and Olivia. At the far end was Feng and Daiyu's bedroom, which they did not enter. The group returned to the living room and down the other hall opposite the entrance, which only had spare rooms and bathrooms. Terrance and Rachel had the room opposite Gwen and Theo, and before leaving them to settle in, the Lius explained where the call buttons were in case they needed something from the help.

The four nodded their thanks, Feng and Daiyu retreating to the living room, and then they stood in silence in the hallway, the reality of the situation sinking in.

"I think I need to lie down," Terrance said, looking sick to his stomach.

"Okay, Terr Bear," Theo said and wrapped her arms around him. "Get some rest. And thanks for coming. I'm so relieved and happy you're here."

"I wish I could say the same, sis," he said, hugging her back.

When they stepped out of their hug, he rubbed the back of his neck and sighed. "Maybe all this will make more sense tomorrow."

"It won't. But hopefully you'll at least feel a little adjusted to it," Gwen replied.

He huffed out air, as if he tried to laugh, then said goodnight as he turned into the room. Rachel waved at them and said, "Goodnight," though her eyes roved over the house, as if she wanted to stay up longer, look around more.

"You don't have to go to bed just because he is," Gwen said. "It's still early."

"I know," Rachel said. "But he seems to be struggling, so I'll stay with him. Maybe I can help talk him through it."

"Thank you," Theo replied.

Rachel nodded and gave them a close-lipped smile, disappearing behind yet another dark gray door.

Gwen and Theo went into their own room, and Gwen flopped onto the bed, arms spread out and looking at the ceiling.

"Honestly, I'm exhausted too," Theo said, turning on a lamp on her nightstand. "I think I'll get ready for bed and doze."

"All right, babe. I'm just going to lie here and think for a minute."

"Okay. But you'll have to scoot over for me eventually," Theo said, leaning over the bed to give her a swift and chaste kiss, then retreated to the bathroom.

Gwen stared at the black ceiling, wondering where Nikki was, what she was seeing at that moment.

Could she see?

Gwen's stomach tightened at the thought, and tears clouded her vision.

No, stop it. She's not dead. She can't be.

She heard the muffled sounds of Terrance and Rachel talking from their room and she flung an arm over her eyes. They'd definitely need a sound silencing spell. More work for her.

Moments later, the press of Theo's body moved the bed, and Gwen adjusted herself, making space and curling under the blankets. Even with Theo's protective embrace, it was a long time before Gwen fell asleep.

Chapter Nineteen

THEY DIDN'T WAKE until late in the morning, bodies weak with fatigue. Groaning, Gwen sat up in bed and stretched before brushing out her hair and throwing on more presentable pajamas. Terrance and Rachel were already in the kitchen when Gwen and Theo went in for coffee and tea, a platter of cold waffles and a pitcher of cranberry juice on the table.

"I didn't expect an underground house to be so fancy," Rachel said, as Gwen and Theo slid into the dining chairs beside her.

"Right?" Theo replied.

"You won't find me complaining about it," said Terrance, stuffing a syrup-filled waffle into his mouth.

After they ate, Gwen offered to make a sound silencing spell for both rooms, and when she stood, so did the others. It was a strange feeling, being the leader. Not traipsing after her siblings, hoping for attention, or pleading with her parents, looking for love. Not even following after Nikki, looking for companionship.

"Don't overdo it, baby," Theo whispered in Gwen's ear, her breath rustling her hair.

"I won't. But we need our privacy," Gwen said, mouth splitting into a wicked grin, picking up Theo's hand and kissing it.

"Ugh, please don't," Terrance said.

"Don't be such a prude," Theo replied, and Rachel snickered.

Gwen spent the next few hours prepping her sound silencing spell. Using a red alder bark decoction as the base, she mixed the leaves of thyme and mullein, added powdered skunk cabbage root, the seeds and dried flower head of thistles, and the berries of English ivy. Theo, Terrance, and Rachel sat in the room while she worked. Rachel offered to help but she didn't have duplicate supplies and Gwen wasn't sure what sort of energy Rachel might accidentally infuse into the mix. Her enthusiasm just might amplify everything.

Once there were enough ingredients to make a spell for two rooms, Gwen pricked her thumb with a knife, dripping her blood into the mix until it was thinner, the trio wincing at her casual self-inflicted wound. As she pulled the magic from inside herself, centering it on her hands, they glowed with gold and silver, healing the cut on her finger, and she wrapped her hands around the blend, at once funneling the magic and the air, as well as the soundwaves of the group's voices, into the mix, letting it know what sound was, what air was, and that it needed to absorb it.

The potion bubbled with the added air and glowed as she infused it, pulsing with light and magic for several seconds after she withdrew her magic, it binding around the mixture according to her will.

Hair matted to her face and neck with sweat, she smeared the mix around the perimeters of both rooms, pulsing an additional infusion of magic around the cracks of the doorframes.

When she was done, Gwen stumbled, head swimming and body weak. Her breath hitched, heart beating a staccato rhythm, and she laid on the bed while Theo and Rachel practiced screaming in their own rooms, ensuring the spell worked.

Of course it did.

Gwen's eyes fluttered open as a cool, damp cloth smoothed around her face.

"Thank you," Gwen whispered to Theo, who wiped away the sweat, then dried her skin.

"No, thank you. You're amazing, you know that, right?" Theo asked.

"Mmm." Gwen replied, lifting her hand, which felt far away and disembodied, to Theo, cupping her face. Theo leaned into her palm but continued to brush the sweat off of Gwen. Through slit eyes, Gwen watched Theo, those hands that fell somewhere between athlete and musician, the delicately sharp curves of her cheeks, her jaw, the way her braids swooped over her shoulder. Heat spread all over her body at Theo's touch.

"You're gorgeous," Gwen said.

Theo looked up at her and smiled, her full mouth widening to show perfect white teeth. She swung her leg over Gwen, straddling her, and Gwen placed her hands on her hips, the muscles taught and lean.

Theo leaned over, hair falling around Gwen's face like a veil, the smell of shea butter and vanilla filing her senses as Theo kissed her below her ear, then her neck, creeping up her cheek to kiss her mouth.

Gwen's hands roamed over Theo's body, feeling every curve and muscle and bone.

"You want to reap the rewards of your spell?" Theo asked, her voice a husky whisper in her ear.

Gwen kissed her in response, opening her mouth with her tongue.

Theo moved her hands, her mouth, down Gwen's body, and she suddenly became very awake.

Mid-afternoon, they stepped into the cold air, the sweat and passion cooling against the winter. Olivia showed them the stairwell that led outside, a steep, spiral staircase that exited from the laundry room. They covered the small trapdoor, barely large enough for a person to climb through, with tree debris and frost behind them.

There was nothing that could be done about the shoeprints left in the dirt, however.

Theo and Gwen meandered the forest, hands entwined, breaths white-gray gusts in the air. A Doug-fir forest surrounded them, a few deciduous trees in the understory. If it had been at a lower elevation, this would have been a great place to forage for truffles. But the thin layer of frost made Gwen stay her hands, not wanting to dig and search through the small drifts of ice.

Instead, they simply walked. Gwen lifted her face up to the pine needles that were the same green as her siblings' eyes, to the sun that none of them could know. It might be the first time she just walked in nature and didn't have an ulterior purpose in foraging and gathering.

It was rather nice, having that lack of intention. She could just exist with Theo, enjoy her and their surroundings, without keeping her eyes on the forest floor for useful ingredients.

It was peaceful.

Her lips lifted in the smallest of smiles. The smile of utter content.

And in that peace, that smile, her gut twisted with guilt. It was so sudden, she nearly doubled over.

Where was Nikki?

Or Xander?

What were they seeing or feeling?

Could they even see or feel?

Were they alive?

The breath caught in Gwen's chest, and she stopped, one sniffle away from collapsing to her knees.

"Baby, what's wrong?" Theo asked.

Seeing the water in Gwen's eyes, the defiant tilt of her chin, Theo wrapped her arms around her in a hug, holding Gwen's head to her chest and smoothing her hair. "I know, I know."

"I just wish I could know if she was okay."

"I know."

"And it feels so wrong to be okay when I don't know if she is. When I don't even know if she's alive."

"I know."

Gwen clung to Theo's jacket, fingers twisting in the fabric. She squeezed her eyes shut, pushing the moisture out of them, and a gate she did not know existed burst open.

Finally, she did not cry just for her lost familiars, her dead flock, or her hateful family. She cried for the hole in her heart that Nikki filled, for her fear of the future, of the enemy they faced, and for the dread of wondering if Nikki was dead.

Chapter Twenty

The Lius woke around dinner, and they sipped on their warm evening blood while Lucas and Olivia cooked a typical spaghetti dinner with bread and a salad that was a few days away from expiring. Gwen took precious bites of the vegetables, wondering when she would get to eat a salad again after this. Wondering how long they would be in the safe house.

After dinner, the Lius beckoned them back to the fire. Rachel and Terrance cuddled on the couch, while Gwen and Theo sat on the floor beside the fireplace.

Standing, Feng said, "What weapons can you wield?"

"Weapons?" Theo sputtered. "What century do you think we're in?"

"There is never an inappropriate era to learn how to defend yourself," he replied, walking to the near wall void of any decoration. Feng pressed something out of Gwen's sight, obscured by the protruding mantle. The movement was followed by a faint, mechanical whir and a low vibration that hummed through the room.

With a gentle creak, the wall disengaged and slid to the side, revealing a panel of tightly packed weapons that stretched the entire length of where the wall had been. Firelight glinted off the dark metal heads on axes and swords and spears of different sizes, ranging from hand axes to battle axes, daggers to short swords to scimitars, throwing spears and spears taller than a person. There were maces, flails, throwing stars, and hammers. They had two crossbows and several bows, both short and long, made of wood or bone. There were pistols, rifles, and shotguns, with boxes of bullets below the mounted weapons.

Gwen's jaw dropped.

Once her mind comprehended the wealth of weapons before her, she looked at Theo, Rachel, and Terrance, all of whom were in various states of surprise. Theo and Rachel's mouths were both open, like hers, and Rachel "ooed" with appreciation, while Terrance's surprise was only apparent in his widened eyes and raised eyebrows.

Gwen laughed. "Of course a secret underground vampire lair would also have a secret stash of weapons."

Feng stood proud, a half grin on his face as he took in his arsenal.

"What calls to you?" Feng asked. "Our personal favorites are already removed and with us. These are all available options."

"Really?" Rachel asked, leaning forward on the couch, eyes wide.

"Really."

Rachel smiled and leapt off the couch, dragging Terrance by his hand behind her to the wall. Theo followed, blinking rapidly, as if she couldn't believe her eyes.

Theo, Rachel, and Terrance approached the wall of weapons, but Gwen remained sitting. She had her magic – she didn't need one of those sharp objects that maim and cripple. All the broken and bent bodies of her flock flashed across her mind, and she stared into the fire, stomach curdling.

"Good choice," Feng said, standing beside Theo. Gwen looked up, Theo holding two engraved silver pistols in her hands.

"Thanks. I haven't ever duel-wielded before. Is there a place to practice?"

Feng's brow furrowed. "Not close. However, I do know a quarry where people practice. Perhaps we could travel there some nights."

"That'd be great. Though, I still want you to teach me how to make bombs."

"Gladly," Feng said, voice lifting with amusement. "Let's do so in the evenings before we go to the quarry."

Feng went to Rachel and Terrance, who spoke with Daiyu, Rachel eyeing a bone bow and needle-like knives, Terrance testing out the weight of a spear and javelin.

Gwen stood beside Theo and asked, "You gonna be a dual pistol-wielding bombmaker now?"

"I'm thinking about it. I've practiced shooting before, but it's been a while. Might be too rusty."

"You have? When?"

Theo smiled wistfully at the memory. "My dad took me when I was thirteen. He took us both, actually. Terr Bear didn't enjoy it, but I did. We kept going until he hurt his back a few years ago."

"I'm sorry, Theo."

She shrugged, still holding the engraved silver pistols in her hands.

"They look good on you. Or with you? Not sure the right way to say that."

"Thanks," Theo said, grinning, and they regrouped with the others.

"I'm not vibing with any of the options." Terrance announced, putting a double-headed axe back onto the rack.

"Why not?" Feng asked.

"I mean, these weapons are cool, but I don't like the lack of protection. I want a shield. If the rest of you are distance fighters, that leaves me up front. I want to have some type of defense."

"Yes, we are lacking in that department," Feng said.

"Until we can find a shield, what feels best?" Daiyu asked.

Terrance turned back to the rack of weapons and tapped a finger on his chin, thinking. He picked up a large, dark metal hammer. He tested the weight in his hands and said, "I like this."

"A fine choice." Daiyu looked at Rachel and Theo. "Feng is adept with ranged weapons. He can teach both of you how to shoot. I can help with the knives and hammer."

Daiyu turned to Gwen. "What would you like to wield?"

"Oh, nothing, thanks. I'm good with my magic."

Feng's eyebrows twitched. "Are you sure?"

"Positive."

Feng and Daiyu hesitated but nodded.

"I suggest we get started straight away," Feng said.

"There is no telling when we will be called to action," Daiyu added.

The group nodded, Terrance and Rachel's eyes wide as they tried to be comfortable with the weapons in their hands.

Daiyu had Terrance and Rachel bundle up, then took them outside to begin training. Theo followed Feng to another room in the safehouse, one previously undisclosed, where he would begin teaching her how to make small, homemade bombs and other, gentler explosives. If you could call any sort of explosive gentle, that is.

Gwen was left standing in the middle of the living room, alone. The safe house grew cold as the fire dimmed, and she retreated to her room to practice magic by herself.

Days passed in a blur, everyone except Theo working their bodies to exhaustion. Theo rambled on about the science Feng taught her, the smoke bombs and grenades, but Gwen let the words wash over her, too fatigued from stretching the limits of her magic to truly listen. Terrance, already muscular, eased into his training more than Rachel, who walked around the house with stiff limbs as the muscles grew and her core strengthened. Slowly, they transitioned to the vampires' schedule, sleeping for most of the day and awakening by night, although since Gwen was mostly in the safe house and did not see the sun or moon, time meant less and less.

Gwen tried to grow the endurance of her magic, practicing summoning and releasing it quickly, stretching herself to the limit of her ability. She practiced throwing out gusts of wind against the wall and experimented with manifesting a wall of air, condensing it into a shield and holding it as long as she could. Nikki's ring on her finger pulsed with the energy in her fingertips, tingling with amplification. It burned at first, but Gwen soon became used to the warmth of the stone on her hand every time magic flowed near it.

One night, restless from being trapped in the safe house and doing the same thing every day, all day, she joined Theo, Rachel, and Feng as they went to the shooting range. It was a deserted quarry, surrounded by tall, still evergreens. Feng set up a folding lamp to offer some light, the illumination highlighting their breaths fogging in the air. As Theo and

Rachel shot, Feng offered corrections and directions. Gwen sat to the side and practiced pooling the magic within her body, trying to speed up the quantity she could gather at once.

A sudden buzzing from her bag caused her to jump, dissipating the magic outside of her instead of returning it to her body, a wave of fatigue settling over her bones.

The buzzing continued at a steady rhythm, harsh against something solid.

Her phone, in her bag, vibrating against the ground.

Gwen's heart leapt into her throat, and she threw herself at her bag, dumping it out until her phone fell to the cold dirt, bright and buzzing.

"Holy shit," Gwen said.

Theo, Rachel, and Feng paused, looking over at Gwen.

"Holy shit, holy shit, holy shit," Gwen said, heart hammering, fingers twitching.

She pressed the green button on the screen and said, "Ina? Is that finally you? Are you okay?"

A muffled sound came from the background before a voice sounded crystal clear in her ear.

"Gwen – what happened to my house?"

Chapter Twenty-One

The quiet scratching of nails on wood broke Nikki out of her rest. If it could even be called that. She hung suspended in the tree, void of hunger or thirst, and had intermittently stopped thinking for so long, she'd faded from wakefulness.

But she never really slept. Flickers of other lives and of her past flashed behind her eyes, voices, words, and things left unsaid haunting her mind.

"Nicoletta darling?" Cat's voice whispered from outside, her nails dragging against the wood, the feel of it sending an uncomfortable shiver over Nikki.

"It's the strangest thing," Cat said, fingertips stopping their trail over the wood. "The pomegranates, they're full of blood."

What? Nikki thought.

"When they dropped, they were normal. But as they decompose, blood seeps out. I picked one up. Pulled it apart. Blood poured over my hands." Cat's voice choked, and she rested her head and hands against the bark.

"Are you dying? Is that what it means? No one in town will speak to me. I'm not sure they are allowed. And Marcus and Titania – the two of

Lilith's disciples who remained to watch me – don't talk to me either. It's as if I am a ghost."

Nikki felt her mom's tears fall on the Tree, as if on her own skin.

"Please, darling, please be alive," Cat whispered, and Nikki's broken heart shattered in her chest. She hung her head, biting back her own tears, her mother so close yet impossibly far. She could not grasp her mother's thread, though she had tried. She could not talk to her through the Tree, nor whisper to her, mind to mind.

Nikki did not know if it was part of Lilith's curse, or if she was too inept at falling through the Earth to find her mother's strand.

What *was* her mom? She had seemed strong and unbending, a redwood, but now she was bent and broken, a willow sapling clutching tight to life, to reality, underneath a howling storm. When Nikki thought of her mother, she came in so many hues, but those were all the colors of the past Cat.

Nikki did not know what she was now. Did not know how to find the thread through time and change.

Even though she was right there.

"You'll find her, in time," Io said, the glitter shifting with the answer. A few glimmers always remained now, in the darkness. It was like having color behind the black of your eyelids. Nothing brightened or illuminated. Nikki did not know what the inside of the Tree looked like, but she was grateful for seeing more than black.

"I hope so. I want to tell her I'm alive." Nikki tightened her face against the rise of her own tears. *"I want to tell her it's not her fault."*

The space around her filled with sadness. *"You will."*

"Something occurred to me," Nikki thought, her breath slowing, tears retreating back behind her eyes.

The sparks lifted in question.

"You said you love all your children equally. That can't be true if you're going to let the vampires dominate humanity. That's favoring Lilith and those who follow her."

Io was silent, thinking.

"If you truly loved all living things equally, you'd find a way to protect them. To find a compromise so neither side is destroyed."

"That was the purpose of imprisoning Lilith. Of making the terms of her punishment conditional."

"Maybe that was the wrong choice," Nikki thought. *"Maybe vampires should never have existed at all."*

"What right do you have to deny them life?" Io asked, tone gentle and inquisitive. *"It is one thing, child, to wish an end to our own suffering. Another entirely to say that all your loved ones, or those who could be loved but are unknown, and even those who are unloved, do not deserve life. Would you have denied your mother, your father, your best friend, the opportunity to live?"*

Nikki was silent, unable to imagine a world without them.

"No, too much of life, of accidents, is too beautiful to destroy. I could not see the path ahead – I was excited and enamored with the new beings, filled with adoration and admiration for the originals. Who was I to make those choices, about who should live and not live? Why not have all life?"

"Humans will not have life if Lilith has her way."

"They will. Only not in the way they are accustomed. Or desire."

"How do you not care about the slavery of humanity, if you love them so much?"

"I believe in their ability to find a way. It was my meddling that caused this problem to begin with. I will not make the same mistake."

"Not doing something will be a mistake. What about at least sending some angels down to fight with us? Surely there are more than just the one that I saw killed."

The flickers twitched like a flinch, and Io said, *"They are guardians, not warriors."* Several seconds passed, and the glimmers rained at a slower speed, winking out in the dark as others appeared. Eventually, Io whispered, *"I will consider your words."*

"Thanks, I guess," Nikki thought. *"Are you ever going to tell me how this started?"*

"Yes, child. Once I untangle my memories from time and can remember the order of events."

"How long will that take?"

The air shimmered with calculation. *"Soon."*

"You keep saying that," Nikki thought, then exhaled hard through her nose, the closest thing to a sigh she would allow herself, with the roots still playing at the corners of her mouth. She hung her head and closed her eyes, and as she drifted into half sleep, her mind wandered to Xander, his bruised face, burned home, and broken heart. She wondered where he was now, if there was any hope for them to be saved, for them to be together.

She wondered if he'd ever forgive her for this. For the danger she brought to him and his family's door.

What would happen to him under Lilith's command? What would she do to him?

Was there any way to stop her?

Nikki's breath caught in her chest, remembering the compelling. Could she do it now that she was in the Tree?

The dark red thread of Lilith wound up from the base of the Tree as Nikki thought of her, her wood-horned head and clawed hands, the terrifyingly beautiful face, eyes as dark as the interior of the Tree.

Wrapping her consciousness around the thread, instead of falling into the earth, she kept herself still, straining against its hold. It wanted her to follow it, but she kept enough of her mind tethered to her body to keep her in place. As she tugged on it, the thread resisted, pulling her back.

With a forceful yanking she thought, *STOP.*

The thread trembled, went still with her command, and then consumed her willpower and flooded her vision with red.

Chapter Twenty-Two

Lilith paused, the cold mountain air lashing against her face. She stood outside the cave, the night bright and sparkling with innumerable stars, the Milky Way a streak across the sky. The cafeteria of the little cult below was aglow, a late-night worship in full swing.

The moment before she transformed to leap into the air, her feet turned to lead, and she stopped. As if something had forced her to stand still.

Her stomach soured, fists clenching, but she poured as much honey into the words in her mind as she thought, *Are you in there, disobedient daughter of mine?*

There was no response. Either the child remained silent, aiming to mask her presence, or she lost her hold on her consciousness and was sent back through the earth.

Or Lilith had hesitated of her own accord.

Lilith laughed. Ridiculous.

"Are you okay, Mother?" Hormin asked, coming to stand beside her on the cliffside.

"Yes. Only thinking." Lilith turned her gaze on her son, his eyes sharp and focused on the cafeteria below.

The wind whipped his salt and pepper hair, and with the mountain scape behind him, he looked every bit a hero. She put a hand on his cheek. "You are so handsome, my son."

Hormin smiled and turned to look at her. "I have you to thank for that."

Lilith returned his smile. Her beautiful boy, how unwavering he had been in his love and loyalty throughout these eons. When so many others had faltered or failed, he had not.

She turned back to the village and asked, "Are you ready?"

"Always," Hormin said, then looked over his shoulder. "What should I do with the boy?"

Lilith followed his gaze, the boy curled into himself, arms wrapped around his knees and head hung low. Cuts and bruises covered his arms, goose-pimpled from the cold. He had gone from whimpering to aggressive by the time Hormin had delivered him to this cave, and it was a struggle to pacify him without injury.

Whatever foolish impulse caused him to fight them had been vanquished. He was humbled now.

They would have to get him a jacket from the compound. She could not have him freeze before she was done with him.

"Bring him," she said. "I'll wait for you."

"Yes, Mother," Hormin responded, retreating to the cave.

Lilith launched herself from the earth. As gravity pulled at her she shrunk her bones and grew her claws, the vampire flesh falling from her human form as she became the screech owl. She screamed into the night, anticipation, hunger, and vengeance filling her spirit with bloodlust.

She descended to a post outside the cafeteria, part of the poorly crafted wooden fence that bordered the property. The whole group was inside that building, the members chanting while the leader spoke gibberish. All the other structures were dark with vacancy.

Lilith waited for Hormin to arrive, amused at the insanity of these humans. A few minutes later, her beloved son navigated the car down the road and parked outside the fence. Despite the noise of the vehicle, the members were too enthralled with their ritual to hear it.

Lilith turned back into her vampiric form but kept the taloned feet and clawed fingers. Hormin met her beside the post, the glowing greatsword slung across his back in its scabbard, and the boy, gagged and handcuffed, dragged behind him.

"What's the plan?" Hormin asked.

Lilith stared through the windows, the silhouettes of the naïve humans undulating.

"Rampage," she said with a smile, then vaulted herself at the wooden door, smashing it wide open.

The humans paused, shock stamped on all of their faces, eyes wide and mouths open.

Lilith leapt to the human closest to her, and with a pathetically easy pull, ripped his head from his body.

They screamed. A high and shrill keen of mortal fear. It filled Lilith with delight, mouth salivating at the anticipation of how those screams would taste.

Those standing made for the door, where Hormin stood with his greatsword, and cleaved two people in half as they tried to pass him.

Those who had been sitting thrashed upward, knocking stools and tables and drinks to the ground.

They ran in confused circles, trying to escape, yet the understanding they could not, that this was their end, was bright in their glassy eyes.

Lilith laughed, threw the severed head across the room, and jumped into the fray, clawing and tearing and ripping apart each human without thought.

Blood rained, dripping from her horns and hands, thick puddles on the ground that coated her feet.

The screams and wails died as the humans did, and with salt and metal and warmth and magic on her tongue, she leapt out of the window that a few humans had escaped from.

She chased down each person, one by one, until there were no footsteps, no sobs.

Only the pure, clean silence of death.

Lilith returned to the cafeteria, Hormin's face and clothes splattered in that most beautiful crimson hue, the blood on the greatsword sizzling away until the blade was clean.

"What now?" Hormin asked, sliding the sword into its sheath, the flames diminishing to a red-orange halo.

Lilith smiled, opened her arms wide, and said, "Feast."

Hormin grinned and walked among the corpses, blood sloshing over his feet, until he found a body he liked. He picked her up, gently cradling her, limbs hanging loose at her sides, Hormin draped her over the side of a table, angling the body so that her blood would move down into her head. He bit into the flesh and let her drain into him.

A trembling from behind Lilith made her turn. The boy, handcuffed to the leg of a table, shivered with tears, his head bent, averting his gaze from the massacre.

Lilith walked over the bodies and through the blood to him. The boy flinched as she approached, and when she grasped his stubbly chin in her hand, jerking him to look at her, he struggled, trying to get out of her hold, to avoid her eyes.

She held firm and forced him to look at her.

His grey-green eyes blazed with hatred, despite the tears that fogged them.

The boy's loathing was such delicious anger, and a heat in her body that she had not felt for a long time unspooled within her. She brought her mouth to his neck, to that delicate pulse below his jaw that clenched and unclenched. The boy's breathing grew heavier, faster, his breath pushing against his skin as if it could escape. Lilith brushed her lips to the pulse point, that rapid heartbeat a delicacy against her tongue. She breathed him in, that sweat and fear, the spice and sweetness that lulled her daughter.

With his heartbeat on her lips, his breath on her neck, Lilith tensed herself, restraining the urge to press their bodies together and sink her fangs into his skin.

She could not do so yet, not with that cursed blood in his veins.

Once Vadasz found the relic, once the boy could be purged of the deceiver, then she would devour him.

Slow and tender, over days or weeks or however long it would take him to give up.

Her lips split in a grin at the thought, and the boy tensed, feeling her mouth move against his neck.

With one last inhale of him, she leaned back, at the wide terror in his wet and hateful eyes.

Lilith laughed and pushed away from him, the boy crumpling back into himself, covering his head with his hands, his neck with his fore-arms, as if he could make it all disappear.

Hormin had pushed the drained body to the side, its limbs askew as it folded over the table and knocked over chairs. He had set up another person to drain into his mouth, lazily letting it pour into him.

Traipsing through the bodies, Lilith picked one that looked appe-tizing – a muscular female with golden bronze skin from long days in the sun, luxurious auburn curls darkened by the smears of blood.

Claw marks and puncture wounds raked her body. It was one of her kills, then.

Lilith brushed the hair out of the woman's face, shifted the clothing on her body so that her heavy, winter skirt was pulled high, and sank her teeth into her thigh, succumbing to the ecstasy of warm blood filling her mouth.

Chapter Twenty-Three

"Gwen – what happened to my house?" Ina asked.

"Looks like it burned down," Gwen said, head spinning with the relief of finally hearing from her.

Theo, Rachel, and Feng approached Gwen, and she flipped it onto speaker.

"I can tell that much. But how?" Ina asked.

"How would I know? I wasn't there."

Ina sighed. "I knew she was coming, but I... I didn't think she would destroy everything."

They were silent, and Gwen's stomach twinged. "I'm sorry that your house got burned down."

After another moment of heavy silence, Ina said, "It's just a house. Just...things."

Theo cleared her throat.

"Hey, Ina, it's Theo. I'm here too."

"Theo?" Ina responded, voice pitching high with her confusion. "What are you doing with Gwen? Are you okay?"

"I'm fine, Ina. I'm with Gwen."

"As I said to Gwen, I can tell that much. But why?"

"No, I mean...I'm *with* with Gwen. She's my girlfriend."

Ina didn't respond, but they heard a long inhale and exhale through the speakers. "What happened to yours and Xanders' good sense? Falling in love with vampires…"

"I'm not a vampire," Gwen spat, gut twisting.

"At least tell me Terrance isn't with a vampire."

"Uhhh, yes and no," Gwen said.

"He's not *with* a vampire. But he is here with us, where there are vampires," Theo replied, slinging the guns onto her new gun belt.

"He's with me," Rachel said. "Hi – I'm Rachel, one hundred percent human. I think."

"What? Theo, what are you doing with vampires? Where are you?"

"We're fine, Ina," Theo said. "These are good vampires. We're in a safe house – they're protecting us."

"'Good' vampires? Have you gone mad? You just let yourself become farm animals."

"Hey, don't be such a bigot. Good vampires exist. Nikki is – was – is? One of them," Gwen said, chest tightening with the ache of missing.

"I'd like to think that my wife and I are one of the good vampires too."

"I think so," Rachel said, smiling at Feng.

Ina took another long breath, as if trying to steady herself. "Okay, fine. We shouldn't be arguing. We need to talk. Where can we meet?"

"You should come here, where it's safe," Feng said.

Ina barked a laugh. "Stay in an unknown vampire's house? I don't think so."

"Well, it isn't really safe for us to leave. We think some of the bad vampires may be after us," Gwen replied.

"Fine," Ina said. "Look, I'm tired. I just got back. I'm going to get a hotel somewhere and sleep. I'll meet you and your hosts outside of their house tomorrow. I will not come in until I assess the situation. Got it?"

"Yeah, yeah, I get it," Gwen said.

"Good. Just an FYI to your host, I'm of the Cradle. Of Utu's Cradle. Understood?"

"We know of your kind," Feng sneered. "But what makes Utu's Cradle so special, we do not know. Nor care."

"You should care. My magic is stronger than many. If you want to keep your skin, you will not test me."

"No harm will come to you if none comes to us," Feng replied.

Gwen sensed Ina bristling on the other end of the line. "Just tell me how to get to this place, would you?"

"Yes, ma'am," Gwen said, mocking, a hot worm of irritation curling in her sternum. "We don't want directions in text. I'll tell it to you if you can write it down."

"Fine," Ina said again, and the shuffling of materials sounded through the speaker. "Go."

Gwen told her the directions as Ina scribbled, the scratching of pencil on paper filling the background.

When they were done with the directions, Ina said, "Keep your heads down and don't do anything rash. I'll see you tomorrow after sunset."

Ina hung up, and they stared at Gwen's phone until the screen blacked out.

"'Don't do anything rash?' What does she think we're going to do in here, host a rager and invite all the vampires?"

"She's just worried," Theo said.

"Join the club," Gwen said, shoving her belongings back in her bag. "I can already tell we're not going to get along."

"Probably not," Theo replied with a grin, leaning down beside Gwen. "In all seriousness, it'll be fine. You're both just stubborn."

Gwen groaned. "Great."

The group faded into silence for a moment before Feng said, "We can deal with her tomorrow. Right now, let's train. We have a few more hours until we need to return underground."

Theo and Rachel nodded, Theo taking her pistols from her belt and Rachel picking up the bow, then returning to their spots in the quarry. Gwen shivered against the cold, simultaneously dreading talking to Ina but desperate for answers.

Chapter Twenty-Four

GWEN AND THEO woke to the smell of bacon and pancakes. Terrance and Rachel walked out of their room at the same time, all four bleary-eyed with poor sleep, yearning for that smell of crispy creature comforts.

After the meal, the group spent the day in anxious silence, waiting Ina's arrival. Too antsy to be around anyone, Gwen spent a few hours checking on her herbs, seeing how dry they were, and trying out some new creations. Near sunset, she went outside and watched the forest swallow the sun, the sky changing from shades of winter to midnight blue. The moon chased the sun, a white smile against dark skin, the stars a splash of freckles across the night's clear visage.

One by one, everyone else exited the safe house and stood beside Gwen, waiting for Ina. They didn't exchange more than pleasantries, a nervous thrum tightening their bodies and clutching the words in their throats.

An hour after sunset, the headlights of a car shone through the skinny and tough trunks of the Doug-fir, casting a stuttering light. The driver passed the dirt road that led to the safehouse, stomped on the brake, then reversed, catching its mistake.

The car rolled up the drive, and Theo gasped, brief and harsh beside her, as if she tried to stifle it.

"What?" Gwen whispered, leaning in, hand tightening in her grasp. "That's Xander's car."

Nausea stirred Gwen's stomach, and she stepped closer to Theo.

The car parked, headlights turning off, plunging Gwen into blinding darkness while her eyes adjusted back to the night.

Ina emerged from the vehicle, a dark silhouette. She looked so small against the towering forest.

A thin circle of light flared in Gwen's vision and she blinked, the brightness of Ina's flashlight roaming over her face, over Theo's, Terrance's, Rachel's, and finally, Feng and Daiyu. "You must be the vampires," Ina said, shifting the flashlight beam from Feng to Daiyu, and back again.

They didn't blink against the harsh light.

"Welcome to our home," Feng said.

"Hmph," Ina grumbled, keeping the flashlight on Feng's face and maintaining a safe distance.

"We are on the same side, I promise you. You can come inside, be warm by the fire. We can talk comfortably in there," Daiyu said.

"Oh? Just waltz into a vampire's lair?" Ina asked. "Tell me, vampire, which side do you claim to be on?"

"The one that opposes the rule of Lilith," Feng said.

"Just because we have a shared enemy does not mean we are on the same side."

"Why ask us about sides to then claim they do not matter?" Feng asked.

Silence filled the forest, nothing but the stiff, cold creak of trees in the breeze.

"Ina," Theo said, clearing her throat. "They've been good to us. We can trust them."

Ina paused, shifting her flashlight and her gaze from Theo back to the Lius. "Do you know what it means to have Utu's blood? His power?"

Daiyu and Feng hesitated.

In that moment of hesitation, Ina turned off her flashlight, but the brightness expanded, and the Lius hissed, hiding behind Terrance and Rachel.

A fleeting scent of burning flesh wafted in the breeze.

Gwen winced, then slowly opened her eyes, peering at the light.

A small orb of glowing, shimmering light suspended over Ina's hand, illuminating her face in brilliant oranges and yellows, her hazel eyes dark with warning. The power radiating from the sun in her hand rustled her hair, the tendrils that were free from her loose bun wisping around her face. The rays of the small sun spilled across the clearing, sporadic and arching like solar flares, casting shadows of the trees, turning the soil a golden orange-brown.

"The sun is in my blood, and I will not hesitate to wield it against you if you prove to be deceitful. Understood?"

"Understood," Daiyu hissed.

Ina diminished the miniature sun in her hand, and the Lius stepped forward.

Feng's face quivered, his hands clenched behind his back. "We invited you into our home, offered our hospitality, and you threaten us?"

Gwen could practically hear the peeling back of his lips, revealing his fangs.

Daiyu placed a hand on Feng's shoulder, and he exhaled, a long deep sigh that dropped his shoulders.

"Forgive us, if we are old fashioned," Daiyu said. "Be assured, you will not come to harm in our home."

Feng closed his mouth, rolling his lips, as if he had difficulty backing down, hiding his fangs.

"As long as none of us," Ina said, indicating Gwen, Theo, Terrance, and Rachel, "come to harm, then neither will you."

"We understand," Daiyu said. "Come, I will show you where to park. Feng, take the children inside."

"Children?" Terrance asked.

"Apologies," Daiyu said with a short shrug. "You are young to us."

"Humans – with me," Feng said, mouth curled on one side with a half grin.

"When you say it like that, I think I prefer 'children,'" Terrance said, and they fell into step behind Feng, back through the small trapdoor to the laundry room and into the house.

The cold, metal garage door creaked as it opened, faint vibrations in the earth. The fire was on in the living room, Lucas straightening the furniture. He took drink orders, Feng asking for two glasses of someone named 'Chris.' Gwen shivered as he ordered, at the knowing of exactly whose blood he wanted to drink.

They sat, silent in the living room, waiting for Daiyu and Ina, the gas fireplace a quiet whir, Lucas's footsteps pattering in the kitchen. When Daiyu and Ina entered from the parking garage, Ina's shoulders were lower and face set, holding onto a little less tension, a little less malice.

Lucas came with the first round of drinks as Daiyu and Ina entered, asking for Ina's order, but she declined a drink. Instead, she remained standing, arms crossed tight across her body, despite how the rest of them sat, postures open and relaxed.

Gwen wrapped her cold fingers around the warm mug of her tea, mint steaming upward from the cup. Theo and Rachel took gentle sips of their gin and tonics, waiting.

Theo cleared her throat and asked, "Why do you have Xander's car?"

A flash of sorrow crossed Ina's brow before her face resettled into a smooth mask. "The police had it. It had been towed, due to illegal parking. Then after the fire, when they were looking for us...they searched it for evidence."

"Evidence?"

"Of foul play. They didn't find any." Ina tucked a loose tendril of hair behind her ear. "I told them my husband and children were still on vacation. I hope I mollified them enough to drop their investigation. We will see."

"Is it true – what you told them?" Daiyu asked.

"No. But where my husband and youngest children are hiding are not your concern. They are far from here. They are safe. Xander...I do not know where he is."

Feng swirled the blood, *Chris's* blood, in his glass, and asked, "Why was your son coveted by Lilith?"

Ina took a deep breath, and in her exhale, she sat on the edge of the couch, but kept her arms locked. "The magic of the first man – of

Adam – is in his blood. And it is that blood, that lineage, that was the key to unseal her from the Tree of Life."

"He's what?" Terrance asked, but Ina ignored him.

"Does that mean Arthur is the descendant of Adam, too?" Theo asked.

"Why was she trapped? And why would his blood free her?" Gwen added.

"One at a time, please," Ina said, and her crossed arms suddenly made her look more like a woman hugging herself, trying to console herself, rather than shutting out the rest of the world.

"The why or how of Lilith's imprisonment is not well known to us. We know there was a falling out with Adam and Lilith. In the aftermath, she became the first vampire. As punishment for the lives she ruined, she was imprisoned, with the knowledge that the true descendants of Adam and Eve would be able to free her. The details of why, and how, are questions for the Creator."

"You're saying Creationism is real?" Theo asked.

"What about evolution? Are we all rela –"

"Please," Ina interrupted Gwen. "As I said, there are many questions only the Creator can answer. But we are not all related. Other pockets of humanity were created to cloak Adam's bloodline, to balance out the scourge of vampirism rampant on the Earth. Hence, the Cradle."

Gwen opened her mouth, but before she could speak, Ina said, "The Cradles of Civilization. Not all peoples of the Cradles were given magic, but some lineages received blessings, became demi-gods, sparking local lore and mythologies. We were given magic, which was used to protect Adam and fight vampires. To create relics to bind them.

For example, I am of the Mesopotamian Cradle, blessed with the blood of Utu, our sun god. My ancestry can be traced all the way back to the great city of Uruk.

"Adam's magic flows through male descendants, and once the next generation is born, his gifts transfer to the child. I was sent to protect Arthur when he was the carrier of Adam's magic. Little did I know who I would find." Ina smiled, lost in her memory. "A disarmingly charming, inquisitive mind, full of energy and childlike wonder at the world. We wed, and then there was Alexander, and I could feel it when the magic shifted from Arthur to our son. But I was with him, and I thought I would be enough to protect him.

"As he grew, I knew him to be blessed with the gift of Compassion, drawing people to him. We adopted Ishaq and Zahra, of the Egyptian Cradle, to hide his light. They are called shields, and my Cradle are called masks. Though Lilith calls us 'deceivers' since the scent of our blood confuses the smell of his. I knew I couldn't keep him home forever, but I thought keeping him close would be enough. The coven here is...docile, compared to many. I thought even if he was sensed, he would be safe."

Ina tightened her arms around her torso, gaze distant. "Now my complacency has put us all in danger. Lilith is free, and my son is gone. We must stop her. And save Xander if he is still capable of being saved."

Silence weighed heavy on their shoulders, all except the Lius staring at Ina as her story unfolded and ended. Xander's unknown fate spilled dread into Gwen's stomach.

Theo stood and walked to Ina, putting a hand on her shoulder. "We'll find him."

Ina nodded, seemed to remember herself, and straightened, the sorrow and worry smoothing away from her face.

"And Nikki," Gwen added. "We'll find Nikki too."

"She is missing as well?" Ina asked.

Gwen nodded. "I haven't seen her since we left your house weeks ago. I heard her once, though, yelling out for help."

The group was silent, thinking.

"Do you suppose," Feng asked, "that she is now in the Tree of Life?"

"It would make sense," Ina said. "If Lilith was freed, she could have had Nikki take her place."

"It would explain why you could hear her, Gwen," Daiyu said. "A small version of the compelling."

Gwen frowned at her cooling mug, heart sinking into her stomach. "All those times she said she heard voices, and I discounted it. It was Lilith all along, talking to her, trying to have her bring Xander to her. I should've listened to Nikki. She wasn't crazy. At all."

"No," Ina said, jaw clenching. "It's not your fault. It's hers. She should have stayed away from my son. If she had stayed away, they wouldn't have found him. None of this would have happened."

Gwen's mouth dropped open as rage seared her chest. "How dare you blame Nikki? She's somewhere, suffering at best, dead at worst. All because she loved your son." Gwen stood, the air rising around her. "Didn't you just say this was all your fault, anyway, because of your complacency? Maybe you should have –"

"There is no point in arguing, now," Feng said. "What's done is done."

"We need to plan our way forward," Daiyu said.

"Right," Gwen replied, dropping the air. Out of her peripheral, Terrance and Rachel sat tensed with fear, and shame sickened her stomach. "So, free Nikki, free Xander, stop Lilith. How do we do that?"

Ina shook her head. "No. First we stop Lilith, then free Xander. Even if we could free Nikki, which I'm not sure how we would do, we don't know what the ramifications would be."

The sick shame she's felt seconds ago turned hot once more, and Gwen clenched her fists. "You're joking. You're just going to leave Nikki trapped? You're not even going to *try* to help her?"

"We don't know what would happen to the Tree without a vessel. Nor would I know where to begin trying to find the spell to release her."

"And you know how to defeat Lilith and save Xander? Like that is so much easier than helping Nikki?"

"It is," Ina said, and Gwen's nails dug into her palms. "That's the point of the Cradle, to manage Lilith and her spawn."

Feng hissed. "Don't call us that. We are not like her."

"Apologies," Ina said, tone flat, keeping her eyes on Gwen. "Lilith is the priority here, followed by Xander. I'm sure everyone would agree that she is the immediate threat. And there is no saving anyone until she is vanquished."

Gwen searched the faces around her for an ally, but the Lius were looking into the fire. Terrance and Rachel avoided her gaze, and her stomach dropped. When she met Theo's eyes, Theo held her stare for a half second, before looking away, and Gwen felt as if the air had been vacuumed out of her body.

"I can't believe this," Gwen whispered, hands unclenching with defeat.

No one answered for several long seconds, and the only eyes that would meet hers were Ina's, determined.

A flicker of sympathy tugged down at the corners of Ina's mouth, and she said, "I am sorry."

The apology sapped the last of Gwen's defiance, and she collapsed back to the floor, strings cut.

No one else prioritized Nikki.

No one else *needed* her.

No one cared about what she had done for Xander.

No one knew a way to release her from the Tree.

She would be sacrificed, forgotten.

Nikki was gone and might be lost to her forever.

Chapter Twenty-Five

SOMEONE PRESSED a fresh mug of tea into Gwen's hands, and she mindlessly wrapped her fingers around it. Conversation continued around her, muffled outside the storm in her mind.

Theo sat beside her, body radiating nervous energy.

As it should, Gwen thought bitterly. How could she take their side? How could she agree with them to leave Nikki trapped?

The Lius were on their second glass of blood, their lips, tongues, and teeth stained red. Ina filled her voice with contempt when she asked if it was necessary to drink blood around them, and Feng had shrugged her off, saying something about how everyone must eat.

Ina grunted with disgust, and Rachel commented that it didn't bother her. She found the whole thing really interesting.

The hot mint tea imbued the fire within Gwen, and awareness returned, sharpening her senses.

"The first thing we must do," Feng said, "is determine who our allies and enemies are."

"Who else in the coven opposes Lilith?" Ina asked.

"No one who is still in the region."

"Not even your coven leader?"

"Tyee? She is more Mother-crazed than the rest of them."

Ina's brow furrowed, and Gwen winced, the expression so much like Xander's. Thinking of him made her think of Nikki.

"I find that surprising," Ina said. "I met with her once and found her quite reasonable."

Gwen raised her eyebrows. "You met with her? Why? Wouldn't that just expose your family to who you're trying to hide from?"

"I met with her before moving here, when scouting for places. She did not know who my husband and son were. When we spoke, Tyee had comparatively unthreatening ideals toward humans. Thus, I thought moving to the area her coven controls would be safe."

Feng said, "She was reasonable, once. Annoyingly so – to the point of controlling. That ended when having a vampire-dominated world became possible."

"I would speak with her. I think I could reason with her."

"What makes you think that?" Gwen asked.

"We have...things in common. Maybe she is being compelled, and I can talk sense to her through it."

"What do you mean, 'things in common'?" Gwen asked, shifting her legs from underneath her, which were tingling with a lack of proper blood flow.

Ina shook her head. "That is not my story to tell."

Gwen groaned and rolled her eyes. "Always with the secrecy."

Ignoring Gwen, Daiyu said, "The compelling is not easy to defy or break."

"Can she even still compel, though?" Gwen asked. "If talking to vampires was possible because she was in the Tree, and she's free, does she still have that ability?"

"That's a good question. One we should aim to answer. Tyee might know," Ina said.

"How do you even know she'll agree to talk to you?" Gwen asked.

"She has nothing to lose either way. If she is on our side, we can know each other as allies. Work together. If not, then the chance of diminishing the Cradle will be too good an opportunity for her to pass up."

"I would strongly advise against this," Feng said. "She is not who she used to be."

"I am not defenseless," Ina said.

"I'll go with you," Gwen said, the words tumbling out of her mouth before she could think about them.

Feng sighed, licking the blood off his teeth. "As will I."

"Me too," Theo said. Gwen looked at her, about to tell her stay behind, to not risk it, but the look on her face was set, and so Gwen bit her tongue, remembering how she asked to not have Gwen make decisions for her.

"I'll stay here, away from crazy vampires," Terrance said.

"Yeah, no thanks," Rachel added, curling up next to him.

"I will remain, then. Ensure that those in the house stay safe," Daiyu said. Feng looked at her with longing, then put his hand over hers, rubbing her wrist with his thumb.

"Very well. How do we reach her?" Ina asked.

"We will have to drive down the mountain to call her. Or we can go directly to her house," Feng said.

"Best to not take a vampire by surprise," Ina said.

"Agreed," Feng said, standing in one fluid motion.

"Wait, are we going now?" Gwen asked, fingers tightening around her mug.

"No time like the present," Ina said.

"Oh, well, okay then."

Theo stood and offered her hand to Gwen, but she did not take it. She was still mad at how quickly she'd dismissed Nikki, how she hadn't stood with her to save her best friend.

Theo's hand curled closed and hurt flashed across her eyes before she turned away. Gwen's stomach flipped with nausea at the look on Theo's face, but she clamped it down beneath her anger.

Feng and Daiyu said their quiet goodbyes, Feng promising to return in one piece. Theo said goodbye to her brother and Rachel, but Gwen did not, refusing to indulge in the idea that they might not return.

Of course they would. They had humanity to save.

The group of three followed Feng into the parking garage and to another Mercedes, this one the size of a small SUV. The drive down the mountain was in silence, with only the whir of the engine and rolling of tires to fill the empty space.

Once within reception, Ina pulled out her cell phone and Feng gave her Tyee's home phone number, explaining that it might not work, as they had set her home on fire.

Ina scowled at him but tried the number anyway.

There was no answer, just a broken line.

"It looks like we have no choice but to arrive without warning," Ina said, shoving her phone back into her pocket.

Chapter Twenty-Six

THE MOON WAS high in its arc across the sky as Feng pulled to a stop, its light filtered by evergreens. They were near the trail to Tyee's house, and Gwen was briefly blinded when the car turned off, the headlights enveloping them in the dark. Even as her eyes adjusted, it was difficult to see in the deep black of the forest, so Gwen and Theo took out their cell phones to use as flashlights, illuminating circles of white light around them.

The sharp bite of cold stung Gwen's cheeks and fingertips as they walked through the densely vegetated trail, Feng leading the way and Ina at the back. Gwen, Theo, and Ina were bundled in layers of thick jackets and gloves, but Feng was dressed in what he'd worn at the house. His breath was a faint puff on the air, and the humans' exhales were dense, visible gusts.

For once, Gwen thought it must be nice to not feel the cold. To have strengthened skin and lower body temperatures.

The ground squelched with mud and debris beneath her feet. Stringing branches grasped at her body, her hair. It had been years since she had come to Tyee's property, having forfeited feigning acceptance as an O'Brennan family member long ago.

The building they found was not the one she held in her memory.

They stopped at the front of what would have been Tyee's property, their flashlights swiveling over wood and structural debris, pieces of the main house and her tree house littered the ground, as did branches and trunks of fallen trees. Burned and downed wood, turned soggy from the mud and rain, rotted into the ground, a dank and moldy scent clinging to the air.

"I didn't mean to do this much damage," Feng said, but there was no remorse in his voice. Gwen glanced at him, one corner of his mouth lifted in a private grin.

All this destruction to free Nikki. A sudden swelling of appreciation filled Gwen's chest – they defied Tyee, burned her house, in the hopes of freeing Nikki, of fixing things.

"Thank you for trying to save her," Gwen said.

The grin on Feng's face dropped, and he nodded. "I regret that it was not effective. In hindsight, we should have brought her to our safehouse. We did not truly know, then, how dire things were."

"Well, I'm not giving up on her yet. Even if the rest of you have," Gwen said, and Theo tensed beside her.

"It'd be a waste of your time, Guinevere."

Gwen and Theo startled, Tyee speaking from behind them. She moved through the forest without a sound, the branches parting away from her, footsteps light enough to not disturb the detritus.

Gwen and Theo raised their lights to Tyee, illuminating the forest patch in which she stood. Tyee stood about twenty feet from them, posture relaxed, hair combed and braided. With the ease in which she stood, no one would have guessed that her home, her forest, had been recently destroyed.

Tyee's gaze flicked to Feng, and her mouth twitched with a repressed snarl. "You are bold to come here, after what you've done. Bold, or stupid."

Feng shrugged, unphased.

"The same could be said for you," Tyee added, looking at Ina. "Fool I was, those years ago when you first approached me, to not see what you were hiding. Now I know better. What a prize you would make to the Mother."

Gwen's heart rate quickened at the malice that crept into Tyee's voice.

She had heard Tyee stern and serious, but never predatory.

Ina stepped forward. "I understand your anger, Tyee. My house was also burned. Please, we've come to speak to you about peace."

Tyee scoffed. "Peace? How many times I've heard that by how many conquerors, and each time 'peace' was brought wrapped up in the massacre of my people."

"You must know that what Lilith plans is wrong. She would devastate the entire human race."

"I see no wrong in that."

"How can you not? When we spoke before, we spoke of our shared humanity, how beautiful it is. You would have that enslaved? Destroyed?"

"It would be a fitting revenge."

"But you said –"

"I've always said what I've had to in order to survive." Tyee stepped forward again, and Ina faltered, taking a step backward at the intensity in Tyee's eyes, the focus and rigidity belonging to lions on a hunt. "I am tired of only surviving. You claim to come here for peace. To convince me of the righteousness of your side. But your side would have me return to the dark. It would have me complacent, obedient. Silent.

"Too many times throughout my life I have watched my people slaughtered. Too many times I have survived by being complacent. Obedient. Silent. You would have me do so again? While you murder all that remains of my family? I think not."

Tyee raised her hands, and Gwen flinched back.

"Finally, it is our time – *my time* – to be victorious. I will not be complacent or silent. Ever again."

A loud crack split the air, rocking the earth, a fissure sprouting from the ground near Tyee's feet.

Gwen stumbled, the fallen branches, logs, and standing trees quaking, as Tyee split open the earth at her feet.

"Tyee – wait!" Ina cried, falling to her knees as the earth shook, hand outstretched, beseeching.

Gwen reflexively grasped at the magic inside herself, every last scrap she could pull, the ring on her finger burning with amplification, and she sent the power out of herself in a large push, the gust wiping the ground clear of debris and detritus, smashing against the trees.

But by the time the wave reached where Tyee had stood, she had disappeared, and the fissure in the earth closed.

Gwen's gust of wind slammed through the forest, howling as it tunneled.

Once it had dissipated, she collapsed to her knees, exhausted. Loose pine needles fell from the trees overhead, raining onto her hair.

Gasping for breath, Gwen stared at where Tyee had stood. But she was gone – swallowed whole by the earth.

Chapter Twenty-Seven

"This is unfortunate," Ina said once they were back in the car and warmed up enough to feel their fingers again. "She would have been a powerful ally."

"Instead, she is a powerful enemy," Feng replied.

Theo tried to support Gwen on the walk back, but Gwen had shaken her off twice, now leaning as far away from her as she could, pressing her magic-warmed face against the cold glass of the car window. She removed her layers to air out the sweat from the rest of her body, the moisture making her colder in the winter air.

Theo rested her head on her hand and stared straight forward, face set and unreadable.

"You gonna tell us this mystery yet? This supposed similarity you have with Tyee that made you think this was a good idea?" Gwen asked.

Ina sighed. "I was silent before out of respect for her. But now if we are to face her as an enemy, I suppose you should know." Ina adjusted herself in the seat. "Her human side is of the secondary Cradle."

"The what?"

"The first Cradle was the six I mentioned earlier. There are another six, blessed later, as both human and vampire populations expanded. She is of the Native American Cradle."

"How is that possible?" Theo asked. "I thought the Cradle and vampires were like poisons to each other."

"They are, which is why hybrids are rare," Ina replied. "Hybrids of the first Cradle don't exist, as our blood is meant to kill vampires. The second Cradle's blood maims. Over time, some communities of Born vampires – those that already had human blood – evolved to tolerate it. And, over time, seemingly impossible vampire-cradle hybrid communities formed. They have extra abilities that the rest of us – Cradle or vampire – don't have. Hence her power to move the Earth."

"So, she's basically a super-powered vampire," Gwen said, filling with dread.

"Yes."

"Great. How do we go about killing someone like her?"

"With great difficulty. Vampires are already hard to kill. With tolerance to the Cradle's abilities, it makes it even more difficult." Ina paused, watching the trees dash past the window in the dark. "I do understand her anger. When she spoke of genocide, she did not just mean from the English settlers. There are many vampires and those of the Cradle who would see hybrids killed. Her tribe was hunted, by both sides, for centuries, if not millennia, before the settlers even thought about crossing the Pacific. She has lost so many. I do not blame her for holding on to what she can. Though I wish she would hold onto the human side, and not the vampiric."

"Yeah, this blows," Gwen said, lifting her head from the cold window. "Feng, did you know this about Tyee?"

He shook his head. "I do not think anyone did."

"It would be a vulnerability of hers if people knew," Ina said. "It makes sense she kept it secret. Especially after so many centuries of persecution."

"Don't make me feel bad for her," Gwen said, sadness twisting in her gut, knowing what it was like to be hated, to be an outcast, and then imagining that multiplied so greatly in intensity that people wanted to kill her. To endure that over centuries was unfathomable.

"What you feel is your choice," Ina quipped, and Gwen rolled her eyes, resisting the urge to slap her. She hated when people said she could choose her feelings, as if they could just be shut away, only appearing when she allowed them to. "But it is good to know where she comes from. Literally and figuratively."

Many minutes passed, Feng speeding to make it home before sunrise. There was a covered, blackened-out hatch in the back, and drivers could switch, if necessary, but he had made it clear his strong preference not to have anyone else drive his car.

"What do we do now?" Theo asked.

"We regroup," Feng said.

Ina nodded. "We need to figure out the specifics of Lilith's plan. Where she currently is, where she is going. I alerted the Cradle while transporting my family, and they are gathering their resources to confront her. Once we know her plan, we can reconvene with them to make our own counteroffensive."

Conversation dropped, and Gwen closed her eyes, letting the gentle whir of the engine, the roll of wheels over asphalt, and passing wind create a delicate lullaby, coaxing her into partial sleep.

In the dark haze of her semi-consciousness, the voice she'd relied on most throughout her life, the voice she'd been missing most, awakened in the back of her mind.

"Gwen?" Nikki asked.

Gwen ached with missing her best friend as Nikki's voice filled her head, knowing she was falling into a dream with Nikki, willing herself to plunge in instead of falling out. Her heart twisted violently in her chest at the depth of her loss, at the sound of Nikki's voice, and the threat of crying nearly broke her out of her half dream.

Gwen kept her eyes closed, willing it to stay.

"I miss you too," Nikki said, sad.

A bump in the road rocked the car, jolting Gwen up in her seat, and her eyes flew open.

Her chest caved at the lost dream, the one place she could talk to Nikki.

"I'm in a Tree. Io, who's basically God, says it's the Tree of Life."

Gwen blinked as Nikki spoke in her mind.

She was awake, but she still heard Nikki.

Unless she was in a very, very realistic dream.

"Am I in a dream?" Gwen asked, but Theo was asleep, mouth open and head lolled.

"No?" Ina said, from the front seat.

"That's what someone in a dream would say."

"You're not dreaming, Gwen."

"Then how can I hear you?"

"What?" Ina asked.

"I don't know – I just found your thread and pulled."

Gwen's heart raced and she bolted forward in her seat. "Oh my God, Nikki!"

Theo opened her eyes, blinking rapidly as she startled.

"What's going on?" Ina asked, turning around to look at her over the seat.

Gwen's body hummed with excitement, and she bounced with energy, a wide smile on her face. Feng's thick brows furrowed in the rearview mirror, and he glanced back at her, worried. Ina and Theo stared at her unblinking, as if she had lost her mind. The sound of Nikki's voice was a light in the dark, igniting a bright hope that surged in her chest. For the first time in what seemed like eons, she felt as if she could breathe again.

Chapter Twenty-Eight

Gwen's excited shouting resounded in Nikki's head, and she smiled, as wide as she could with lips closed. Her heart leapt at Gwen's voice, at finally being able to talk to her.

She had seen Gwen's thread, thicker and brighter than ever before, and followed it down into the earth. Nikki saw her in a car with Theo, Ina, and Feng, traveling down a dark road. She tried speaking to Gwen, but Gwen's head was so full, so loud, she couldn't hear Nikki until she drifted to sleep.

If not for the tips of plant tendrils at the corner of her mouth, Nikki would have laughed at the sheer joy of it. Hearing Gwen, she no longer felt so alone. So trapped.

The glimmers in the air around her flickered with amusement and satisfaction.

"*Was this you?*" Nikki asked.

"*It was,*" Io replied. "*It is why I've been distant. Quiet. For so long. I wanted to build that thread for you.*"

"Thank you," Nikki said. "*But if you don't want to stop Lilith, why help me?*"

Io's contemplation filled the space within the Tree. "*Peace. I wanted to give you peace.*"

"You've given me something better."

"What is that?"

"Hope."

Io's energy buzzed with trepidation, warning. *"Hope is dangerous."*

"Right now, I don't care," Nikki thought, the excitement leaving her body, easing into acceptance. *"I am grateful. Thank you."*

"You're welcome, child. Do not fear, I will maintain the thread for you."

"Then I'll be able to reach Gwen any time?"

"Yes."

Nikki's heart cracked with the relief, and if so many tears hadn't already been shed, she might have cried again.

"Darling?" Cat said, hand pressing against the Tree. "The leaves – your leaves- are changing. Are you well? I do not know if that is good or bad. The pomegranates have all but bled and rotted into the soil, yet the Tree's leaves are budding." Cat rested her forehead against Nikki's bark. "I miss you so much, my darling. I'm sorry. I'm so sorry."

Nikki squeezed her eyes, dulling her mom's voice to nothing more than background noise as she searched for Io. *"What is my mom talking about?"*

"A different fruit for each month. The fruits feed the keepers of the Tree, fitting their needs. Your Mother and her keepers are the only ones left here. Thus, the fruit bleeds for them, instead of making fruit flesh, as it would for a human."

"Can you tell her that? She is so worried, and I don't know how to reach out."

"She is beyond me as well, child. Her sorrow is too great. It blocks her mind."

Nikki's heart sunk again, the elation of finding Gwen then hearing her mother speak with woe playing with her heartstrings.

The gold, silver, and copper flickers of Io danced in her vision, the thread of Gwen wavering below her feet. As her mother pawed and sighed at the outside of her – of the Tree – Nikki wished she could be anyone and anywhere else. She looked back to that green thread, that wonderful connection to Gwen, and thrust her consciousness back down, leaving her body and the Tree behind.

She rolled through the dark and light spots of the Earth until she once again looked through Gwen's eyes. The midnight silhouettes of trees and vegetation whipped by as Feng barreled down the road and toward their destination.

"Nikki!" Gwen said, her excitement vibrating against Nikki's consciousness. "We went to see Tyee, but that didn't go so well, so now we're heading back to the Lius' safehouse."

Gwen still spoke out loud, Theo and Ina watching her, Feng trying his best to keep his eyes on the road, despite how they darted to her in the mirror.

"Gwen, just think. You don't have to talk out loud."

A pause, silence. "I can't organize my thoughts like that, Nikki. I need to think out loud."

Nikki filled with amusement and affection – it was odd, having feelings without the physical sensation of her body. But she could still sense them, the lightness, the adoration she had for Gwen, in some other, energetic realm outside of the physical.

"Where did you go, just now?" Gwen asked.

"Oh. I was shocked at finally finding you. I went back to the Tree for a minute. Does Ina know where Xander is?"

"She doesn't. We think he's with Lilith, but we aren't sure."

"What is she saying?" Ina asked, eyes wide. "Is she asking about my son? Does she know where he is?"

"She doesn't. Right, Nikki?" Gwen said.

"I wish I did."

"What is she saying?" Theo asked.

"Does she know where Lilith is? What she wants?" Ina asked.

Nikki felt Gwen's body constrict with irritation. "Hold your horses, folks. I can't have multiple conversations at once. Just let me talk to Nikki for a bit."

"Actually, I do know where Lilith is going. I vaguely know where she is now, somewhere in the southwest. I don't know the name of the town though. Somewhere with a cult."

"Ugh, that's not helpful. There are so many cults over there."

Feng raised an eyebrow in the rearview, and Theo furrowed hers.

"I know. But she's going to the Olmec Heartland. Have you heard of it?"

"Uh, no, I have no idea. Let me ask Ina." Gwen poked Ina, but she was already turning around at the sound of her name. "Hey – do you know where the Olmec Heartland is? That's where Lilith is going."

Ina's face turned to stone. "That's where the Mexican Cradle is. I need to warn them."

A sense of confusion teased Nikki's edges. Io had spoken of the Cradle, but did not go into specifics of where, and why.

Ina pulled out her phone, fingers flying across numbers, repeatedly bringing it to her ear, as it rang and rang and rang without answer. When no one picked up, she switched to texting.

"Gwen, tell me everything you've learned."

"Sure thing. As long as you do the same," Gwen said.

Nikki remained in Gwen's head through the rest of the drive back to the Lius' safe house, filling each other in on everything they had learned. Tears swam in Gwen's eyes when Nikki told her about her dad, and she quickly moved on before they could linger too much on the pain. When the group returned to their new home, and Gwen was barely conscious with exhaustion, Nikki left her mind so she could rest and then careened back through the world.

She collided back into her own body, where there was no soft bed, no steaming dinner, no fresh air, no arm of her beloved to hold her.

Just the same old dark, Io's distant presence surrounding her, and the Tree clasped tight around her wrist and ankles, binding, leaching.

Chapter Twenty-Nine

Gwen and Theo awoke in the evening, the smell of breakfast once again waking them up. Gwen lingered in bed longer than normal, processing her conversation with Nikki. Her chest ached at the loss of Miguel. She hadn't spent much time with Nikki's father, but he was always supportive and kind to her. He had been like the cool uncle she'd wished was her dad.

Wandering into the kitchen with sleepy eyes and yawns, they found Ina at the dining table, glasses low on her nose, hair falling out from its messy bun. Her clothes dropped on her shoulders and notes littered the table as she wrote, drew, and read, trying to figure out Lilith's plot. Gwen noticed the photo she found at Ina's house beside the notes, the greasy gleam of fingerprints over the film showing just how much Ina relished it. Gwen hadn't realized Theo gave it to her, but she hoped it brought Ina some joy.

Lucas hummed while cooking pancakes and greeted them as they entered, offering them orange juice, coffee, and tea. Gwen and Theo took the hot, caffeinated beverages with grateful grunts. Despite the heating system, the winter cold seeped into the ground, chilling Gwen to her bones.

They sat at the table, brushing aside Ina's scribbles. Ina looked up at them, bags hanging under her amber-hazel eyes, overhead lights glinting off her glasses.

"Did you sleep?" Theo asked.

"No. No time," Ina said. "Lucas, another coffee, please."

"Yes, ma'am," Lucas replied, continuing to hum as he refreshed her mug and returned to his cooking.

"It looks like you've been...productive," Gwen said, nudging the array of papers.

"Hardly," Ina said. "There are too many variables. Too many paths Lilith could take. Too many conflicting motivations. I don't know what she is prioritizing," Ina tapped the eraser of her pencil on the table. "Can you ask Nikki if she has any other information?"

"I can try," Gwen responded, then asked, "Nikki?"

Even though Nikki had said she could just think, it felt weird to talk without speaking. Her thoughts were so often images, she didn't know how to make them into quiet words in her head.

"Nikki? You there?" she asked again.

But her head was quiet.

Gwen looked at Ina and said, "Nikki's not home right now, but please leave a message after the beep and she'll get back to you as soon as she can."

Theo smirked into her mug while Ina's face grew stern.

"Beep," Gwen said, laughing to herself despite Ina's pinched mouth of annoyance.

"Excuse me, ma'am," Lucas said, hovering over them with plates and utensils, trying to set the table.

Ina made a noise, something between a sigh and growl, as she stacked all the papers into a chaotic pile. She gathered her notes and coffee, then left the room. Theo and Gwen remained behind with Lucas, who resumed his humming while setting the table.

"You're in a good mood this evening," Gwen said, sipping her earl gray.

"Why shouldn't I be?" he asked.

"Imminent overthrow by an ancient vampire demi-goddess," Theo replied.

Lucas shrugged. "That's not on my doorstep yet." He looked at the stack of pancakes on the table, then at the batter near the stove. "Do you think we'll need more?"

"Terr Bear can eat his weight in pancakes, so yes," Theo said.

"You know, I've been wondering," Gwen said, setting down her mug but holding onto it tight, "why do you work here, for the Lius? I'm sure you and your sister had other prospects in life than being servants to a vampire couple."

"We're not servants," Lucas said, pouring the dry ingredients into one bowl and mixing them. "We're employees."

"But don't you give them blood?"

"Well, sure, but lots of people donate blood to those who need it."

"Being a vampire and having a blood disease are different things."

"That doesn't make their need any less." Lucas whisked together the wet ingredients, then folded them in to the dry. "They're kind to us and pay us well. We feel safe here. I'm not sure what else there is to say."

"Have they promised to turn you? Or given you their blood?"

Lucas hesitated. "No to the former, yes to the latter."

"You do know that humans consuming vampire blood will make them addicted, like to an insane degree, to that vampire."

"Gwen," Theo interjected, whispering, "you might not want to talk about this here."

"No, best to clear the air. I've seen the pitying, wondering look on your faces ever since you arrived." Lucas set the bowl down carefully, but as he turned, Gwen saw his jaw clench with repressed irritation. "And do you know that it takes, like, an insane amount of consumption for that to happen? We've had a little. Enough so that we don't get sick, so that we can live a little longer with slightly stronger senses. What's the harm in that?"

"The harm is that if you become addicted, you'll be a mindless slave." Gwen spat. "I've seen their other servants, in the main house, and they're not well. I wonder if they haven't committed suicide with the Lius' absence."

"They haven't," a soft yet steady female voice said from the doorway.

Gwen looked at Daiyu and felt her face enflame.

"They may have felt some withdrawals, but they should be well, by now. We talked to them before we left, gave them instructions for care," Daiyu said, crossing the kitchen to the fridge.

She pulled out a pitcher of blood, poured it into a mug, and popped it in the microwave.

"I do not expect you to understand our methods. However, I will let you know that it is not as malicious as you might think. We want them to be healthy and strong. We want those we care for to feel good."

"And if they become so loyal they are physically dependent on you, that's just an added benefit to their good health, huh?"

Daiyu grinned, and the microwave beeped. "Exactly."

Daiyu retrieved the mug, took a sip of the warm blood, and said, "Do not worry. Lucas and Olivia's intake is moderated. They will remain as they are."

"Well, that's good," Gwen said, stabbing a pancake and sliding it onto her plate. Theo was already two pancakes and nearly a cup of syrup deep. That woman had quite the sweet tooth.

Daiyu licked the blood from her lips and said, "Once you finish your breakfast, meet us in the living room. There is much to discuss."

"If we must," Gwen said, shoveling a large slice of pancake into her mouth, the barest hint of cinnamon and nutmeg in the batter.

A few minutes later, Terrance and Rachel joined them in the kitchen, quietly eating breakfast. None of them were morning people – even Rachel's usual cheeriness was dulled until she had at least one cup of coffee.

Breakfast done, they went to the living room where the fireplace was on, with Feng, Daiyu, and Ina huddled in a semi-circle around it, Ina's notes between them.

For being so resistant and hateful of vampires, Ina had accepted being in their presence quickly, taking the spare bedroom beside Rachel and Terrance's. Maybe it was because she had nowhere else to go, or maybe she was just using them, but despite how irritating she could be, Gwen was grateful to have someone with them that could give them guidance.

Or try to.

Ina swallowed, her loose jacket drifting off her shoulder. "We need to take a more proactive approach."

"Meaning?" Gwen asked.

"The three of us," Ina said, nodding towards Feng and Daiyu, "have decided to leave. We are going to hunt Hormin and Lilith."

"You're just going to leave us here?"

"Only if that's what you wish," Daiyu said. "You may come with us, or stay. The choice is yours. You would not be expected to fight."

"However, you three have shown great improvement in use of your weapons," Feng said to Terrance, Rachel, and Theo.

"We've only been training for a couple weeks. I don't think any of us are ready to fight," Terrance said, shifting from one foot to the other.

"Especially considering the strength of our opposition," Theo added.

"If you join us, you will not be on the front lines," Ina said. "Feng, Daiyu, and I have already discussed this. We will lead our offense against Lilith. We would like you to join us, as our allies grow slimmer every day, but we will not force you. However, we do not have time to debate this. You must make your decision now."

Gwen's blood hummed, and she shifted on her feet.

"We will keep you safe," Daiyu said, "as best as we can."

"So, will you join us?" Ina asked.

"Obviously," Gwen said, while Theo, Terrance, and Rachel exchanged hesitant looks before nodding their heads.

"I understand you are still weaponless, Gwen. You need to choose now. Before we leave," Ina said.

Gwen remained sitting. "I don't need one of those weapons. I already have my magic."

"Which you use incorrectly," Ina said.

"Excuse me?" Gwen replied, snapping her head back to Ina, the heat of fury spreading through her chest and up her neck.

"You don't use your magic correctly. That's why you fatigue easily. If you used it right, that wouldn't happen."

"How would you know anything about my magic? Our sources – our abilities are vastly different," Gwen asked, rising, blood ringing in her ears. This one thing was always hers, what she had honed her entire life, and this stranger dared tell her she is doing it wrong? "What gives you the right to tell me I'm using my own magic incorrectly? I've been practicing it for over a decade – I think I know what I'm doing."

"Just because you think that doesn't mean it's true," Ina said, standing to face Gwen. Even though she was shorter than her, the severity in her eyes and set to her jaw was intimidating. "And just because my magic is different than yours doesn't mean I know nothing about it. I have met witches other than you, Gwen. I have seen when magic is used correctly, and I can assure you – yours is not. The only thing you're right about is that our abilities are vastly different. I, for example, can use mine without fainting. You think that's how it's supposed to be? You think it means your magic is strong?"

Ina was hallowed by the fire, and Gwen clenched her fists, resisting the surge of power raging inside her, the rising wind at her fingertips, wanting to extinguish the demon before her.

"Nobody who is purely self-taught can be a master. Thinking so only means you're a fool."

"Is that so?" Gwen asked, through gritted teeth, taking deep breaths to abate the million insults stampeding through the blood that rang in her head.

"Everyone needs a teacher, Gwen. I'm not denying that you have power. You do. But before you, or any one of us, can depend on it, you need to learn how to use it correctly. Imagine this: We're fighting Lilith, or Hormin, or any other strong vampire, and we only depend on your magic. What happens if you exhaust your magic? If you pass out? Where would that leave us, besides dead?"

Ina's words hit her like a slap, and she squeezed her eyes shut, the memory of all the little broken and bloodied bodies left on her doorstep flooded her mind. At how she failed to make the right spell, to protect them, to keep them safe.

Gwen groaned, the sound transforming into a yell as she turned around and shot the wind across the living room away from everyone, letting out her anger and sadness in her defeat.

The release of power left her body tired, calmer.

"Why don't you teach me then?" Gwen asked, turning back to Ina, lip curled in disgust at her emotional outburst. "If I'm so terrible, why don't you teach me how to be better?"

Ina scoffed. "I would never teach a vampire. No offense," she added, glancing at Daiyu and Feng.

Feng shrugged and said, "None taken."

"I'm not a vampire," Gwen said, tensing.

"You are."

"I am not."

"You are. I can prove it." Ina looked at Theo, Terrance, and Rachel. "Can one of you please come over here? And bring a dagger?"

They hesitated, shifting on their feet and glancing at each other, waiting to see who would volunteer.

"I'm not going to hurt you. The dagger is for me," Ina said.

"Fine," Terrance replied. He took a knife from Rachel and stood beside Gwen in front of Ina.

Ina took the dagger and made a small cut on her forearm, barely wincing with the pain. She dabbed a finger on the cut, swabbing up blood. Ina took Terrance's arm and swiped her finger on his skin.

"See?" Ina said. "He is human, so his skin doesn't react to my blood."

"Mine won't either," Gwen blurted, and Ina's face twitched with pity before returning to steel.

Ina dabbed at the cut again, and taking Gwen's arm, smoothed her blood over her skin.

The skin under Ina's blood grew warmer and warmer, until it was hot, and then burning.

Her skin sizzled and peeled and cracked, just like Nikki's did in the sun.

As her flesh burned away, she yelped with the pain, the horror, reflexively pulling her arm close to her mouth to suck away the pain, to bring the cooling relief of her saliva to the searing wound.

Ina snatched her wrist, stopping her from bringing the blood to her mouth. "Do you want your insides to burn, too?"

Reality slapped Gwen and she lowered her arm, slow. Disbelieving as she heard the flesh sizzle, watching it burn away, even as tears burned in her eyes.

Ina swiped the remnants of her blood from Gwen's wound, most of it having burned away, and said gently, "I told you – you're not the first witch I've met."

Gwen stared at the burn wound on her arm, an oval in the shape of Ina's finger.

"No, no, no, no, no," Gwen murmured, tears glassing her vision.

There were so many things she had never been in her life: never a beloved daughter, never a welcomed sister, never an accepted coven member, never a good student, never able to control her emotions. Never, never, never...

The only never that she liked was that she was never, never a vampire.

For all she tried to help Nikki feel confident in herself, she didn't blame her for not wanting to be a vampire.

Gwen didn't either.

She never wanted to be a bloodsucker. A leech. A monster.

She couldn't be a vampire – she was a vegetarian, for Christ's sake.

Now that singular 'never' that she had held close to her heart, to her sense of self, that was taken away from her too.

In truth, she had never been human.

Loss filled her heart like a flash flood, and she stuttered a broken inhale, rushing out of the room before the tears could roll down her cheeks for everyone to see how pathetic and naïve she was. She had never been that smart either, had she?

If the blood of the good guys burned her, did that mean she was a monster, after all?

Theo shouted after her, but the sound was in a seashell, distant and muted, as Gwen navigated to the bedroom behind hazy vision, body aching like the air had been punched out of her.

She closed the door behind her and locked it. She knew Theo was on the other side, wanting to be there for her, but she didn't want Theo right now. She didn't want pity or false comforts.

"Nikki?" Gwen cried. "Nikki, are you there? Can you please talk to me? Please, please..."

Gwen collapsed to her knees and cried into her hands, Ina's burned fingerprint still searing and throbbing on her arm while she called out for Nikki.

Only Nikki would understand how much it sucked to be a vampire.

Chapter Thirty

Nikki was watching Lilith when Gwen cried out. She was better at maintaining her sense of self while in Lilith's mind, her consciousness separate, instead of melding with Lilith's thoughts and feelings. She could peel those layers back if she wanted to, but the rage and malice in Lilith sickened her.

Nikki watched the world through Lilith, aching for a glance of Xander. She had yet to find out what relic Lilith asked Vadasz to hunt, and she had yet to find his, Aella's, or Uase's thread. She hoped that the Cradle would know. That Gwen and Ina could find the relic before Lilith had her hands on it, before she could drain Xander dry. The sensual desire that rose in Lilith as she hovered near Xander's neck made her stomach turn.

So, Nikki watched, and hoped, for proof that he was alive. Asking for him to be well seemed a step too far. But if he was alive, there was hope.

Lilith stood in a small house in the middle of nowhere, maybe somewhere in Northern Mexico, waiting for Hormin and Xander to catch up.

In the part of her consciousness still rooted to herself, Nikki asked,

"Io, how does Lilith still communicate with Hormin? I thought the telepathy was tied to the Tree."

Io's presence grew, as if rising from a meditation so deep it was near sleep, and the hazy glimmers around her shifted. *"Hormin shares much of her magic. It isn't telepathy, more like…magnetism. They can sense themselves in each other, the corrupted magic, and it binds them. They will always sense where the other is."*

"Dangerous," Nikki thought. *"We can't fight them simultaneously, but it will be difficult to separate them."*

Io didn't respond, and Nikki refocused on her consciousness within Lilith. Lilith rifled through clothes in the home, claws red and chin wet with the blood of the people she had killed. Lilith wondered at the concept of clothes, having either been in her owl skin or nude in her vampiric form. She had never worn them on her own skin, only through the bodies of the descendants she watched, possessed.

The female's clothes were too petite for her tall, muscular, and woody form. The male's clothes fit, but they sagged and hugged the wrong places of her body. The tag itched the back of her neck, the rough spun cotton cloying and suffocating against her skin –

"Nikki?" Gwen's voice cried.

Nikki detached from Lilith, leaving her to her musings and discomfort of clothes, tumbling fully back into herself, heart thudding at the desperation in Gwen's voice.

"Nikki, are you there? Can you please talk to me? Please, please…"

Nikki clasped the wavering green thread that reached up toward her suspended feet and shot her consciousness through the world to Gwen. Her vision was glassy with Gwen's tears.

"What is it? Are you okay?"

"Nikki!" Gwen gasped. "Terrible news, I'm a vampire."

Nikki was silent, not knowing how to respond. Gwen sensed her uncertainty and shifted their gaze to a burn on her forearm, in the shape of fingerprint.

"What happened?" Nikki asked.

"Ina – her blood – it burns me, and I – I –" Gwen hiccupped and took stuttering breaths through her words.

"Gwen, breathe. Then tell me what happened."

Gwen took a few deep breaths, the caught air in her lungs and throat releasing out on a slow exhale. Then Gwen told her of the conversation with Ina about weapons and magic, about how she used it wrong, how Ina swiped her blood on her arm just to prove that Gwen could burn like a vampire.

Nikki threw part of her consciousness back to the Tree, to Io. She shared the vision of Gwen's arm and asked, *"How is this possible? There is nothing else vampiric about her."*

"She has the flesh of a vampire but the spirit of human. It is the nature of witches."

"Then why doesn't she burn in the sun, too?"

"The Cradle's magic is not the same as the sun's. Their magic is a balance to vampiric power, which includes the magic of their witch offspring. The vampirism in Gwen will react to the Cradle's power, despite withstanding the sun."

Turning her mind back to Gwen, vision split between the glimmering dark of the Tree and the curtain of Gwen's frizzy red hair over her burned arm, Nikki said, *"You're not a vampire. You're a witch."*

"But witches are vampires," Gwen said. "I thought I was different. That I wasn't a monster. No offense."

"None taken," Nikki thought, despite the sharp twist in her sinking heart. *"You* are *different Gwen. Don't let Ina tell you otherwise. Io said you have the body of a vampire and the spirit of a human. You're a witch, so you are different. You don't drink blood. You can stand in the sun. Don't let Ina bully you into thinking you're a monster. You're not. You're the most compassionate person I know. Besides Xander, maybe."*

"I wish I could agree. I feel like I no longer know who or what I am. I mean, I knew I came from vampires, but to see my skin fall apart like a vampire in the sun, it just…I don't know what I am anymore."

"You're Gwen. The most badass witch out there."

Gwen huffed a laugh, false and full of sorrow. "I'm not. My flock is dead because of me. Between that, this burn, and what Ina said about me not using my magic right…I don't think I'm a good witch, Nikki. I'm a bad witch, after all."

"You're not a bad witch, Gwen. But it might not hurt to find a teacher."

Gwen's heart fluttered with a pang of irritation, but it smoothed out, turning into heaviness in her gut.

"Yeah, I guess. And then," Gwen said, perking up, "I can shove it in Ina's face how powerful I am. Prove her wrong about me."

"Good plan," Nikki thought, pleased Gwen was boosting herself up. Despite the extremes of her emotions, Gwen also had an ability she envied – to snap out of them quickly instead of dwelling.

"Thanks, Nik," Gwen said, standing and going into the bathroom to wash the wound. "I'll put some salve on this and then talk to Theo. I kinda slammed the door in her face."

"Okay," Nikki said. *"I'm glad you're feeling better. Call me when you have news. Lilith is still in Northern Mexico."*

"Okay, I'll let the team know," Gwen said. "Talk to you soon?"

"Please," Nikki thought. As she stripped her consciousness from Gwen, she whispered, *"bye,"* then shot along the thread through the earth, returning to her trapped body, heart sinking with longing.

Chapter Thirty-One

Theo was not waiting for Gwen outside their door as she had expected. She hmphed to herself, stung that she gave up on her so quickly, but smoothed the sting away. She couldn't blame Theo for giving her space when she shut the door in her face.

Thankfully, Theo believed that Gwen talked to Nikki and wasn't just losing her mind.

Hushed voices echoed down the hall, firelight reflecting dim orange on the dark walls. She smoothed her hair back one more time, tucking the wild strands behind her ears. Gwen ensured the wrap around the burn was tight, and touched her face, checking it for puffiness. She put a cold compress over her eyes and cheeks after talking to Nikki, hoping it helped the swelling.

Back in the living room, the group was huddled near the wall, holding their different weapons. Feng glanced at her with a twitch of a thick eyebrow, then resumed his quiet conversation with Rachel and Terrance. Daiyu and Ina talked by the fire, Theo stood alone on the far side of the wall, eyeing the myriad guns.

Stepping farther into the room, the heat of the fire and her shame pushed against her skin. Ina left Daiyu and stood in front of Gwen, who stiffened in response.

"I did not mean to upset you," Ina said. There was no remorse in her voice, but she spoke gently, as if to calm an animal.

Gwen's lip curled, and she said, "Guess that explains why a tablet I found at your house exploded in my face."

Ina's face fell. "You destroyed one of my artifacts? Those are irreplaceable –"

"I didn't do it on purpose. I was trying to salvage belongings for you when it inconveniently and annoyingly erupted into dust that took days to get out of my hair."

Ina's mouth tightened into a thin line, and Gwen pushed past her to Theo.

Theo held a smooth silver pistol in her hand, rubbing a finger over the metal and testing the weight in her hand.

"I'm sorry for storming out like that."

Theo scoffed and shook her head, twisting the pistol in her hand, looking at the fine engravings along the barrel. There were thin vines and small leaves twining around it, catching in the shifting light.

"That's it?" Gwen asked, heat creeping up her neck and into her cheeks. "My whole sense of identity crashes around me, and when I apologize for my reaction to that, you just scoff?"

Theo looked at her, eyes flat and jaw set. "I don't care if you storm off. I do care about having a door slammed in my face."

"Yeah, well, as I said, I'm sorry. I was overwhelmed."

Theo picked up the sister gun sitting on the stand, holding one in each hand. "I guess I would have been too."

"So...you forgive me?"

"Sure. But I'm still mad at you."

"Well, I'm still mad at you for the whole abandoning Nikki thing, but I also still love you."

Theo's face twitched, part wince and part smile. "And I still love you, too."

Gwen gave her a close-lipped smile, not feeling the joy in her heart, just a small sense of relief. She stood on her tiptoes and kissed Theo on the cheek.

Ina cleared her throat. "So – the plan. We need to pack up our belongings, weapons, and then we need to pick up my sword."

"Your sword?" Gwen asked.

Ina nodded. "It was Arthur's, actually, but as he is in hiding, we thought it would be better kept with me. I gave it to a friend to repair before driving up here. I hope it is ready."

"Is it a magic sword?" Rachel asked.

Ina pinched the bridge of her nose between her eyes, and Gwen finally saw the resemblance between her and Xander. It was in the shape of the eyes, the eyebrows, the mannerisms. The recognition twanged her heartstrings – Ina wasn't just a Cradle member trying to protect the earth, she was a mother missing her son.

"It's magic, right?" Gwen asked. "It's being repaired by magic."

"Yes. Thank –"

"What kind of magic is it?" Rachel asked, perking.

Ina massaged the bridge, eyes squeezed shut. "I'll explain when we're on the road." She dropped her hand and opened her eyes, glancing at them in turn, Feng and Daiyu casual and calm. Feng slung a sash that held knives and homemade bombs around his waist and a rifle across his back. Daiyu wrapped a belt around her that held space for daggers and fan blades. Theo held two pistols, pointing downward, Terrance grasped the hammer, and Rachel had daggers tied at her waist and a bow in her hand.

Ina stared at Gwen. "You still need to pick a weapon."

"I don't want to."

"Your magic cannot be your only weapon. Not until you have been taught."

Gwen glanced at all the deadly, sharp objects in the room. The menacing guns and bone short bow. Her pulse ratcheted. "I don't want to hold any of those things."

"You need something to defend yourself," Ina replied, irritation creeping back into her voice. "We just went over this, Gwen. What don't you understand?"

A cool, firm hand landed on Gwen's shoulder. Daiyu stood beside her, large black eyes searching. "I have an idea. Come to this side of the rack."

Daiyu led her to the wall nearest the fireplace. "You have spent much of your life outside foraging, correct?"

"I have," Gwen replied.

"And did you use your bare hands, or any tools?"

"Tools, usually. I had a bark stripper, sickle, knife, trowel...all kind of things."

"As I thought," Daiyu unhooked a sword with a short handle and deeply curved blade from the rack and angled it out for Gwen to take.

Gwen stared at the handle, the crescent moon blade shining in the low firelight. Her heart beat hard in her ribs, and she clenched her fist to still her trembling fingers before reaching out to take it.

"It's a sickle sword," Daiyu said. "I understand why you do not wish to wield a weapon, Gwen. I was once that way myself. I thought, perhaps, this form that is somewhat familiar to you might make it easier."

Warmth and appreciation flooded Gwen's rapidly beating heart, lumping in her throat. It did feel strange to hold, larger and heavier than the other tools she had used, but Daiyu was right – it wasn't as foreign as holding a bow or long sword. She could almost pretend it was an oversized gardening tool.

"Thank you," Gwen choked out.

Daiyu smiled at her, close-lipped, and gave a small nod of recognition.

"Now that that's settled," Ina said, clearing her throat. "Let's pack up and head out."

The group broke apart, and walking down the hallway to their rooms, Terrance asked, "So, we're headed to Mexico?"

"No. The Pelican State."

Chapter Thirty-Two

In the dark of the Tree, with Io glimmering around her and her mother resting against her bark, Nikki tried to find Vadasz. Or Aella. Or Uase. She also looked for Atoc and Ozcollo, but their threads were equally elusive. She knew Lilith's path, and as much as she wanted to see Xander, to see proof he was living, she wasn't sure how much more her heart could bear watching him be abused. It broke her to see the new bruises bloom across his skin, the bags that grew darker under his eyes, the weight that fell from his body, clothes getting baggier. She wished that the telepathic bond she had with vampires through the Tree also applied to humans, and that she could reach out to him directly. That they could talk through everything that happened.

That she could tell him she was sorry.

But she could try to figure out where Vadasz and his crew were, what they were looking for. She could tell Gwen, and they could intercept them, protecting Xander from Lilith's plans for him.

When Gwen had told her that they were prioritizing stopping Lilith first, she wasn't surprised, although her chest emptied. It made sense to stop Lilith first, to protect the majority of people before her. But to hear that they didn't know how to get her out, that she might be stuck in here forever...

She tried not to wallow in despair as she usually did. She tried to be like Gwen, to think of what she could do, not what she couldn't.

She could still help if she manipulated the threads that connected her to the vampires, but it was so hard to reach others. It made sense why she was drawn to Lilith, due to her bond with the Tree, and Io had helped establish her link to Gwen, but she could not summon the threads to anyone else. When she thought of Vadasz, his terribly beautiful face, long fangs, the skin melting from his carved skin, sometimes she saw – or sensed? – a glimmer of dark purple, so deep it was almost black. The dark purple of the midnight sky.

Or one of Xander's bruises.

Lilith and Gwen's threads wavered at her feet, easy ties to her now, but no other strands appeared for her to pull on.

"You are in better spirits," Io said.

Nikki's eyes opened, the metallic glitter swimming in her vision, and she realized her eyes had been closed as she thought.

"It's nice not being completely in the dark," Nikki thought, and her body clenched with the repressed laugh.

It was a terrible joke.

Sad amusement swarmed around her, and Io said, *"I am glad."*

Nikki tried moving her arms, her hands, an instinct to check if her arms were dead. The shoulders shifted, but nothing else moved or tingled. Only the roots inside of her skin twinged. *"I still feel like I am missing a lot of context. There's so much I don't understand. Can you tell me now – why are things this way? How did this happen?"*

"Yes, I think I am unraveled enough. Where should I start?"

"From the beginning." A nervous hum zigged through Nikki's body, a trembling of anticipation. *"Please."*

"That is a long story."

"I'm not going anywhere."

The glimmers stilled, shifting more silver as they twisted in the air, which grew heavy. *"I suppose not."*

Pressure in the Tree grew, as if Io took a deep breath.

"I do not remember the beginning. All I know is that I was nothing, and then I was something. As it is for all living things. There was much

darkness and yet so much light. The glow of billions upon billions of stars, the swirl of galaxies, the beautiful dust of nebulas –"

"Oh. Hold on. When I said the beginning, I meant about vampires. This mess with Lilith. Are you talking about the beginning of the universe?"

"No. As I said, I do not remember that. I do not think I was a being, then."

"Are there others like you?"

"Yes, numerous. We travelled the universe as it expanded, as it aged. It was glorious. Full of creation and destruction. Full of color, yet dark. Full of matter, yet empty. It was – is – a wondrous thing."

Nikki's mind spun, trying to imagine the unfolding of the universe. It made her queasy.

"Others of my kind, they unraveled from time, impatient, wanting to see everything, everywhere, immediately. I, however, enjoyed the slow crawl of time once I discovered it. Instead of seeing the creation of life and death of a planet all at once, I could watch it. It fascinated me. The combination of elements, the pull of other planetary beings. How everything interacted. Or how it did not.

"This left me behind the others. They ascended to a different dimension. There were others like me, who liked time, but we were few and far apart. I grew adept at being at once within and without time – traveling through space and time with more efficiency, but able to stop and unravel when I desired.

"Which I did, when I found this one, unique planet. It was young, relatively, and so vibrant. So...complex. After eons of physics and chemistry, I finally found biology."

Chills wound up Nikki's spine. "*You didn't create life?*"

The air shimmered, like a chuckle. "*No. I found it here already. It was during what your scientists call the Cambrian Explosion. Not only had I found life, but I also found so much more than I had ever imagined. And it was the first time I contemplated myself. Realized that I was alive. It was a great time for Earth's biodiversity, and my introspection.*

"I stayed, and I watched. Half within and half without time. Over those millions and billions of years, I watched millions upon billions of species rise and go extinct. Each one unique. Each one distinctly beautiful.

For once in all my eons of travel, I did not want to leave. I wanted to stay. Not only did I want to stay, to watch, I wanted to engage. I wanted to help. I wanted to see what I could do, as I finally realized what I was and that I had power other creatures did not.

"My interference was small at first. Adding an abundance of carbon dioxide into the atmosphere for plants to grow. Blowing the wind for early invertebrates to find their food. Shifting the currents for marine life to swim toward cleaner waters. Encouraging leaves and grasses to grow for Gastonia to eat."

"Gastonia?"

"It's a dinosaur."

"Oh."

"I loved them all. Each species that lived in their own way – whether plant, animal, or insect. But I knew the cycle of our universe, after having watched the billions of years of stars form and fade. Of black holes eating everything around them. Of the birth of stars in the dust clouds. I mourned each extinction, despite accepting it as necessity.

"After a time, the first humans evolved. At first, I did not find them special. They were not so different from other creatures, except with bipedalism. Even then, other species were oft times bipedal, and I had seen the extinction of two other bipedal species before humans.

"Humans stayed and expanded, continued to evolve. They did so in marvelous ways. Tools. Fire. Then consciousness sparked in and out of some of them, language carving through. It was not a sudden ripple of aware-ness. There were several species of humans at the time, all diversifying and evolving in their own ways. And, as is the nature of life, of all things in the universe, they destroyed. Absorbing and killing other species.

"Yet, consciousness continued to establish itself. They, too, could create. They, too, could influence their surroundings. Not to the same extent as I, of course, but I remember that day when I realized the boundless potential – the utter beauty – of humanity despite the violence.

"I saw the intelligence, the passion. I wondered – what if I made my own? What if I took this species, and gave them part of my magic? What wondrous things could they do with it? I did just that. I made my own humans from the dust of the earth and gave them some of myself. Thus came Adam. And Lilith.

"My first son. My first daughter."

Io's voice ached, the air around Nikki tightening with sadness.

"They were beyond beloved. I miss those early days when they were new to the world. Everything was so pure, so beautiful, to them. And I finally had creatures to share in the joy of magic, of life. I found that with them, too, I developed emotions. What an equally wondrous and disastrous thing that was for us all." Io hesitated. *"Gwen calls for you."*

"What?" Nikki asked, snapping out of her reverie.

"Hey, Nikki, you there? I have another update for you, kind of?"

Nikki ignored the green thread that reached up for her.

"You can't leave the story there. We were just getting to the relevant part!"

"It is all relevant, child."

"Helloooooooo? Nikki? I have a question for you..."

Nikki exhaled, the sigh so deep her chest caved, and plunged mind first into Gwen's consciousness.

Chapter Thirty-Three

GWEN SHOVED her belongings into packs and bags. Although it was several weeks since her last relocation, she was irked at having to leave again. She didn't even get a chance to settle in. But maybe she would never have settled into a vampire dungeon, anyway.

"What's your question, Gwen?" Nikki asked, her presence peeling into the back of Gwen's mind.

"Do you know what the Pelican State is?"

Theo shouted from the bathroom, "I'm telling you it's Louisiana!"

"I believe you!" she shouted, then dropped her voice to whisper. "Is it Louisiana, Nik?"

Nikki was silent for a moment, then said, *"Yes. According to Io. Why?"*

"Ina says that's where we need to go, although she hasn't specified exactly why."

"She must have allies there."

"I guess so," Gwen said, packing up all her herbs and witchy supplies, which she actually packed with care, unlike her clothes that she dumped in haphazardly. "Anyway, that was my only question. I just wanted to hear your voice. Or the thought of your voice? Is it even your voice?"

"No, it's not. It's an interesting question though – if you hear my voice the way you used to hear it or if it's how I think of my voice and projected to you."

"You don't sound any different."

"But do we imagine my voice the same?"

"I can't handle these types of questions right now, Nik. They hurt my brain."

"Sorry. I have nothing better to do now than hurt my brain."

Gwen hesitated, mouth scrunching with the inability to provide comforting words. "I'm sorry, Nik. I wish I knew how to get you out."

"Me too." A pause. *"I'm glad you are on the move. It gives me hope for Xander."*

"We'll get ya boy."

Gwen sensed a pained relief along the back of her skull, Nikki's own feelings pressing into her.

"I still can't find Vadasz and his companions. Or Atoc and Ozcollo. Let me know if you find anything out about them. Any detail, no matter how small. It might help me connect with them. I don't know what they're doing, and it worries me. Especially Vadasz."

"Yeah, him being on a special quest for Lilith can't be good."

"My thoughts exactly. She wants to make Xander drinkable. I don't how she plans to do it, but Vadasz has something to do with it. Maybe pick Ina's brain."

"All right, Nik, will do," Gwen said, tying off her bag of ingredients. Nikki's presence eased from her mind, like a pressure lifted. "You don't have to go."

Distant, Nikki's sadness crept down Gwen's spine. *"I need to keep an eye on Lilith. Try to find the others. But thank you. Keep me posted. And stay safe."*

"I will," Gwen said, heart dropping.

Theo stepped out of the bathroom, all their hygiene products and towels neatly tucked into an extra suitcase from the Lius. "All set?"

Gwen nodded. "Thanks for packing the bathroom."

"No problem," Theo said. She set the suitcase down and put her smooth fingers under Gwen's chin, lifting her gaze up. "Everything okay?"

"I'm just worried about Nikki. She sounded so...defeated."

Theo tucked a wild strand of hair behind Gwen's ear. "We're not defeated yet."

"'Yet' doesn't fill me with hope. As if our defeat is inevitable."

"That's not what I meant. I meant it's too early to give up."

"I know," Gwen said, standing and wrapping her arms around Theo, sighing her shoulders loose as Theo returned her embrace. "It's all just so scary. Like, are we really about to hunt down Lilith? The craziest, most evil vampire out there?"

"I guess so. But we're not alone. There are experienced people with us. And we've been training, too. I think everything will turn out the way it's supposed to – where the good guys win."

Gwen wondered if she was a good guy, glancing at the burn mark on her arm. "Yeah, I hope so."

Gwen released Theo and shook her anxiety out, plastering the brightest, fakest smile on her face, wanting to dispel the somber expression from Theo's. Theo asked, "Are you ready to ride in our war caravan?"

"As long as I don't have to ride with Ina. That woman is intense," Gwen said, looping her backpack over her shoulders. "I mean, can you imagine being in a car with her for...however long it takes to get to Louisiana?"

"She's not *that* bad once you get to know her."

"Whatever you say," Gwen said, forcing a laugh, but it felt hollow in her throat.

Before they left the room, Gwen looked at it from the doorway. The silence pushed against her ears, nauseating her. She missed the sounds of the woods, of her flock flying and chirping, the squirrels chittering and rabbits crunching. It was always quieter in the winter, but despite what Theo had said about finding a flock in the spring, about having the companionship of others, she was more alone than she had ever been.

Gwen slammed the door, yelling "whoops!" afterwards, as if she hadn't done it on purpose just to drown out that horrible, oppressive quiet.

Chapter Thirty-Four

Both Theo and Gwen had to sit in the same car as Ina. For some reason, Ina felt it necessary to assign them seats, and she refused to have her ideas changed. So, Gwen and Theo sat with Ina and Feng in Feng's car, while Terrance and Rachel got to be in his Jeep with Daiyu.

Gwen thought the latter setup sounded a lot more fun.

And safer, since Feng packed crates full of his explosives in the car. Despite their potential utility in a confrontation, if they got in a car accident, they'd go up in wild flames.

Gwen mused at how interesting that crime scene would be, since not only was the car packed with explosives, but it was also packed with blood. The Lius had expensive, tightly sealed and well insulated coolers that they stored blood bags in for the trip. In a contentious argument, the Lius and Ina agreed that when the Lius ran out of stored blood they could hunt as long as they promised not to kill anyone. If they got in a car accident before that point, it would be an extra bloody mess for emergency responders.

Lucas and Olivia remained at the house, both for upkeep and as a point of contact in case someone had to return without Daiyu or Feng. They had food and drinks packed for them; Olivia's eyes glassy with tears as Daiyu hugged her goodbye. Lucas's face was downcast, a frown pulling at the corners of his lips, but his eyes were clear when shaking their hands, promising to take care of their house and his sister.

Gwen hadn't realized just how attached Olivia and Lucas were to the Lius. It was obvious they liked them since they would have to if they were willing to live in an underground bunker and give them blood. But even more surprising to Gwen was how attached the Lius were to Olivia and Lucas in return. Feng and Daiyu's faces contorted with worry when saying goodbye, and seeing the sorrow in Olivia's face, the restrained longing in Lucas's, it felt as if a family was breaking apart.

Feng's car was at least more comfortable than Terrance's, large and plush. Gwen hadn't been outside the bunker in so long that it felt strange when the car pulled out into the frigid night.

"Snow!" Gwen shouted when her eyes adjusted, soft flakes falling slow and small, a thin layer of white on the ground and evergreen branches.

Theo groaned.

"What – you don't like snow?" Gwen asked.

"No. Not at all. First, it's a safety hazard. Then it becomes gross. When it melts and mixes with all the sludge."

"But it's so pretty. And it's only sludgy and gross in the city."

"Don't care. Still don't like it."

"Hmmm..." Gwen said. "We'll have to change that. I love snow."

Theo shivered and burrowed into her jacket, so Gwen turned her gaze back to the snowfall, the shimmers of white against the black.

Feng drove slowly, cautious of the frozen dirt roads and black ice on the highway as Ina directed them to her friend's house, which was in the opposite direction they needed to go. Instead of heading east, they traveled west, back into and over Portland, past the rolling hills that faced the city, and into those that swallowed the southwest neighborhoods.

"What are we going to do when it's dawn?" Gwen asked.

"Keep driving, of course," Ina said.

"Don't 'of course' me when we have two made vampires. Don't you explode in the sun, Feng?"

"So I have heard."

"Okay then. Again, what are we going to do when the sun rises so that they don't incinerate?"

"The back of the car can be modified to block out sunlight. We also have large, UV proof travel bags. We will hide in there before the dawn."

"You're going to sleep in a bag in the trunk? Sounds degrading."

"And if we get pulled over with bodies in the trunk, that will look pretty bad," Theo added.

"Don't get pulled over then," Feng said, shrugging. "It is what we must do to survive."

"Turn here," Ina said, pointing. "It'll be the second house on the right."

Feng followed her instructions and parked in front of the indicated house, the only building on the street with the porchlight on. It had a large, bare maple tree in the front yard, edges lined with shrubs. It was two stories, the upper story coming to a point at a sharp angle, a small window shining warm light through it.

Terrance parked behind them, and the group congregated at the door.

"This should be quick," Ina said. "Cora knows we are in a hurry."

Ina lifted her fist to knock, but the door creaked open before her knuckles landed on the faded wood. A willowy woman with ice-blue eyes and flaxen blonde hair smiled wide at Ina, stepping back from the door to let them inside.

"My friend, it is so good to see you again," Cora said.

"As it is you," Ina replied, smiling back. The two women hugged like old friends.

Ina made introductions, Cora beaming and welcoming each person individually. She did not seem surprised at having vampires in her presence, and Gwen wondered if Ina had warned her, or if vampires were just so normal for her, she didn't blink.

Cora had one of those comforting handshakes where she took your hand in both of hers as if trying to warm it.

Gwen liked her immediately.

When Gwen shook her hand, encompassed in the warmth of Cora's, Cora paused as her hand retreated, looking at Nikki's ring on her finger.

The smile on Cora's face grew wider, her gaze wistful. "You have one of my daughter's rings."

"Really?" Gwen asked, twisting it. "This ring, when I put it on, it's like…I feel stronger. It's not mine though." Gwen looked at Ina. "Xander bought this for Nikki on her birthday. Because he loves her."

Ina's lips tightened, and Gwen grinned, feeling lighter at reminding Ina of the love between her son and a vampire.

The best vampire.

"Yes, my daughter is a gifted mage," Cora replied. "She doesn't quite understand the extent of her ability, but some stones are incidentally imbued. Like this one."

"Maybe she should be fighting along with us, if she's so powerful."

Cora's smile faltered, but she still held Gwen's hand. "I would rather keep her out of this."

"Don't worry," Ina said, putting a hand on Cora's shoulder. "Rhea doesn't need to be involved."

"Thank you," Cora replied. "But speaking of Rhea and her magic, follow me."

They followed Cora through the house to a dining room, where a large item wrapped in brown paper lay on the oak table.

As Ina unwrapped the item, Cora said, "I just told her it was a repair of a family heirloom for a friend. She didn't ask any other questions."

The paper crinkled and fell away, tumbling to the floor.

When all the wrapping was gone, light glinted off metal, and Gwen's mouth dropped.

A gleaming sword lay before her, the hilt a deep walnut woven with silver and gold. Attached to the hilt was a small ring, the pommel rounded and glimmering with precious metals. The blade was a deep silver, shot through with verdant hues ranging in shades of winter to evergreen.

Rachel oohed as Terrance asked, "Is that what I think it is?"

"It is," Ina said, a small grin on her face as she wielded it.

"But, I mean, it's not really Excalibur, is it? Terrance asked.

"No, it's the replacement."

"The replacement?"

Ina nodded. "Excalibur was destroyed in battle. This one was first given to King Aruthur by the Lady of the Lake as its replacement. It must have also been shattered and lost in battle, as so many centuries later, the Lady gave it to Arthur when we were on our honeymoon."

"But...why?" Theo asked.

Ina set the sword on the table, the dark metal and veins of green reflecting the orange overhead lights. "King Arthur was a descendant of Adam. Hence, Arthur and Xander are also his descendants."

"So, Arthur is a family name," Gwen said.

"In a sense," Ina replied. "Although, I do not think it is conscious. Long ago, the Cradle decided that Adam's bloodline should not know what they are. That it would be safest for them to be ignorant in case they got too close to a vampire. Or became too arrogant and started the war between vampires and the Cradle themselves. So, Arthur does not know what he is. He was given the sword, but the why is a mystery to him. I pretended to disbelieve his story about the Lady to keep the secret safe."

Gwen's stomach clenched, and her mouth pursed. "So, you lied to your husband your whole relationship."

Ina stared at her, jaw clenched. "I did not lie. I kept him safe."

Biting down on the inside of her lip, Gwen took a deep breath, assessing how many people were around them. Despite wanting to shame Ina, she said, "Whatever."

"How did your daughter fix it?" Theo asked Cora.

"She's a geomancer," Cora replied, the corners of her lips tilting up with pride. "A very skilled one. She blended the shards together. These veins of green," Cora said, running a finger gently over the sword, "are her bindings of the sword, created from her own stone and metal."

"Wow," Rachel said. "I had no idea there was so much magic in the world. And so many different kinds."

"Me neither," Gwen murmured, although her voice did not have the same lilt of excitement as Rachel's.

"Thank you, Cora. And please, thank Rhea as well. This is beautiful," Ina said.

"I will let her know. I trust you will use it well."

"Does it –" Gwen started.

Ina threw up a hand. "We will have time for questions in the car." Ina looked at Cora. "We should be leaving."

"Of course," Cora said, nodding her head in understanding. "Is there any other way I can help?"

"My friend, I was both hoping you would and would not ask," Ina said. "I would not put you in harm's way, but we could always use someone with your talents."

Cora inhaled, chest expanding with the breath, but her voice did not waver, nor did her eyes leave Ina's, as she said, "I will not leave you to face such things alone."

Ina laid her hand over Cora's and squeezed it. "Thank you."

Cora nodded. "Do not wait for me. I need to pack – I will catch up with you."

Ina released her hand from Cora's and picked up the sword, heralding the group out the door as Cora returned to the recesses of her house.

Questions bubbled within Gwen. What was the power of the sword? What did it mean to be a descendant of King Arthur? What abilities did Cora have, and which Cradle was she from?

The questions hummed an anxiety beneath her skin, and she fidgeted in her seat, waiting for Ina and Feng to stop discussing their route, for them to sit still, so that she could ask.

When they were on the highway and the navigational conversation ended, Ina said, "Gwen – I can feel your uncontrolled energy. Please take a breath before spewing out your questions."

"'Spewing?'" Gwen spat. "You bring us into another witch's house, show us new magics and relics, and think I won't have questions?"

Theo put a hand on Gwen's, heat rising in Gwen's chest.

"First, she is not a witch. She is a mage. There is a difference. Second, you may ask questions, but please control yourself."

"Are you kidding? I've been controlling myself this whole time! While you two have been chatting about this or that road to take, I've been waiting for answers!" Gwen looked at Theo. "Am I wrong? I swear every day I find out a different way we're kept ignorant of the full picture."

Theo hesitated, hands shoved into her jacket pockets. "No, I agree with you. There's so much we don't know...but we're also going to be in this car together for days, Gwen. We'll be adequately informed when it's the right time."

"Well, I think the right time is now," Gwen said, slouching in her seat, eyes fixed on the back of Ina's head.

Feng flicked on the wipers, the snow melting on the windshield, blurring their vision.

Ina sighed. "Fine. What do you want to know?"

"Let's start with Cora. Who is she? How do you know her? Which Cradle is she from? What's her magic? How is a mage different from a witch?"

"Cora isn't from the Cradle. There are more lineages with magic than just vampires and the Cradle. She is from one of those other bloodlines. I don't know how she got her magic, or where, but she seems to come from a long line of geomancers. As for the magic Cora has herself, it isn't physical like ours or her daughter's. It's more...psychic. She's a diviner."

"What does that mean?"

"It means she senses things. Sometimes about people, sometimes about their past or future. It's a very unpredictable ability, but can be among the most useful when fate allows."

"So, her magic is useless until it's not. How illuminating."

"The same can be said for everyone, Gwen. Don't be spiteful just because you finally have to face the fact that you're not that special."

"Excuse me?" Gwen stammered, the spark of heat from her core rising up through her neck, warming her cheeks and tensing her jaw. She leaned forward, the air around her rising, crackling static.

"Hey, now," Feng said. "No magic in the car."

"Then tell her stop being a bully!" Gwen yelled, trying to drop the air, but crinkles of static still kept the hair on her arms raised.

"This is going to be a long car ride." Theo sighed, arms crossed and eyes closed.

The fight in Gwen disappeared at the disappointment in Theo's voice, and she settled back in her seat, the heat in her face changing from anger to shame.

"Okay, so geomancers and diviners, blah, blah. What's the deal with the sword? I know you said it was King Arthur's, but what makes it special besides being older than dirt?"

"It is incredibly old magic, but to understand the magic of the sword, you need to understand the magic of King Arthur, and therefore the magic of Adam's bloodline. All descendants of Adam are blessed –"

Ina cut off as the car swerved, tires lifting as it hydroplaned, sliding across the road, and Gwen's vision spun as the car whirled, the trees and headlights churning.

The seat belt yanked against her, locking her body in place and knocking the air from her lungs as she jerked against it and the car slammed to a stop.

For a second, the only sound was their breaths, ragged and scared as their vision stabilized.

"What the hell was that?" Gwen asked, smoothing the hurricane of her hair away from her face.

"We have company," Ina said.

The car was turned perpendicular to the highway. Gwen looked over Theo, whose hands shook as she righted her hair and straightened her clothes, adjusting the seatbelt where it cut against her neck.

Outside, two cars barricaded the way forward, three figures standing in the snow.

"What do we do?" Theo asked.

"Stay here," Ina said, stepping outside and conjuring an orb of sunlight in her palm.

Feng growled, low in his throat. He turned the car off and followed Ina into the night, standing far enough away to not be burned by the sun in her hands.

Theo and Gwen looked at each other, searching. Gwen took Theo's shaking hands, kissed them, and left the car, with weapons in hand.

Behind them, Terrance's car was also turned perpendicular to the road, having swerved to avoid their spin out. Terrance, Rachel, and Daiyu got out of the car, fixing their clothes, checking each other for injuries, and looking over their shoulders, worried. They grabbed their weapons from the trunk and moved towards Gwen's group.

Gwen looked past them, spotting where another car had stopped right behind Terrance's jeep, blocking them in. From her vantage point, she could see three individuals in the car, but she could not make out any of their faces.

Tensing, Gwen followed Ina and Feng, who stalked forward to meet the three figures blocking the way. When she reached them, she stood beside Ina, the warmth of the miniature sun melting the snow in the air and warming her cheek.

"Of course it would be you," Gwen hissed, the light from Ina's sun catching the shimmering deep red hues of her sisters' hair.

Bridget stepped forward, illuminated by the light but not yet burning. Gwen's two other sisters stepped up beside her, faces flickering in the sun's flares.

"Of course it would be you, dearest sister, who continues to cause problems," Bridget said. "And of course, we are here to stop you."

Two more figures stepped from behind Bridget, tall and broad with fine features and straw blonde hair.

The Ivarssons.

The fourth figure moved into the light, posture calm and chin raised, dark, thick braid hanging over one shoulder.

Tyee.

Gwen sensed the heat of Terrance and Rachel, smelled the soft jasmine smell of Daiyu as they approached, closing ranks.

Then there was the sound of another pair of footsteps, the cold of the air amplifying the scent of old forests and pine needles in winter. Gwen whispered, "Farrell."

He stood beside her, tall and sharp, eyes dark with foreboding. She searched his face, the one most similar to hers that had been friendly, even if not familial. The one sibling who had not completely abandoned her, or hated her.

"Why?" Gwen asked, eyes roving over his merlot hair and diamond cheekbones as if they would tell her the answer. "How could you do this to me? I thought ..." Gwen stilled her quivering chin, widened her eyes to reabsorb the tears, "even if you weren't on my side, you at least weren't against me."

Farrell startled. "I'm not against you. I didn't –"

"You're boring me!" Bridget yelled, and Gwen turned her focus back to her terrible sister.

"Quiet!" Tyee barked at Bridget, then turned to Gwen and the others. "We cannot let you proceed," Tyee said, looking at Ina.

"How did you know where to find us?" Ina asked, the flares of the sun shining on the dark asphalt, the lines of her face.

"Someone's phone is still on," Brienne said, staring at Gwen.

"We smelled you when you came to visit our dear brother and knew you would resurface eventually," Bridget sneered.

Ina glanced at Gwen, disappointed. But how was she to know they could track her phone?

Tyee stepped forward. "You can come with us, back to my cells, or die here and let your bodies freeze over."

"You know we cannot do that," Ina said.

"And we will not be the ones dying here," Feng said.

"There is no other choice," Tyee replied.

"There is. There always is," Ina said, raising her hands.

As Ina raised her hands together to expand the sun, the Lius stepped back.

Tyee lifted her hands in front of her, fingers pointed straight like daggers toward the earth, and as she pulled her hands apart, the asphalt below opened with a loud, splintering crack. Gwen stumbled with the rumble, and the ground swallowed Ina, demolishing her sun. Gwen blinked in the sudden darkness, the light of Ina's sun extinguished.

Tyee thrust her hands together, clasping them into a joined fist, and the asphalt and dirt closed around Ina, leaving all except her head trapped in the ground. Gwen's head swam with the dizzying motion of the earth opening and reforming.

Ina squirmed, but she could not move.

Terrance dropped to Ina's side, trying to pull her up from the crevice.

"Please, Tyee –" Daiyu started.

"No. I no longer have a coven, and therefore I am no longer Tyee," she said through a clenched jaw.

"Please," Daiyu said again, taking a step forward. "I don't want to fight you. You were there for us when nobody else was. You cared for us when nobody else would. Is there no other way to solve this? Can we not be on separate sides, yet not harm each other?"

"You're an idealistic fool, Daiyu, just like your husband, and always have been." The woman who was once Tyee spat. "I am, quite frankly, surprised that you would side with... them. After so many years of wanting more authority, more thralls, when you finally have that freedom at your fingertips, you would deny it?"

"This is not the way we wanted it. You know that."

"The conqueror cares not for the method of claiming their land, as long as it is theirs in the end," she said. "It appears I overestimated you, in thinking you had that same immovable fire required to meet your goals."

The air puffed in front of Gwen's face as she pooled her magic into her core, ready for release whenever that time came.

But Terrance remained near Ina, and the Lius did not step closer to their ex-coven leader. Her sisters did not move, nor did her brother or the Ivarrsons. Theo stood close to her, and Rachel sidled close to Terrance. Each side not willing to give ground, yet not willing to attack without provocation.

But something had to give.

The loud whir of a car engine approaching thrummed through the night, the wheels kicking up melted snow. As it approached, it sounded as if it was getting louder, the wheels spinning faster and the engine working harder. Headlights flashed against the concrete barrier and over their cold skins.

"Watch out!" Terrance yelled, launching upward to push Rachel, Theo, and Gwen to the side as the car screeched, slamming on its brakes despite the speed.

It veered into the shoulder lane then made a sharp turn when it passed them, crashing into not-Tyee with the horrid twisting of metal and a screech of pain. The car crashed into the two vehicles that had created a barrier, shoving them aside and pinning not-Tyee between steel.

Not-Tyee screamed, but the shock passed quickly and she snarled as she tried to push the vehicle away to free herself.

She coughed, and blood burbled from her mouth, dripping down her chin.

A tall, thin figure stepped out of the recklessly driven car, and swayed on their feet.

"I hope I'm not too late," Cora said, then buckled.

Feng sprang forward, catching Cora before her head met the road, and gently laid her down, swiveling on his heel as Bridget and Brienne leapt toward him, daggers in their hands.

As he swiveled, he pulled a dagger from his boot and slashed, causing the sisters to jump back.

Gwen met Bronwen's eyes, wide and frozen, as she backed into the crashed cars. Bronwen looked stunned, disbelieving, as if she had always gone along for the ride and had finally been slapped with the reality of the situation she found herself in.

"Go!" Farrell yelled, pushing Gwen and running to enter the fight, jumping onto Bridget while she slashed at Feng once more. They crashed to the ground with the sickening crunch of bones on asphalt, and Farrell pinned her flailing arms beneath his hands.

Looking over his shoulder, Farrell yelled again, "Go, Gwen! Get out of here!"

Not-Tyee's hands crunched the metal hood of the car that pinned her, and the Ivarssons rushed to help release her. With few seconds before she was freed, Gwen turned to her friends.

"Terrance, smash the shit out of the ground with your hammer – we need to get Ina out!"

Terrance nodded and dashed to where Ina was trapped, then brought the hammer down, down, down on the fissures in the ground. It cracked and splintered under his blows. Daiyu held one hand over Ina's eyes so that the splatter of asphalt from the hammer would not eviscerate them, and dug her fingers underneath loosened chunks of asphalt with her other hand to fling them out of the way.

Farrell struggled against Bridget, who flailed, screamed, and tried to claw her way out from under him.

Feng and Brienne slashed and dashed around each other with their knives, and Gwen pulled the magic from her core into her hands, concentrating it into a dense ball of air.

"Theo and Rachel, go pick up Cora and her things and take her into one of the cars. Each of you get behind a wheel and be ready to drive as if hell is on your heels."

Gwen couldn't see or hear their responses, focused as she was on funneling every scrap of magic into her hands, but she saw their silhouettes in her peripheral run forward, rummaging through Cora's car, then dragging her body back to Feng's vehicle.

Not-Tyee's hair fell loose from her braid, slicked with sweat to her face, as blood dribbled down her chin and her abdomen continuously healed from the crush of the car. She placed her palms on the vehicle and pushed. The Ivarssons surrounded the car and tried to push it off of her, but the metals were twisted and locked.

"Stop her!" Not-Tyee shouted, pointing at Gwen. With worried looks on their faces, the Ivarssons turned their attention to Gwen and ran toward her.

A bright flash and bang resounded in front of her, momentarily stopping her magic funneling. A haze of smoke billowed where the Ivarssons were, Theo standing beside her with guns wielded. The Ivarssons coughed and not-Tyee yelled, the smoke filling her lungs.

"It's just a screen – meant to disorient them. They'll recover soon. We don't have much time, Gwen," Theo said.

"I know," Gwen said through gritted teeth, pushing her magic together as much as she could, feeling it drain from every nerve of her body, Nikki's ring burning with added power. "I told you to wait in the car."

"I'm not leaving you."

Chunks of dirt and asphalt flew to her side, Daiyu and Terrance finally smashing through the layers of asphalt and digging Ina out from the ground, their nails broken and bleeding from clawing her out.

Bridget had flipped herself over so that she was on her back beneath Farrell instead of being face down, and blood stained his clothes where she clawed at him, screaming.

Feng, noticing movement, brought his fight with Brienne closer to the vehicles, letting her chase after him.

Bronwen had long faded into the darkness.

When Daiyu and Terrance pulled Ina from the ground and carried her to the car, her ribs crushed from the clutch of the earth, and Feng was at her side, Gwen released her magic with a scream, throwing out her hands, sending a gust of wind so strong it sent Farrell, Bridget, the Ivarssons, the cars, and not-Tyee careening through the air, landing in a crunch of metal and bones.

Darkness crept at the corner of her vision, exhausted, spent. Farrell's body flipping through the air made her sick, wanting to chase after him, but there was no time, they had to go, they had to leave.

She cleared the path, and consciousness would not be with her long, as every scrap of magic within her had been funneled into that wind.

Feng and Brienne, who were fighting behind her and therefore out of reach of the gust, paused at the sound of bodies and cars flipping over the road.

Feng grabbed Brienne's wrists, twisting them with a sickening crack of broken wrists. He brought her right forearm down against his leg, snapping the bone in half.

Brienne screamed, and Feng grabbed her other arm, wrenching it with his hands, and it split in two, splintered bones peeking through her ragged, bleeding flesh.

Gwen stumbled toward the car, her legs becoming heavier with every step, vision tunneling. Leaving Brienne screaming on the road with her mangled flesh and broken bones, Feng scooped Gwen into his arms and ran to the car, her vision bouncing with his footsteps.

Warmth surrounded her, a car door slammed, and she heard shouts, someone yelling to "Go, go, go," and tires squealing as the gas was floored, her body jerking with the sudden movement.

Arms kept her from falling, from slamming into the front seats.

Beloved hands cupped her face, the scent of shea butter filled her nose and Gwen wondered if she was on her way to heaven, and then there was only black.

Chapter Thirty-Five

Nikki tumbled through the earth when Gwen went unconscious, forced from her mind. She'd sensed Gwen's distress when they encountered not-Tyee and her sisters, and she'd followed Gwen's thread. She watched the confrontation in horrified silence, not wanting to distract Gwen. But when her best friend lost consciousness and she was sent back to her body, Nikki struggled against her bindings, wishing she could help. She was so isolated. *Useless.*

"Gwen will recover, child," Io said, voice soothing her mind in gentle brush strokes. Nikki gritted her teeth and exhaled, raging against her imprisonment, trying to stifle the need to scream.

"I wish I could help them. I wish I could be with them. Not stuck here doing nothing but spying. They're hurting, and I can't do anything."

Io's presence thrummed around her, considering, but did not respond.

When Nikki's adrenaline drained away, leaving her tired, she hung her head, thinking of the events of the night. The other woman, who Gwen thought of as Cora – just who was she? Nikki caught a flash of Gwen's memories, where Ina mentioned she had magic but wasn't from the Cradle.

"Io?" Nikki asked.

"Yes, child."

"That other woman, Cora. What is she? Ina said she isn't from the Cradle. But some other type of mage. What does that mean? I thought it was only vampires and the Cradle who had magic."

Io's glimmers flickered in the dark. *"We are not at that part of the story, yet."*

Nikki suppressed a groan. *"Can we get there?"*

Io pulsed around her, like an exhale. *"Where were we?"*

"You were telling me how you wanted to make people of your own. Sounds like we're not made in your image, then."

"Image?" Io asked, amused. *"I do not think I even have one."*

Nikki didn't know how to respond to that, instead trying to imagine how one had form but no image.

"No, humans evolved on their own. All I did was hasten the process. I made my own from the clay, dust, fire, and water of the earth, and gave them my spirit. What you call magic. Adam and Lilith. They were nameless, then, when first created. They chose their own names over time, as they learned of themselves, of each other, of the world.

"With them came the invention of love. It had, of course, existed in a way previously. There were bonds among friends, kin, tribes. But nothing that burned so bright as this. Over time, as much as they loved, they hated. Their fights blazed through the garden I created for them, destroying and creating in equal turn.

"Their lives were destined to be long. My gift made it so. They aged, and learned, and loved, and burned. Lilith yearned to learn of the wonders of magic and earth, whereas Adam wanted the marvels of power and flesh. In this, their disagreements, their bitterness grew.

"Lilith would not conform to Adam's ever-increasing controlling and dominating ways. Nor would Adam yield to Lilith's whimsies, her own subtler ways of maintaining him. The memory of that day, when Adam came to me and begged for a new wife, the flames of the garden still blazing behind them from their last fight, is clear like crystal to me still. I was blind to and in denial of their misery until that very moment.

"I admit, I succumbed to what was to be his manipulation of me. I did not realize it at the time. Lilith wanted the world, and Adam wanted to be King, so I granted them their wishes. I banished Lilith from the

garden, giving her the world. Adam remained to lord over his home, to cultivate the remains of the garden into a flourishing piece of the earth. As he requested, I gave him Eve. Made of the same clay and dust and fire and water, but with his bones, so that they would be peaceful with one another.

"And they were. But I did not account for the depth of betrayal Lilith would feel. I did not realize that while Adam only burned in distaste for her, she still burned with love for him.

Io paused, the air growing heavy, tasting of sorrow and regret. *"I failed her. My first daughter, I failed her miserably. Betrayed, doubly, by both her husband and her creator. None had experienced such love, or such betrayal, prior to Lilith. She was the first to consciously feel these. There was no one to explain to her that these emotions existed, that they could happen. I did not even know they could. To this day, I regret the decisions I made then. To have her be the first woman to know betrayal. I do not know how, exactly, but Lilith knew when I spun Eve into existence. She may have sensed the change of magic in the wind – she was always adept at noticing such things. She did not view the banishment as a gift, as I had thought. She did not want the world alone. She wanted the world with Adam.*

"The banishment, the betrayal, the rejection...knowledge of Eve is what broke Lilith, what began the corruption of the magic within her."

"Why did you not make Lilith a new husband, like you gave Adam a new wife?"

"She would not take one," Io said, and the space around Nikki contracted, as if she was a heart being squeezed in a broken chest. *"I saw the corruption take hold of her – twisting the magic within her black and vengeful. I came to her, in the cave she had carved for herself, and begged her to tell me what she wanted. She refused to answer. She would not even acknowledge me. I left that cave not just a failing god, but a lost parent.*

"Not long after the creation of the garden, I created the angels from space dust and myself, so that they could travel the world as an extension of my will. Thus, I sent Senoy, Sansenoy, and Samengalof to watch her. She ignored them as well. Lilith weaved a spell to hide my view of her, and I left her to heal her wounds. I knew injured animals ofttimes want solitude. So, I turned my gaze back to Adam and Eve, who had proliferated. Their chil-

dren were glorious and powerful, shining with magic and surrounded by the vibrant energy of the garden, which they had restored. Eve was kind and complacent, as Adam had hoped. Yet, she too, had a hunger for knowledge.

"But that is another story.

"Many years later, long past when Adam and Eve had transformed the garden into a vibrant city of glowing stone and abundant vegetation, drawing the attention and desire of other human civilizations, the angels told me Lilith wished to speak with me. Fool that I was, I was excited. There was something about Lilith, her inquisitiveness, her intuition, that resonated with me. She was an extension of me – my first daughter, and I never lost that love for her.

"Lilith had changed in the intervening years, the corruption black in her veins. Yet all I could see was my hurting child, and all I wanted was to make it right. So, when she asked permission to reenter the garden, I said yes. She had been quiet all these years, alone. I sensed nothing malicious within her, despite the corruption of her magic. I thought that perhaps being back in the purity of the garden, the corruption would purge itself from her being.

"I was wrong. Instead of the garden purging her corruption, she corrupted the garden. Lilith weaved a spell to alter the barrier that kept her out, and tainted the garden so that it recognized her more than it recognized Adam and his children, so that she would never be excluded from the garden again." Io paused, the floating flakes of metal dimming. "Lilith ensnared as many of the children as she could before the angels could stop her. Adam, Eve, and their adult children fled the garden, scattering across the land. Thus started Lilith's pursuit of his family, and the consequent hunting of her by the angels."

Io's flickers faded, barely visible against the dark. Voice distant, Io said, "I think I would like to stop there for today."

Nikki remained silent.

"Maybe now you understand how all of this is my fault. Understand why I no longer wish to interfere with the events of life on Earth. Yet, you must also understand that I am a being of spirit, magic, and intuition. Never had I dealt with beings who had cunning. I was a young and naïve god. I did not even know that such a concept of cunning could exist. For me, *there was only truth. Suddenly, there were lies. Deceit. Manipulation. What a terrible evolution."*

Nikki thought of the secrets she kept from Xander, his outrage and hurt. "*It really is.*"

"*I am sorry,*" Io whispered, then left the Tree, the pressure easing around Nikki.

Full darkness descended upon her as she contemplated the broken heart of a god.

Chapter Thirty-Six

NIKKI HOVERED IN THE DARKNESS, the echoes of Io's story in her head. How Lilith corrupted the magic within herself, becoming the first vampire.

That's all vampires were then, corrupted magic.

Cat shuffled outside the tree, faint footsteps like mice scattering. It sounded like she might be cleaning, but then another voice came, the male watcher, Marcus. Nikki strained to hear his words, but they were muffled beyond the bark.

Nikki reached for Gwen, but still could not find her thread. Heart sinking, she stared at the bottom of the Tree, willing it to reach up for her. But there was only bottomless black.

What had Lilith been like before she was corrupted? What about Adam? What happened once Lilith conquered the garden? Where was it now?

An ache filled Nikki's chest, a distant sympathy for who Lilith had been. The demi-goddess she could have been, the demon she became.

Lilith's muddy red thread glowed near her feet, and with a sharp exhale through her nose, the closest she could get to a sigh, Nikki plunged her consciousness down into its pull.

Lilith flew over a dark forest, the warmer southern temperatures a blessing on her aching wings. Despite how close she was to her destination, she would need to land soon. Would need to rest for the day before continuing the journey.

She flapped her wings, the wind a gentle beat around her body, caressing her feathers. The night was deep and humid, with thousands of stars overhead and a mountainous jungle beside her.

Turning and rising up along one of the mountain slopes, she spotted a discoloration in the landscape, a haze rising from the jungle. She soared toward the light, her little bird heart fluttering with excitement. Lilith perched on a stone ledge, a castle of old white stone, thin pillars and winding pathways rising from the jungle. It was an old maze of a castle; a beautiful place she would have once made her home. Below was a fire, with two people curled around it. Although it was warmer here than in the north, there was enough of a chill that these pathetic, ragged human creatures would feel a bite of cold.

Lilith dove toward the forest interior, transforming midair, peeling off her owl skin and feathers, cracking her bones larger and regrowing into her vampire form. The owl body collapsed with a wet thud behind her.

She stretched, arms and horns touching the surrounding foliage and stone. Encompassed by cold pillars, broadleaf trees, and shrubs with leaves larger than her face, she breathed in the dank, humid air, filling her lungs with the beautiful scent of life, decay, and freedom. Of flesh roasting over an open fire.

Lilith crept through the jungle castle, peering at the humans and their fire. They were well-equipped, with stuffed packs reeking of preserved food and plastic.

One man passed a flask to the other, a rosy sheen on his cheeks, a distance in his gaze.

Lilith grimaced. She hated the taste of alcohol in blood.

But it would have to do. It was better than no blood at all.

She took a step forward, and then abruptly jerked back, one of her wooden horns snagging on a low hanging branch. In the stumble, she crunched the moist foliage beneath her feet and growled in frustration. The two men startled, turning their gaze to the jungle.

While she didn't need the element of surprise, she always enjoyed that look of shock and horror on the faces of her prey. The moment they realized their life was over. That she was taking it.

With another snarl she yanked her head forward, pulling her horn through the snag, snapping the branch.

She stepped into the firelight, and the men's eyes widened, taking her in at a snail's pace, from her horns to her clawed hands and her feet, still in the shape of talons.

One man froze, his mouth dropping in terror, while the other shot to his feet, stumbling over the rock he sat on, and turned to run into the jungle.

Lilith grinned, the smell of their adrenaline mixing beautifully with the humidity.

She launched forward, catching up to the running man before he made it a step away from the fire, and snapped his neck, a satisfying crack echoing against the trees.

The other man screamed, finally shifting from frozen to fleeing, and he fell, crawling backward while she stalked toward him, his mouth agape with horror, crying out for all his false gods and saints to save him.

Lilith dropped to her knees and grabbed him by his shirt, pulling him toward her, ready to drink him fresh –

Except she didn't pull him forward.

Her arm was paralyzed, stuck in place. She willed it to move, but it would not.

The man grabbed a knife from his belt and swiped it against her arm. She recoiled with the sudden sting, the surprise, and released him.

He got to his knees and ran into the jungle, the maze of walls and pillars and stairwells, and Lilith tried to rise herself, but she was stuck, rooted to the ground like a tree.

Like a tree...

Lilith snarled and screamed. Her voice rebounded then was swallowed by the jungle. Growling, she fought against her invisible chains and closed her eyes to envision her thread – she never knew what color it was – and she dug her hands into the earth, soil moist and warm from the fire. When she caught the thread, a glorious red the color of earth and blood, she wrenched it free from her daughter's grasp.

She panted with the release, sensing the shock of her daughter, shaking in the back of her mind. She knew that surprise. The first time one controlled another was disorienting, your consciousness entwined with their nervous system before being thrust back into your own.

Lilith stood, her body aching from the flight and the invisible fight. She walked to the nearest tree, a beautiful broadleaf with smooth bark, and placed her hand on it.

"*I know you're there,*" Lilith said, her daughter's starbright blue thread in her mind's eye, stretching from the Tree of Life, through the Earth, to this tree, and into Lilith.

The thread quavered, but the child did not respond.

"*I am impressed that you stopped my whole body your first time. It took me years to control more than just a limb.*"

Hesitation, then a breath, no more than a whisper in her mind. "*I didn't want you to kill anyone else.*"

"*It makes sense that passion would increase the ability. Yet, this is an issue. You have been following me this whole time, haven't you?*"

She did not reply, but there was a sense of discomfort.

Lilith's mouth peeled back. "*I thought so. You may have found the gift of the Tree, but I cannot have you know my plans.*"

Lilith removed her palm from the bark. "*I have not tried this before. It may hurt.*"

Keeping her eyes closed, she spun magic from the jungle, from the air, plants, soil, rock, and creatures, and funneled it into herself. She wound it through the thread that bound her consciousness to her daughter's, and pulled, cutting it quick and clean like the landing blade of a guillotine.

The child gasped in her mind and sweat trickled down the side of Lilith's face.

The thread's remnants burned beneath her magic, her power, her hate, and then faded – a soundless sizzle that broke the connection between her and the child.

Lilith stumbled back with the sudden release of the magic as her thread ruptured.

Eyes opening, she touched the tree, and searched for any signs of a connection.

She sifted through the corners of her mind, prodding for the sense of being watched.

There were no threads.

There was no voice.

Lilith smiled, despite the dropping in her stomach, and her fingers stroked the tree as they pulled away.

How long had she depended on those threads to see, to hear, to feel? To learn, to grow, to communicate?

No matter.

It would be harder to talk with Vadasz and the others now, but there were other ways.

And there would always be Hormin.

With the watchful eyes of her enemy blinded from her, she leapt back into the jungle, salivating at the promise of still beating blood.

Chapter Thirty-Seven

"*Io?*" Nikki cried in the dark.

The parts of her body that she could feel shook, the intensity of Lilith's acknowledgement, her wrath, pouring fear deep into her bones.

"*Io!*" Nikki yelled again, with as much mental force as she could, imagining her voice booming through the ethers.

How did she summon a god?

How did Lilith banish her? Would she ever be able to know Lilith's path again? To see Xander, and know he was alive?

The air condensed around her with the weight of an approaching storm, and the tell-tale glimmers of Io's presence appeared before her eyes.

"*Why is it so hard for you to come back to me?*" Nikki spat, desperate.

"*Dear child,*" Io whispered, "*when I dissipated myself into the magic of the world, I became lesser. As I was used over time, I became less and less. It is difficult for me to become a sentient being once again after floating through time and space.*"

Nikki hesitated. "*Does talking about Lilith hurt you that much? That you had to dissipate yourself again?*"

"*I would not say 'again.' I can never return to what I was. I bound myself to the spirit of the world, those empty spaces where magic lives. Like water, I compress in a glass but spill outside of it. When I leave my compression here, then I return to the rest of me that pours around the world."*

Nikki took a deep breath, watched the flickers of Io shiver in the dark. *"Please. Don't leave me. You're...you're all I have, now. Even Gwen feels distant."*

Io was silent, and the glitter jumped with curiosity. *"Why do you quake?"*

"Lilith saw me. I don't know how she did it, or even exactly what she did, but she tore apart the binding thread. It forced me back here."

"That is...curious."

"That's it? Did you know she could do that? Will the thread return?"

"No, I did not know it could be severed. I do not know if it can be, permanently. Let me see."

Part of Io left, lifting the pressure from around Nikki, and she was grateful that some of the gold and silver shining through the dark remained while They searched for answers.

Sometime later, Nikki sensed Io return to the Tree, and Io said, *"The thread remains, but it is cut. I do not know if the ends will rejoin, or how long it will take."*

"Can you help? Like you did with Gwen?"

Io paused. *"I do not know if that is the correct path."*

"Why not?"

"It is an interference. Which I swore to never again commit."

Nikki clenched her jaw, letting her fangs jab her lip to satisfy her anger. *"Inaction is still action. You are making the choice to let Lilith kill all these other people you claim to love equally. Hardly seems fair to me, how you favor her."*

"Perhaps she deserves vengeance. Perhaps she is right."

"Perhaps she was – countless millennia ago. Why do people have to suffer the consequences of events they had no part in? Why does Xander?"

Io hummed with consideration, a buzzing in the air.

"This isn't the right path, Io. I understand you feel guilty for what happened and want to make things right with her. But letting her massacre innocent people isn't the way to do it."

"You would have her murdered instead. I would not."

"Even if it saves innocents?"

Air swirled around Nikki like a sigh. *"The greater good argument has been used too many times, by too many evils. No one can predict the ramifications of their actions. Therefore, no one can truly know what the greater evil is in the long term."*

Nikki squeezed her eyes shut, heart beating against her caving ribs, fighting against the defeat in Io's words. *"No, we can't see the future. But we can see the short term and try to make the best choices we can. To make the short term as good as possible. And hope that translates into a greater good in the future. So many people will die, Io, and can you really be okay with letting that happen? As you said, this is partially your fault. Not just what happened to Lilith, but what is happening to everyone else right now. Adam's lineage, the Cradle, the descendants of other humans you loved so much that you decided to mingle with them. Can you really say that you're okay with them being butchered? And once you ask yourself that, can you really think that once Lilith has sated her bloodthirst against the Cradle and Xander that it would stop there? That she would ever peacefully sit back and return to a quiet life? If you do, you're a fool. She wants to rule the world. Once she decimates the Cradle and no one opposes her, this balance you created for vampires will be no longer, and humans will be no more than cattle."*

Contemplative silence surrounded Nikki, Io twinkling before her, the rain of metal slowly forming and dissipating.

The quiet enflamed Nikki's core, the rage clenching in her lungs. *"Hello?"*

"I heard, child. I will consider your words."

"You said that before. I don't know if you actually did. If it meant anything."

"It did. It does. I will contemplate all you have said, all I have seen. I will not act in haste."

"The people out there don't have a lot of time. I hope you can think fast. For their sake."

"I will take the time needed."

Nikki exhaled, releasing the tension in her body as she heaved out her defeat.

There was nothing more to say to Io, now. Though she had more questions, she did not want to engage further. Not yet. Let Io contemplate the situation, and maybe next time they spoke, Nikki could get more information out of the god.

Unlike those outside, she had all the time in the world.

Chapter Thirty-Eight

GWEN BLINKED, hazy light filtering through the cracks of her eyes. She groaned as sensation returned to her body, dull lurches rumbling through her as the car rolled down the road.

She was on her back, legs scrunched against the side door of the back seat. Her head was elevated. The comforting scent of sugary shea filled her nose.

As her vision focused, she saw a dense gray smog hanging outside the window, smothering the sunlight more than the overcast clouds of the Pacific Northwest. Ina drove, and Cora sat in the passenger seat, soft classical music playing.

Gwen groaned, pushing herself up with her elbows.

Hands untangled from her hair, and Theo said, "Careful."

Gwen's head swam, but she pushed up until she was sitting, the swirl of her mind making her queasy.

"Where are we?" Gwen croaked, looking at the modest neighborhoods framed by imposing mountains as far as the eye could see in both directions.

"Salt Lake City," Ina said, glancing at her in the rearview.

Gwen groaned and settled back in her seat, muscles tired and weak. "How long was I out?"

"About twelve hours," Theo replied, brushing her hair out of her face. "How are you feeling?"

"Like a sack of mashed potatoes."

Theo's face softened with concern, and she laced her fingers through Gwen's.

"I take it Feng is in the trunk?"

Theo nodded. "It's early afternoon right now. If I wasn't used to gloomy days, I might not believe it, given how dark it is."

"No kidding," Gwen said, turning around to peer at the heavily tinted back windshield. "Is it legal for it to be that dark?"

"Probably not. Here, you sound like a frog," Theo said, handing her water.

At the sight of water sloshing in the clear plastic, the dryness in Gwen's mouth worsened, and she snatched the bottle from Theo's hands. "My hero," she said, unscrewing the cap, then chugging the bottle until it was empty.

The water sat heavy in her stomach, and Gwen grimaced as it gurgled, until she burped loud and strong.

"Much better," she said, then flopped back into her seat.

Ina's hands clenched on the steering wheel, squeaking on the leather, but Gwen caught grins on both Theo's and Cora's faces.

"I also assume our companions behind us are fine?"

"Yes," Cora said. "We've figured out a system – they flash their lights when they need to stop."

"Good," Gwen said, closing her eyes, ready to fall back asleep.

Theo squeezed Gwen's hand and she squeezed back, but Theo continued to clench it, so Gwen peeled her eyes open and lolled her head to the side to look at her glorious girlfriend.

"You're a badass, you know," Gwen said, recalling the smoke bomb Theo set off, how mighty and sexy she looked dual wielding those pistols.

Theo's mouth twitched in a brief smile. "Thanks. You are too. But... I was worried about you. A lot. Please, don't exert yourself that much again."

"Yes, perhaps now you understand why I pressed the importance of choosing a weapon. Of finding a teacher," Ina said.

The melting she had felt in her heart at Theo's care hardened to stone when Ina spoke.

"Oh, excuse me for saving all of our lives."

"It was a joint effort."

"Pfft. By some, sure, but not you. You were stuck in the ground. But Cora – nice move barreling into Tyee. Formerly Tyee. Are you hurt from the crash? I have some healing ability if you need it."

Cora gave her an appreciative, close-lipped smile, and as her head turned, Gwen noticed the cuts and bruises and bandages on her body. "No, thank you. I'm fine. Only minor injuries here."

"You need to rest anyway, Gwen. Restore yourself before using magic again," Theo said.

"You're probably right. But I do have some salve if you need it. I let Nikki use it for her gums when her fangs were coming in, and it seemed to help her a lot."

Cora considered. "Perhaps at our next stop I'll take you up on that."

Gwen dozed, the rumble of the car a lullaby for her bones. In the haze of half sleep, she thought of Farrell, lunging at their family for her, wondering where he was now, how he was doing, if he was still alive.

She woke again when they stopped at a rest area, the humans stepping into the daylight to stretch their bodies. Gwen had a grumbled reunion with Terrance and Rachel, who both had bags under their eyes. It seemed they had a harder time sleeping in cars than she did.

When night settled and the vampires stirred from their blackout bags, they played musical cars, Cora joining Daiyu with Terrance and Rachel. Ina drove for a while longer as Feng woke up, her nose crinkling with disgust while he drank his cold blood.

In this way, changing drivers and taking short, periodic breaks, they traveled over mountains, down valleys, through vacant crop fields, over rivers, and between city streets, the sun and moon chasing each other across the sky.

Nikki peeked into Gwen's head during their second day of travel. Although it hadn't yet been two days since they left the Pacific Northwest, it felt like ages had passed. They were somewhere in eastern Texas, and Ina said they would arrive by the end of the day. Nikki whispered her concern for Gwen's health and wellbeing, then told her how Lilith found her, how they were running out of time now that Lilith knew she had been watched, that she had broken the thread. Nikki said Io thought the thread could be restored, but it wasn't yet, so Nikki didn't know where Lilith was anymore.

Which was just so great. Super-duper.

Late evening, when the sun had barely set, Gwen bouncing in her seat with restlessness and Theo demolishing her nails in her mouth, they drove by endless barren agricultural fields. The density of houses and croplands increased, growing closer together. The vampires were in their bags in the trunks, but Feng still joined in conversation, equally restless and unable to sleep.

Gwen did her best to not ask if they were there yet, just to be able to fight with Ina and have some energy released.

Finally, Ina indicated for Cora to pull down a private road, ambling down an open field studded with two houses.

The car rolled to a stop close to the front house, and Ina said, "We're here."

They parked and got out of the car, the group from Terrance's vehicle joining them.

"This is it?" Gwen asked, staring at the modest wood house in front of them, the lawn covered in desiccated shrubs and stiff, frosty grass.

"No. But it's where our guide lives."

"Our guide? To where?" Rachel piped up, stepping in behind them.

"To the epicenter of the Native American Cradle in the United States."

"Oooohhh, cool," Rachel said, and the group took a step forward as one.

Chapter Thirty-Nine

Fanned around Ina on the porch with all of their belongings, the group shivered against the winter air, somehow different from the winters in the Pacific Northwest. More like a cold hand, rather than sharp needles of frost that bit through their clothes.

Ina rang the doorbell, a soft ding-dong reverberating through the house. From somewhere inside, a dog barked and padded to the door. The white floorboards of the porch, paint chipping away, creaked beneath their feet as they shifted, lights flipping on one by one from within, footfalls sure and steady approaching the door.

It swung open a moment later, a burst of warmth brushing against Gwen's face.

"Ina!" The broad man behind the door shouted, nudging an excited golden retriever away from the door. He stepped back and extended his arm into the interior. "Come on in before all the heat leaves."

"Thanks, John," Ina said, stepping over the threshold.

Gwen shook as warmth spread over her, her body expelling the cold. The inside of the house had several old but well-cared-for pieces of furniture, a mix-match of color and texture that was both fun and comforting. The dog ran in circles, sniffing and licking the hands of the humans while giving the vampires no more than a passing glance.

"This is Sunny," John said, patting the dog's head. "You didn't tell me you'd be arriving so late. I could've stayed up and been presentable," John said, indicating the sweatpants he wore. He was taller than most of them except Terrance, but he was muscular and broad, creating a presence that was much bigger than he was. His glossy, thick black hair hung loose over his shoulders, framing the sharp features nestled into his oval face, golden-brown skin gleaming in the low light.

He squinted as the Lius walked past him. "You also didn't tell me you'd be bringing vampires into my home."

Ina hesitated, folding her hands in front of her and lifting her chin. "They're peaceful, John. And our interests are aligned. To be frank, I am not sure what would have become of us these last few weeks without them."

Feng's thick eyebrows twitched with surprise, and Gwen had to give Ina props for vocalizing appreciation for people who just a few weeks ago she had considered her mortal enemies.

Feng flashed a wide smile at John, showing all his silvery, sharp teeth, and extended a hand. "A pleasure."

John deepened his squint but after a second of thought grabbed Feng's hand and shook it. "As long as you keep your fangs to yourself, bloodsucker, we will have no issues."

"Consider them kept," Feng replied.

John grunted but moved past them, waving his hands to usher them deeper into the living room, motioning for them to sit.

"Where's your brother?" Ina asked, settling on an armchair.

"I'm not sure, but I'd guess hunting." He flicked an anxious gaze toward Feng and Daiyu, whose jaws clenched. John ran a hand through his hair and said, "Anyway, you must be hungry and thirsty. I'll be right back."

John disappeared to the shadows of the house, and Gwen sat behind Theo on one of the couches, a long, low-backed floral blue sofa straight out of the 1980s. She tucked herself against Theo, who stretched her arms over her shoulders. Terrance and Rachel sat on the other side, curling up together. Rachel's excitement had dimmed, and she could barely keep her eyes open as she nestled against Terrance's chest.

God – or Io, Gwen supposed – she wished for sleep.

No one should have to travel that far over so short a time by car.

Was it really only a couple days ago they fought with not-Tyee and the others?

The clank of a pitcher and glasses, and the rustle of plastic on the coffee table, pulled Gwen from her near slumber, eyes jolting open, though her lids remained heavy.

Rachel snored delicately, but everyone else remained awake, even if barely.

John assessed the room, the awake humans silently drinking water. He ran a hand through his hair, the beautiful strands falling in sleek layers that a model would envy, and said, "I want to know what this is all about, but I think we should wait to talk until you've all had a chance to rest. There's plenty of space in the guesthouse. Ina – you remember where it is?"

"I do," Ina said, standing. "Thank you, John. I hope you forgive us for the imposition."

John waved a hand, dismissing her. "No imposition at all. This is why we exist, right? To help each other out?"

Ina gave a close-lipped grin. "That is part of it." She turned her gaze to the group and said, "Come on, let's get some rest."

"Do you have somewhere appropriate for us to sleep? Somewhere without sunlight?" Daiyu asked.

"The only place without sunlight is in my basement. It's not cozy, but we can move a mattress down there. I haven't had to host vampires before."

"That's fine," Daiyu said. "Thank you."

"Perhaps we can go on a walk first?" Feng asked. "While it is bedtime for you, it is the middle of the day for us."

John hesitated, running his hands through his hair, then folding his arms. "I don't have a delicate way to say this..."

"You don't want to go to sleep with us still awake," Feng guessed.

"I'm sorry," John said, and he looked both sincere and uncomfortable, "there is a lock on the basement, as we have had to keep protected relics in transit there sometimes..."

"Not ideal, but we understand," Daiyu said, before Feng could retort. "Do you have a television?"

The relief washed off John's face, and he said, "Yes, now that is something I can help with. Let's get you setup."

The group broke apart, the Lius going with John to move a mattress and television into the basement. The rest of them followed Ina through the kitchen to the backyard, the shadows of hibernating plants, flower beds, and raised vegetable gardens standing in the dark. Ina lit a small sun in her hand and led them to the guesthouse adjacent to the main house, the inside of which was a basic lodging space that reminded Gwen of how movies depicted orphanages. It was a series of individual beds throughout a long hall, two bathrooms set at the back.

Gwen plunked down on a bed, the metal creaking under the thin mattress. Theo picked the bed beside her, and when they looked at each other, silently communicating how they didn't want to sleep apart, Gwen crept to Theo's bed and forced herself onto it, curling into her body.

"I wish we could do that," Rachel said from opposite bunks, Terrance barely being able to fit on the bed himself, let alone leaving space for Rachel to join him.

Gwen grinned and nestled further into Theo, whose arms wrapped around her, and chin settled on top of her head. Theo's braids and Gwen's mane mingled on the pillow case. She didn't care if they regretted this setup in the morning. There was no other way she ever wanted to sleep again.

Gwen drifted off with the feel and smell of Theo around her and a smile on her face.

Chapter Forty

Dull slants of light filtered through the windows when Gwen awoke, her shoulder stiff and neck cricked from pressing into the firm bed for too long. She smacked her mouth, dry yet cottony. She must have been snoring.

Theo's arm was still flung over her, chest pressed to Gwen's face. Gwen kissed up her body, her collarbone, her neck, her chin, and Theo rose from unconsciousness, hands moving up Gwen's back, pressing her closer.

"I have morning breath," Theo said, voice a low growl with waking. Checking the time she said, "More like afternoon breath."

"Perfect, I do too," Gwen said, tilting her face up and meeting Theo's mouth, parting her lips and joining the sweet staleness of morning on their tongues.

A voice cleared behind them.

"This isn't a private room," Terrance said from the walkway between beds, already dressed.

Theo and Gwen detached their lips but kept their bodies close, Theo glaring at her brother.

Rachel, standing behind Terrance put a gentle hand on his back and said, "It will be once we leave."

Gwen sat up and looked around the room. Everyone else was gone already.

Rachel nudged Terrance forward and winked at Gwen, and Gwen smiled her mischievous grin.

"Ugh," Terrance said, but did not resist Rachel's push, and they left the building with a high squeak of the door.

"Maybe we should go, too," Theo said, stretching and rubbing one eye.

"I think not," Gwen said, flipping over on top of Theo, her mane cascading around them, closing them off from the world. "We can talk about all that crazy, saving-the-world stuff later. Besides, the Lius probably aren't even awake yet, and what can we really do without them?"

"Mmm," Theo said, hands running up Gwen's sides, sending an anticipatory hum though her body. "You make a good point."

"It's something I can do, every now and then," Gwen said, grinning. She lowered her face, nuzzled their noses together. "Thank you for taking care of me when I was passed out. There's nothing better than waking up to your hands on me."

"Is that so?" Theo breathed, one hand wrapping in Gwen's hair, the other playing with the waistband of her pants.

"It is," Gwen said, lowering her face to open Theo's mouth with her lips, slow and wanting. Pulling back, she said, "It's only fair I show you how nice it is to wake up to my hands."

Gwen sidled herself down Theo's body, kissing her way lower, hands exploring every glorious inch.

Basking in the chance to finally have some privacy, and not knowing when they would have another opportunity, they took their time. Relieved of tension and her heart full of love, Gwen fell asleep in Theo's arms once more. When she awoke a couple of hours later, they took a joint shower and left the guesthouse to join the others in the main one. The sun was low in the west, and despite the short walk, the cold turned Gwen's wet hair into ice. Theo put an arm around her, the frost-crusted grass crunching beneath their feet.

They knocked at the back door of the main house and then let themselves in, finding everyone except Feng and Daiyu settled in the living room, a roaring fire with real wood crackling.

Gwen plopped herself in front of the fire, raising her hands to let the heat burn her palms. She swung her loose, wet waves in front of her, hoping the fire would loosen the ice and help it dry faster.

Man, she missed real fire.

"I understand the urgency, Ina, but I made an oath to not open the portal without consulting with the Council first."

"Portal?" Rachel and Gwen asked at the same time Theo and Terrance said, "Council?"

Ina ignored them.

"Did you not also make an oath to protect humankind from vampires? The longer we wait, the more she will kill. This is our fastest way to intervene. We know she was heading for San Lorenzo. She could already be there, killing our cousins and the civilians who live nearby. I think the Council would understand."

"I could lose my seat."

"You can throw me under the bus if you want. Say I forced you. Isn't it better to save lives? What's that phrase? It's better to beg forgiveness than ask permission?"

John sighed, then ran a hand through his hair and leaned back.

"What if we get this mysterious council on a zoom call?" Gwen asked.

John huffed a laugh and shook his head. "A few of them are... traditional. They barely agreed to own a landline. And for something this important, they'd want to come here in person."

"Well, how far away are they?"

"The farthest is in New Orleans."

Gwen looked at him, blank-faced.

"It's about four hours by car."

"That's not so bad."

John shook his head again, slips of hair falling over his shoulders. "You don't understand. They would walk here. They wouldn't arrive for over a week."

"But why would they do that?"

"We rarely meet to discuss time-sensitive matters. For less important ones, we do talk on the phone. However, for use of the portal, we'd need to discuss it in person. The walk gives us all time to think about the issue, to gather our thoughts and come together with clear opinions we know how to articulate."

"They can't make an exception just this once?"

"They do not make exceptions."

"This is why," Ina interjected, shooting daggers at Gwen, "I am trying to convince John to act now. An attempt that you are interrupting."

Gwen's face heated, not just from the flames. "You know, we were in the car for almost forty hours straight. You could have given us this context at any time. About the Council, about whatever the hell portal you're talking about. Maybe I wouldn't be interrupting if you had thought to tell us this before we got here."

Ina's jaw clenched before she jutted it out and said, "Maybe if you hadn't exhausted your powers, like I warned would happen, and you had been cognizant enough to ask more questions, to actually demonstrate a capacity for learning, I would –"

"Enough," Cora said, throwing up her hand. "That's enough."

Gwen and Ina glared at each other for several seconds before Gwen turned back to the fire.

"John," Ina said. "You can feel it, can't you? Deep in your bones, your gut? The world as we know it is on the brink of collapse. Lilith may have already slaughtered the people of San Lorenzo, may already be moving on to our other cousins, murdering innocents along the way. We know she has already done so, from the U.S. down into Mexico, she has massacred."

"How do you know her path?"

"Her friend," Ina nodded in Gwen's direction, "has replaced Lilith in the Tree and has thus been granted its ability to move into the consciousness of her kin."

"You forget," Gwen said, "She's not just my friend. She's also your son's girlfriend."

"How could I forget such a thing when it's her fault my son has been found and taken?"

Gwen clenched her fist, burning from the fire. She launched to her feet and stared down at Ina, the air in the space around her heeding her call, pulling towards her, "How dare –"

"No," Cora said, rising to her feet. "This is inefficient, and frankly, stupid. Gwen, come with me."

Gwen dropped her fists and the air, a low gust pulsing through the room. Cora walked to the door, but Gwen remained frozen. Breaking the stare-down with Ina, she looked to her friends, Terrance and Rachel avoiding her gaze. Theo met her eyes, and shrugged, at a loss for how to help. John's eyes were wide, eyebrows raised in surprise.

"You're a witch," he said.

"Gwen, come on," Cora beckoned from the back door.

With a huff of an exhale, she left the group in the living room, with their warm fire and secrets, to join Cora out in the cold.

Burrowing into her jacket, stomping her feet on the crunchy grass, Gwen snapped, "What?"

Cora gave a close-lipped smile, somewhere between amusement and fatigue, and said, "Let's go on a walk."

Gwen fell into step beside Cora, the brightness of Cora's blonde hair amplified in the fading winter daylight, the sun barely hanging on to the horizon, the sky to the east already fading to deep blue. Their breaths puffed in their faces as they walked through the property, full of dead and hibernating plants, past a chopping block, shed, miscellaneous tools, and a push-mower.

"You and Ina are so much alike," Cora said, "Someone needs to run interference."

Gwen sputtered. "I am not like her."

Cora smiled and chuckled. "That is something she would say."

Gwen grunted and tensed her shoulders, the neck of her jacket moving up to enshroud the lower half of her face.

"Gwen, I've known her for a long time. She has always thought in black and white. But she is changing now, bit by bit. Never would I have thought she would ally with vampires, let alone *like* them. For someone as stubborn as she is, with who her family is, bending to a new worldview is both difficult and terrifying. She has had to be black and white to protect her family. But she is learning to think in grays, and that new thinking will apply to you too, someday. Just be patient with her."

Gwen paused, absorbing Cora's words. "She makes it so hard sometimes. She's just so...prickly with me. One could even say downright mean."

"I know," Cora said, stopping and looking up at the fading sun before turning to Gwen, her cheeks rosy with cold. "I don't think it is personal, though. When she looks at you, she sees all that has happened in the past few months, a lifetime of fears that has led to her son being taken from her."

"But Terrance and Theo were his actual friends, so why doesn't she get mad at them? Wouldn't they be more of a reminder?"

"When she sees them, I think she recalls the happy memories. She can think of when they and Xander played, not the methods by which he was taken. It is different with the Lius, as they had no hand in Xander going missing. But you are the closest link to Nikki, and with Nikki and Xander's fates entwined, that is all she can see." Cora's bright blue eyes pierced Gwen, and Cora extended her palm. Gwen placed her hand in Cora's, and the other woman wrapped both of hers around them, soft and warm with life. "I ask you to please be patient with her. She is hurting more than she shows."

"She doesn't have a monopoly on pain," Gwen said. It felt as if the air was knocked out of her every time she thought of Nikki trapped and alone. Of how she had to fight her own family. Of how she was uncertain if Farrell was alive or not.

"I know," Cora replied with a sad smile. "But she is blinded, and you are not."

Gwen shuffled her feet and looked to their clasped hands. She knew Cora was playing on her ego, and yet she didn't care. She straightened her back then laughed, surprised at the wave of relief that washed through her. "Do you know who I am? Asking me to back down from a fight is like...asking a bird not to fly. I can try, but I make no promises."

Cora smiled, eyes crinkling. "Consider it a learning experience then. Perhaps it is time to try being a penguin rather than an owl."

Gwen laughed again and said, "Sure, I can try."

They continued their walk, and after several minutes, Gwen asked, "Do you have other abilities besides clairvoyance? I mean, I'm kind of surprised I didn't fight you about this. I actually feel kind of calm, instead of angry?"

"I seem to have that effect on people," Cora said. "But no, I think that is more about my temperament than any magical ability."

"Hm," Gwen said, burrowing her face back into the jacket, the temperature plummeting as the sun set.

Cora stopped again during their walk back to the house. "Gwen. There is another matter."

Dread sank into Gwen's stomach. "Yes?"

Cora hesitated, tucking a strand of hair behind her ear, her eyes boring into Gwen's soul before growing distant. "The portal will be opened. What is on the other side... I cannot see, but I know it is covered in blood. Do you truly believe you and your friends are ready for battle?"

Gwen's stomach curdled, fear creeping into her nerves. She shook her head. "I know that I am. In some ways, I've been fighting my whole life. But the others...no, I don't think so. They've been practicing with their weapons for several weeks, but they've never used them in a real fight, except for when we were fleeing not-Tyee and the others. But against Lilith and whoever else is with her? Probably not."

"You must make a choice, then. You are the fork in the road. The one who decides who remains and who leaves. But..." Cora's gaze refocused on Gwen, "...you must be careful not to speak your answer."

"You know," Gwen mused, "I always thought the movies exaggerated when they portray seers as vague. Starting to think they're on to something."

Cora chuckled. "I sense more than see, but I understand your point. If you think about it, however, it makes sense. Once you tell people your plans, you give them reign to change it through their own will."

Gwen hummed. "Guess I have some thinking to do."

They reached the backdoor of the main house just as the sun dropped below the horizon, their approach activating the backdoor light.

Arm outstretched, hand wrapped around the door handle, Cora said, "You do. However, there is little time to decide."

"What do you mean?"

"You'll see," Cora said, swinging open the door and ushering Gwen back into the warmth of the house.

The fire still roared in the living room, the skin on Gwen's face relaxing as the cold left it. The Lius were awake, standing beside the fireplace.

Cora returned to her vacant seat and Gwen stepped behind Theo, placing a hand on her shoulder, and then playing with her hair, braiding her braids. Theo tilted her head back and smiled at her, taking one of her hands and kissing the back of it before returning her attention to Ina and John, who seemed to have come to an agreement. Gwen's stomach clenched at Theo's smile, her heart leaping with adoration as guilt settled in her, thinking about what she had to do to ensure Theo was safe. To ensure that smile remained in the world.

"You've barely had any rest," John said, looking at Ina, then at the rest of the group. "I can see the fatigue on your faces, not to mention the vibrant bruises on your skin. If I were to open the portal, it won't be until tomorrow, at the earliest."

Ina's mouth popped open to argue but John cut her off. "No, don't argue with me. In good conscience, I couldn't let you all throw yourself into danger without at least one more night of rest and healing. You need to recover your strength."

"Lilith could kill so many more people tonight before we get there. How would that sit on your conscience?" Ina asked.

"There is no way for me to come out of this with a clear mind, feeling like I made the right decision. But if I let you go now, still weak and tired, and she slaughters you all as well, then what? It would mean I led you all to a massacre, and she would keep killing. No, I won't let that happen. Right now, you all are the front lines to Lilith. We need your expertise. And the hope you will instill. If you fail, I fear what would happen to the morale of the Cradle while we are still trying to amass our members."

Ina's jaw clenched and unclenched. Through gritted teeth, she said, "Fine. But you will take us at first light."

John threw up his hands and leaned back. "Yes, yes, fine. First light it is." He glanced at the Lius, cleared his throat, then said, "But I can't take them. I'm sorry, but I can't let vampires through the portal."

"You can't or you won't?" Feng asked.

John swallowed. "I won't. Sorry. It's against the rules. All of this is, really."

Daiyu laid a hand on Feng's arm, stopping his retaliation. "It's fine. We will remain. As long as we can stay here and protect the new home base."

"Oh," John said, fidgeting. "Yes, sure. You can stay here, but the same rules remain about being locked downstairs while I sleep."

Feng snarled, lips peeling back and showing his teeth, glinting dark orange in the firelight.

Daiyu squeezed his arm again and said, "That's fine." Turning to her husband, she said, "It's only temporary, love."

Feng sighed, a deep growl in his throat, then crossed his arms and leaned against the wall beside the fireplace.

Silence descended over the room, broken up by the crackling and spitting of wood as it burned.

"So.., um," Rachel murmured, "I'm actually pretty hungry?"

Terrance, Theo, and Gwen exclaimed their agreement, Gwen's stomach suddenly twisting with the hunger pains she had been too distracted to notice.

John leapt to his feet, "Of course! I'm so sorry. I wasn't thinking. I wasn't expecting so many people. I have a few pizzas in the freezer? Anybody gluten free?"

The group shook their heads, and Gwen said, "No, but I'm vegetarian."

"I think there's a veggie pizza in there, let me go check." John sidled out of the room to the kitchen.

Ina looked at each of them in turn. "Any of you are welcome to stay with the Lius. Continue training, protect this house, and recover until we move on. I do not want anyone who feels unprepared to join us."

"I'll stay," Cora said. "I'm not much use in a fight."

Ina nodded, then looked at Terrance, Rachel, Theo, and Gwen.

They all remained silent.

Gwen's stomach roiled, and as butterflies lifted in her body, they moved bile into her esophagus. Yes, Theo had been using guns for a long time, but it had been a while since she shot, and she had only done so at non-moving targets. She had small smoke screens and bombs, but those could be used against her, against all of them, if she wasn't careful.

Terrance was strong, fast, and imposing, and a hammer could do some serious damage, but how much could it really hurt an ancient vampire with skin as tough as stone? One missed swing and it could turn against him, crushing his own head...

And Rachel was small, quick, and had impressive aim, but her muscles were still developing, and she was so easily distracted...

No, Gwen, didn't think any of them should go with them. Yet none were volunteering to stay behind.

Her heart plummeted into her stomach, hands stilling in Theo's hair.

"You okay, baby?" Theo asked, taking one of Gwen's unmoving hands and twisting to look at her.

"Oh, yeah, just thinking about...everything."

Gwen caught Cora's eyes, and Cora gave her a small, knowing nod.

Ina squinted at Cora and Gwen but held her tongue.

Gwen moved around the couch and sat beside Theo, clasping her hand tight, hoping the grip would steel the nerves in her fluttering body, hating what she would have to do.

Hating to break her promise.

The group descended into nonsense chatter, and John returned after having put the pizzas in the oven. All the conversation dropped into the background, Gwen mentally running through all the potions and ingredients she had with her, formulating a plan that could cost her the most important relationship she'd ever had.

She understood a little better now why Nikki had done what she had done with Xander. Keeping him in the dark to keep him safe.

It sucked.

The humans ate in silence, all devouring their food except for Gwen, the pizza like ash in her mouth. Guilt squashed her appetite, but she forced herself to eat anyway, knowing she would need her strength and unsure of when she would be able to eat again.

Ina ushered the humans to the guesthouse for bed, insisting they get as much rest as possible, as no one knew what they would face on the other side of the portal to San Lorenzo. Only Cora stayed behind, talking with the Lius, promising a tired John that she would keep an eye on them and lock them up when she was headed to bed.

In the guesthouse, Gwen sat on the bed parallel to Theo. When Theo cocked an eyebrow at her, Gwen said, "You know I love you, I just slept really stiff last night and my neck hurts. Thought maybe we'd sleep better if we had more room to stretch."

"Okay..." Theo said, brow furrowed with confusion. She took her hygiene bag and headwrap to the bathroom, and while she was gone, Gwen rummaged through her bag, finding a vial of her blood and crushed plants just as Theo's footsteps returned behind her. The vial was cool and congealed, so Gwen held it tight in her hand, tucked beneath her head and the pillow.

"You're not going to brush your teeth? Or get into pjs?" Theo asked.

"I'm too tired," Gwen said, stomach souring with the deceit.

"You're gonna feel gross tomorrow if you don't."

"That's a problem for tomorrow," Gwen said, trying on a fake smile.

Theo's lips pursed, and she gave Gwen a hard stare, but after a minute she rolled under the covers and onto her side, facing away from Gwen.

Gwen wanted to vomit.

Or cry.

One by one, the lamps on the nightstands clicked off as everyone settled into bed.

Gwen rolled onto her back, vial clutched in her hands, trying to warm it. She stared at the ceiling, her heart thundering in her ears, pushing against her rib cage so hard she thought it might burst from her chest.

Gwen waited until the breaths of everyone evened out, deepening in slumber.

She waited until the faint slants of moonlight filtered through the window at such an angle, she guessed it was close to midnight. Hopefully, everyone would be deep asleep by now.

Gwen sat up in her bed, the frame letting out a quiet creak beneath her shifting weight. She raised the vial, and in the moonlight, she saw that it was more liquid than solid now and moved with the regular viscosity of blood.

Her heart still a drumbeat in her head, she shifted out of bed, vial clutched to her chest. The sickle sword rested on her nightstand, which she picked up with sweaty palms. Gwen crept on tiptoes to Ina's bed, Ina's eyes shifting behind her eyelids and hair fanning around her.

Gwen placed a hand on Ina's shoulder, and Ina's eyes flew open as she startled awake.

Gwen put a finger to her lips, and thankfully, Ina did not speak.

Gwen tilted her head, indicating for Ina to follow. Ina squinted at her, uncertain and questioning. Still, she slipped out of bed, the groan of the floor beneath her feet pushing Gwen's heart to her throat, the noise so loud in the silence of the night.

Ina looked at the sleeping bodies and then at Gwen, understanding dawning on her face. She set her jaw, then gave a terse nod, pulling the sword out from under her bed. Gwen and Ina slipped through the guesthouse as quietly as they could, although a few floorboards compressed with dull creaks beneath their feet.

Outside, Gwen heaved an exhale. She'd held her breath that whole time, as if that's what might wake the others.

The bitter cold snarled at Gwen's skin, as if reprimanding her for this betrayal.

"Are you sure about this?" Ina whispered as they walked to the main house.

Gwen nodded. "They're not ready. I think they know it, deep down, but don't want to admit it."

"They will not be pleased with this, Gwen."

Gwen hesitated, imagining Theo's expression when she woke to find her gone. "I know," she said, then opened the back door to the main house, voices coming from the living room and dim light crawling across the floor.

"Someone want to explain what's going on?" John asked, voice deep with recent sleep.

Cora, Feng, and Daiyu stood with him in the living room, Feng wearing a belt of grenades and bombs, a rifle slung across his back.

Gwen's fingers shook as she unclenched her fists and stepped forward, her throat thick. "We need to leave. Now. Before the others wake up."

"Why?"

"They're not ready," Ina said. "We need them to stay here, and keep training, but they will not freely admit it."

John sighed, rubbing his face in his hands. "You think it's a good idea for just you two to go?"

"Feng will go, too," Cora said.

"I've already told you I won't let a vampire through."

"You must, if you want Ina and Gwen to have a chance at survival."

John groaned again. "I'm too tired to argue this, and I doubt I'd win anyway. But if the Council threatens me, I'm going to say you forced me against my will. I won't lose my job or my seat for you."

"I've already told you that's fine," Ina said. "Let's go. Now."

Feng and Daiyu had a quick, chaste goodbye, Gwen and Ina saying farewell and thank you to Cora, who had clearly seen the decision on Gwen's face and knew to find them more help.

Weapons strapped across their backs or in hand, Ina, Feng, and Gwen followed John back out into the night, walking down the dark porch and through the front lawn to John's car.

Every rustle of wind and crunch of their footsteps roared in Gwen's head, maybe they'd get away without anyone finding out, maybe they'd just wake up with them gone and it wouldn't be such a big –

"Hey!"

Gwen turned, Theo running after them, the guesthouse door swaying on its hinges. That would surely wake up Terrance and Rachel, too.

"Stop!" Theo yelled, her long runner's legs making ground, hair neatly wrapped in her scarf and her pajamas loose on her body.

Gwen's heart melted and tears sprang into her eyes. Theo hadn't even bothered to put on a jacket before she ran after her into the dead of a winter's night.

"We have to hurry," Gwen said, turning her back on Theo even as it broke her heart.

But Theo was a winning sprinter in high school for a reason, and she caught up with them fast. As Theo's form grew closer and more detailed in the moonlight, the others barreled into John's car. Gwen unstopped the vial of her own blood and ran as fast she could to spread it in a long line, then crushed the glass in her hand to bring out the more fresh, powerful blood.

Calling forth the threads of magic within her body, she funneled the gold and silver into pools in her hand and thrust it at the line she made. Pulling on her blood, willpower, and magic that she had poured onto the ground, she forced it upward, casting a stiff barrier. With the added blood on her hands mixed with burning magic, she pulled on the ends of barrier and extended it outward as far as she could, a blazing ripple of the shield twisting like a heat wave in the air as it grew horizontally and vertically. It shimmered once more with her magic, Gwen reinforcing the barrier as sweat slicked down the side of her face.

"No!" Theo screamed as she approached the shield.

But Gwen had been working on a shield as long as she could remember. It was one of her oldest and strongest spells.

Theo hit the barrier and stopped, screaming. She pounded her fists against the shield, yelling, "Gwen! No! Please don't do this! You promised! Don't leave me! Don't go!"

Eyes glassing, Gwen stepped backward.

"I'm sorry," she whispered, and she spun on her heel to run back to the car. Theo's fists pounded against the shield louder than the sound of Gwen's drumming heartbeat in her head.

"No! You promised!" Theo screamed one last time as Gwen threw herself into the stuttering car and John drove away.

Gwen looked over her shoulder through the back window. Theo crumpled to her knees and clasped her hands to her bowed head as she collapsed, forehead touching the ground.

Theo pulled herself back up to her knees and screamed, a long, blood-curdling howl filled with anger, sorrow, and betrayal.

Gwen threw her hands to her ears and curled her legs up on the car seat so that her knees touched her forehead, tears moistening her pant legs.

A firm, cold hand squeezed her shoulder, but she could not move, could not think, not after hearing the sound of Theo's heart breaking.

Chapter Forty-One

Around ten long and quiet minutes of driving past agricultural fields, John made a few turns and the land flattened out into maintained grass with pockets of trees. There were no streetlamps to guide their way, the sky dark and covered in clouds.

John parked where the road widened into an oval pullout spot, with several covered wooden benches.

"We will walk from here," he said, and they stepped out of the car, Gwen shivering with the sudden cold. Her heart sat heavy in her gut, and she tried not to think of Theo, of her pained screams, fists bashing against her shield.

Feng slung his belt of explosives and knives around his waist. Ina held her sword in one hand and a flashlight from John in the other, which she turned on and aimed at the ground, the frigid white light illuminating them in a small circle. John pushed his hair over his shoulder and took a small pocketknife from his jeans, then pricked his finger with one of the blades. Without explanation, he smeared a line of blood down Ina's forehead, but she did not flinch or question it.

John turned to smear the blood on Feng's forehead, and Feng flinched back, lips peeling back in a startled snarl.

"I am not a sun bearer, vampire. My blood will not harm you."

"That does not mean I want it."

"It marks you as one of my guests. Allows the earth to welcome you. If you want to join them, you must take my blessing."

Feng's shoulders stiffened, but he said, "Fine."

John rubbed a line of his blood on Feng's forehead, Feng's body and face rigid. True to his word, the flesh beneath the blood did not sizzle or burn.

Feng frowned, his thick eyebrows heavy over his face. "It itches."

"Try not to scratch it," John said, turning to Gwen. Her heart rate increased, the burn of Ina's blood on her arm flaring with old pain. She held her breath as John smoothed his warm blood on her forehead, and she exhaled her relief as it didn't so much as itch.

"Ready?" John asked.

They nodded, and John took the flashlight from Ina, leading the way.

They walked over mowed grass toward a hill looming before them.

"What is this place?" Gwen asked.

"Poverty Point," John answered. "The earliest city in the Americas, and the center of the Native American Cradle. If you look at the aerial imagery, you can see the concentric circles of what the great city was once, and the scattered mounds of what were pyramids. It is now a World Heritage Site, owned by the State of Louisiana."

"And the portal is here, somewhere?"

"*Portals*, multiple. You will see."

"And the state doesn't know about them? You're not going to get in trouble for just waltzing us through here in the dead of night?" Gwen asked as they approached the base of a mound where a paved walkway led forward and up, to a point that was over seven stories tall, with the whole mound several hundred feet wide.

"We prevented them from digging. This was our land, our city, first, after all. What they do and do not know, I cannot be sure. But I do know they would not dare interfere with the workings of myself and the Council. I believe there are similar...understandings in other locations of the world where portals reside."

Ina nodded. "There are."

John led them up the paved walkway but stopped as they reached the set of stairs that would take them higher up the mound. He stepped to the side, then took out his pocketknife and sliced open a long cut across his palm. He laid his palm flat on the grassy wall in front of him, blood flowing down the hill. Once enough had pooled, he used his fingers to draw a long straight line down the mound wall.

Again, he laid his bleeding hand over the line of blood, and as his hand rested on the elevated earth, glimmers of bright gold and silver and white flickered from beneath the grass, illuminating the earth. It flowed in brilliant streaks through the ground and into the line of his blood, until it was illuminated in all colors of magic.

John stepped away from the wall, squinting at the light.

A low hum rumbled beneath their feet, and first the grass, then the layers of old soil peeled away, a door-sized opening forming in the earth.

John shone the flashlight within, then looked over his shoulder with a satisfied grin at the surprised looks on Gwen and Feng's faces. "Come on," he said.

They followed him into the space below the earth, a passageway so narrow they walked single file. As they moved deeper below the mound, the ceiling rose above them, the walls reinforced with stone, clay, rock, and wood, thrumming with the familiar warm buzz of magic.

"So, you said you don't wield the sun," Gwen said, running her hand across the wall beside her, their footsteps echoing in the halls. "I thought everyone in the Cradle did?"

"No, only the primary," Ina replied. "The secondary Cradle have other abilities."

"Oh. Like what?"

"Including moving of the earth, like John and ex-Tyee's abilities. Though there are many others."

They approached the center of the mound where the peak was highest. It opened into a large, open cavern. Circular platforms rose to an altar in the middle. Around the platform, in a perfect circle, were six wide archways that led to nowhere.

"This is incredible," Gwen said, the surging thrum of power all around her as comforting as a cocoon.

"Isn't it?" John said, walking to the center. They stopped around the altar and he asked, "You want to go to San Lorenzo, correct?"

Ina nodded, "Yes."

"Do each of you speak Spanish?"

Ina said, "I do," as Gwen and Feng said, "No."

"Okay then," John replied, and motioned for them to stay put as he went to the wall near where they entered. There was a tall shelf there, filled with strange objects.

He had Gwen hold the flashlight when he returned with a pouch of herbs covered in red dust and a small, frog-shaped pipe. John sprinkled the herbs into the bowl of the frog's head and pulled a lighter from his pocket.

"What's in that?" Gwen asked.

John's eyes flicked to Feng before answering. "It's an old combination of imbued herbs, further enhanced with our blood."

"What herbs?" Gwen asked, the shelves of her mind opening to add them to her list of ingredients, of potential abilities.

"It's a trade secret," John said, and Gwen rolled her eyes.

"What is its purpose?" Feng asked.

"You'll see," John responded, lifting the pipe to his lips. As he lit the mixture of blood and herbs, magic pulled from the air, flickers of it shifting and winding around them as it followed the flame into the bowl, brightening the contents as John smoked.

He breathed and breathed and breathed, until his chest was full of smoke and the contents of the bowl were gone.

John closed his eyes briefly, then opened them and blew the smoke in an arc, puffing it into all their faces.

Gwen coughed, the smoke catching in her lungs unexpectedly. Feng and Ina cleared their throats and gave small coughs but did not choke the same way Gwen did.

"What the hell was that?" Gwen asked through her coughs, smoke puffing out of her mouth.

"Language is no barrier to you, now," John said, setting down the pipe, smoke still flowing out through his nose like a dragon. "For the rest of your lives, you will understand them all."

"Oh," Gwen said. "Well, that's convenient."

"Indeed," Ina agreed, and Feng sneezed.

"Are you sure about this?" John asked.

"Yes," Ina replied. "Feng? Gwen?"

Feng nodded, and Gwen said, "Let's do this." She clenched her fists to hide her trembling fingers.

John led them to the southeast archway, and as the flashlight brightened the stonework, Gwen noticed the intricate carvings on it, whirls of leaves and vines that wrapped all the way up and around it. Each archway was slightly elevated on its own platform, and at the base of each pillar of the arch was a small bowl.

John stretched out the hand he had cut, reopening the wound that had started to congeal, blood moving freely down his hand again. He leaned over the first bowl and let his blood drip into it. Once the bowl was half full, he moved to the other one and filled that as well, squeezing his hand and wincing as he pushed his fingers into his wound to encourage more bleeding.

John stepped back, and from his seemingly endless pockets, pulled out a bandage that he wrapped around his hand.

The blood from the bowls moved up the archway, filling the leaf and vine carvings with red. As the blood filled the pillars, the magic that hummed around them grew closer and denser. It peeled away from the walls and ceilings, thin glowing threads winding through the air to the center of the archway, where the threads of bright color whirled together in a slow vortex. As the blood moved to the top of the stone, both sides meeting each other, the ends of the threads merged into the vortex, leaving them standing in front of a large, spiraling circle shining in golds, whites, silvers, and bright gemstone hues that swallowed, morphed, and regrew as it all mixed together.

The light and warmth of the portal encompassed Gwen's vision, so bright it almost blinded, yet it didn't hurt to look at.

It was the most beautiful thing she had ever seen.

She wished Theo could see it.

Her heart gave an unpleasant squeeze in her chest.

As the portal whirled, it sucked her forward, pulling on her clothes and hair, beckoning her into its gravity.

John turned to look at them and said, "Be safe."

"Thank you, John. We will not forget what you have done for us," Ina said and stepped toward the portal.

Standing directly in front of it, Ina's hair moved forward, as if there was a breeze behind her.

But no, it was the portal beckoning her.

Ina looked over her shoulder. "You two ready?"

Gwen and Feng nodded, and Ina stepped into the light, disappearing without a sound.

Feng looked at Gwen. "Go on. I'll be right behind you."

She nodded, hesitant.

Gwen's heart thrummed with the ferocity of a frightened moth's wings, as it could not escape the flame that would kill it.

Gwen took a deep breath and stepped into the light.

<h1 style="text-align:center">Chapter Forty-Two</h1>

Nikki lost the thread to Vadasz. Again. It slithered at the base of the Tree, a deep purple vine stretching up for her. Yet, every time she attempted to plunge her consciousness into it, she barely made it down the thread before she was repelled back into her own body. She sensed Lilith's thread reforming, but was too weak to follow. Maybe with more time she would be able to track her again.

Perhaps it was the wards on his body, the ones that had prevented Gwen from scrying for them, that also got her expelled from his mind.

Frustrated, she stared into the void and rolled her neck, the only part of her body she could move, the glimmers of Io raining around her.

Io's presence was warm and attentive, but not smothering, as if Their consciousness was half in the Tree, half spilled around the world.

"*Io?*" Nikki asked. She tried to flex her fingers, but she could not tell if they moved. They had long surpassed the point of tingling with blood loss, moving into a state of complete numbness. Yet she still tried, having nothing better to do.

"*Yes, child?*" Io replied, the flickers hesitating, then shifting toward her, as Io's attention came to rest on Nikki.

"*What happened next with Lilith? After she infiltrated the garden.*" Pressure in the Tree grew as Io focused Themself. "*Understand, that in her cloak of darkness before she corrupted the garden, the first brood of vampires were created. She hid herself from me so completely, the protection extended to her children as well. Hormin came from that first generation of born vampires, rich with magic and loyalty, as were all his siblings.*

"Though Lilith's children waited at the fringes of the garden to help her massacre Adam and Eve's family, only one child was captured. Their first daughter, Aclima. There was such power in Adam and his family, the first brood could not contend with it. Yet, Lilith was at first satisfied with only that kidnapping. She took Aclima to her enclave, and in vengeance, turned her into the first made vampire.

"That did not go as expected. She thought by making a vampire they would have even more strength, more loyalty to her than her born children. She was wrong. Lilith could not bend the blood of Aclima like she could her children, could not touch Aclima's mind with hers. She was likewise unprepared for what the process of turning would entail, and despite the violence she had incited on others, it disgusted her, what Aclima had become. In her mind, Aclima was a being who lost her grace, failed to achieve the glory of what she believed was a true and beautiful vampire. She believed Aclima a monster.

"I believe this is where Lilith's hatred against the Made began. Yet, this did not stop her children, and her children's children's children, ad infinitum, from continuing to turn humans. At least those that could survive.

"Lilith expelled Aclima and focused on expanding her lineage. Instead of turning humans, she killed them in her wild hunt to find Adam and his family. At this time, I blessed the Cradles of Civilization, encouraging those brilliant speckles of civilization to form in pockets around the world, to protect and shield Adam and his family. As I mentioned before, magic used to be more abundant in this world, as an extension of myself, and thus the first of the Cradle were immensely powerful, inspiring their own mythologies and legends. The abundance of my essence in the world is what led to the creation of other genealogies with different abilities. Some individuals learned how to grasp my essence from the matrix of the world, whether the air, water, fire, or earth, and it integrated into their bloodlines. This is how mages, such as Cora and her daughter, came to be.

"As with vampires, the magic in the Cradle and mages has diminished over the eons.

"Lilith and her ever-growing species rampaged through humans, battled with the Cradle, and killed them where they could. This blood trail eventually led the angels to her, where they captured her and, under my direction, stored her in the Tree."

"I don't understand why you did that. Why not just kill her?"

"She was still my first daughter, and I still loved her. I felt...guilty for what she had become. The Tree, which I made as an anchor for perpetuating life on earth, had struggled to sustain itself through the strands of magic that ebbed and flowed through the air, the soil, the water. But with a vampire as its core, it would have a consistent, never-ending source of life. I thought – I hoped – that time in the Tree would soften Lilith's edges. That in the absence of bloodlust, she might return closer to whom she once had been."

Nikki hesitated, considering. *"Why make Adam's bloodline the solution for her release? It seems that would only make her focus on her enemies more."*

"Again, I was a naïve god and trickery was new to me. The intention of Adam's bloodline being her release was meant to be one of reconciliation. The hope was that a strong enough peace between humans and vampires would be obtained. That the peace would lead to the blood being freely given. That Lilith would be intentionally released in a time of peace. I regret I did not think of how she would abuse this binding rule."

Nikki could not think of a response that wasn't biting or cruel, so held her tongue.

"The flaming sword was given to protect both Lilith and the Tree from those who would harm it, as it had wound its way into human lore. The sword was never meant to leave this island. Two additional events I improperly foresaw."

Nikki bit down on her lip, fangs jabbing into them, as she mulled over Io's words. *"So you put Lilith in here to calm her, punish her, and protect humans. But the Tree already existed, and you said it was struggling to survive. Does this mean that the Tree will always need a vampire inside of it?"*

Io pondered, the flecks of light pausing with thought. *"I have not thought of another way."*

"So, I'm stuck here forever."

"Unless someone takes your place."

"Unlikely," Nikki replied, the heaviness of dread and acceptance settling low in her gut.

Several minutes passed in silence, Nikki absorbing the information, knowing that she would never really have a life again.

This was it.

Forever.

Once that feeling curled itself into her heart, turning it into a brittle stone, she asked, *"Where is the garden? What happened to it after Lilith corrupted it?"*

The space around her tensed with a long-ago ache, and Io said, *"The corrupted garden was a constant reminder of my failings. Of the loss of simplicity and beauty, always in the periphery of my awareness, as it pulsed with magic both pure and tainted. I could not bear it. Thus, I purified the corruption and sunk it. Where on the ocean floor it lies now, I do not know."*

Loss filled both the air around and within Nikki, for a glorious civilization, a beautiful ecosystem, forgotten and eroding in the dark abyss of the ocean.

Maybe she'd be in this Tree long enough to see the day when humans found it.

Perhaps that was something to look forward to.

Chapter Forty-Three

GWEN FELT it was no different than emerging from water or changing altitude. There was a shift in pressure, a pop in her ears, along with a sense of warmth and comfort and blinding brightness and –

Her foot landed on solid ground. Blinking away the spots of light, eyes adjusting to the dark, she saw Ina's silhouette standing before her, back turned. As her vision focused, she realized they were in another underground temple, but with a shallower ceiling, a rectangular room, and eleven portals in a line to either side of the one they stepped through. The room was held together by the same threads of magic found in Poverty Point. Lit sconces framed the opposite wall, casting flickering orange light on the yellow, aged stones. A second portal, directly to her right, was open. It churned with the same magical vortex, pillars of old stone vibrant with blood in the carvings.

Sweat trickled down the side of Gwen's face, and she tugged at the collar of her shirt and jacket. It was warm here.

Too warm.

Feng stepped through the portal behind her, bumping into her with a surprised "oomph."

Ina turned to them, hands on her hips and lips in a tight line, and said, "Something is wrong."

Feng took a deep breath. "There is blood in the air."

"Come," Ina beckoned, hand tight on her sword, and Feng slung the rifle over his shoulder. Gwen's fist was slick on the handle of the sickle sword.

Feng and Gwen fell into step behind Ina, flanking her sides. Their footsteps echoed in the tunnel-like temple, ears straining for any other sound.

But between the footsteps and her escalating heartbeat, Gwen couldn't hear anything else.

"There is someone weeping outside," Feng murmured.

Ina whirled. "Then we must hurry. Can you lead us to them?"

"I can try," Feng said, taking the lead and breaking into a slow run for a vampire, perfectly paced for the speed of a human, following the sound of the voice only he could hear.

They twisted through the temple, tight turns that disoriented Gwen. They sprinted past empty bedrooms, halls, kitchens, dining rooms, and living rooms with minimal furniture and décor. Gwen's clothes were sticking to her body now, from the heat of the air and the effort of her running. When finally they stumbled upon a winding staircase, made of the same old stone of the temple, dim light shone through onto the steps with the promise of the outside, yet the air grew thicker, heavier.

Feng bolted up the steps, Ina and Gwen behind, Gwen gasping as her lungs burned and legs ached.

Maybe she should have trained with the others.

They ran up and up and up, and when Gwen thought her legs would give out beneath her or her lungs would burst, flesh growing hotter with every passing second, they finally broke above ground.

"No," Ina whispered, and Gwen's mouth popped open.

The world was on fire.

Bodies, broken and bloodied, littered the ground.

They stood on the top of a hill, the night sky hazing with smoke but bright with flame that licked at the grass and burned the edges of the ruins around them.

Gwen bent, putting her hands on her knees to catch her breath, eyes stinging, blurring. Her stomach clenched against rising bile as the stench of burning flesh, spilled blood, and the char of smoke filled her senses.

Breath caught, she lifted herself, and with a quick burst of power pushed air against the smoke, shoving it out of their faces, however brief the reprieve was.

"Someone lives. This way," Feng said.

Ina lifted an arm to cover her face, and Gwen peeled off her jacket as they followed Feng through the smoke and crumbling stone, around the fire, and over the twisted, lifeless bodies of the Cradle that covered the earth like leaves in fall.

"*Gwen, are you okay?*"

"Nikki." Gwen coughed, surprised, stepping over an arm that had a bone protruding from the middle of its bicep. "When did you get here?"

"*Just now. I felt your distress. What – what happened? Where are you?*" Nikki's voice rose as she saw the massacre through Gwen's eyes.

"We're in San Lorenzo," Gwen wheezed, hacking out the smoke that rushed to fill her lungs. "I don't know what happened yet."

Nikki's presence was heavy with sorrow. "*Be careful.*"

Gwen nodded, unsure if Nikki could sense the movement.

Sniffles broke through the crackling fire. With another quick burst of air from her hands, barely calling on her magic in order to preserve her dwindling energy, she cleared the way before them. The smoke parted, and the flames peeled away from her wind.

But they separated only for a second before they roared higher. Gwen's mouth popped open, the air she summoned only fanning the flames.

"Gwen!" Ina chided. "Why would you think that was a good idea?"

"I had to do *something*."

"How about use your brain?"

"I thought I could smother the fire, okay? I didn't think I'd make it worse."

Ina tsked and shook her head. Finding their way around the fire, Gwen saw a child, no more than twelve years old, dragging a man out of the ruin and down the hill where the fire had not reached.

Sirens blared in the distance, but Gwen could not see how far they were through the smoke, could not gauge their distance with the roar of fire in her ears.

They rushed to the child, Ina shouting, "Cousin!"

The girl startled and dropped the man, shifting into a defensive stance. Her eyes flicked to Feng, and they widened, and as she lifted her arm, a flare of sunlight manifested like a whip in her hand.

"Wait! He won't hurt you!" Gwen yelled, and although she didn't speak Spanish, the words warped in the air and the child seemed to understand her.

Feng stayed back as Gwen and Ina approached the girl, who remained stiff and tense, but extinguished the flare whip.

Ina formed a ball of sunlight in her hand, and the child's face flickered through several emotions. Shock, relief, sadness.

"Cousin," Ina repeated, standing a few feet from the girl. "What happened?"

The child gulped, looking at the dead man at her feet, then threw her gaze over her shoulder. Gwen followed her line of sight, a row of bodies lined up down the slope.

"*So many dead,*" Nikki mourned.

Turning back to look at Ina and Gwen, the girl clutched the cross around her neck and spoke, and although Gwen could see that her lips took a different shape, the sounds of the words bent between them, reforming into sentences she could understand.

"The ancient evil came with her son and two others while we slept. A few of us heard the commotion outside and went to check it out, but no one came back. More and more left, with none returning. Soon we heard screams and shouts, and felt the heat of the flames. When I came aboveground, so many were already dead..." Her voice cracked, and the fire danced in the tears in her eyes. "But the evils would not die beneath our suns. They burned, but the flesh regrew and their skin, like marble, would not crack. My uncle, he told me to go to our cousins in Caral, to seek their help and give them warning. I fled back down to the underground and began the ritual to open the way there, but the evil found their way to me. I was sure I was dead, too, but...the ancient one simply thrust me aside." The girl exhaled, steadying herself. "When I came to, the evils were gone, and everyone was dead but me."

Ina's eyes widened. "Lilith went through the portal?"

The girl nodded, hesitant.

"Then we must as well. Come!" Ina shouted, turning on her heel.

"Wait!" Gwen yelled after her. "We can't just leave her here."

"We have to," Ina said. "Gwen, of all the times to fight me, this is not it."

"You're just going to let her deal with all the bodies and the fire alone?"

"She's right," the girl said. "You must stop them. Help will come," she added, nodding to the sirens in the distance.

Gwen shifted on her feet.

"*Go with Ina, Gwen. She will be okay.*"

"At least tell me your name."

"Isabella," she said, twisting the cross in her hand.

"Isabella." Gwen nodded. "I'm Gwen, and we will come back, or find people to help you, I promise."

Isabella's eyes shone. "Thank you."

"Gwen – come on!" Ina yelled, and with one last look at Isabella, who stooped down to resume dragging bodies away from the flames, Gwen followed Ina and Feng back through the smoke and flames, the bodies and ruins, and then down the stairs and through the winding halls of the temple.

With a rush of adrenaline coursing through her body, her aches lessened and the rasping of her breath was muted. Her heart raced not just with the exertion but the disbelief and fear that they were flinging themselves headfirst into a battle with Lilith, who waited just on the other side of the portal.

Who were the other two vampires with her and Hormin? Had the Cradle at Caral already been massacred?

Would they be able to beat them?

Beat Lilith?

They crested the corner into the sanctuary with the portals, and Ina ran straight into the one to Caral without pause, disappearing in the blink of an eye.

Feng put a hand on Gwen's shoulder, stopping her before they stepped through.

Gwen sucked in scratchy gasps of air, and Feng placed both hands on her shoulders, looking her square in the eye, his dark gaze solid and strong like obsidian.

"Catch your breath. Brace your body."

Gwen's hands trembled, but her breaths evened out as she timed her breathing to Feng's, steady and sure.

"Good," he said, squeezing her shoulders. "This is your last chance to return, Gwen. You may go back to Poverty Point and await reinforcements. If you come with us to Caral, you must be prepared to lay down your life. We may not be able to protect you. We do not know exactly what awaits on the other side. Defeating Lilith and Hormin, and whoever else they have with them will not be easy. It is unlikely to occur without sacrifice. Do you understand?"

Gwen clenched her shaking fists, the faces of Nikki, Theo, Terrance, Rachel, Xander, Cora, Daiyu, Farrell, and John flashing through her mind. All these people who fought so hard and were so deserving of life. She may not be able to save Nikki, but if her death meant ensuring the lives of those she loved, and even those she would hate but deserved life anyway, she would do it.

"Yes," Gwen rasped. "Let's kick some evil vampire ass."

Feng smirked, squeezing her shoulders, eyes gleaming with battle lust.

"Yes," he replied, his smirk breaking into a wide smile, revealing all of his silver, pointed teeth. They flashed bright in the light of the portal, like the glint of the sun against the blade of a sword. "Let's."

Chapter Forty-Four

Intense pressure and release.

Blinding light gave way to darkness.

Heat became a pleasant chill.

Gwen stepped away from the portal so that Feng did not walk into her again. He arrived looking as sure and steady as he'd been on the other side. Ina was nowhere in sight.

"How do we get out of here?" Gwen asked, surveying the large room. It was made of quarried stone and river rocks, held together with soil, clay, and threads of magic. The base of the room was rectangular, walls angling closer together as it reached the ceiling, creating a trapezoid. Eleven portals circled the space, all on raised, terraced platforms, facing the center of the room.

A shudder went through the earth, sand and stone sifting from the ceiling. Gwen flinched and covered her head.

"We follow the sound," Feng said, brushing the debris from his clothes and hair, then wielding his rifle.

Gwen fell into step behind Feng, not bothering to remove the soil and dust from her hair. It would take a good washing to get it out.

Her grip tightened on her sickle sword as they walked through the temple, passing empty room after empty room, no sound but the patter of their shoes and the raggedness of her breaths.

The structure rippled like a roll of thunder coursed through the stones and Gwen's stomach leapt to her throat. "Maybe we can try to get out of here faster? I'd really rather not be crushed to death."

"Can you run?"

Gwen nodded, though her legs were wobbly and her lungs sore. Feng broke into a sprint and she bounded after him, hair flying behind her. The magic that kept this temple in place infused the air with power, playing at the periphery of her aura, and she felt that, if she could only reach out, she could somehow harness it for herself...

As they ran, she tried to beckon the magic that thrummed around her, but it did not respond, and she did not know how else to ask. Maybe the only magic she could have was within herself.

Feng finally found the exit, a wide staircase that led directly above-ground, the doors wide open to the clear night sky. The clangs of metal against metal echoed down into the chamber where they stood.

With a quick glance at each other, they dashed up the stairs, the balmy night breeze whisking away the sweat on Gwen's skin.

They stood at the top of a terraced pyramid, one side overlooking a green valley and river, the other spreading out over sandy, barren ground. The ramp down from the pyramid led to a circular plaza where bodies clashed and voices shouted in battle, bursts of sunlight winking in and out of existence.

Blood smeared the ruins of the pyramid where bodies of the Cradle were pulverized and torn apart. Carried on the gentle breeze, the metallic scent of war flooded Gwen's nose, along with the shouts of those who still stood to fight.

Gwen made to run down the ramp, but Feng threw out an arm to stop her. "Wait."

He stared at the circular plaza, eyes roving over the forms below that Gwen couldn't discern.

"About a dozen unknown people remain fighting alongside Ina. Ozcollo is dead."

"You can see that from here?"

Feng nodded. "Thirteen against Lilith, Hormin, and Atoc."

"Now fifteen."

"I do not like these numbers."

"At least one is down already?"

Feng folded his arms, thinking. "The combat is too close quarters to use any explosives. And I will have to stay away from the sun bearers. I am not sure how much use I will be in this fight, trying to avoid the weapons of both sides. You, Gwen" – he turned to look at her – "stay away from Lilith if you can. Let the Cradle handle her. And Hormin as well."

"Maybe," Gwen gulped, "we can both go after Atoc? Take him down first?"

"Yes, good plan. Then the Cradle can focus on the other two. Let's go."

Gwen sucked in a deep breath, balled her shaking hands into fists and pulled at the warm power within her body. She pooled it into her core, winding the threads up into her arms and fingertips, lighting up with the shifting flow of magic beneath her skin.

The cries, grunts, and shouts grew louder, as did the bashing of weapons and tearing of flesh. Ina fought against Hormin with a few others outside the plaza, Lilith and Atoc within.

As they breached the plaza, the world quieted around Gwen as she finally saw Lilith for the first time, her inhumanly tall, muscular body made her alien-like. Feet like owl talons and hands outstretched into claws only added to the effect, especially with wooden horns protruding from her skull and ears. Dark red blood stained her chin, and Lilith laughed as she launched herself into the air before kicking someone in the chest, sending them flying and skidding across the ground. From their spot in the dirt, the person flung an orb of sunlight at Lilith, but she spun out of its way, the flash of light illuminating her gray skin, lined like wood and padded with thin patches of bark.

Feng yanked on Gwen's arm, bringing the world back into shattering focus, just as Lilith stomped through the person's chest, their ribcage breaking with a disgusting crack, blood spurting into the air, a shocked wheeze escaping the man as he died.

Lilith ground her feet in his chest cavity then bent over to rip his head from his body, the skin stretching and tearing and –

A whip of sun lashed against Lilith's back. She snarled in response, dropping the man's head mid-tear, staring down at the group behind her, all of whom were poised with balls and whips of sun in their palms.

"WHERE IS MY SON?!" Ina screamed, hurling light at Hormin who danced away from her attack and the attacks of the others.

"Oh, I'll never tell." Hormin laughed, jumped, and dodged through the attackers. As he shifted position, he saw Feng and Gwen, and his eyes widened before running away from the plaza into the field.

"Don't you dare run from me!" Ina screamed, chasing after him.

"Come on, Gwen," Feng said, pulling her arm.

Atoc fought against three of the Cradle. They stood near his brother Ozcollo's body, whose head was neatly separated from his torso in a clean, burned cut.

Atoc's spear lashed through the air and one of the women dodged, rolling under the attack and swinging her legs to sweep him off his feet. He leapt over the kick and turned midair to bash a sun-wielding man on the head.

The sunlight kissed Atoc's skin and his shoulder sizzled, but the knock against the head prevented prolonged contact. Stunned, the sun dimmed from the man's hand and Atoc pushed him to the ground with the butt of his spear, stabbed him with the head, and rolled away as the whoosh of thrown suns and angry screams followed him.

Atoc rose like a cat, poised low to the ground, the skin of his shoulder melting with the burn. He heaved deep breaths and glared over the shoulders of the Cradle at Gwen and Feng.

Atoc's lips peeled back from his face, and he snarled, "Traitor."

Feng and Gwen stood beside the Cradle, who did not dare to look away from Atoc.

"You two should go," Feng said to the Cradle, setting his rifle to the side. "We can handle him."

The women hesitated, gaze roaming over their fallen comrade before turning to search for those who had disappeared to chase Hormin. Lilith was also hot on her son's heels, leading the others out of the plaza to regroup closer to Hormin.

Finally, their gaze shifted to Feng and Gwen, assessing Feng's weapons, as well as the magic shimmering beneath Gwen's skin. They nodded and ran backwards a few steps until comfortably out of range, turning their backs on them and charging after the rest of the Cradle.

Atoc straightened himself, eyes following the retreating women. He rolled his burnt shoulder and asked, "How does it feel to be a traitor?"

"How does it feel to be a mindless slave?"

The snarl on Atoc's face deepened, and Feng lowered his body into a defensive stance, hands on the hilts of his daggers.

Gwen pooled her magic into one hand, grasping the sickle sword with the other, tightening her grip against the sweat in her palm.

Atoc leapt forward, pushing himself hard off the ground and snatching the spear out from the man's chest. The man gasped with the sudden pain, apparently not dead, but Atoc ignored him and launched himself into the air, spear pointed down at Feng –

Gwen thrust out her left hand, a swift gust pushing Atoc out of his lunge and into the stone wall of the plaza with a loud smack. He landed on his feet, fingertips on the ground, before righting himself with a growl deep in his throat as Gwen and Feng spaced themselves out, like a deadly game of monkey in the middle.

The plaza was empty except for the bodies on the ground, and as they circled Atoc, they wound closer to the middle and away from the wall.

Atoc stood eerily still, spear held in both hands perpendicular to his body, waiting for the next to strike as Gwen and Feng stalked in a slow circle around him.

When Gwen faced his back, Atoc twisted hard and fast on his heels, jumping forward and slashing his spear at her. She gasped, heart leaping to her throat at his lightning-fast movement. He was too close for her to react, to blast him away, so she instinctively flinched backward, but the spearhead still caught her cheek, ripping open the skin just under her eye.

Gwen froze, stunned by the sting.

Atoc grinned.

Dread curdled in Gwen's gut. The smirk and sinister gleam in his eye made Gwen feel like a mouse caught under a lion's paw.

Gwen hopped backward and Atoc followed, a predator following the scent of fear. She tripped on a body behind her, narrowly missing the swing of the spear that would have collided with her head if she had not fallen. The weapon came rushing toward her and she screamed, rolling away as the point sliced through her shirt and skin, ripping both flesh and fabric.

A flash and bang of light burst from behind Atoc, haloing his body in orange, and Atoc screamed.

Gwen crab walked back, and as Atoc turned to face Feng, she saw the aftermath of the vampire's small explosive, the torn flesh and muscle and exposed bones of Atoc's back.

Bile rose to her throat and burned her esophagus, and her hand slipped on another cooling corpse, slick with blood. She flinched away with a surprised shout and looked at the mangled mass of skin and muscle she had touched. She bent forward, vomiting thin strands of bile, her stomach too empty to produce anything of substance.

Panting with the ache of her dry heaves, she got to her feet, hot liquid pouring down her cheek, her side. Gwen clasped a hand to the gouged flesh in her torso and willed the blood to clot. She was no healer, and would not risk the complication of full healing, nor the amount of power it would take to mend it completely. But scabbing? She could do that.

Her head spun as her blood congealed. Feng and Atoc moved in a flurry of kicks and stabs, punches and lunges, cutting and bruising each other in equal measure.

Gwen hobbled over the bodies, pulling at the diminishing magic in her body, letting its warmth and power fill her hand. She waited until Feng jumped away from Atoc far enough that she could send another blast of wind careening into Atoc, throwing him off his feet and onto his back.

"Shield!" Feng yelled, retreating to Gwen and pulling a grenade from his sash, popping the cap with his teeth and throwing it at Atoc's slowly rising body, his exceptional stamina finally starting to wane. Gwen waved the hand with magic and blood in an arch in front of them, summoning up the wind and forcing it to condense into an impenetrable barrier in front of them, holding on to it tight as sweat and exhaustion threatened to shut down her body.

Atoc leaped backward just as the grenade exploded at his feet in an impressive, thunderous BANG, and Gwen flinched, squeezing her eyes shut reflexively. She kept the wall firm, the shrapnel rebounding off the shield and back at Atoc, hitting him with the shards of metal not once but twice.

"You can drop it," Feng said, rising from his crouch behind the wall, bleeding from numerous spear cuts.

Gwen opened her eyes and dropped the shield, sweat mixing with the blood on her face.

They approached Atoc with caution. To Gwen's horror, he peeled himself up from the ground, sticky blood clinging to what remained of him.

He knelt on the stubs of his knees, one leg below the knee blown off, the other hanging on by a thin, muscled thread. His torso, arms, and face were decimated with cuts that both shredded through him and embedded in his skin, neck, and left eye.

He was barely more than muscle and bone and blood.

Atoc wheezed, metal rattling in his lungs and throat. But he lifted his chin as they stood before him, and somehow, the mangled mass of his face managed to sneer.

"You will lose, and you will die. All of you."

Feng shrugged. "Most creatures that walk the earth do."

"Not the Mother," Atoc growled, and with the fervor of his dying strength, he ripped a fragment of metal from his body and lunged toward Feng, slicing the shard along Feng's inner thigh.

Adrenaline rushed through Gwen's body – Feng could not die here, they needed him, *she* needed him – and before she could think, her hand shifted on the sickle sword and swung it through Atoc's neck. Her weapon sliced through skin, every muscle and tendon and bone, and then open air.

Atoc's shredded face thumped to the ground, his mangled body slumping to the side with an indelicate plop.

The sudden silence was suffocating.

"Oh my god," Gwen said, hands shaking. "I just killed someone."

"And I thank you for it," Feng said, clutching at the cut on his leg.

The trembling of her hands released her grip on the sword and she dropped it, the red on her hands blurring in her vision.

Whose hands were those?

They couldn't be hers...could they?

A firm, marble hand landed on her shoulder. "Gwen."

She blinked through her tears, gaze shifting from her stained hands to Feng's, his obsidian eyes bracing.

"Did he...did he get your artery?" Gwen stammered.

"No. It just hurts. Terribly. No one has done that to me before."

"Well, there's a first time for everything," Gwen said, voice wavering on the edge of hysteria, pitch rising higher.

"Gwen," Feng said again, squeezing her shoulder. "You did the right thing. I am sorry that before we entered the portal I did not also ask you if you were willing to take a life."

"Oh, well, you know." Gwen's voice shook, and she wrung her hands together, smearing the blood. "I knew it was possible, but I never really thought about what it would feel like."

"I understand. But Gwen, you can't afford to process now. We must help the others."

"Yes, of course. More...more fighting. Yay."

Feng knelt to pick up her sword and placed it in her hand, then retrieved his rifle. With a steady hand on her back, they limped out of the plaza, away from the field of bodies and blood, following the intermittent flashes of sunlight that burst into the air.

Chapter Forty-Five

Feng's injuries stitched together as they walked. He twitched his fingers, flexing and unflexing, as though resisting the urge to scratch the itch. Gwen's breathing steadied and her nerves settled, but a persistent, anxious hum vibrated through her blood, a disturbed hive of bees in her veins. The blood on her face and side cooled, gumming to her skin, the pain ebbing to a dull throb.

Lilith, Hormin, Ina, and the rest of the Cradle had moved far from the plaza into the rest of the ruins. Hormin leapt backwards, farther away from the temple, all while dodging and slashing. Lilith whirled around the crescent of the Cradle, trying to pick off those at the sides, but streaks of sunlight and the whip of flares lashed ever outward, burning her skin and driving her back.

Feng frowned, moonlight spilling over his sharp features. "They are leading them away. Xander must be in the opposite direction."

Gwen looked over her shoulder at the dark, looming temple and the line of trees behind it. "Should we look for him?"

"No." Feng shook his head. "Let's help them first. However we can. We can find Xander once they're defeated."

Gwen nodded, heaviness filling her chest, imagining Xander all alone somewhere in the dark. They passed by three more bodies, one with a broken neck, laying stomach down but with its vacant eyes cast toward the sky. Two others were alive but severely wounded, one with deep claw gouges in her stomach and across her face, holding another person whose breaths were ragged and short, clutching their bleeding gut while a femur protruded from their leg. They gave a passing glance to Feng and Gwen when they walked by, barely able to see through the blood that ran down their faces, over their eyes.

Those who still fought came into focus as Gwen and Feng approached, illuminated by the conjured aspects of sun. The grunts and shouts and heavy breaths of battle grew louder. Feng winced, breaking out in a sweat, as the flashes of light from the sun stole over his skin.

Gwen hated that he did not feel what she felt. To her, these moments of sun, of warmth and light, were welcome signs of hope in the dark.

"Are you going to be okay?" Gwen asked.

"As long as none touch me, I will survive. Albeit uncomfortably. I should stay back, in case," Feng replied, and his arm left Gwen's shoulder, staying close enough that he could shoot, throw an explosive, or intervene if needed, but not so close that a sun or flare would hit him.

The bees within Gwen rose to a frenzy, and she turned away from Feng, closing the distance to the Cradle, to Lilith and Hormin, alone.

Gwen tugged at the magic within her, calling it into her hands. Light flickered beneath her skin, delicate threads dancing within her body.

She had one more attack or shield within her, maybe, until she was spent.

Gwen stepped beside Ina, whose chest heaved and hair was matted with sweat to her face, throwing orb after orb at Lilith and Hormin, who jumped and rolled and dodged the barrage of attacks aimed at them. With the crescent of the Cradle stretching around Lilith and Hormin, they could do little more than avoid the whips and miniature stars hurled at them, both of their faces twisting with rage, teeth bared and eyes wild.

Lilith's gaze flashed to Gwen when she stepped into the formation beside Ina, and she seethed, "You."

"Oh, you recognize me?" The cut on her cheek flexed with a twinge of pain as she spoke. Gwen raised a hand, magic pooling into her fingertips. "I'm flattered."

Hormin side-stepped a flare, and the fighting paused, disturbed by their speech.

"You could join me, daughter. Despite the weakness in your blood, you are one of mine."

Gwen grimaced, stomach sickening.

Lilith straightened from her fighting crouch, black gaze boring into Gwen's. "I could teach you magics you never dreamed of. Grant you power you could never obtain on your own. Join me, and no one will doubt your strength again. You will be the most powerful witch who ever lived."

The mark of Ina's fingerprint seemed to burn anew on her arm, a harsh reminder of what she really was. Where her blood dictated she belonged. The faces of her family rushed through her mind, a lifetime of fantasies for revenge and bringing her power down on those who bullied her, neglected her, called her weak, all just one word away, the taste of vengeance bittersweet on her tongue –

"I don't need you to become the most powerful witch. So no, I don't think so, bitch," Gwen said.

Lilith snarled, lips pulling back to show the thickest, longest fangs Gwen had ever seen, shining white against the blood on her face.

A burst of sunlight streaked across Gwen's vision, slashing through half of Lilith's face, melting away the snarl.

Lilith's head whipped back with the force. When she turned back to the crowd, bile rose in Gwen's throat at Lilith's melted skin, her face sloughing down her chin onto her chest, the white of her skull gleaming and the jelly of her eye pouring from the socket, the stench of burnt flesh and hair staining the air.

A deep growl rumbled from Lilith's chest, and Hormin yelled, unsheathing the glowing greatsword, dashing forward and slicing the head off the perpetrator in one fluid motion, too fast for the eye to see, too fast for anyone to stop it. The head of the woman toppled to the ground and rolled away from the body that fell beside it.

A beat of stunned silence passed, and then the world exploded with sunlight. Gwen squinted with the manifested anger of the Cradle blazing in the dark as those closest to Hormin formed whips and lashed them against his limbs, the flares wrapping around his wrists and ankles, forcing him to drop the sword. He screamed with pain and rage as the whips burned and bound him, and the Cradle tugged at the strands, forcing him to his knees.

At the same time, the four closest to Lilith, including Ina, funneled sunlight into their hands to form one large sun, the tendrils of heat and light swirling together before them, growing and growing until Gwen was nearly blind.

Lilith screamed when Hormin was brought to his knees, the flesh and hair on her melted face regrowing with sickening speed. Straining against the growing light, Lilith curled into herself, growling as wings grew from her back, large and feathery like an owl's.

"Hurry!" Ina yelled. "Don't let her fly away!"

Gwen lashed out her last threads of magic, a gust that pushed against Lilith. It barely moved the other woman, feet sliding back less than a foot, but the additional second was enough for the Cradle to bear the sun down on her, encapsulating her in its light.

A bloodcurdling scream rippled through the air the moment the sun, taller than any person and just as wide, descended on Lilith, but the scream was cut off abruptly, the sun pulverizing Lilith's vocal cords in an instant.

"No!" Hormin screamed, writhing against his bonds.

The Cradle kept the sun over the space where Lilith had stood. It flared and burned and sizzled with all the strength of the sun on a clear summer's day, burning away the ground. The energy from it created its own tempest, rustling through Gwen's hair, bringing with it the perfume of Lilith's burning body.

The sun diminished slowly as the Cradle funneled it into Lilith and the earth, ensuring it incinerated every part of her body.

With a wink, the sun was gone, leaving a bright spot in Gwen's vision where it had once been. She blinked it away, adjusting her eyes back to the dark.

Dropping the arm that shielded her from the light and wind of the sun, Gwen stepped up beside Ina and the three other Cradle members, all heaving with exhaustion, staring at the remnants of Lilith.

In a shallow, blackened crater, Lilith's skeleton lay still, oddly human with the absence of horns and wooden flesh. Only the large fangs would identify the remains as vampiric.

A black pulse shifted under Lilith's rib cage, and Gwen squinted at the skeleton. With the last vestiges of her power, Ina manifested a small sun, shining light on the body.

Beneath the ribs, a black heart pulsed.

Gwen gasped. "What the hell?"

Dark threads burst from the heart, winding around the rib cage, reforming organs, tendons, and ligaments. They repaired the broken bones and the body plumped out with layer after layer of muscle, skin stretching over the form, horns sprouting from the head and ears, streaks like wood forming on the skin, hair regrowing from their roots.

Eyelids opened into empty sockets, and the optic nerve appeared, the jelly of eyes forming into black orbs as Lilith's face reformed and her full lips broke into a vicious grin over her fresh mouth.

"Fools," Lilith said, rising to her feet. She stretched, body absent of any injuries, looming over them as wings sprouted from her back. Gwen, Ina, and the others took a step back. "You think I can be killed, when it is my blood that fuels the earth?"

"Perhaps not," a man holding a whip on Hormin said. "But he can."

The man shot power through the whip, extending the flare so that it wound up Hormin's arm, singing his flesh in a vine-like pattern, and the three other Cradle members that held him down lengthened their whips too, the flares climbing up his limbs. Hormin grimaced with pain, biting back a howl.

Lilith snarled, features contorting with rage. She leapt into the air, diving toward the group that held her son.

A deafening bang reverberated through the field, and Lilith's body flinched midair, left side twisting back.

In the distance, Feng crouched, rifle aimed at Lilith.

Lilith growled and removed her hand from her side. Gwen's jaw dropped as it came away without blood.

Surely it must have at least hurt, even if it couldn't pierce her skin.

Lilith hovered in the air, looking down at them, a commander assessing the battlefield.

Gwen and Feng, plus eight Cradle members against the two of them.

The startling shot gave Hormin a moment of reprieve from the twining flares, and in that split second, he lunged for the greatsword. Struggling against the flares, he slashed the sword through the air, forcing the nearby Cradle members to jump back, loosening his bonds.

With a frustrated scream, Lilith dove for her son, the talons of her feet digging into his shoulders. In a powerful beat of her wings, she lifted him off the ground, the sun flares snapping loose from his body, the force of the release sending two of the Cradle to their backs as they had tried, and failed, to hold on to him.

Ina, gasping for air, ran after them, fixing her eyes on the pair as they rose into the night sky, flying eastward back to the temple.

A hand fell on Ina's shoulder, stopping her.

Ina yelled, shrugging off the touch. "Are you idiots? We have to go after them – we have to stop them. We have to find my son!"

"Ina," the man said between breaths. "We have him, don't worry."

Half of the Cradle fell to their knees, exhausted, watching Lilith and Hormin fly away.

"How?" Ina asked.

"We wouldn't be very good shields if we couldn't sense what we needed to protect, now would we?"

Ina looked at the man, brow raised.

"We sensed him as soon he touched our ground. Those of us who were awake woke up the others. We sent a small group to get him, and kept most of the force at Caral to distract Lilith and the others. Your son should be well on his way to Aspero."

"Thank God," Ina sighed with relief, collapsing to her knees.

While the Cradle huddled to check on each other's injuries, Gwen walked on shaking legs to Feng, who kept his distance.

"Nice shot," Gwen said.

"Thank you," he replied, eyes fixed on the night sky. "She will not be pleased when she realizes Xander is gone."

"No, she won't." Gwen followed his gaze, watching the diminishing silhouettes of Lilith and Hormin, until the dark swallowed even the light of the greatsword.

Chapter Forty-Six

Nikki left Gwen watching Lilith and Hormin fade into the night sky, mulling over Lilith's cryptic words and frightening immortality. Despite the horrors she'd witnessed through Gwen's eyes, when she settled back into her own body, her shoulders sagged, a burden relieved.

Xander. Xander was safe.

Xander was *safe*.

The tightness of fear unwound from her, cold goosebumps dancing over her skin as the tension released, her lips curling and eyes closing, holding back the tears.

The last she had seen of him was at the compound, bruised and battered. Now whatever Vadasz was looking for didn't matter.

Xander was safe.

Once the rush of relief faded, images from the night streamed through her mind's eye.

All those poor people killed and wounded.

So many murdered, massacred, mangled, all for the sake of Lilith's vengeance.

"Io?" Nikki called.

The bright metallic flickers shivered in the air, twisting toward her with Io's attention.

"Have you seen what Lilith is doing?"

The rain hesitated.

"I have seen," Io replied, sorrowful and distant.

"Tell me you aren't really okay with this."

Silence grew heavy around her body. A hot coil burned in her gut as the quiet built, flashes of bones shoved at odd angles through skin marching through her mind's eye, the blood-covered ruins and smell of burning flesh assaulting her senses.

"Are you?"

The air around her rose, the glitter lifting and dropping like a sigh.

"This behavior does concern me."

"Concern you?" Nikki spat, stomach acid souring. *"I'm glad the massacre of dozens of people concerns you. Such morality."*

Io constricted the air around Nikki like a hand squeezing her body, and she exhaled sharply. The moment her mouth had opened, the tree's tendrils that had been braced against her jaw wound their way into her mouth, down her throat –

With expert practice, Nikki clamped them off with a solid bite, ground them between her teeth, and spat the mulch to the ground.

"You forget, child, who I am. I have born witness to endless ages of violence. Have seen massacres greater than this. Incomparable genocides. They have all disturbed me, but it is not my place to change the way of humanity. As you are now aware, creatures of the Earth have manipulated me before. Your sarcastic chiding will not be an effective tactic in changing my mind."

The air released her, and Nikki sucked in a deep breath through her nose, the heat in her belly subsiding to a swaying sickness.

"I'm sorry," Nikki said. *"I'm scared for my friends and their families. For all of humanity. Surely you can see Lilith's path better now and understand what she means to do."*

"I am not yet convinced that her actions will become more than revenge."

"Even if that were true, how could you be okay with it? With her killing all of the Cradle? Those are your blessed people. Don't they deserve your protection since they are in this position because of the choices you made? You chose them. Gifted them. And now abandon them."

"It's not abandonment if I am still here."

"You're right. It's worse. It's neglect."

Io remained silent, the sifting of light falling lighter.

"Io, please. Please intervene. Do...something. Anything. You're the only one who can stop this. Lilith has killed almost a third of the primary Cradle now. Who will be left to defend humanity once the remainder is gone? If she only wanted revenge, if she didn't want to enslave and dominate humanity, then what would be the point in annihilating their protectors? If it was just for revenge, she could slaughter those directly involved and move on. But that's not what she's doing."

An indeterminate amount of time passed in silence as Io contemplated those words. Nikki's head dangled, facing down into the depths of the Tree.

"Even if I decided to intervene, I would not know how," Io whispered.

"You could tell us how to defeat her," Nikki replied. *"If the combined sun of the Cradle can't kill her and a bullet can't pierce her skin, I don't know how we can stop her. She's so much stronger than the rest of us. Even combined."*

"Yes, she has surpassed my expectations. She has outgrown the power balance of this world," Io said, a reluctant pride coloring her tone.

Nikki sensed the weight of Io's presence easing away from her. She opened her eyes, the glimmers fading out one by one, until there was barely more than a handful of shifting stars.

"Where are you going?" Nikki asked, the sudden and unexplained departure filling her with dread.

"To collect information."

"Oh. I see," Nikki said, biting back another sarcastic response, not wanting to enrage Io again.

"Do not worry, child, I will return to you. I will not let the swollen loneliness of your heart consume you."

Nikki flinched, Io's words scraping open a tender wound in her heart.

"I feel the weeping of my blessed ones, the bleeding of their tears into the rivers and oceans, the seeping of blood into the earth. It...it hurts me, tearing at the fabric of my essence imbued into this planet. Perhaps you are

right, that action must be taken. But I must leave you, to determine what that action will be."

"*Okay,*" Nikki said, inhaling deeply to alleviate the sinking of her heart. "*Thank you. For listening to me.*"

Io swirled around her, warm and loving like an embrace before fading away, leaving her once again in total, empty black.

Chapter Forty-Seven

Gwen walked down the road from the cramped house in Supe Puerto toward the ocean. The house would have been a fine size if not for the fact that everyone left of the Peruvian Cradle had joined them, cramming multiple people into each room. Even the living room had people sleeping in it. Feng was lucky to have the basement to himself, but with having to sleep on the hard concrete, maybe he wasn't so lucky after all.

The previous night the group made their way from Caral to Supe Puerto, which was home to one of the old Cradle civilizations that had made up the larger Caral – Supe Cradle. They arrived within an hour of driving, squeezing into cars at the base of Caral, all struggling to walk from injuries and exhaustion.

The moon was still high in the sky when they pulled up to the Council member's house where it was decided they would regroup, the weathered paint of the exterior dull against the darkness.

Ina rushed inside the home, Feng and Gwen on her heels. Xander sat with a cup of tea steaming in his hands and a blanket wrapped around his shoulders, hunched over on the couch. Two people sat with him and one bustled from room to room, welcoming them in and pressing bottles of water into their hands.

Xander looked up from the steam, gaze distant.

As his eyes focused on the people before him, tears glassed his vision and his mug dropped out of his hand, shattering on the floor.

"Mom," he sobbed, and Gwen's chest ached at the cuts and bruises on his face, his arms, one eye swollen shut.

"My sweet boy," Ina said, voice breaking, and she ran to his side and wrapped her arms around him, rocking him and smoothing the back of his head while Xander cried into her shoulder. "I've got you. It's okay, I've got you. You're okay, you're going to be okay," Ina repeated over and over. Gwen turned away, swallowing the lump in her throat, her vision turning hazy with her own tears.

She followed the sound of voices through the house, letting Xander and Ina have some privacy. In a back room she was bombarded by hands that appraised her injuries, stitched up the wound in her side, and sent her to bed.

Gwen was asleep the moment her head hit the pillow on the floor, someone else having already claimed the bed in that room. She woke up a few times, fitful and feverish, but there was always a pair of hands to wipe the sweat from her face and pour cold water into her throat.

It was late in the afternoon by the time she fully awoke, disoriented in that first moment of consciousness before remembering where she was, what had happened. She shot up from the floor, the tear in her side searing with pain, and she hissed through her teeth.

A pair of clothes sat beside her, so after finding some food and a shower, she set off down to the ocean to get some much-needed space from the clamor and claustrophobia of the home.

It was not a far walk to the ocean, the sun beginning its descent and reflecting gold and yellow flickers over the endless water. It was perfect weather, just warm enough to be comfortable but not so warm she was hot. A weak, intermittent breeze blew the salt spray into her face, filling her nostrils with the timeless smell of the ocean.

How long had it been since she last visited the coast? It must have been with Theo, before the weather turned.

Gwen's stomach soured as Theo's face flashed in her mind, her terrible howl as Gwen left her behind. Even if Theo didn't forgive her, at least she was safe. And she hadn't seen all the terrible things Gwen had the previous night.

The twisted and broken bodies, heads shorn from their necks.

Gwen swallowed the bile in her throat and lifted her chin, the wind billowing through her hair.

The beach was busier than she hoped, so she walked around the curve of the shore and scrambled over some rocks until she came to an isolated, pebbly section where there was no one else. She could still see those who lounged on the sandy beach, but at least she couldn't hear them.

Gwen settled on the ground, wet cobbles and stones pressing into her, but she didn't care. She breathed deep of the ocean breeze, the fresh and immense saltiness exfoliating and refreshing.

Gwen stared into the distance, watching the sun curve across the sky. She thought of how it felt to slice through Atoc's neck, the pale glow of her hands in the dark as she sheared it from his body. Nausea curled in her gut, and she remembered the feel of the sword slicing through his lacerated neck, moving through each layer, what it looked like as it rolled off his body and slumped to the ground –

She shivered, expelling the thought.

Gwen didn't feel guilty, exactly. He had killed so many people, would have killed more, would have killed Feng, but...

He was a flame she extinguished.

One that would never rekindle, never again see the moonlit earth or feel the wind on his skin.

The more she lingered on it, the less guilty she felt. He deserved to die. And she would do it again if it meant protecting innocents.

Her mind wandered from Atoc's broken body to wondering where Lilith was, how everyone was doing now, what they would do next, until all her thoughts spun out and she simply existed as one small part of the great world.

The clack of talons on rock startled her out of her meditation. To her left, three sooty black birds, a little over a foot tall, walked and jumped on the shore about ten feet from her. They had red beaks with slashes of yellow near their mouths and long white whiskers.

"Hey there," Gwen said, heart heavy with the reminder of her lost flock. She opened a palm and wound a peanut sized ball of magic into her hand, warm and bright. The birds cocked their heads and hobbled forward, assessing.

"I don't have any food, but I can give you a little energy? A little competitive boost."

The birds came within a foot of her hands then stopped and shifted, until one bird came forward tentatively, head cocking back and forth as it tried to figure out what was in her hand.

"What a cute little mustache you have," Gwen said, seeing clearer the long white whiskers that stretched out from the bird's face.

The bird looked at her as if it understood the compliment, the mustache bouncing with the movement.

Gwen tilted her palm closer to the bird, and with a quick motion, it pecked at the magic. At the same time, Gwen released it, letting it flow from herself to the bird. It startled as the threads wound into it, blending with its body.

"I guess your friends haven't tattled on me." The bird cocked its head, looking at her, and the other two walked forward. "I'm a bad witch, you know."

Extending out both hands, she made two more small orbs of magic for the other birds to absorb, each of which took it cautiously.

With a blink and shutter of their bodies, the three birds flapped their wings and lifted into the air.

Gwen watched them fly away, a small smile on her face, feeling the whirl of air around their wings, the freedom in their flight like a distant memory.

Chapter Forty-Eight

Gwen arrived back at the house just before dark, the western sky still orange and aglow with the faint traces of sunlight over the ocean. Her steps were lighter on her way back – she would have to figure out what that bird was, what it liked, and see if she could find it again. She could still sense the birds through her magic, but it faded with every passing second. Soon, whatever power she lent them would be gone.

Inside, Feng sat by himself in the living room, paler than usual, face sunken and wan.

"Are you okay?" Gwen asked, pulling hair over her shoulder and sitting beside him.

Feng flinched a smile and leaned back, arm stretching out over the couch. "Yes. Simply hungry."

"Ah, of course," Gwen said, twirling a strand of fire-tinted hair in her fingers. "You didn't bring any blood with you?"

Feng shook his head. "I did not think Ina, or John, would appreciate that."

"You're probably right. Guess we should get you back home – or, to John's home – soon," Gwen said and shifted her legs under her feet, angling towards Feng. "Look, I wanted to say thanks. I don't think I could have gone through last night without you."

Feng lifted a brow.

"You gave me words of encouragement when Ina just rushed through, and you stayed by me while we were fighting. I don't think I could have stomached any of it, could have plucked up the courage to walk and fight my way through if I had been alone. So, thank you. For being by my side."

Feng nodded, and shifted his eyes to her torso and her cheek. "How are your injuries?"

"They're fine," Gwen said, running a hand over the cut on her abdomen. "Someone healed them up when I got here and got me through whatever fever I was having last night, so I think I'll be alright."

"Good."

"How are your injuries?"

"What injuries?" Feng said, smirking, lifting up his sleeves and shirt to reveal perfectly smooth skin.

Gwen tsked. "Not fair."

Feng shrugged and patted his clothes back into place. "How are you feeling about your first kill?"

"You know, I was thinking about that today. Or rather, thinking about how I should be thinking about it? I don't think I'm as upset as I should be about taking a life. I actually realized I'd do it again in a heartbeat."

"I'm glad to hear you are handling it well. Not everyone does. If your thoughts change and you need someone to talk to, I am here."

"Thanks," Gwen said with a small smile. "So, where is everyone?"

"Some returned to Caral while their Council, or what remained of it, stayed here. They're talking with Ina."

"About what?"

Feng paused, as if listening. "Still debating if they can trust me."

"That must be getting old for you. Everyone automatically assuming you're bad or untrustworthy."

"I'm used to it," Feng said, but his fingers curled into a small fist.

Gwen hesitated, but allowed the subject to wash over them. "Have you spoken to Xander, yet? I haven't had a chance."

"No. I do not think he is ready to speak with a vampire. But you should speak with him. He is resting upstairs, in the third room to the right. I will call to you once the Council is ready to speak with all of us."

"Thanks," Gwen said, and peeled herself off the couch, the foot she had sat on tingling as blood poured back into it.

She walked through the dark house, flicking lights on and off as she went, voices from Ina and the Council echoing from a room far down the hallway, the sound disappearing as she made her way up the creaking stairs to the second floor.

A sliver of warm light shone through the cracks of the door, which hung ajar, and the floorboards squeaked beneath her feet. Blood pounded in her ears, and she chided herself for being so nervous. This was just Xander, after all. There was no reason to be worried.

She cleared her throat and smoothed the hair back from her face before she lifted her fist and knocked, the door creaking open as her knuckles rasped against the wood.

From inside, Xander gave a startled inhale. After a beat, he said, "Come in."

Gwen pushed the door all the way back and stepped into the room, Xander sitting upright in bed, leaning against the metal wire headboard, pillows stuffed between him and the frame. Bandages wound around his arms, one loose at his side and the other across his abdomen. His legs disappeared under the thin blankets. His head was tilted back, long wavy hair spilling down his shoulders and over the pillows, scruffy beard unkempt. One eye remained swollen shut, and the other gazed vacantly at the ceiling.

"Hey, Xander," Gwen said, pulling a chair from the opposite wall and setting it beside the bed.

Xander blinked and exhaled, leveled his head, and turned his good eye on Gwen. "Hey." He swallowed, Adam's apple bobbing in his neck. His voice quavered when he said, "It's good to see you."

"It's good to see you too," she replied, giving him a close-lipped smile. Gwen reached out to hold his hand, but at her movement, he flinched, arm pulling close to his body.

As if he was bracing for being struck.

A piece of Gwen's heart broke.

Hands hovering in the air, she clenched her fists and brought them to her lap, holding them tight.

"Do you – did Ina explain what's going on? Do you know?"

Xander's jaw ticked. "Yes, she explained. I know who – what – I am now. Would've been useful information to know before this all happened."

"I know." Gwen curled her fists together, rubbing her knuckles against each other. "I'm sorry. But everything is going to be okay now."

Xander scoffed. "That's what everyone keeps saying. But is it really, Gwen? Is it really going to be okay? As far as I can tell, we're all fucked," he spat, voice tightening as he spoke through an ever-clenching jaw, and his swollen gaze burned into hers.

She lifted her chin and returned the heat of his gaze. "Yes, Xander. It's going to be okay. We're going to stop Lilith, and Hormin, and we're going to save the world."

Xander laughed, but Gwen kept her face straight, chin held high.

"I'm serious."

Xander's features smoothed out from his laugh, and when his face slackened from anger to resigned hope, Gwen continued.

"Your mom has been working on summoning the Cradle, and we've all been training, getting stronger. We're going to gather all of our allies, all of our resources, and put a stop to this. We won't let her win."

"What do you mean by 'we?'"

Gwen filled him in on the past several months, from staying with the Lius to Terrance, Rachel, and Theo training with them, fleeing the remaining coven in the PNW and getting to Louisiana, what they saw at San Lorenzo and Caral. Apparently, Xander had been kept nearby during those attacks, but they had tied him up out of sight to avoid having the Cradle find him. They had dragged him through the massacre at San Lorenzo, so he knew what had happened there, but he had no idea there'd been a battle at Caral.

Gwen sucked in a deep breath and said, "And then there's Nikki."

Xander's eyes widened, but then he turned his head away and clenched his jaw. "What about her?"

"Well, she's still trapped in the Tree, but she can travel into born vampire minds, and my mind, like Lilith could. She's also been talking to God – who likes to be called Io – so I guess that almost makes her like a god now, too. At least a saint, I would think."

Xander remained silent, eye cast toward his feet, and his fist clenched over his stomach.

"If you want to talk to her, I can try reaching out."

His eyes squeezed shut, and his lips peeled back as he grit his teeth, fist clenched, as if he was fighting against someone twisting his heart.

When the wave of pain passed, he kept his eyes closed as he said, "No – I don't know whether to be mad at her for lying to me or sad that she's trapped or relieved that she's alive. I promised I'd save her when – before – before –" Xander's voice staggered and he sucked in large, deep breaths, steadying himself. Gwen placed a hand on his, and although he flinched, he did not pull away.

He blinked his eyes open and swallowed hard, shaking his head and relaxing his clenched fist. "No, thanks. I don't want her to see me like this."

"Okay," Gwen said. "But she just pops up at any time, she could even be here right now already, so..."

Silence filled the space within and without her, indicating Nikki was not with her.

"But she didn't chime in, so probably not. I'm just saying you don't necessarily have control over when she'll see you, whether you're ready or not."

Xander grunted. "About time somebody gave me warning about something."

"Look, she feels really bad about the whole thing. I don't want to speak for her but–"

"Then don't," Xander spat, then winced at the harshness of his tone. "I'm sorry. Please don't, Gwen. I can't – I can't do this right now."

"All right," she said, and squeezed his hand one more time before letting go. "I'm glad you're with us now. Theo and Terrance are going to be so happy to see you again. Just shout for me if you need anything and I'll bring it to you."

Xander nodded, and Gwen put the chair back in the corner.

"Turn the light off on your way out?"

"Sure," Gwen said, flipping off the light, hearing Xander shuffle himself deeper into the covers, the bed squeaking under his weight. She closed the door behind her and chewed on her bottom lip as she went back downstairs. There were many wounds she could heal, many salves she could make, but there was nothing she could do for the wounds Xander currently suffered from.

Chapter Forty-Nine

GWEN PASSED the hall of echoing voices as she made her way to the living room, where Feng sat on a chair reading a magazine that had been on the coffee table. She sat on the couch opposite him and asked, "They're still not done?"

Feng shook his head.

"Ugh," Gwen replied and laid down, tucking her arm under her head and closing her eyes, wanting to sleep again despite having only been up for a couple hours.

She was quickly swept under the cloak of darkness, vaguely aware of a blanket being draped over her body, warding off the dropping temperature as night descended. In a half dream of Theo asking when Gwen would teach her how to fly, a cold marble hand touched her shoulder, gently nudging her awake.

"Huh?" Gwen asked, eyes fluttering open, reorienting herself after explaining to Theo she didn't know where to buy wings.

Feng stood over her, hand on her shoulder.

"They're ready for us."

"About time," Gwen said, swiping the drool from cheek and raking her hands through her hair.

Gwen followed Feng, who tracked Ina and the Council by the

sound of their voices, to a room with a large circular table surrounded by chairs. Half of the chairs were empty, Ina and four other people spaced evenly around it, ranging in heights and hair color from dark auburn to black. Two looked familiar, and images of them creating a sun with Ina flashed through Gwen's mind. They had been there, fighting Lilith.

"This is it?" Gwen asked after introductions were made, scraping a chair back as she pulled it out and sat down. "I thought the Council would be bigger."

"Three of us died fighting Lilith," Carmen, a woman she recognized from the fight, responded. She had light brown skin and black hair, shorter on the sides and longer on the top, slicked back.

"All Councils of the Cradle are only seven members," Ina explained. "Six for each primary cradle, and one for God."

"Io."

"Excuse me?" Carmen asked.

"God prefers to be called Io, for Infinite One," Gwen said. "I have an inside source."

Ina sighed, and as her head dipped, the bags under her eyes grew darker and larger. "We're not here to discuss God's – Io's – name. We're here to discuss what's next."

"You haven't been doing that for the last several hours?"

"What my Council does and does not discuss is none of your concern, witch," Carmen spat.

"Whoa there, take a chill pill." Gwen threw up her hands. "I didn't mean to offend you. I just thought you were doing that already."

Carmen's face twisted, lip pulling back into a sneer, and as she opened her mouth, Ina raised a hand to stop her.

Ina gave them both sharp looks and said, "Carmen – Gwen and Feng have been useful allies. I understand they are not part of your Cradle, but they deserve our confidence. And Gwen, the people before you are powerful, and very experienced. Please try to show them respect. Especially in their own home."

Gwen and Carmen stared at each other, then both nodded, the other Council members shifting in their seats.

Ina continued. "First, we discussed how Lilith was able to find this

Cradle to begin with. This Cradle is made of shields, those with blood-lines and scents invisible to Lilith. We suspect that Atoc and Ozcollo, of a Peruvian coven, were able to somehow find this location. This means no Cradle is safe if they can be discovered so easily. Concluding this, we took a rough assessment of our losses and discussed the fighting tactics witnessed. We think it's best to split up forces. The Council here will either remain to rebuild our resources in Caral, or rejoin Isabella at San Lorenzo to assist her. We also need someone who will travel to the other Cradles to tell them what has happened, help them prepare for what's next. Feng, Gwen, my son, and I will return to the United States and continue our hunt of Lilith."

Ina paused and looked at each member of the group.

"I will remain here, as head of the Council," Carmen said, and Ina nodded.

"I will go to our allies in San Lorenzo," a man named Hector said.

"As will I," the other man, Cesar, replied.

Ina looked at the last person, who had tan skin and shoulder-length dark auburn hair. They were also at the fight with Lilith, and had a square and muscular build, as well as a refined and sharp jawline. "Alessa?" Ina prompted.

Alessa's gaze roved over Gwen and the others and said, "First, for the newcomers, refer to me as they/them."

Gwen nodded, filing that information away.

"Now, tell me," Alessa continued, drumming their knuckles on the table, one arm slung behind their chair, "how do you plan to defeat Lilith? Have you unlocked some secret since last night, when neither our sun nor bullets could harm her?"

Ina hesitated, lacing her fingers together. "No, I don't have a plan for that yet. I hoped discussing this issue with other members of the Cradle might mean we will be able to find a way. Or perhaps," she said, glancing at Feng, "there is secret vampire lore that could help us."

Feng shrugged. "None that I know of."

"So, figuring out how to beat her is the next step. Not actually beating her," Alessa replied.

Ina nodded, lips drawing into a tight line.

"What were her words, when she reformed?" Alessa asked.

"She said that nothing could kill her when her blood fueled the Earth."

"How wonderfully cryptic."

Butterflies fluttered in Gwen's stomach, lifting hope into her chest, and her eyes widened.

"It's not cryptic," Gwen said. "Lilith messed up – she just told us how to beat her."

"What do you mean?" Ina asked, all heads turning to Gwen.

Gwen smiled, ear to ear, chills waving over her skin with excitement. The butterflies in her stomach leapt up through her chest.

"It means we have to free Nikki first," Gwen whispered.

"Repeat that, Gwen?" Ina asked, leaning forward.

"It means we have to free Nikki first," Gwen said louder, smile widening. Excitement bubbled through her body, and she slammed her palms down on the table as she stood. "Ha! It means we have to free Nikki first! Nikki is her descendant, so has her blood, and Nikki is in the Tree of Life. So, her blood is the fuel for all life. She can't be killed while a vampire is in the Tree."

The room was silent, and Gwen looked at each person's face as glee tore through her body. They would save Nikki now. They would free her. She'd have her best friend again.

When she met Ina's stony face, Gwen thrust out a finger and pointed at her, "I told you."

Ina's nostril crinkled with annoyance, and Gwen bounced with joy. She bent her elbow and thrust out her finger, pointing at Ina again and again as she repeated over and over, "I told you! I told you! I told you!"

Chapter Fifty

"GWEN, CALM DOWN," Ina said, jaw tightening as her lips drew into a thin line.

"No, I don't think I will," Gwen replied, smirking. "I told all of you we should get Nikki first, and no one was on my side. On Nikki's side."

"Not from dislike of Nikki – "

"Oh? Really?"

"Don't interrupt me, Gwen. Just sit down and listen!" Ina snapped, rising from her seat, fingertips perched on the table. "You wanted to free Nikki first from selfishness, not because you knew we needed to do so to defeat Lilith. So do not pretend you know more than we do. Secondly, even with this new information, the same issues apply. We don't know how to get her out. We don't know what will happen to the Tree without a vessel."

The steam fizzled from Gwen's body, and she tapped a finger on her cheek, thinking. "Couldn't we get her out the same way we Lilith got out? With some of Xander's blood?"

"Doubtful, since Lilith wove her own spell with Nikki's father's blood to trap her. Even if Xander could release her, I would not ask him to bleed again."

"Pretty sure he would be willing to sacrifice a drop of blood to save his girlfriend."

The faces of the Cradle twitched with various looks of surprise, from widened eyes to lifted eyebrows and opened mouths. So, Ina hadn't told them that part.

Ina pinched the bridge of her nose and sighed, slumping back into her seat.

"She has a point, Gwen," Feng said, angling to face her. "The magic Lilith used to trap Nikki is sure to be different than the one Io used to trap Lilith."

"Hmmm," Gwen replied, dropping into her chair. "So, any ideas on how to get her out?"

"That's not the only issue, as Ina stated," Carmen said, leaning her face against her fist. "Can the Tree survive without someone – or *something* – inside of it? If it cannot be a vampire, then what are we left with? Sacrificing one human a generation to feed the Tree until the end of the Earth?"

The room was silent, brows knit.

"It is an unpleasant idea," Feng began, "but is it less pleasant than being exterminated by Lilith and her followers?"

Alessa straightened. "If it comes to it, I will be the first sacrifice. We should try to find another way to end this, but if there isn't one, I will go in first."

"Alessa –" Hector started, eyes wide.

"No," they replied, bringing their hand up to stop him. "If it must be done, it must be done. And we waste time debating it."

Ina swallowed, and Carmen's eyebrows drew together.

"Yet still, even with a"–Cesar's eyes darted to Alessa– "replacement, we do not know how to get the current vampire out of the Tree. And one point that has so far been neglected is that we do not even know where the Tree *is*."

"I could scry for Nikki," Gwen said,

Carmen scoffed. "If after tens of thousands of years we do not know where it is, the simple magics of a witch won't be able to locate it."

"Well, it's not like it'd hurt anything."

"We won't get anywhere sitting here," Ina said, cutting off Carmen from whatever she was going to say next, mouth hanging open. "We need to disperse as discussed and try to gather information from our allies. We still have each other's phone numbers. Let's check in periodically, even if we haven't figured out anything."

Hesitant, the group nodded their heads and vacated the room, chairs squeaking against the hard wood floors as they pushed back. Alessa stated they would join Ina and her team, a spark of irritation in Gwen's gut that she was just considered a tagalong to whatever Ina was doing.

All of the Peruvian Cradle left, heading back to Caral, where the rest of them would meet them the following night. Ina argued that Xander needed one more day of rest before being moved, and Gwen sighed a breath of relief that she would actually be able to sleep, instead of mobilizing once again.

Adventures were exhausting.

Why do so many stories forget to mention that?

Chapter Fifty-One

THE DRIVE to Caral was dark and quiet, as was the temple exterior. Carmen met them near the entrance, where they exchanged keys and pleasantries. Like John, Carmen sliced a cut in her palm and smoothed it against the stone. The stone absorbed the blood and with a faint rumbling, crunching sound, the stones peeled back into the shape of a doorway, leading them through another entrance.

Gwen expected to climb the temple again, assuming they'd go in the way they came out, but she was grateful for this other route. She had not looked forward to climbing more stairs.

Lit sconces framed the stone hallways, and their footsteps echoed all around them as Carmen led them past the same rooms Gwen and Feng had seen two nights prior.

"How is everyone doing?" Ina asked Carmen as they passed a room where a handful of people sat in somber silence, cleaning bloodstained clothes.

"It has been a tough two days," Carmen said, running a hand through her hair. "There are many bodies to move, many family members to notify...and not many of us left to do it."

"I'm so sorry we did not come in time."

"Even if you had, what could be done? They are strong and determined creatures. We know now what to expect in the future. Do not put too much blame on yourself, cousin."

Ina's jaw tensed, but she nodded.

Carmen led them to an open room, larger than the others, with training dummies bordering the walls. Alessa stood with two others, one male and one female, talking in low tones, weapons strapped behind their leather-armored backs.

Hearing them approach, Alessa turned and said, "Ah – you are here!"

Carmen turned to Ina. "I must prepare the portal room. Alessa will take you."

"Thank you," Ina said, and Carmen left with a solemn nod.

"Ina, Feng, Gwen, Xander," Alessa said, pointing at each in turn then throwing their thumb over their shoulders to indicate the other two they were with, "meet Julian and Elena. They are two of my best warriors and have agreed to join us on the front."

"Pleasure to meet you, cousins," Ina said, giving a head nod so deep it was nearly a bow.

"You as well," Julian replied, mimicking the nod toward Ina and Xander. But he did not show the same respect to Feng and Gwen. Elena searched them with a cocked head, Julian's brow furrowing.

Feng smiled, showing them his pointed teeth.

Julian grimaced and Elena's features smoothed out, hiding her reaction. Gwen stifled her laugh. One of her favorite parts of the last few months was learning that Feng had the same vindictive streak she did.

"We will learn to get along, I am sure of it," Alessa said. "Ultimate evils encourage the strangest bed fellows."

"Mom," Xander said, quiet. "What are they saying?"

"Nothing to worry about, son," Ina replied, putting a reassuring hand on his arm. "They will be joining us. When we get back to Poverty Point, we will put you under the same linguistic spell so you can communicate."

Xander's fingers twitched, and he shoved his hands into his pockets. "Okay."

"He speaks only English? We can speak some. But it may not be so good," Alessa said, switching languages. A small pressure around

Gwen's ears released, the spell no longer bending the words in her head, and her heart thumped with the surprise, not having previously felt the presence of that magic around her.

"Come. Let us go to the portal – Carmen is likely ready for us."

"Lead the way," Ina said, and Alessa stepped in front.

"Gwen, come speak with me," Alessa said when they passed, and Gwen fell into step with them as they walked through the quiet halls.

"You are a witch, yes?" Alessa asked, russet eyes searching. "I saw you fighting. You have the flesh of a human but the...aura of a vampire."

"Love hearing that," Gwen murmured.

"Hm?"

"It's nothing. My relationship with vampires – with sharing their blood – is complicated for me."

"Yes, it would be for me as well, if I were you." They stepped around another corner, moving deeper into the pyramid. "Who is your teacher?"

Gwen bristled, and her chest tightened, retreating. "Myself. Why?"

"You do not use your magic correctly."

"Ugh," Gwen sighed. "People keep saying that but they don't tell me what that even means."

"You need a teacher."

"Yes, that's also something I keep hearing, but no one is stepping up to the plate."

"What plate?"

"The – never mind. You know, like, nobody is offering to be my teacher."

"I see," Alessa said, staring into the distance for a moment. They came to what was once a doorway, the door and bar that had been used to lock it blown from the hinges and now resting against the wall. Bright white light poured from the room into the hall. Alessa turned to Gwen, the illumination highlighting the red in their eyes. "We must find you one. You are strong, but for this war, we need you stronger."

"Well, if you have suggestions, I'm all ears."

Alessa nodded. "I will think on it. I have met few witches before. While I can see when magic is used correctly and when it is not, I do not know how one is taught to use it the right way. Perhaps as our journey progresses, we will find someone who does know."

The group stepped into the portal room from a different entrance than her and Feng had previously exited from. The portal was now more blue than silver.

Carmen wrapped her hands over Alessa's. "Be safe. Be brave, yet smart. And keep in touch."

Alessa nodded. "We will."

"Thank you, all of you." Carmen said, looking at each of them in turn, even though she swallowed hard at thanking a vampire and a witch. "Your presence, your courage, saved lives. We will rebuild, and rejoin the fight stronger than before."

"Until then," Ina said, shaking hands with Carmen before stepping through the portal.

Alessa, Julian, and Elena followed her through. Xander hesitated on the platform, fingers clenching and unclenching.

Gwen, standing behind him, lightly touched his shoulder.

He flinched.

"Hey," Gwen said. "It's going to be okay."

Slowly, Xander nodded and stepped through.

Feng, then Gwen, stepped through the portal, leaving Carmen, Caral, and the blood-stained temple behind them.

Chapter Fifty-Two

NIKKI HEARD Cat scurry and murmur around the Tree, hands raking against the ground. The slice of her nails on the grass sent shivers through Nikki's body, as if delicate fingers trailed her skin. Her mom seemed distressed, anxious. The muffled voices of her mother's keepers rippled through the Tree, but Nikki couldn't understand what they said. By the tone of the voice, they sounded exasperated.

Cat spat out a response in that terse tone Nikki feared as a child, voices rising back and forth in an argument.

Cat's hand rested on the Tree and her voice rang around her, booming. "My child is in there! You will not tell me how to care for these grounds. Mind your own business."

The voices responded, annoyed.

"Just leave me be," Cat pleaded, then her voice twisted with spite. "What does it matter to you what I do in our prison? Go farm people like sheep, or whatever horrible thing it is you do."

A heavy sigh and retreating footsteps.

Cat braced both hands on the Tree, forehead resting on the bark. "Oh, my darling Nicoletta, what are we going to do?"

Royal purple seeped through the Tree, the essence of Cat's consciousness winding into the bark and wood. Nikki expanded her own consciousness, reaching for her mother, if only she could just grasp onto her, she could talk to her –

But her mother's essence oozed like molasses tears, seeping down the inside of the Tree and disappearing into the dark.

Nikki's heart sank, watching the connection to her mom fade, and Cat's hands released the Tree, returning to her cleaning of the grounds.

Nikki reached for Gwen, but could not find her thread. She must've still been resting from the fight, and Nikki's heart thudded hard in her chest, hoping Gwen's wounds would heal without issue.

Several dark red threads erupted from the base below her dangling feet and Nikki startled, heart leaping into her throat. She barely restrained a surprised yelp as it wound around her body, clawed into her consciousness and forcefully dragged her down into and through the Earth. The threads channeled her through the dark black and brown soils of the world until she resurfaced in a mangrove, face to face, or bark to face, with Lilith. The brief moment of excitement she had at finding out where Lilith was, at claiming her thread again, quickly diminished when she saw Lilith's black eyes hot with fury.

Lilith stood knee deep in water, the roots of the mangroves protruding from the surface, leaves and branches filtering the moonlight. Hormin leaned against a tree, the sheathed greatsword at his side.

"There you are," Lilith sneered, lips curling back to show her thick fangs as she gripped the thread between them so tight Nikki could not escape.

Back in her body, Nikki's heart pounded with adrenaline, a dull beat at the back of her mind. "I thought I rid myself of you before, but it must not have been an effective enough cut if they still found me. How else would they know where to look if they didn't have their little spy?'

Lilith's claws dug into the wood, pressure tightening in Nikki's consciousness, an energetic suffocation.

"Nothing to say for yourself?" Lilith asked, leaning closer, voice turning to a growl. "I lost something precious because of you. If you think they have suffered already, wait until you see what I do to them next."

Lilith leaned so close her warm breath gusted over the mangrove. "Your friends and family will suffer ten thousand deaths before I free them from their mortal coil. Not only have you failed to protect them, but you have ensured their pain."

"*Wait –*" Nikki cried, but Lilith stepped back, and as her hand peeled from the Tree, the blood-red thread followed. It pulled from Nikki into Lilith's palm, the sudden yank of energy through her stopping her thoughts.

"Time to ensure you can no longer follow me."

Lilith spread the thread, webbing it between her hands and fingers, and illuminating it with the ethereal glow of pure magic. When the thread glowed full white instead of red, she summoned the fire within her spirit and infused the magic with her hate. Nikki saw Hormin watch with dim fascination, eyes barely widening, hands sliding over the sheath.

The threads burst apart with light, evaporating fragments into the air and shoving Nikki along her bleary blue thread and into her own body, causing her to gasp as her mind and physical selves collided.

Tendrils inched into her mouth and she bit into them, into her lips, writhing against her bonds, her helplessness.

"*Io!*" she cried, numb limbs and fingers uselessly twisting.

Cat's hands rested on the wood. "Darling?"

"*Io!*" Nikki screamed again, flickers of light manifesting around her, sifting like gentle rain.

"*What is it?*" Io responded, distant.

"Darling? I can see you rustling. Please, tell me what is happening," Cat whispered, slinking to her knees.

"*She did it for real this time,*" Nikki said, the cool of Cat's hands somehow steadying on her bark. "*Lilith broke the thread permanently.*"

"*Impossible,*" Io replied. They disappeared, pressure easing in the Tree and light fading.

Nikki heaved several breaths in and out, focusing on the feel of her mother's soft palms, her knees on her protruding roots. Nikki had been so close to being able to track Lilith again. So close to being useful. Now, that opportunity was gone forever.

Nikki's ears popped, and she opened her eyes, the glimmers of Io filling her vision.

"*I cannot find her. The thread is gone.*"

Nikki cursed. *"What are we going to do now? If I can't see her, if I can't tell the others what she is planning, how are we supposed to stop her?"*

Io didn't respond, but an uneasy shifting, like a boat on rocking waters, swirled around Nikki.

"Can you help build the bond between me and Hormin? Or with Vadasz? Or anyone of his crew? We can't do this blind."

Io vibrated in the air.

"Please, Io. Please. We need your help," Nikki begged, filling her inner voice with as much determination and pleading as she could. *"Please don't let her kill everyone."*

Heaviness, like sorrow and regret and... disappointment, emanated from Io.

With a resigned sigh and a fading voice, Io said, *"I will see what I can do."*

Chapter Fifty-Three

"They're back!" Rachel yelled, leaping from a chair placed in front of the portal when Gwen and Feng stepped through.

"Thank the heavens," Daiyu said, rushing to Feng and throwing her arms around him, burying her head in his neck. His arms wrapped around her lean body, and he closed his eyes as he rested his face in her hair.

Rachel stepped beside Gwen, whose eyes traced the room, Theo and Terrance standing beside Xander. Theo's gaze roved over Xander's face, and Terrance had a firm hand on his shoulder, smiling in relief. Xander's head was turned away, so Gwen couldn't see if he shared in their joy or not.

Theo's eyes slid over Xander's shoulder to Gwen. They locked eyes, and the corners of Gwen's mouth quirked up, hesitant. Theo's face smoothed into neutrality and looked back to Xander.

"How bad is it, on a scale of 1 – 10?" Gwen asked.

"100," Rachel replied, arms folded and following Gwen's gaze. "It doesn't help you missed Valentine's Day, too. Did you at least bring something back for her?"

"Oh, shit," Gwen said with a groan. "No, I totally forgot, with the whole fighting an ancient evil and all."

"Fair point." Rachel looked up at Gwen, taking in the cut on her cheek. "We were really worried about you."

"I know," Gwen said, a lump catching in her throat. "I'm sorry."

"Don't apologize to me. I'm only glad you're okay."

"Thanks."

Rachel shot her a quick grin and went to Feng and Daiyu, leaving Gwen standing alone in the humming sanctuary.

John, Ina, and the Peruvians talked near the center, John prepping his frog pipe. When he called Xander over to them, the three friends split apart, Xander heading toward his mom. Terrance looked at Gwen, gave her a small shake of his head, and joined Xander in the center.

Gwen froze in place, Theo's stern eyes upon her, as she approached with steady, sturdy footsteps.

Her neck tilted back as Theo came closer, and her gut twisted with the dark bags under Theo's eyes. Theo crossed her arms, hands splayed on her forearms, nails bitten to shreds. Gwen's heart hammered in her throat. She wanted to reach out, to clasp Theo's hands and smooth salve over her damaged fingers, tuck her hair behind her ears and apologize, but all words stuck in her mouth, all actions frozen in her frayed nerves.

"Nothing to say, huh?" Theo asked.

The words hit Gwen's sternum like a punch, knocking the wind out of her.

"I'm sorry, Theo."

"You should be. You *promised* you wouldn't do that to me."

"I know, but I – I didn't want you to get hurt. I didn't know how else to avoid it."

"And you don't think I don't want *you* to get hurt? That it's not worse sitting here and not knowing when, or even if, you'll come back?"

"I understand why you're upset," Gwen said, straightening, leveling her gaze with Theo. "I'm sorry for hurting you and scaring you, but I won't apologize for the decision I made. It was...horrible, Theo, and I'm not sorry for protecting you from that."

Theo's lips curled. "Well. I'm glad you're alive."

Theo stepped away from her and Gwen shouted, "Theo, wait –"

"Not here," Theo spat, turning on her heel and pointing at Gwen.

"Don't think we're done talking about this. I'm beyond pissed at you. But this is not the time or place to talk about it."

"Fine," Gwen said, watching Theo storm away, back to the center where her brother and friend stood.

John enchanted the Peruvians and Xander with the same language spell. Rachel and the Lius stood beside Gwen, Rachel explaining that he had already done it for her, Terrance, Theo, Daiyu, and Cora the night before. All five of them had traveled to the temple the same night Ina, Feng, and Gwen left, Theo's screams waking everyone else up. They took turns going back to John's house for food and water, using the restrooms at the park when they were open. The hidden doorway to the temple wouldn't open when other people were nearby, so they avoided being noticed by park visitors, of which there were few. Cora was back at the house, waiting for them and taking care of the dog. They brought John's and Terrance's cars, so when the spell was done, Xander and the Peruvians coughing and sneezing away the smoke, they piled into the vehicles and returned to John's home. Gwen shivered against the cold, already missing the warm, balmy air of Peru.

Sunny barked excitedly and wagged his tail when they returned, licking John's palms and bouncing alongside him. Cora greeted Gwen and Ina with a smile and hugs.

"Well done," Cora whispered into Gwen's ear as they embraced. "Everyone's in one piece."

"At least physically."

Cora gave her a sad smile when they pulled apart, hands on Gwen's shoulders. "You know what they say – all will be well in the end. And if it isn't well, it isn't the end yet. Don't worry, Gwen, everyone's heart will be fine."

"Is that a premonition or are you just being encouraging?"

"It is a dream I'm manifesting."

"I don't know if that's supposed to make me feel better or not, then."

Cora smiled, cupping a motherly hand on her cheek and avoiding her cut. "It should."

"I'll take your word for it."

Cora's smile remained as she removed her hand and followed John, the Lius, Terrance, Rachel, and Theo inside, Ina guiding the Peruvians and Xander to the guesthouse.

Torn between two paths, breath frosting in front of her face, Gwen shivered and turned left, icy grass crunching beneath her feet as she walked to the guesthouse.

Ina talked to Alessa, Julian, and Elena on the opposite side of the room, close to the back, while Xander sat with his head hung and hands limp between his knees, staring at the ground.

She grabbed a container of salve from her pack and stepped hard when she walked to him, making sure her approach was heard. "Hey, come with me."

Xander looked up at her, hair lank over his purple and yellow bruised face. He blinked, nodded, and rose to his feet, sluggish.

She guided him to one of the bathrooms and had him sit on a bench beside the shower. Uncapping the salve, the air exploded with the scent of mint, and Gwen's heart twisted at the remembrance of Nikki, at how silly and sad she was about her fangs coming in.

Gwen sighed and smoothed the salve as slow and gentle as she could over Xander's face, though he still flinched with the first touch. Soon, however, his face relaxed as the salve worked its way into his skin, easing over the pains.

After a couple minutes of silence, Xander asked, "She left it, huh?"

"What?" Gwen replied. She followed his gaze down to her finger, where the ring he bought for Nikki gleamed. "Oh." Gwen hesitated, a knot of guilt twisting in her stomach for wearing this ring that wasn't meant for her. "I mean, you broke up didn't you? It probably made her sad to keep wearing it."

"Yeah, sure. I get it," he said, tone harsh and quiet.

"This was a good find, you know," she added, not knowing what else to say, feeling that whatever she did say would be awkward, but wanting to say *something*. "It's an amplifier, made by –"

"Gwen, it's fine. I don't know why I brought it up. I don't even want to talk about it. Just surprised to see it, I guess.

Gwen hummed, but let it rest. Once she was done smoothing the salve over his face she motioned to his shirt and said, "off."

"You don't have –"

"Nope, zip it. Up and off, then turn around."

He stood, and with a wince, pulled the shirt over his head, dropping it to the floor. Gwen gasped.

"What did they do to you?" she breathed, eyeing the wealth of cuts, scratches, and bruises that littered his back.

He huffed out through his nose and moved the bench out so he could sit with his back to her. He leaned forward, elbows on his legs, the wounds stretching as his back bent.

Through the sting at the back of her eyes and the flame in her chest, Gwen swabbed salve over his back, over each red line and misshapen bruise.

"At first, she said to be careful with me," Xander said, quiet. "I thought maybe they wouldn't do...this. But things didn't work out the way she wanted, and she grew frustrated. Every time either of them were upset, I became their punching bag. If I looked at them the wrong way. If I breathed too loud. Or too quiet, and they wanted to make sure I wasn't dead."

"I'm so sorry this happened to you," Gwen said, the crumbles of a scab falling off his back as she rubbed the salve over it. She blinked back the tears in her eyes.

"Yeah," he murmured, then turned to look at her over his shoulder. "Thank you, for coming to save me."

"Of course."

Xander nodded, then hung his head, relaxing his shoulders and letting the soothing balm wind through his muscles. Gwen sat on her knees to smooth the salve over his lower back, the tile of the bathroom cold through her jeans.

They both stood when she finished, and she hissed as he turned, his chest just as damaged as his back. Fine lines cut through his chest hair, along the definition of lean muscle in his abdomen.

"I can do this part," he said, taking the salve from Gwen's frozen hand.

"Right. Of course."

They locked eyes, his long hair hanging in front of them, the longest tendrils reaching past his chin. There was something missing in his gaze, something not quite present, and she wished her salve was strong enough to reach his heart.

He turned away from her with a twitch of his jaw, standing in front of the mirror, looking over the wreckage of his body.

Gwen turned to leave, but with her hand on the doorknob, he said, "She'll forgive you, Gwen."

She looked over her shoulder, and they locked eyes in the mirror's reflection. "Are you sure about that?"

He nodded, swiping the salve across a cut that stretched from his collarbone to his sternum.

"Does that mean you forgive Nikki?"

He paused. "That situation is a little different than this one."

"Is it? Because all Nikki did was try to protect you, and that's why I did what I did to – for – Theo."

Xander sighed, dropping his hands to the sink counter. "I don't know if I forgive her. Everything I feel for her and about what's happened, what is happening, is too tangled up for me to understand. I miss her, but I'm so mad at her." His Adam's apple bobbed, and he cleared his throat. "I suspect I won't know how I really feel until I see her again. If I see her again."

"You will. We all will."

"You sound very sure of that."

"Haven't you heard? That's our next step in this whole shitshow in beating Lilith – getting Nikki out of that damned Tree. And I'll make sure it happens even if it's the last thing I do."

"You shouldn't say that, Gwen."

"Why?"

"No one wants you to go that far – no one wants you to sacrifice yourself. Nikki wouldn't want that either."

"Well, tough shit. Hopefully it won't come to that, but I haven't slept right since she's been gone."

"Me neither."

His admission took the wind out of her sails, and Gwen's ruffled feathers settled. "I don't plan on sacrificing myself. I'm just saying."

"Well don't let Theo hear you 'just saying.'"

"I don't plan on it."

A beat of silence passed, and Gwen flicked a small grin at him. He blinked at her, and his mouth twitched, as if he tried to mimic her expression but couldn't quite figure it out.

Gwen opened the door and shut it quietly behind her. When she turned around, she ran into a body and yelped, startled.

There stood Theo, with her arms crossed and jaw clenched, lips disappearing into a fine, angry line.

Gwen sighed.

"Goddamn it."

Chapter Fifty-Four

"How much of that did you hear?" Gwen asked, trying to step away from the door, but Theo did not budge.

"Enough." Her eyes narrowed. "So, you're gonna disappear again, leave me behind again, to play the hero?"

Gwen's eyes flicked over her shoulder to the door. "Do we really have to talk about it right here?"

"I don't care if Xander hears."

"Well, I do."

They stared at each other, unmoving except for Gwen's curling fingers into her palms.

"Fine," Theo relinquished, spinning on her heel and storming through the guesthouse then out the front door.

Fists clenched and heart pounding, she followed Theo, grabbing a jacket slung over the foot of her bed. She stepped into the brisk night, skin pimpling with the cold as she slid the jacket over her arms.

They walked to the back of the property, the air still and quiet, and Gwen's chest ached with missing the shush of evergreens in the winter breeze, the rustle of fallen leaves and debris, the patter of rain on muddy ground. The night sky was dark and clear, and she wondered when she'd once again see heavy fog clinging to the cold ground, gray clouds that stretched from horizon to horizon.

Theo stopped walking with a huff and faced Gwen.

Seconds as long as minutes passed, staring at each other's dark forms.

"So let me have it then," Gwen said.

Theo's body tightened, but she did not say anything, and Gwen's nails dug into her palms.

"What are you waiting for? I know I messed up, and I'm sure you'd love to explain to me how, so –"

"Do you know how hard it is to be with someone who's in love with someone else?" Theo asked, quiet.

Gwen's mouth popped open, stunned.

"What are you talking about?"

"You," Theo said. "You're in love with Nikki."

Gwen laughed and immediately regretted it, Theo bunching her body tighter together.

"That's ridiculous, Theo. She's my best friend. I would say she's like family except that my family sucks, so she's better than family. But I'm not in love with her."

Theo shook her head. "Every time something is wrong, she's the one you want to talk to. *She's* the one you'll go to the ends of the earth for. Who you'll sacrifice yourself for if you have to. Your willingness to die so that she lives – how do you think that feels? That you'd be okay leaving me, and everyone else, behind?"

"Theo, you've got this all wrong," Gwen said, stepping forward and trying to reach for her hand, but Theo stepped back, dodging her, and Gwen clasped her fist closed in the empty air. Then she dropped her hand, palm slapping against her thigh.

"I don't know how I can explain my relationship with Nikki to you in a way you'll understand. You know my family doesn't, and never did, love me. All throughout my childhood, my sisters picked at me, at my appearance, at my intelligence, at my attention span. At my love with animals. Everything about me was a joke, a disgrace to the family. You know how many times they 'joked' about burning me at the stake? At throwing me in the river to see if I would sink or swim? My parents and Connell just stood there. My grandfather protected me until he died, and Farrell did what he could, but he isn't the most authoritative person in our family, so he really didn't help much.

"All this is to say that Nikki is the only consistent, true person I've had my whole life. We've been together through everything when no one else was there for us. Not only that, but she's the only one who understands how messed up our world is, how hard it is to navigate this wack vampire culture in a world where we have to hide it."

Theo sneered. "You don't really expect me to feel bad for you, do you? Poor rich, magical, woman living in a world most humans only fantasize about."

"I don't expect you to feel bad for me, but I expect you not to minimize me!" Gwen yelled, and the wind lashed around them. Theo startled and stepped back as the breeze pushed her.

Gwen sucked in a deep breath and settled the air around them.

"Look, I won't pretend to know what bullshit you've had to deal with in your life, but I would have given everything to know what unconditional love feels like." Gwen's voice broke, and she cleared it, stilling the lump. "Nikki's the only one who gave me that, my whole life. No matter when I was annoying, or mean, or bonkers, she was there for me. She forgave me, and loved me anyway. And that has always been a two-way street for us.

"You're right, though. Most people fantasize about the lives we have. But if you haven't been able to tell by the nightmare we find ourselves in now, fantasizing about this life is delusional. People see the old wealth, the agelessness, the beauty, and think that's all it is, but it's not even close. You know most vampires die from suicide or homicide? Being a vampire, living with vampires, is a life of betrayal and paranoia. It's wondering who is after what you have, who is trying to kill you in some perverse power grab. It's blood, pain, and death. How anyone glorifies that, I don't understand. And neither does Nikki. She hates it. We both hate the situations we've been born into, but at least I don't have to hurt people to survive." Gwen laughed, pushing her hands through her hair. "My whole 'I'm a badass witch act' is just that – an act, Theo. I've always felt weak and useless and unloved, and frankly I don't know if I would have lived this long without her. I don't know if she would have either. Do you understand yet? I'm not in love with her. I've never been attracted to her or interested her in that way. But we're each other's life lines. We're closer than family. We wouldn't exist without the other. Being without her, knowing she's trapped, it's like...living without part of myself.

"But Theo," Gwen stepped forward and cupped a hand to Theo's cold, tear-streaked cheek, "living without you is like living without air. It's like trying to walk when someone has carved out my heart and there's nothing left to pump my congealing blood. I'm just an empty, fleshy, husk without you."

Gwen's eyes glassed, and Theo's silhouette wavered. "The whole time I was away, I wished you were with me. For the good parts, I mean, not the fighting and the – things I saw. I didn't think of Nikki at all except for when they said we could free her. But I thought of you when I saw the sunset on the Pacific, when I tasted lucuma ice cream, when I felt the warm sun on my skin. When I saw the interiors of the other temples – they're just incredible. But not as incredible as you. Yes, I would sacrifice myself if it meant saving Nikki. I'd do the same for you, except I'd make the world burn tenfold first for any pain it brought you."

Theo hiccupped a laugh, and rested her forehead on Gwen's.

"I'm serious."

"I know," Theo said, warm breath rushing over Gwen's face. "I really wanted to yell at you. To tell you how much you hurt me, how scared I was I'd never see you again. But it's hard to stay mad at you when you talk like this."

"I'm sorry I left you like that. Cora gave me some vague premonition, and it scared me, the idea that you would be hurt. I didn't have a lot of time to think things over, all I knew was that I wanted to keep you safe. I didn't know another way to do that."

"You promised me, though, that you wouldn't ever do that to me. That you'd let me make my own decisions about what I will and will not face. If you get to decide to sacrifice yourself, it's only fair if you give the rest of us the same respect to make our own decisions, too."

Gwen's chest squeezed, and she pushed her hands through Theo's hair, holding her braids away from her face. "I'm sorry. I won't do that again, even if every fiber of my being screams to. I mean it this time. I'm sorry I broke that promise before."

Theo nodded, and Gwen kissed away the streaks of tears on her cheeks, then wrapped her arms around Theo, holding her tight. Theo hugged her back, hands brushing through her hair, cheek resting on her head.

"Nikki isn't the only one who loves you anymore, Gwen. I love you, too."

Gwen smiled, and squeezed her arms tight around Theo, causing Theo to huff hard as the air expelled from her lungs.

"I know. I love you, too."

Chapter Fifty-Five

Everyone was huddled in the living room of the main house, crammed onto furniture, sitting on the floor, or leaning against the walls when they returned. Xander's hair was pulled back in a low ponytail, ringlets dangling in front of his face. He leaned back against the couch, and Gwen smiled at the fact that the salve had eased his pains enough for him to recline.

"Gwen, Theo," Ina said, as the two stood beside the fire, the Lius moving out of the way for them to warm their cold hands. "We've made some decisions in your absence."

"Great, so we know how to get Nikki out?"

"No, but we know who might. The only issue is that we do not know where to find her. Could you ask Nikki? Ask her if Io knows?"

"I can try," Gwen said, rubbing her palms together. "So, who is this person?"

"Her name is Aclima, a daughter of Adam and Eve. Legend says she was the first Made vampire, and that with the fall of the garden, she disappeared. There is no hint of her death." John added, "The last record of her is several millennia old, reporting a sighting of her in Alaska. But that's a huge area, and could be old information."

"Why do we think she knows anything? Especially if she's been MIA for so long."

"We do not know for certain if she does know anything, but having been part of this feud from the beginning, she is the only one on our side who might know where the Tree is or how to get Nikki out."

"And you're certain she is on our side? That she would actually help us?"

Ina's mouth thinned, and her eyes flicked to John. "No, but we know she is not on Lilith's side, so we can hope that means she is on ours. At least enough to give us guidance."

"All right, I'll ask."

All eyes in the room stared at her, and a knot of wood cracked in the fireplace.

"Oh, you mean right now?"

"We don't have much time to waste," Ina said.

"Right. Okay." Gwen glanced at Theo, who nodded, then Gwen cleared her throat, and said, "Hey, Nikki, got a second?"

She looked around the room while she waited, and when Gwen met Xander's eyes, taking in the purple and yellow bruises on his face, the cuts on his skin, Gwen turned around to stare down into the fire.

"Nikki? I need to ask you some questions." A few seconds later, pressure built in the back of her head, the sense of a second silent person on a phone line creeping up her neck.

"Hi, Gwen, What's going on?"

"Hey, Nikki," Gwen said, smiling. "It's been a minute."

"Not a good one, either."

"What do you mean?"

Uncertainty swam in her skull, and Nikki said, *"Lilith broke the bond with me for good. I can't sense her or see her at all anymore."*

"That's not good at all." Dread sank heavy in Gwen's gut.

"What's not good?" Ina asked, but Gwen ignored her.

"Are you with everyone?"

"Oh, yes, we're all in John's living room at Epps."

"I thought we were alone. Why are you facing the fire?"

"Oh, that." Gwen spread her hands in front of the fire, wagging her fingers then smoothing them on her legs. "Well, Xander doesn't want you to see him right now."

"You didn't have to tell her that," Xander said. "Or say it in front of everybody."

A sting zipped through Gwen's mind, and Nikki asked, *"Why?"*

"Um, I'll explain later."

Nikki's presence grew heavy, like a long sigh. *"Fine. Anyway, I'm trying to find the bond with Hormin, Vadasz, or someone with them, but it's difficult."* Nikki paused. *"I'm useless to you now."*

"That's not true. There's information only you have, especially with your direct line to God."

"Io isn't always particularly helpful." Nikki's presence shrank momentarily, then she whispered, *"Sorry, Io, but it's the truth."*

Gwen grinned.

"So – you said you have questions for me?"

"Have you heard of a vampire named Aclima?"

"Io brought her up recently. Said she was the first made vampire and the first daughter of Adam and Eve. Lilith tried to get revenge on them by turning her, but her connection to the made is weaker than those who are Born. She was also repulsed by the transition into a made vampire. Her disgust plus inability to control them is why she hates the Made now."

"Weird bias for someone who rips heads off bodies and drinks corpses dry, but okay."

Nikki chuckled. *"Why do you ask?"*

"We hoped she might know where the Tree is – wait, have *you* asked Io where you are?"

"I have, with no result. They are wavering on how much help to provide us. They are still attached to who Lilith was, before all of this. They're wary of tipping the scales too much and causing unforeseen conse- quences."

"That sucks."

"You're telling me. I think They will come around, though. They just need some time."

"Well, as Ina always tells me, we don't have much time to waste."

"Try giving that argument to an infinite being. It doesn't mean much."

"I suppose it wouldn't."

"Last Io said, They don't know where Aclima is. Let me ask again – I'll be right back."

"Thanks."

Gwen looked at the group over her shoulder, too many eyes upon her back. "She's going to ask Io right now. She'll be back soon."

"How is she?" Xander asked, leaning forward.

"She's as good as she can be."

"Why did you say, 'That's not good'?" Ina asked.

"Lilith permanently broke her bond to the Tree, to Nikki, so we're blind to her movements from here on out."

"Damn," Ina breathed.

"Yeah."

Pressure returned between her ears, and Nikki asked, *"Gwen?"*

"Yes?" she said, snapping her head back to the fire.

"Aclima wove a spell around herself to hide her from Io's gaze. Io does not know where she is, but has not felt her energy redistribute back into the spirit of the world, so believes her to still be alive."

"Well, that's better than nothing."

"Sorry we can't be more helpful."

"Don't worry about it. We'll figure it out. Just work on Io and let me know if you find out anything from other connections."

"I will. Tell Xander..."

"Tell him what?"

"Nothing," Nikki said, presence like a heavy storm cloud. *"Never mind. Please be careful out there, Gwen."*

"I will. Be kind to yourself in there. We're coming for you."

A bittersweet surge filled Gwen's head, then slowly, reluctantly leaving, Nikki's presence slipped away, leaving a hollow ache in Gwen's chest.

With a deep breath and tightening of her fists on her legs, she took one last look at the fire before turning around.

"What did she want to say to me?" Xander asked, breathless, eyes wide and hopeful.

"She didn't tell me," Gwen replied, and Xander's expression shuttered. "I'm sorry."

His jaw ticked, but he shrugged and clasped his hands together, elbows on his knees.

Theo knelt beside her, and Gwen wrapped her fingers through her girlfriend's steady hands, then filled the group in on the rest of her conversation with Nikki.

"Alaska it is, then," Ina said, standing.

"Logistically, how do we do this?" Alessa asked, arm draped over one uplifted knee, sitting in front of the couch where Elena and Julian sat. "Where is this place, how far away is it, how do we find her?"

"We'll have to drive –"

"Drive? To Alaska?" Gwen blurted.

"Now? And in the winter, too?" Terrance asked. "Why can't we just fly? There's gotta be flights to Anchorage or Fairbanks."

Ina shook her head. "It's too risky. Lilith can fly – if she knows which plane we're on.... it's over."

"How is an owl going to take down a whole plane?" Rachel asked.

"Fun new development," Gwen replied. "Lilith can fly without turning into an owl."

Rachel, Theo, and Terrance's mouths popped open.

"Yup. Just sprouts big nasty wings from her normal back and takes off. We saw her carry Hormin and the greatsword, so if they were determined enough, they could down any plane we're on."

"So, we drive to this far away place, and then what?" Alessa asked.

"I can help you there," John said, standing. "One moment."

Gwen looked around the room. "This group keeps getting larger and larger. Are we really all going? Seems that if we wanted to be incognito, we wouldn't travel in such a big group."

"There is strength in numbers," Ina said, "and I won't let Xander out of my sight again. Which means Alessa, Elena, and Julian must join us for their shields."

"We won't sit idly while others go to fight," Feng said, and Daiyu nodded.

"Me neither," Gwen added, glancing at Theo.

"And if I go, she goes," Theo said.

"If my sister goes, so do I," Terrance chimed.

Rachel sighed. "Guess I'll go freeze with the rest of you, too."

All eyes turned to Cora, finger twining in her long hair. "I will go. I think I may be useful as well."

"We're going to need another car," Gwen said as John returned to the room.

"What are we talking about?" he asked, smoothing over an item in his hand, sitting back down at his place on the couch, Sunny on his heels.

"We don't have enough space for everyone to travel," Ina replied.

"Oh, don't worry about that," John said, "you can take mine. I'll ring Joseph and tell him to come back so I'm not stranded out here."

"If you're sure," Ina said, and John nodded. "Thank you. What is that?"

"It's an enchanted Clovis point," John replied, opening his palm to reveal an oblong, pointed chert stone that shone, wisps of ethereal light winding through it. "This, I think, can help you locate her. At least it should, in theory. It was often used to find missing people on hunts, both for animals and vampires. It works by recognizing the blood and intention of the bearer. And you," John said, gaze on Xander, "are a very distant relation of Aclima. It should respond to your blood."

At the furrowed brows and frowns of the group, John said, "Here, I'll demonstrate."

John pricked the edge of the Clovis point on his finger. His blood welled, then spilled over the point and down the stone. He set it flat on his palm, and the stone glowed. "I'm going to ask about my brother first." He clenched his fist around the point, closed his eyes, and after a moment opened both. The Clovis point flashed white, then blue, then swiveled on his palm like the arrow in a compass.

It settled, and he said, "So, my brother is southeast of us. Which is good, since that's where he is supposed to be. Now, I'll ask about my mother."

He closed his fingers and eyes again, and when he opened them, the Clovis point glowed, then spun, settling in a new direction.

"Roughly north. Her house is that way, and since she should be sleeping right now, that makes sense."

John swiped the blood off the Clovis point and extended it out to Xander, who stared at it, then took it with a deep heave of his chest.

"Do I need to bleed on it every time?" he asked, turning it over in his hands, fingers running over the flute at the bottom.

"Not every time, just as long as your blood is on it."

"We can stock up so you don't have to keep cutting yourself," Gwen said, "I always have extra vials with me, we can use some to store your blood."

Xander blanched but nodded.

"It only works for finding relatives who still have blood in them, so if she's dead and desiccated, nothing will happen. No finding long-lost ancestors."

"You should test it," Ina said, gentle.

"How do I do this for someone I'm not familiar with? I mean, I don't even know what she looks like. How do I know it won't direct us to Dad, or some other random blood relative?"

"Think of your father first, then again with Aclima. If the directions are different, that is a good sign," Ina replied.

Leaning forward with elbows on his knees and curls around his face, Xander flipped the stone over in his hands several times. Shifting under the weight of everyone's eyes, he lifted the point to the tip of a finger, and after a couple seconds, pressed it down into his skin.

He followed the same steps as John, and when he opened his palm to show the glowing, blood-streaked stone, it swiveled and stopped, pointing east.

Xander glanced at his mom, and Ina nodded. "He is in that direction. Try again, for Aclima. The first daughter of Adam, the first made vampire. Your very distant aunt."

He sighed, and wrapped his hand around the point. After many seconds, he opened his palm and eyes, and the glow filled the room as the point spun, then settled northwest.

The room stared at it, stunned.

"It appears that the centuries old intel isn't too far off after all," Ina whispered, then lifted her gaze to John. "Thank you. For this, for everything. Everything would have been so much harder without your help."

"Of course," John replied, leaning back with his hands behind his head. "Just do me a favor and kill Lilith, would you?"

"I wish I could say no problem, but I'm sure it will be."

John's grin fell, and silence sat heavy on Gwen's shoulders.

Ina sighed and rubbed her eye. "We'll leave tomorrow night. Get some rest everyone, while you can. Gwen – tell me immediately if you hear any updates from Nikki."

Gwen saluted, "Aye-aye, captain."

Ina's face twitched, eyes crinkling as if amused but mouth thinning with annoyance.

Gwen took it as a win.

Chapter Fifty-Six

DREAD SAT in Gwen's stomach as she climbed into the car the next night, the idea of sitting for another week straight in the car making her want to tear her hair out. Nikki didn't have any news for her, so this was the way they had to go. Even if they did know where Lilith was, there was the question of how they'd transport all their belongings, especially the weapons. Surely those wouldn't get through security. They discussed all potential ways to get to Alaska, but taking a ferry posed similar risks as an airplane. The fastest route was through Canada and they didn't have time to waste.

Gwen was not built for sitting still in a cramped space with so many other people. Cramped spaces with her flock, her animals, was one thing. But they didn't talk as much.

At least now with Xander back she didn't have to ride with Ina. Xander, Ina, and the Peruvians piled into Feng's car. Terrance, Theo, Gwen, and Feng were in Terrance's car, with Daiyu, Rachel, and Cora in John's. While she wasn't in the girl power car, it was a more relaxed space without Ina's stiff hands twisting the leather on the steering wheel, glancing in the rearview mirror at her every five seconds.

Theo, Rachel, Gwen, Daiyu, and Feng agreed to do musical cars at rest stops so they could all get time with their partners, though once day broke, Daiyu and Feng would be separated into different blackout trunks.

"I understand drugs now." Gwen groaned as she laid down in the back seat, the fatigue from battle, anxiety, and an overuse of magic weighing down her bones.

"I don't have any for you, sorry," Theo said, brushing her hair back.

"You want some of my blood?" Feng asked, smirking.

"Ew, no," Gwen replied, "I don't even know if your blood would do anything for me. Just let me sleep forever and I'll be okay." Gwen flopped an arm over her eyes, the rumble of the car over the broken road jostling her body.

In her ever-magnanimous way, at the first rest stop, Ina let them check their phones for ten minutes, doling them out one by one. At all other times they had to be turned off and with Ina so that she could be sure they weren't being tracked. Everyone spread out in different directions, stretching, walking, and checking emails and texts. Terrance, Theo, and Rachel contacted their parents, still pretending to be on an extended vacation. As it didn't seem like the police were tracking them, Gwen supposed their parents bought the lie. Gwen slapped her phone against her palm, wondering who would even care to know if she was well.

Farrell.

Io, she hoped he was okay.

Twining a finger through her hair, she called him, each ringtone magnifying her worry.

"Gwen?" Farrell answered, breathless as if he had run to the phone. "Are you all right?"

"Hey," she replied, "I'm fine. I can't tell you where we are, and I won't have my phone on long for obvious reasons, but I wanted to see how you were doing. I assume you're not trapped in not-Tyee's dungeon."

"No, thankfully not," he said. "Gwen, listen. I'm sorry about what happened. They confronted me when they caught your scent after you visited. I tried to convince them it was nothing. That it was simply the smell of items from your studio I brought into the house. But they did not believe me. I heard them leave that night, snickering about how they were going to capture you. I tried to stop them. Again, I failed. There was little I could do but follow." He took a deep breath. "I wish there was more I could have done."

Gwen couldn't remember a time her brother had spoken so much, let alone apologized to her. "It's okay, I know it wasn't your fault. I appreciate you trying to throw them off course, but they've always been out to get me. There's nothing you could have done to stop them."

Farrell sighed. "Thank you for saying that. But there's something else...they're gone."

"What?"

"Everyone's gone. Tyee, or 'not-Tyee,' as you called her. Plus the Ivarrsons and our sisters. They're gone."

"I don't understand what you mean by 'gone'."

"As in they're not here. I've been the only one home since that night. I haven't heard from anyone, either. I even plucked up the courage to go to both not-Tyee and the Ivarrsons' houses, but both were empty."

"They could've been hiding from you."

"You truly think they would have hidden from me after what I did? I'm surprised they let me get away that night at all."

"They were probably too worried about not-Tyee."

"True, but they never came after me. They aren't here, and they left me alive. Alone, but alive. I haven't even heard from Connall."

"Maybe they're scared of the Irish vampire mafia," Gwen said, trying to lighten the mood despite the foreboding that settled heavy in her gut.

"I don't think that exists."

"Why wouldn't it?"

Farrell sighed. "Will you please tell me what the hell is going on? Everyone has been unpleasantly sparse on details."

Gwen chewed on her lip and glanced at the group, each member strolling back to their cars.

Ina waved to Gwen, motioning for her to return. Gwen held up a finger, asking for one minute.

"Please?" Farrell asked.

With a sigh, Gwen told Farrell everything as succinctly as she could, Ina's disapproving glare boring into her.

Gwen held her ground, talking to Farrell as long as she could, until Ina walked over to her.

"I have to go," she rushed, "but I'll call you as soon as I can."

"No, wait, I want to –"

Gwen hung up as Ina stepped in front of her, arms crossed and lips tight.

"Good call?" Ina asked, extending her hand to get Gwen's phone back.

Gwen nodded, and with a sigh, turned off her phone before handing it over.

"I was talking to my brother," she said, and fell into step with Ina as they walked back to the cars. "He said everyone's gone."

"What does he mean gone?"

Gwen groaned and filled Ina in, the other woman's brows knitting closer together as she talked.

"They could be anywhere," Ina said.

"Yup. Exciting, huh?"

"Ask Nikki if she can find where they are."

"I will," Gwen said. "I need to call him again as soon as possible. We got cut off."

Ina scowled but said, "You can call him tomorrow."

"Yes'm."

Ina looked at her, unamused, and returned to her own vehicle.

In the first round of musical cars, Gwen and Theo were in John's car with Cora. Theo took over the driving for the next stretch, Cora lying down as best she could in the back seat to sleep.

The plains of the Midwest stretched before them, dreary and flat, with little more than the red backlights of the cars in front of them to break the dark.

Theo bit at her nails, the clicking and snipping turning into irritating pinpricks of noise.

Gwen rested her hand on Theo's leg and asked, "What's up?"

Theo snapped a nail off her finger, adjusted her position, and said, "I'm worried about Xander. He's not himself."

"Would you be yourself, after what he went through?"

"No, of course not, but he seems so far away." Theo cleared her throat before continuing. "I thought he'd be relieved to be free, but he doesn't even seem to notice it. It's like he's still stuck there, with Lilith and Hormin."

"He is."

"You're supposed to be helping me feel better, not worse. What if he never comes back?" Theo asked, swiping under her eyes with one hand.

Gwen squeezed Theo's leg. "He will, but it'll just take time. At least until this is all over, and probably even longer than that. He's had a very traumatic experience."

Theo sniffled and nodded.

"In the meantime, we'll be here for him. We'll make sure no one hurts him again, and we'll support him however he needs. That's all we can do right now."

Theo twisted her hands on the wheel. "Life will never be the same again, will it?"

"I don't know. Even if it's not, it doesn't mean that's a bad thing." Gwen tugged one of Theo's hands away from the wheel, and laced her fingers through them. "Let's just focus on one thing at a time. We'll find a way to free Nikki, slaughter Lilith, and we'll worry about what happens after when it's all said and done."

Theo nodded again and sighed, shoulders relaxing.

"I have to talk to Nikki now. Do you mind?"

"No, go for it."

"Thanks." Gwen leaned her head against the cold window, gazing at the abyssal landscape. Conjuring Nikki's pale, sad face in her mind, she asked, "Hey, Nik, you got a sec?"

Chapter Fifty-Seven

No matter how long and hard Nikki thought of Hormin, of his wild eyes and eccentric personality, his vibrant orange thread never appeared again.

Lilith must have severed the Tree's bond to him as well. Interesting that it didn't harm them to have their consciousness unbound from the Tree of Life. Was there no consequence? Or was the effect more subtle?

Nikki hovered in the Tree, turning the situation over in her mind, looking for some angle that could possibly help them. But no matter how many times she thought on it, she came up with no ideas. They were in the dark more than ever. Who knew what damages Lilith and Hormin were causing now, and where.

Nikki had turned her focus to convincing Io to help bind the thread to Vadasz, Aella, or Uase. She could glimpse their glimmering threads, complementary hues of teal, violet, and jade, but her consciousness could not plunge along theirs for long. Before her eyes would open through the nearby vegetation, she would lose their trail and funnel back to her own body.

It had been so easy with Gwen and Lilith. Thanks to Io's help with Gwen's thread and Lilith's connection to the Tree, she could hop to their minds so easily. But finding a thread, then following it to a region, then a specific set of vegetation that was pulled by their energy, was beyond her ability.

Io, at least, was disturbed by Lilith's violence against the Cradle and pockets of humanity she came across. With each ruthless slaughter, Io caved more to Nikki's arguments. Nikki was careful of their push and pull, knowing if she pushed too hard against Io, then the entity would disappear. In their conversations, Nikki dropped comments about the help they needed, about the harm Lilith caused, and how Gwen and the others could stop her, letting the seeds of her argument take root in Io's consciousness. Io was distant when Gwen reached out for her, and Nikki hoped that meant Io was in the ethers, working on strengthening one of the Scythian's bonds to her.

Nikki didn't want to leave the Tree in case Io returned, so when Gwen's thread reached into the base, Nikki only half grasped it. She kept part of her mind in the Tree, while the other barreled to Gwen.

In the half of herself that was with Gwen, she sensed cold night air smothered by heated air conditioning, and the whir of movement.

"Where are you?"

"In the middle of bumfuck nowhere," Gwen replied. "How are you doing?"

"Same old, same old."

"That exciting huh?" Gwen joked. "In other exciting news, not-Tyee as well as my sisters and the Ivarssons have vanished."

"What do you mean 'vanished'?"

"Like poof – gone. Farrell told me they all up and left one day without telling him where they were going. I was hoping you knew. Or could ask Io."

"Things just keep getting worse and worse, don't they?" Nikki thought with a sigh.

"Yeah. But hey, at least we'll be getting you out soon. That's something to look forward to."

"I guess. Though, I feel bad that someone else will have to be the vessel."

"Yeah, that sucks, but I'm just excited to see you again."

"Me too." Nikki pulled herself out of Gwen's body, reconnecting with her own in the Tree. She called to Io, but They were distant.

There was nothing to do but wait.

Chapter Fifty-Eight

The caravan approached a snow-dusted Omaha by the time Nikki got back to Gwen. Gwen and Theo were back with Terrance, the vampires still hiding from the daylight. Gwen and Theo dozed while Terrance pounded energy drink after energy drink.

Nikki's voice jolted Gwen from her sleep. *"Io found your sisters, not-Tyee, and the Ivarssons. The Ivarssons are on a plane over the Atlantic. Not-Tyee and your sisters are in British Columbia and heading north."*

"Where are they all going?" Gwen asked, blinking away the sleep crust in her eyes, the sun blindingly bright against the snow.

"We don't know the Ivarsson's final destination. Io believes Lilith realized she let slip information she shouldn't have when she told you she can't be destroyed as long as a vampire is in the Tree. Io thinks Lilith came to the same conclusion we did, that Aclima is the only one besides herself who knows how to unlock the Tree, so sent not-Tyee and your sisters to stop us from getting that information. I guess her sources also had her last located in the northwest of the continent as well."

"You know, I was really hoping you'd say that they all died of some sudden, inexplicable vampire disease and we wouldn't have to deal with them anymore."

Nikki chuckled, but it wasn't believable. *"I wish it wasn't this way."*

"How are they even locating her? Do they have a magical arrow compass too?"

"I don't know. But considering not-Tyee can split open the Earth, I'm sure she has plenty of other tricks up her sleeve."

Gwen groaned. "In any case, thanks for the head's up. I'll tell Ina at the next stop. She's gonna be thrilled."

"Good luck with that conversation."

Gwen grinned, and Nikki faded from her mind, presence disappearing with a small pop in her ears.

The next stop was at a mall to get sub-zero clothing. Night had not yet clawed its way over the sky, so the vampires remained in the car, blanketed by the parking garage so they could at least get out and stretch.

When asked what clothes they wanted, Feng and Daiyu laughed, saying they would not perish from something as simple as weather.

Lucky them.

The mortals had the most tedious shopping spree, paid for by the seemingly endless funds of the Cradle. They resupplied their water and snacks, and bought layer after layer of special gear for the winter. Alessa, Julian, and Elena's teeth clacked just from the brittle chill in Omaha, so they were sure to be miserable in the frigid, freezing conditions of Alaska, even with their sun summoning.

Gwen filled Ina in on her conversation with Nikki, who replied with little more than, "We must brace ourselves for another battle."

Encouraging words, indeed.

Despite Feng and Daiyu's resistance to weather, Gwen still bought them a few layers. Just because they could resist it didn't mean they wouldn't be uncomfortable, right?

Before they got back on the road, Ina redistributed the phones and Gwen called Farrell again.

"I want to join you," Farrell said.

"You what?"

"I want to join you. I detest sitting here doing nothing while this mess is occurring."

"You know that means becoming enemies with our sisters, right? And most other vampires."

"I know. I've thought about this all day and night. I haven't been able to sleep since we spoke. You know there's no love lost between me and the girls. And I think there would be many vampires against Lilith's scheme of world domination if they knew it was happening. I'm not worried about my reputation. What's right is right. I don't want to live in a world where genocide and slavery is normal."

Gwen's heart squeezed in her chest, like an adoring hug tightened with fear. "I understand. Let me talk to Ina and see where we can meet."

In the next round of musical cars, Gwen, Theo, and Cora ended up with Ina. After a couple minutes of settling in to the new arrangements, Gwen cleared her throat and said, "My brother wants to join us."

"No," Ina replied.

"What do you mean 'no?' You didn't even think about it."

"I don't need to," Ina said, the pleather on the wheel squeaking as her hands twisted around it. "We've reached our vampire quota for this group."

Gwen rolled her eyes. "Yes, having strong, difficult to kill allies against the most evil thing on this earth is just terrible."

"She's not the most evil thing," Cora chimed in.

"Was that supposed to be comforting? Because it wasn't. At all."

"Sorry," Cora said. "Ina, Gwen has a point. There's no reason to avoid letting him join our side if he wants to."

"Except for his blood-thirst," Ina snapped.

"He can control it. Like the Lius do. If Cora isn't getting any bad vibes from this idea, I don't see what your issue is."

"No bad vibes here. Far from it."

"See? Trust the psychic."

"Clairvoyant."

"Sorry," Gwen said.

"How certain are you that he told you the truth? How do you know he didn't betray you and then lie about it? He could be against us, playing on your desperate need for familial love and attention to get to us."

Gwen felt as if Ina punched her in the gut, the wind knocked from her being. How dare she call her out like that? She wasn't *desperate* for her family.

Even though it would be nice to be unconditionally loved by somebody.

"Ina," Cora chided. "Apologize."

Ina sighed. "Fine. Sorry. If you both trust him then I will let him join. But I will not trust him until he proves himself. If he missteps, I will incinerate him without blinking. And we're not going out of our way to get him. He can meet up with us somewhere, or not at all."

"Let me know when and where, and I'll let him know at our next stop."

"We'll have to keep him updated. Hard to say where we're going exactly."

"True. I'll at least let him know we're going to Alaska for now."

Ina nodded, knuckles turning white on the wheel.

Gwen smirked. "Thanks for being so agreeable, for once. You're really growing."

"Don't push me, Gwen," Ina replied through gritted teeth.

"But it's so easy. And so fun."

Ina inhaled deeply and exhaled slowly. Theo put a staying hand on Gwen's knee. Gwen didn't say anything else to irk Ina, but the glee at doing so remained.

Chapter Fifty-Nine

Hours blended into a hazy mix of daylight and darkness, alternating between different cars and companions. They made a last stop before the border crossing at a deserted pullout, huddling in the winter chill under the deep cloak of night. Counting passports, Gwen was the only one without, having never been deemed worthy to join her parents or siblings on their travels. She stiffened at the bitterness crawling through her skin, pretending her stoniness was just from the creeping cold. They piled as many weapons as possible into John's and Cora's cars, putting suitcases and duffel bags in Terrance's, leaving Gwen to huddle in the trunk of the Lius' vehicle. She fluffed some jackets beneath her to cushion her bones, and Ina pulled the blackout cover over her, promising they'd get her out as soon as they could, before closing the trunk.

Gwen imagined Ina had a hidden satisfaction at locking her in the trunk, even though there was no expression on her face indicating that was true.

The car rolled back onto the road, the tires scratching on the gravel before meeting the smooth asphalt. Gwen buried her face in the pillow of jackets and curled tight into a fetal position. She would not let the stirring tempest in her chest ruin their chances of getting into Canada. If they failed, it wouldn't be her fault, for once.

Every time the car slowed, her heart leapt to her throat, wondering if they were finally at the security check point. But each time the car picked up speed again without any voices, and soon her anticipation was so intense, her pulse beat in her ears, drowning out the whir of the car.

Finally, they came to a complete stop, and Gwen covered herself with jackets as best as she could. She heard Ina shift the car into park and roll down her window.

"Good evening, sir," Ina said.

A sniffle, then a deep voice said, "Don't get a lot of travelers this time of night."

"Or season," a second, tired voice added.

"These other cars with you?"

"They are," Ina said.

"Where y'all headed?"

"To Alaska, just taking the scenic route."

"Through Canada, in winter?" the tired one asked.

"Some of us have a fear of flying."

"I see. Y'all got identification?"

"Of course," Ina replied.

A set of footsteps walked around the car, slapping against the road as they moved to the next car in line, and Gwen held her breath as they passed.

The first man, who Gwen deemed Sir Gargle, cleared his throat again, the laminated documents shuffling between hands.

"You okay, son?"

"Huh?" Xander asked.

"Your face. What happened to it?"

"Oh, I, uh, got into a fight?" he answered, voice rising at the end.

Damn it, Xander, Gwen thought. Way to convince nobody.

"Hmmm," Sir Gargle replied. "Ma'am, I'm going to have to ask you to open your trunk."

"Why?"

Gwen stifled her groan. That was also not a response devoid of suspicion.

His throat cleared, and feet shuffled away from the car. "Ma'am, please step out and open the trunk."

Gwen imagined Ina's face pinching in poorly suppressed irritation as the driver door clicked open and another, lighter pair of feet walked around the vehicle, followed by Sir Gargle.

Gwen's heart was near to bursting through her chest, pulsing in her fingertips. What was she supposed to do if he found her? Explode air at him? Say she fell asleep? That she wasn't supposed to be there? Maybe she could say they didn't know her, she was just trying to escape, and then she could meet up with Farrell and –

The trunk opened, and the canvas snapped back.

A flashlight swished from side to side, the muted light pouring through the jackets.

She felt something tug at her hair and ice formed in her gut as it was pulled. Sir Gargle hummed with concern, picked up a lock of her hair, then threw back the clothes. Gwen blinked against the harsh light, the flashlight directly in her eyes, and when they were focused, Sir Gargle's aged, pockmarked face was nearly as surprised as her own.

"Boo!" Gwen blurted, all good sense leaving her body.

Sir Gargle's face twitched through too many expressions: shock, amusement, concern, and worst of all, as his hand dropped to the weapon at his belt, it landed on disciplined fear.

"Miss, I'm gonna need y—"

Feng crashed into his body, slamming the officer to the ground.

"Feng!" Ina cried as Gwen jumped up and out of the trunk, mayhem erupting.

"What?" Feng asked, knees pressed into the officer's back. The officer's arms were wrenched back at painful angles, wrists held in Feng's stone grasp, his legs uselessly flailing against the ground.

Daiyu slithered around from John's car and pounced on the other officer, looping her arms through his armpits and hands resting on the back of his neck, then pushing him to his knees on the ground. His hands waved, trying to swat her, but the more restless he became, the more forceful her stance, until his neck was bent so far, he stared at the ground, his shoulders surely straining in their joints.

"Stop!" Ina yelled again, freezing the group in motion, as everyone had leapt from the cars and surrounded the officers, who still flailed and gasped against the vampires' clutches. "What have you two done?"

"We handled the problem," Feng said, nowhere near breaking a sweat, despite the grand efforts of Sir Gargle beneath him.

"This was not the way to do it."

"I suppose you wanted to try talking," Feng replied, sneering.

"Yes! That's what reasonable people do before they launch into violence. They talk."

"No, that's what fools do. You think there was any way to talk ourselves out of this? You think they wouldn't have checked all the trunks after finding Gwen? Those of us not shot on the spot would have been arrested, and your whole plan to save the world would have ended here and now."

Ina's mouth pinched, and she crossed her arms, exhaling in a huff. "It might not have gone into that worst case scenario. But we'll never know now." Ina took a deep breath and then let out a long exhale. "I don't know what to do with them now."

"We could drink them," Feng said with a smirk.

Ina's face fell. "No, absolutely not."

The officer that Daiyu held, who Gwen nicknamed Mister Weasel, whimpered, "You – you could let us go. We wouldn't tell anyone, right, Travis?"

"Absolutely not, these scum bugs gotta –"

Feng pushed Travis's head down into the ground, gravel filling his mouth, causing him to sputter.

"See? This one isn't agreeable. No way he would've let us go. Even with his life on the line, he won't give in."

"What?" Mister Weasel squeaked. "Please don't kill us. Or me, at least. Please don't kill me!"

"We're not killing anyone," Ina said.

"It's true, my love, we don't want a murder investigation on our heels," Daiyu said.

"And it's wrong," Ina replied, shooting her a dark look.

Rachel piped in. "Don't any of you know some binding spells? Like something that will tie their tongues or prevent them from speaking about what happened? Or any memory erasing spells? I feel like with how many magic users are around, there's gotta be something we could do."

All heads turned to Gwen.

"What?" she sputtered. "How would I know how to do that?"

"You are a witch," Ina said.

"You think I just go around binding people's freedom of speech for fun?"

"How would we know what you can and cannot do? You have lived a life of secrets."

"Well, well, well, look at the pot calling the kettle black."

Ina's mouth puckered and jaw stiffened. While Ina and Gwen stared each other down, the Lius dropped their heads to the necks of their victims.

The gasps of the officers drew Ina and Gwen's attention, and Ina yelled, "No! What are you doing?"

Ina fell to her knees beside Feng and Travis, just as Feng released Travis's neck. Feng sat upright, keeping his knees on the officer's back. Blood dribbled down his chin onto his shirt.

Daiyu released her fangs from Sir Weasel, who shook and shivered as the blood ran down his neck.

In tandem, the Lius bit into their own wrists and dripped a few drops of blood into the reluctant mouths of the officers, grasping their jaws to force their mouths open.

The officers sputtered and spit, blood staining their lips and chins.

"Now we'll always know where to find you," Daiyu said.

"If you report us, follow us, or cause us any trouble at all, we will come after you and everyone you hold precious," Feng finished, nose barely an inch from Travis's wide, horrified face.

"Do you understand?" Daiyu asked.

Mister Weasel nodded and whimpered, while Sir Gargle cleared his throat and whispered, "Yes."

"Good," Feng said, pushing Sir Gargle back and letting him stand. "Now, let us through."

Travis looked at the other man in Daiyu's grip.

"I'll release him once you open the gates and let the cars pass," Daiyu said through glistening red lips.

Travis nodded and stumbled over his feet as he ran to the station, releasing the barricade so it swung open.

Everyone else piled into the cars and drove into Canada, Daiyu walking her captive behind them.

Once they were all through and Daiyu back in Cora's car, they continued the trek through the wintry north, silent except for Ina's twisting hands wringing the stiff leather of the wheel.

Eager to break the uneasy quiet, Gwen said, "Well, that could have gone better."

Ina glared at her through the rearview mirror. "Maybe next time you should find something better to say than 'boo' when confronted by an officer."

"You're blaming me? You're the front lady, and you acted so weird."

"I did not."

"Did so."

"No, I did –"

"Mom, Gwen, stop it," Xander said, "It doesn't matter now. It's over. If I didn't look so...damaged, we probably could have gotten through fine."

Gwen's heart plummeted, remembering how Cora asked her not to give in to fighting with Ina. Combined with the dejected tone of Xander's voice, Gwen changed the subject. "Don't blame yourself. It's not your fault."

"On this, the witch and I agree."

A beat of silence passed, and Ina called Feng through the Bluetooth in the car.

"Going to scold me?" Feng asked, when he picked up.

"Not this time. As my son said, what's done is done, although I do think that could have gone better."

"Yes, I do wonder, what did you say to make him so suspicious?"

The leather squeaked beneath Ina's hands again, and she said, "I didn't say anything to make him suspicious."

Feng chuckled, but didn't goad her.

"When we cross into Alaska, let's try it again. Hopefully, things will go better. I'm wondering, how do we know they won't report us anyway? They might have just thought you and Daiyu were mad. Not supernatural."

"Mmm," Feng said. "We don't have to worry. I could taste it."

"You could what?"

"Taste it. Their fear, their acceptance. In a few months, it will be nothing more than a bad dream to them. And in a few years, they'll wonder if it was even real."

"The more I learn about vampires, the more disgusted I am."

Feng paused, and Gwen imagined him stiffening in the other car. "You're welcome," he said, then hung up. Gwen didn't know if it was a sincere response or not.

"You really should be nicer to your allies," Gwen chided.

"I don't need advice from you."

"Apparently, you do. I mean, I understand not holding your tongue —"

"You don't say?"

"But there's no point fighting internally. The Lius have saved us over and over again."

"Doesn't change the fact that they're vampires. They hunt humans. Disturb the natural order."

Gwen groaned. "You are such a bigot."

"Excuse me?" Ina asked, voice rising to a yell.

Xander groaned and pinched the bridge of his nose. "For the love of God, or Io, or whatever, please stop bickering for once."

Gwen leaned back in the hatch of the SUV, looking at the heads of the Peruvians who sat in the back seat. "You three are awfully quiet. What do you think about what just happened?"

Alessa looked at her over their shoulder. "We are here to shield the son of Adam, to fight Lilith. We are not here to judge the methods of how it is done."

"True neutral, I like it," Gwen said, and settled back down in the trunk, wondering what the conversations in the other cars were like. She imagined Rachel asking Daiyu all kinds of questions about other vampiric sanguine abilities, while Terrance and Theo listened. In the other car, perhaps Feng was complaining about Ina while Cora defended her. Or maybe Cora agreed with Feng that Ina was too harsh.

In either case, Gwen was sure being in another car would be more fun than this one.

At the next stop, they played another round of musical cars, the Lius preparing for the sunrise and hiding in the blackout of a trunk while Gwen joined Theo in Cora's car. Before Ina snatched her phone away, Gwen called Farrell, who was already on the road northward. They agreed to stay in touch as much as they could to meet up, with the Clovis point turning ever westward the more north they traveled.

Days and nights blended together, restlessness filling everyone's bones, leading to anxious tapping, leg jiggling, and pointless bickering to release some of the pent-up energy. But nothing of consequence happened as they traversed the snowy and icy terrain of Canada, winding through flatlands and mountains, enduring sleet and sunshine, until they finally reached the Alaskan border.

Xander's cuts and bruises were less noticeable thanks to Gwen's salve, and they agreed for this round of security to keep him in the back-seat where his wounds would be less obvious, obscured more by shad-ows, even if a flashlight flicked in his direction.

Gwen hunkered down again in the trunk while everyone had their passports checked, and they got back into the United States without another bloody incident, much to everyone's relief. Losing track of time as the sun and moon chased each other through the sky, Gwen vowed to come back in another time of her life, to enjoy the varied scenery, the change in vegetation, that she could not adequately appreciate as cooped up as she currently was. Worries about the future, and about Nikki, swam through her mind, as Nikki seemed more distant with each passing day. As the confrontation with Lilith and not-Tyee grew farther away, the unknowns grew, and it was difficult to maintain the glimmer of hope that this ragtag team could save the world.

It seemed everyone else was bogged down by similar thoughts, as faces grew long and weary, sentences became terse, and gazes turned ever to the horizon, to the road ahead.

Chapter Sixty

FINALLY, just as it seemed like they had entered a limbo where they'd be on the road forever, they made it to Fairbanks. After experiencing open roads and endless vegetation for so long, Gwen was surprised to see an actual city. She knew she shouldn't have been. Even more surprising was her relief at the sight of buildings more than one story tall, of the paved roads and sidewalks piled high with snow. She never would have guessed civilization would bring her such relief.

The hot cocoa in a heated café was even more of a blessing, as they all settled in to stiff chairs around a wooden table. With baggy eyes, they sipped at their drinks, except the vampires, all somehow fatigued from sitting for days on end, watching the scenery pass. Gwen wrapped her hands around the porcelain mug, grateful to feel something besides plastic or paper against her skin.

Ina and Cora called hotels, looking for places with availability while the rest waited. Once they had chosen a destination, the group grabbed extra hot drinks and pastries, then piled back into the vehicles. They were able to reserve two suites, so although there wasn't complete privacy, there was enough. Ina, Xander, Cora, and the Peruvians shared one suite, while everyone else took the other.

Thankfully, Ina didn't summon a meeting after they checked in, but let everyone eat and rest on real beds, saying they'd reconvene to discuss their next steps the following night. The humans in Gwen's suite all ordered room service, too tired to find somewhere else to eat, wanting nothing more than to curl under real covers, feel an actual pillow beneath their heads.

While they waited for food, Gwen called Farrell, telling him where they were. To her third surprise of the evening, he was already in Alaska, and would be in Fairbanks the next day. Gwen stuffed her face with French fries and a plant-based burger. Satisfied both physically because of the food and mentally because her brother was safe and nearby, she curled into bed and between Theo's arms, sleeping the deepest, blackest sleep she'd had in what felt like eons.

Their sleep schedules were mixed the next day, as the humans went to bed early in their exhaustion. The Lius forced themselves to stay awake until sunrise, explaining how they wanted to enjoy the longer nights while they lasted. Ina waited until the late evening, when everyone was awake, to call a meeting in the restaurant on the bottom floor of the hotel to talk about their next steps. Farrell continued to send updates, anxiety humming in Gwen's veins as he grew closer, estimating he would be there around midnight. After the long, deep sleep in a real bed, Gwen's bones were less stiff, her muscles less sore, and she made her second vow of the journey – that once this was said and done, once Lilith was defeated, she would never again sleep overnight in a car.

As the day wore on, Gwen's legs jumped more and more, fingers tapping against whatever surface was nearest – a table, an armrest, a mug between her hands. She checked her phone so often, waiting for Farrell to say he had arrived, even though she knew he wouldn't during the daylight hours, to the point where Theo took her phone away from her. But despite the group's attempts at distracting her, her mind could not stop spiraling to him, the one brother who had, when it came down to it, rejected their family and sided with her.

Even though he had been the only one to ever stick up for her, she would never have dreamed that he would choose what was right, would choose *her*, over loyalty to the rest of the family.

It made her heart swell with so many emotions – joy, pride, worry at the expectation – that it brought tears to her eyes if she lingered on the thoughts too long.

Night unfurled over them like a downy blanket, and when the Lius were up everyone gathered in one suite. Shortly after Gwen received that call from Farrell saying he was in the hotel lobby, and Gwen's leaping heart jolted her to her feet. With a stammered shout at the others that her brother was there, she ran from the room and down the stairs to the lobby, skidding to a halt a few feet before his tall frame.

He stood as still as a statue, hands in his pockets, face turned toward the sliding glass doors, reflecting the interior against the dark of night.

Slowly, his head turned toward Gwen, and even slower, the corners of his mouth tilted upward.

"Hello, little sister," he said.

"Hi, big brother," she responded, throat tightening around the words. Her fingers twitched. She knew her family wasn't affectionate – she could count on one hand the amount of times anyone had touched her with love – she knew they weren't huggers, and yet...

She threw herself at Farrell, wrapping her arms around him and squeezing with all her might, knowing that even with all her strength, she couldn't hurt him. She buried her face in his shirt, breathing in the familiar, ancient, frost-dusted mossy forests, and wondering if maybe this meant that when this was all over, she would have someone to call family.

Farrell chuckled, and all doubts about her forward behavior vanished as his arms wrapped around her, his head resting on hers, seeming to take in the comfort of her scent, too.

"I'm so glad you're here," Gwen said, giving him one last squeeze before pulling back, blinking away the moisture in her eyes. "I was worried about you, on the road all by yourself."

Farrell put a hand on her shoulder and said, "Everything was fine. One could say that the coven has put me in the rearview mirror."

Gwen chuckled and wrapped one hand through his, tugging him to the hallway. "Come on, let's get you settled in and over to meet every-one. Be warned, Ina can be...difficult. Especially toward vampires."

"Oh?" Farrell asked, grabbing his suitcase and following her through the hotel, keeping his hand in hers. While they walked, Gwen filled him in on their motley crew, who and what they were, Farrell's face becoming more drawn, losing its good humor.

"Out of the flame and into the frying pan," he muttered.

Gwen gave his hand a reassuring squeeze. "They've learned to get along with, and dare I say, even *like* and trust the Lius. I'm sure they'll come around to you too."

"And what about you?"

"Ina and I don't really get along, but it's fine with Alessa and the others. With Ina, our personalities just clash." Gwen shrugged, and let them into the suite he'd be sharing with her and the others. Once they dropped his belongings, they crossed the hall to the other suite.

"Ready to join the madness?" Gwen asked, fist raised to knock.

"My darling sister," Farrell said, attempting a grin, "as a vampire, madness might as well be my middle name. Let's do this."

Gwen smiled and knocked, rocking on her feet, waiting for the others to let them in.

Chapter Sixty-One

Nikki followed the tangle of the Scythians' purple and teal threads through the earth over and over again, until finally her consciousness came to rest without being snapped back into her physical body.

Pride swelled in that distant heart, brushing against her mind, at finally making progress.

But when she focused on the threads, they skittered away from her, outside the tree she had traveled to. She couldn't see or hear them now. There were lines of color, the vibrations of noise, but nothing distinct that she could make out.

"What am I supposed to do now?" she thought, frustrated as the threads shifted around her.

The sunlike warmth of Io glimmered in the dark.

"Reach," Io said. *"Listen."*

"I'm trying, that's the problem."

"You restrict yourself to one, when you should be of many."

"Can you be more specific?"

"You remain in one trunk, one tree. Yet, the forest is connected. Disperse yourself amongst it. Become the woods. Feel the vibration of their words against your foliage."

"You make it sound so easy."

"It is, once you learn to let go of the individual."

Nikki's body released a tense sigh while her consciousness focused on itself, carefully unweaving from the Scythians while trying to remain grounded, resisting the pull back into her body. Once she could no longer feel her physical body, Nikki focused on the tree she was within, the exhalation of oxygen and intake of carbon dioxide to and from the leaves, the upward movement of water and downward flow of sugar in the veins.

With one part of her mind, she followed the exchange of gas from the leaves, where they overlapped with neighboring trees. With the other part, she followed the sugar down to the roots, where they entangled with mycorrhizae and other roots.

Tree by tree, Nikki breathed from leaf to leaf, and crawled from root to root, slow and precise to prevent losing her connection to these woods.

Soon, she tapped into the larger network and with a rush like being sucked into a vacuum, her mind was pulled into hundreds of shrubs and trees, their exchange in the air and soil binding them all together, binding Nikki to them. Her mind split into dozens, then hundreds of different organisms. She almost lost herself in the sudden and severe fracturing of her consciousness, cracking into innumerable pieces like broken glass. Nikki fought to maintain awareness of herself as sensations of the forest crashed through her, the push of wind on each tree trunk, the slant of moonlight on every leaf, the scurry of insects through low-growing shrubs. Her mind scrambled to make sense of the cacophony of unfamiliar sensations and a whole new way of being. She focused on tying all the threads of the forest together, and just when she thought she would lose herself entirely the pieces clicked into place, and she wasn't hundreds of beings, she was the larger system composed of all of them.

She breathed with the whole forest.

Felt the skitter of insects across bark and foliage, worms between roots.

Rode with the intake and output of nutrients in the dirt, the roots, the fungi.

She was many beings at once, and yet, somehow, only one.

Just the pulse of the forest, stretching over dozens of acres.

When the Scythians spoke, their voices carried on the air and pushed against the plants closest to them until the forest absorbed them. As their footsteps fell softly over her roots, she traced their movements. She could not see them with her eyes, but could sense their shapes through the vibrations of the forest, and their voices transmuted from simple background noise to words.

"...camp," Aella said.

"Soon. There are some hours of night yet remaining," Vadasz responded.

They were silent for a long time after that, traipsing through the forest without conversation. Nikki shifted her web of consciousness to follow their footsteps. The Scythians found a stand of hollowed out trees to spend the day in, and once thick canvas was spread over the openings to dull the sunlight that would filter through, they sat around a small fire, sucking blood from unsuspecting rodents.

"So much work, for such a little trinket," Aella groaned, stretching out her legs.

Uase paused his blood drinking to grunt in agreement.

"A powerful little trinket," Vadasz corrected. "It was foolish to think we'd find the ring so easily in such a vast world."

"As long as we get the reward promised, I don't care how long it takes."

"But the Mother does. The sooner she can dispel the magic from the boy, the sooner she gets her long-awaited vengeance. The sooner she can end the transference of his m –"

"Yes, yes, I've heard her speech too. The sooner she can remove his magic, the sooner Adam's bloodline ends. Though, they've been rather harmless the last dozen or so generations. Doing nothing greater for the world, focused on their own little lives."

"Perhaps they do not know what they could do if they put their minds to it. Long past are the days of kings, let alone great ones."

Aella tsked. "A shame. I preferred those times."

Uase grunted, tossing a desiccated rat over his shoulder.

"We all do," Vadasz said. "Those days will be upon us again once

Lilith destroys the Cradle and ends Adam's bloodline. Our kind will be kings and queens, with Lilith as goddess over all."

Aella sighed. "Then let's hope we find the Ring of Dispel soon."

"Every clue we eliminate, the closer we are to finding it. Patience, sister. We will retrieve it and receive the promised relics."

Aella rose to her feet and dusted the dirt from her leather armor. "I'm going to sleep before day fully breaks. Don't keep me up with chatter."

Uase grunted, and Vadasz chuckled. "No risk of that."

The Scythians settled in for the day, and as their breaths deepened, Nikki unwound herself from the weave of the forest, pulling back from the leaves and roots into one tree. Her awareness of her surroundings changed, from a vast network to a dozen individuals to just herself, the pull of her body yanked her consciousness back through the earth and into herself.

Nikki blinked in the dark of the Tree, the change from feeling interconnected with the earth, to feeling not just each part of the whole, but the whole itself, back into only being her, this small, singular being, shocked her mind. When she was the forest, she was outside of time, experiencing space and life in a whole new way. There had been the breath of the whole forest, the pulse of nutrients through the earth into each plant, and now there was only her heartbeat, her one set of eyes, blinded.

Her isolated heart dropped into her stomach at the loss.

Would she ever be the same, knowing what it was like being both the parts and the whole of a natural system?

Blinking in the darkness, glimmers of gold, silver, bronze, and white filtered into her vision as Io's presence grew. Io's warmth spread throughout her body, and Nikki became more grounded in herself, the feeling of being the forest fading like a dream, although part of her yearned to go back to it.

"You did well. It took Lilith many decades to bypass her rage in order to accomplish such a feat."

"Thanks. It was...amazing. Even that word feels too weak. It was indescribable."

"Yes, I imagine it would be, as human consciousness was not designed to interpret the world through a forest's eyes."

The loss sank deeper into Nikki at Io's words, and to shake the feeling from her mind, she shifted her thoughts to the Scythians.

Where were they?

She hadn't sensed they carried large packs, nor were their footsteps heavy enough to indicate wearing thick clothing. If they were human, she would have guessed they were somewhere warm, but with vampires being able to tolerate a wider range of temperatures, all she could surmise was that they were not in the arctic or Antarctic.

But they ate free roaming rodents, which meant it had to be warmer.

Were they somewhere in the Southern Hemisphere?

Distracted as she was by breathing and seeing as the forest, she hadn't thought to sense the shape of the leaves. They weren't needles, which meant they weren't evergreen, but were they broadleaves? Maples? Poplar?

She didn't know.

Maybe she could travel back and figure it out.

But she had other questions that needed answers first.

"Io – what's the Ring of Dispel?"

Io flickered in the space around her, a hesitation.

"An ancient relic, intended to dispel magic. It was typically used to remove curses or negate the effects of a potion."

"It sounds like Lilith wants to use it on Xander. Would it remove the boons he has from being Adam's descendant? Or from having the blood of the Cradle?"

"I do not know if it would work on inherited magic. That may be wishful thinking on Lilith's part."

"But what if it does work? What would happen to him?"

"If it does work, and if it could remove both blessings, then he would effectively be mortal. She could drink his blood without consequence." Io paused, a heaviness settling in the air as the glimmers stilled. *"And Adam's bloodline would forever be gone from the Earth."*

Ice crept over Nikki's skin. *"She'd kill him."*

"I do not know if she would. But she could."

"I know she would, if she could. That's what the Scythians were talking about." Nikki heaved a sigh, clenching the muscles in her abdomen and thighs, trying to move even a little bit. Doom crawled closer, and still she was trapped.

Useless.

"So, we either need to find the ring first or kill Lilith before she can put it on Xander." Nikki exhaled a defeated laugh, fine roots edging to the corners of her lips. She did not bite them off, but let their earthy taste fill her mouth.

They were only harmless roots.

"Must Lilith be killed?" Io asked, sorrowful. The glimmers dimmed, fading into the dark.

"I don't see another way to stop this, unless you have some ideas."

But Io was gone, and she received no response.

"Cool, thanks," Nikki thought, hanging her head.

After a few minutes of silence, mulling over this new information, still wishing she could feel the rush of wind on her leaves, the feel of voices against her bark, she decided to reach out to Gwen.

They should know what she'd learned. Maybe the Cradle would know where the ring was, and would know how to stop Lilith from finding it. Before it was too late.

Chapter Sixty-Two

Ina did not look happy. Her lips pinched into a thin line, and she sat rigid as rock, all muscles tensed. She tried to act normal, but her gaze flitted back to Farrell every few seconds. Despite how he helped them escape, she was clearly uncomfortable with an unfamiliar vampire in her midst.

Her discomfort made Gwen smirk.

As soon as they'd walked through the door to the hotel suite, Gwen had introduced her brother to everyone, with even the Peruvians being more welcoming than Ina. To Gwen's surprise, Farell spoke Spanish, and she wondered what else she didn't know about him. She supposed when one had centuries of life to live, learning languages was a good pastime. Farrell's hand wrapped around Alessa's in greeting, their gazes lingering for a little too long. His gaze roved over Alessa's muscular form, their thick hair, and a blush rose to their cheeks before they cleared their throat and looked away from Farrell.

Rachel's mouth popped open upon seeing Gwen's brother, and Gwen could see the gears in her mind turning, wanting to bombard him with questions. But Terrance nudged her, snapping her out of her reverie, and she held her tongue to focus on the discussion before them.

Though Gwen was sure Farrell would be bombarded with questions later.

Gwen glanced at Theo, but whatever spell Farrell had cast over her the first time was no longer evident in her expression. Maybe she was used to the beauty of vampires now.

"So," Ina began, her hands turning white as she squeezed them together in her lap, "we've been making inquiries. The Clovis point indicates a northwest direction from here, but we are running out of travel roads. Looking at maps and talking with the locals, it seems Aclima is hiding somewhere in the Brooks Mountain Range. There is a small town north of here in the mountains, Wiseman, that I propose we travel to and make our base before heading out on foot to find her."

"You want us to walk through an entire mountain range, in Alaska, in winter, to find one vampire?" Rachel asked, eyebrows raised.

"It shouldn't be an entire mountain range, but yes, that is the gist. That is why we stocked up on winter supplies in Omaha. I don't expect everyone to go, as we will need people to stay behind and be a point of contact to the outside world in case we go missing. We can make further inquiries in Wiseman. Maybe the locals have rumors or legends of a creature in the mountains."

"And maybe we'll spot our sisters and not-Tyee, who we can follow," Gwen said.

"That is the least ideal option, but yes," Ina replied. "I doubt we'd be able to follow them without being noticed, and I'd rather not have another confrontation with them, but if we see them, then we may know we are on the right path."

"And once we find this Aclima, what do we do?" Alessa asked.

Ina's stiff shoulders shrugged. "That depends on Aclima. I don't know what to expect of her personality or her motivations. Maybe she'll be eager to help us, or maybe she'll need convincing."

Alessa grunted in understanding, and the conversation dwindled into the immediate logistics of leaving this hotel and planning for the trip forward.

"Why does Ina look so upset?" Nikki asked, her voice a faint whisper in her head.

Gwen startled, Farrell stiffening and Theo jumping beside her in response.

"Oh, hey, Nik," Gwen replied, and all heads snapped in her direction. "Farrell's here, now. I think Ina doesn't like how many vampires there are."

Ina's mouth narrowed further, and Gwen turned her head to Farrell so Nikki could see him.

Farrell's eyebrows quirked, his deep green eyes sparkling with curiosity, but he said, "Hey, Nikki."

"I'm happily surprised to see him. I didn't expect any of your family to stick with us."

"She says 'hi', too."

Something in her face must have given away her lie because Farrell looked at her with disbelief. But he didn't call her out on it, just continued to stare at her expectantly. As did everyone else.

"So, what can we do ya for, Nik? How's the Tree treating you?"

"I finally found the Scythians."

"That's great! Where are they?"

"I don't know."

Ina cleared her throat. "Care to fill us in?"

"Have you ever tried having more than one conversation at a time? It's hard."

"Never too late to practice your multitasking abilities."

"I can multitask wonderfully, thank you." Gwen's gaze flicked to Xander, and something hopeful yet full of pain gleamed in his eyes, tugging at Gwen's heartstrings. "All right, I'll try to do this more efficiently."

Nikki sent her thoughts to Gwen's mind, and Gwen repeated them aloud to the group on the condition that no one interrupt or ask questions until Nikki finished explaining. Gwen watched everyone's faces shift with growing horror or defeat, or some twisted combination of both, as Nikki explained how she didn't know where the Scythians were, except somewhere likely in the southern hemisphere. But she did know what they were looking for. Ina's face grew paler than Gwen had ever seen when it was revealed, filling Gwen's stomach with a cold pool of dread. To Gwen's surprise, rather than his face dawning with fear at what could be done to him, Xander's face fell flat, showing less emotion than a statue.

She had never seen his face so lifeless, and that was more troublesome than Ina's drained expression.

Did he no longer care what happened to him? Did he think his chances of survival were so slim?

Gwen felt Nikki's crushing twist of hurt as they watched Xander, and Gwen averted her gaze to spare them both from seeing his pain.

"I'll check in later," Nikki said, fading and sorrowful. *"Once you all have had time to process and discuss. I'm going to see if I can get a more precise location on the Scythians."*

"Okay, Nik," Gwen replied, words of well wishes turning to ash in her mouth. What could she say to her trapped friend? The weight of the room crushed her optimism, her desire to add levity to dire situations.

"Will it work as Nikki fears?" Gwen asked.

Ina stared into the distance, thinking for several moments before she said, "I don't know much about this artifact. But I doubt it is nuanced enough to take away only one, or only part of a blessing. Do you know anything of it?" Ina asked the Peruvians.

They shook their heads, and Julian answered, "We know little of this ring. I was not even convinced it was real until now."

"Maybe it isn't," Feng added. "Maybe they're on a wild goose chase."

"Yes, that's the best-case scenario. We can hope for it, but not plan on it. We have to assume it would erase both the blessings from the Cradle and from Adam if she were able to put it on Xander," Ina said, voice tight as she tried to keep it from shaking. Cora put a comforting hand on her back.

"But what can we do about it?" Feng asked. "We don't know where it is, and we're across the world from the Scythians."

"We can't do anything except keep Xander safe and as far away from the ring as possible. Hopefully Nikki can keep watching them and let us know if they find it, if they seem to be getting close to us."

"I don't think that's important," Xander said, so quiet everyone leaned forward. "Keeping me safe, I mean. Wasn't the purpose of keeping me away from vampires to prevent Lilith from escaping? Well, she's free now, so what's the need to make sure I'm away from her? What else can she do to me?"

Ina's mouth popped open, her eyes wide. "She can kill you."

"Right, but I don't see why that's important anymore. The worst that could happen with my blood has already happened. The focus now should be on preventing things getting any worse. By that, I mean stopping her from turning humanity into slaves by any means necessary. If I'm a casualty, then so be it. I wouldn't be the first one, and I probably won't be the last."

Gwen was frozen in place, Theo stiff beside her. Everyone stared at Xander, stunned, but none more so than Ina, whose eyes glistened with tears. Swallowing thickly before she spoke, she asked, "What are you saying?"

Xander stood and took a deep breath. "I'm saying if it's a choice between killing her or letting me die, then let me die. Let her put the ring on me and use it as an opportunity. My blood doesn't matter anymore."

Gwen's vision glassed, and she was grateful Nikki had left before she heard this. It would have shattered her already cracked heart.

Xander turned to leave, fingers twitching at his sides, and Ina grasped his arm. "I won't let you die, I won't let harm –"

"Your blood does matter, son of Adam," Alessa interrupted. "What you carry, what you are, is more important than you could ever know. The grace you carry, the light you represent, gives many of us purpose. We can't let Adam's bloodline disappear from the Earth. It is hope. It is a reminder of all things good in this world."

Xander yanked his arm from his mom's grip and stared down at Alessa, scrunched on the floor. "But that's just the point! Adam's bloodline doesn't matter anymore now that Lilith is free. And bloodlines die off all the time. Since everyone failed at keeping it from Lilith, what's the point of it anymore? What's the point of *me*? You all value me for what I am, not *who* I am, and that's not how I want to live." Xander shot his mom a hard glare. "Did you even love Dad, really, for who he is? Or were you just trying to protect what he is, like he's nothing more than an asset? Is that all I am to you?"

"Of course not, Xander, I love you so –" Ina stretched out to grab for him again but he reeled back, out of her reach.

"Don't," he seethed. "Just don't. I don't want to hear it. I don't want you to touch me." Xander looked around the room, at the sad and horrified faces of his friends, of the strangers. His cheeks reddened, and he clenched his fists and closed his eyes, taking a deep breath. When he opened them again, he said, "Just...leave me be. Stop focusing on me so much. I don't matter in this. Not anymore."

He turned on his heel and swept from the room, running a hand through his long hair in the way Gwen knew Nikki adored. As the door shut behind him, all life drained from the room, leaving a vacuum of silence, all staring at the space he had just occupied.

Theo snapped at her brother, jolting everyone out of the stunned silence. "Go after him!"

"Right," Terrance said with a nod, coming back to reality, untangling from Rachel and following Xander out of the suite.

Gwen looked to Ina, who stared at the closed door where her son had left, overhead lights glistening in the tears streaking down her cheeks.

Chapter Sixty-Three

After the meeting, Theo joined Terrance and Xander, gnawing on her fingernails as she disappeared from view. Farrell and Gwen meandered through the hotel hallways, Gwen wanting to stretch her legs after the limbo of driving for days on end but not wanting to endure the subzero temperature outside. Ina and the others remained, plotting details that Gwen didn't care to sit and listen to any longer.

When she was sure they were out of earshot, at least for the humans, she said, "Welcome to the madness. What did you think?"

"The amount of drama is unsurprising for a group of mortals," Farrell replied with a small shrug. "This Xander speaks sense. I admire him for his insight."

"What do you mean?"

"Sometimes one must be sacrificed for the good of the many."

"That's not going to happen."

"How do you know?"

"I won't let it. None of us will."

"Sister, I know you are fond of him, as it appears many are, but it may be necessary. How many other lives is one life worth?"

Gwen stiffened, and she bit the inside of her lip to suppress the barbed words that bubbled up her throat. "We're not going to let Xander die. End of story."

"Fine, fine," Farrell said. "Now, tell me more about this Alessa."

Gwen shot him a sly glance. "They're part of the Cradle, bro. You know, your mortal – immortal? – enemy."

"But no longer, correct? They are fierce. Striking. I would have them."

"Drinking their blood would melt your face off."

"That is not what I mean."

"You know, you're old enough to be their grandpa."

"Darling sister, are you ageist?" Farrell asked with a grin.

"No, I just mean..." Gwen sighed, releasing the strange tension that Farrell's inquiry had curdled in her chest. He was her brother, and his interest in Alessa didn't mean that she would be put aside again. "I don't know much about them, honestly. We haven't spent much time together, and they are always paired up with Xander and Ina in the car. But I wouldn't get too attached. They've offered themselves up as Nikki's replacement in the Tree."

Farrell hummed and tilted his head back to look up at the night sky. "Fierce indeed."

"That didn't deter you at all, did it?"

"It is a complication, but it only increases my interest."

"Well, good luck with that," Gwen replied.

They walked around the hotel without conversation, the only sounds were of their muffled footsteps on the thin carpet. Every once in a while they'd pass a window, the outside faintly visible thanks to streetlamps. There weren't as many evergreens in Fairbanks as there were in the Pacific Northwest, but they made her heart heavy, wishing for the beautiful simplicity of home.

Of the comfort of her studio, her flock, and Nikki. Now all lost to her.

Gwen thought of the birds in Peru, at how they didn't fly away from her, and she smiled. Maybe someday she'd have a flock again. Maybe someday she wouldn't lead all her beloved birds to slaughter. How long did the magic last within the tern? How much of herself would she have to supply to maintain any future connections?

Musing on the future, she didn't notice when they arrived back at their suite, where Theo, Terrance, Rachel, and the Lius watched television.

Gwen laughed at the normalcy of it after so much chaos. Everyone looked at her with confused, questioning faces while she tucked herself between Theo's legs on the floor in front of the chair Theo sat in.

Gwen wrapped her arms around Theo's legs and tilted her head back to look up at her. "How's Xander doing?"

"Strangely calm, which is worrisome," Theo replied, taking Gwen's hair in her hands and combing out the wind-swept knots.

"Why is that worrisome?"

"It means he's decided," Terrance said. "When he gets calm and distant like this, there's no getting through to him. No changing his mind."

Gwen hummed, and Theo added, "He's more easily persuaded when he's emotional, heart wide as an open door. But it's closed off now and nothing can get inside."

"How do we open that door?"

"I'm not sure we can," Terrance replied, and Rachel weaved her fingers through his, giving his hand a squeeze.

Chapter Sixty-Four

They checked out of the hotel the following night, much to Ina's annoyance. She had argued that they should mobilize sooner, but she'd been outvoted. Everyone else had decided they needed one more day of rest before they headed back out into the unknown.

As soon as the sun set, Ina banged on the door of their suite, commanding them to get up and go. By the time Gwen and the others were packed and ready, those in Ina's suite were huddled around the cars, shifting on their feet as they waited. Ina stood with arms crossed and mouth tight, clearly displeased with the delay.

Xander leaned on Feng's car, surrounded by his mom and the Peruvians, hands tucked into his jacket pockets and the breeze ruffling his curls. Gwen tried to make eye contact with him, and although his chin was held high, he looked away.

She furrowed her brow, wondering how to bring him back to himself, how to prevent him from becoming a martyr.

Although the idea of sitting in a car again filled her with dread, with the addition of Farrell's vehicle in the mix of musical cars, there was more choice and more space to spread out. She and Theo jumped in with Farrell, while the others dispersed amongst the remaining cars.

The roads were dimly lit, narrow, and covered in compacted snow, so the drive took most of the night. Gwen asked Farrell about their family, but he didn't have any more information about them, apparently cut off as much as she was. Last he had heard was what he'd already told her, that Bridget and Brienne were with not-Tyee, and Bronwen had disappeared. Connell was with their parents hiding in Ireland, cowardly waiting for the whole thing to blow over, to side with whoever came out on top, not caring about anything more than their own survival.

Farrell and Theo had stilted conversation, trying to get to know each other a little better, but couldn't quite figure out the right cadence. The awkwardness eventually dwindled to silence, which stretched for the rest of the car ride. Gwen didn't mind, though. She knew they'd get to know each other naturally over time, and found the attempts thus far endearing, the awkwardness funny. She was too tired to smooth out their conversation with her input, so she half-listened, the other half of her brain hoping they found Aclima soon, and that she knew how to free Nikki. She also hoped Nikki could bring Xander back to himself.

Despite how long the drive took, the nights were still longer, and they arrived at the cabins a few hours after midnight. With large stretches and groans from the mortals, the group lugged their belongings inside once Ina had figured out how to get in. There were two cabins for them, so they split up the same way they had in the suites at the hotel, Ina for once too tired to demand they plan their next steps before resting for the day. Gwen thanked Io for this one grace. In more relaxing circumstances, she would have loved the cabin aesthetic, the wintry getaway, but all she cared about now was another day of sleeping on a real bed because who knew what the next day would bring.

Farrell, the Lius, Terrance, Rachel, Theo, and Gwen found extra sheets and blankets, blacking out the cabin as much as they could, the vampires claiming the darkest rooms to rest. Gwen laid down on the pullout couch next to Theo without changing into pjs or brushing her teeth, falling asleep immediately.

When she woke up, there was still faint light outside. Gwen bundled up and ventured out to the cold wooden porch steps of the cabin, sipping her steaming tea. It was a beautiful and serene landscape, the snow a bright blanket on the ground, surrounded by evergreens nestled against the mountainside.

The mountainside. They were in the mountains.

The realization struck Gwen with a new sense of dread. How far, and how long, would they have to travel through this mountain range to find Aclima? Was she even in this range? Did they have enough supplies for such an excursion? She trusted Ina's planning abilities, but it seemed so absurd for them all to traipse through these mountains looking for one person who may not want to be found.

"Thinking deep thoughts?" Theo asked, startling Gwen as she sat down beside her.

"More like cold ones," Gwen replied. Theo followed her gaze up the slopes of the mountains and nodded.

"We'll be fine. We have plenty of winter gear and dehydrated food. Plus, we have sun wielders with us. That will help a lot with building fires and keeping us warm." Theo put an arm around Gwen's shoulders. "Don't worry. We're prepared."

"But are we, really?" Gwen asked, flashes of slicing Atoc's head off his shoulders flashing through her mind alongside visions of Lilith ripping apart the Peruvian cradle.

Catching Gwen's shift in meaning, Theo said, "I hope so."

They watched the sun fall behind the mountains, then the stars brighten the darkening sky. Lights from the insides of the cabins flipped on and shone golden light across the snow. Eventually, the vampires, Rachel, and Terrance met them outside, and the group walked to the other cabin.

Inside, the smell of warmed bread and melting butter flooded her nose, her stomach clenching with sudden hunger. They were ushered into the dining room, which was laid out with plates and silverware, golden rolls steaming in a basket, while Cora and Ina finished dancing around each other in the kitchen.

Xander sat at the table, framed by his bodyguards, and didn't give any of them more than a terse greeting.

"What's going on?" Gwen asked him, hoping to pry him out of his shell.

"My mom thinks we need some comfort food after the past several weeks. Guess she stocked up on some meals under our radar to surprise us."

"Wow," Gwen said, surprised, although she knew she shouldn't be. She had such a hard time envisioning Ina as a mom rather than their stern leader, despite Ina having more experience in the former than the latter.

"It smells so good," Rachel said, a chair squeaking as she pulled it out.

Terrance's stomach rumbled in response, and they all chuckled, except for Xander, whose mouth barely curved into a grin.

Ina and Cora brought out macaroni and cheese, burgers both made of meat and plants, vegetable stir fry, and a box of cookies.

"How did you hide all this? And keep it from spoiling?" Gwen asked.

"As if hiding things from you is hard."

"Well, you're not exactly the most subtle person."

Ina scoffed. "I went shopping in Fairbanks and kept it all on ice since then."

"And," Cora chimed in with a grin, coming around the corner from the kitchen and dangling several bottles in her hands, "there's wine."

The group cheered and clapped, whooping their appreciation while Cora opened the bottles and passed them around, filling their glasses, except for the Lius, who could not have it. They pretended not to mind, but Gwen could tell by the averting of their eyes, the resigned twitch of their lips, that they wished they could indulge. Farrell, able to tolerate the wine thanks to the human in his DNA, raised the glass to his lips. Gwen noticed his gaze flick to the Lius, and then he put the wine back down without tasting it, his expression turning blank.

Gwen leaned over to Theo and whispered, "I'll be right back," before leaping from her chair and scurrying back to their cabin. She rummaged through the fridge until she found the thermoses of blood politely hidden toward the back. She grabbed one out, and while everyone was distracted dishing up their plates, Gwen poured blood into mugs and heated it in the microwave, then poured it into wine glasses for Feng and Daiyu.

The glass warm against her hand, she brought the cups to the Lius and her brother. Feng's eyebrows jumped with pleasant surprise while Daiyu beamed, a smile splitting her face wide.

"Thank you," Daiyu said, "this was very thoughtful."

"It didn't sit well with me, you sitting here without anything while everyone else enjoys the meal. There's more in the kitchen."

"Thank you, Gwen," Feng said, bringing the glass to his lips. Farrell raised the glass to Gwen in thanks, and at the vampires' satisfied smiles, Gwen smiled too, glad they weren't left out.

But when she turned back to return to her chair, Ina stared at her with a set jaw and stern eyes.

"Don't scold me," Gwen said before Ina could open her mouth. "They deserve to be included too. It isn't fair to keep treating them as outcasts, even though we've been with them since before we were with you."

Elena and Julian looked a little uncomfortable, bodies angled away from the Lius and mouths twisted in a grimace, but they held their tongues.

Alessa cocked their head, observing Feng and Daiyu, the blood in their hands, and then said to Ina, "The witch is right. It is better this way. Besides, it looks not so different from the red wine in ours, yes?"

"Sure. If one ignores the thick streaks of blood down the sides."

"Then ignore it," Alessa said. "We are all together in this." Gwen saw Alessa's gaze snag on Farrell's, and he grinned at them over his glass of blood and wine, a faint blush blooming on Alessa's cheeks before they turned their focus to their food.

Ina let them eat before weighing them down with what they were going to do next, waiting until utensils scraped on empty plates and stomachs were bulging. The brief respite they had from the severity of their circumstances, the delusion of being on vacation, faded into the background as quickly as the sounds of eating, leaving a hollow, heavy silence.

"So," Ina began, throwing the napkin from her lap onto the table, "each cabin should have four sets of snowshoes. Meaning most of us could go, but we need to discuss who stays behind. Given that we will be hiking outside with no known campsites or cover, I would suggest the vampires stay here."

Gwen's gut twisted. "Is that really a good idea? They're stronger than us and have better senses, so they could find Aclima or warn us of not-Tyee and my sisters approaching before anyone else could."

"We're also more tolerant to the harsh climatic conditions than you mortals," Farrell added.

"None of those benefits are useful if you die in the sun though, are they? Besides, we can wield the sun. That should be enough to keep us warm. And we need people here in case not-Tyee and your sisters come through this way. Maybe they can be stalled here and not interfere with us. And if we don't come back within a reasonable timeframe, you can alert the Cradle and have them send a search party for us."

"Ina has a point," Daiyu said. "We don't know what protection from the day we can find out there, and if they're wielding the sun to stay warm, we'd have to stay far away from them to not be bothered by it. We also do not know if Aclima would welcome the presence of vampires if she was unwillingly made into one."

"We don't know if she'd be welcome to the Cradle, either, though," Gwen said.

"We'll just have to hope and see," Ina replied.

From there, groups quickly broke off. Rachel and Cora would stay behind with Feng, Daiyu, and Farrell, with everyone else heading out into the mountains. Rachel and Cora would drive them as far as they could until the roads disappeared. If they saw anyone on the way, they'd stop and ask about the lore of creatures in the range. As there were still almost twelve hours of darkness every day, between camp set up and break down as well as meal times, there'd barely be any time for hiking. Dread pooled in Gwen's gut at the thought of the excursion taking weeks.

Ina wanted to head out when the sun rose, shifting their schedules back to human waking hours so they weren't wandering the mountains at night. Meaning tomorrow would suck. They'd be up for nearly 24 hours before getting rest again, because there was no way Gwen was getting a nap in now with the impending departure ahead of her. Leaving the Lius and her brother behind filled her with dread and sadness. The Lius had protected them for so long, had been so good to them, she didn't feel as safe without them. And she had just gotten her brother back, but now she had to leave him again? What if they did encounter not-Tyee and her sisters – would they and the Cradle be enough to take them on? Could they win without balancing the playing field with vampiric strength and ability?

Before dawn broke and the vampires hid from the sun, Farrell took her aside.

"You're going to be okay, Gwen," he said, putting hands on her shoulders and squeezing gently. "You're strong, and the group you're with is strong."

"But so is not-Tyee. And our sisters. What do we do if they've already convinced Aclima to be on their side? Or they've killed her? Or if we have to confront them?"

"Our sisters have no practical fighting experience. They rely on instinct. They only have their speed and strength. They don't wield any weapons. Keep your distance, and you'll be fine."

Gwen nodded. "And not-Tyee?"

"She relies on her ability to weave the earth. Keep your senses open to the ground shifting so you don't get trapped, and you'll be okay."

"Okay," Gwen said, taking a deep breath.

"Don't forget we have the satellite phones. If anything happens to you, I'll be there as soon as I can. But I think you all will be fine."

"I never took you for an optimist," Gwen said with a grin, hoping to alleviate the mood.

"I'm not. I'm a realist. Which is why you should believe you'll be fine," Farrell said, returning the smile, and then pulling her into a hug.

After the split second of surprise, Gwen wrapped her arms around him, the familiar smell of kin and home comforting her. Despite his strength, he was gentle, his heart a slow beat against her ear.

Gwen's vision was hazy as she pulled back, heart full with the unfamiliar feeling of familial love.

"Knock 'em dead, sis. And don't break a leg," he said, grinning.

Gwen laughed. "That sounds like something stupid I would say."

He shrugged, "Maybe you're rubbing off on me."

"Uh oh, better watch out."

"There are worse things."

They shared one more smile, Gwen's heart both sinking at leaving him and soaring with his encouragement, a strange splitting sensation running through her torso. He nudged her toward the door, where the others waited outside. Then he turned toward the darkness of the house while Gwen walked into the dawning sun.

Chapter Sixty-Five

Following the snow berm lined road out of town, Gwen marveled that they could drive at all. This part of the world seemed abandoned, with no houses or other human development she could see. It was just naked trees and endless snow, with a gloomy sky casting the area in an ethereal, hazy glow.

After what felt like endless miles, they passed a man shoveling snow off his driveway. Gwen mused at what it would be like to live out here by yourself, with only the harsh terrain and your own mind to keep you company. She'd hate it.

They slowed down to a stop, Gwen guessing that Ina, who traveled in the car in front of them with Cora, Xander, and the Peruvians, made Cora stop to talk to him. Gwen rolled down her window despite the bite of winter air crisping in the daylight to overhear what they discussed.

"Excuse me, sir, do you have a moment?" Ina called from the car.

The man hesitated, hands resting on the handle of his shovel, assessing the two vehicles with eyes barely visible beneath his large winter cap, before grunting and walking closer to the vehicles.

"Odd time of year to be up here," he grumbled. "You lost?"

"Yes and no," Ina replied. "We're just exploring the area. Heading out for some backcountry backpacking and –"

"I'm gonna stop ya there. No offense, but you all look a little... soft for the backcountry here. I suggest you save your hides and go back to where you came from."

Gwen snickered, and rested her head in her hand. Ina was not prepared for this conversation.

"Thanks for the concern, but that's not an option," Ina replied.

"Why? Y'all in some sort of suicide cult or something? Think dying up there will bring you closer to god?"

"We won't die –"

"Ma'am, you surely will. There's a reason not many people live out here. It's an unforgiving landscape with even crueler weather."

"Look, we won't change our minds. Can you just tell us if there are any local legends about creatures in the area?"

The man assessed Ina, pushing his tongue against the inside of his bottom lip. Seeming to give up the fight, he sighed and said, "You're gonna have to be more specific than that. There are a lot of creatures in the area."

"Not typical animals, but those of the paranormal or supernatural sort."

"Oh, I see now. You're those types of people, are ya?" he said, voice thick with judgement.

"What types of people?" Ina snapped.

"The idiots who poke around small towns hoping to find something out of the ordinary, to make their little lives feel less small, but just end up getting killed. Then our lives are disrupted with searches and shows documenting your tragedies," he spat, leaning on the shovel. "We don't need any trouble here, ma'am. Go on back home."

"It was a harmless question –"

"No, it wasn't, but I don't expect people like you to understand how disturbing your little failed adventures can be to our nice and quiet way of life. Now, good day and good luck. When you turn up dead, nobody can say I didn't warn ya," he turned away, continuing to shovel snow with his back turned.

After a moment, they pulled back onto the road. Rolling up the window, Gwen sighed. "Why is Ina the voice of our group? She has no charisma."

"No, but she's the ballsiest," Terrance replied.

"Maybe," Gwen said, wondering if that were really true.

They took the road as far as they could before it came to a dead end, stopped by thick snowpack. They were wedged between two mountain slopes, a semi-frozen creek running beside them.

While they geared up, putting on their snowshoes, backpacks, and weapons, Ina said, "We'll follow the creek through the range until the point directs us to change course. On the way here, it was still pointing mostly westward. We'll only walk a few miles today since we're all fatigued, but expect to pick up the pace tomorrow."

Gwen surveyed their surroundings while Theo fitted the snowshoes for her, having never worn them before. It was a beautiful area, with sunlight dancing off snow and patches of dark evergreens dotting the slopes. It was strange, being both warm and cold, her face chilly against the air but the sun and insulating clothes pulsing warmth through her body. She wrapped a scarf around her face, shielding all but her eyes from the cold, and she laughed to herself when she looked at the group. Weapons stuck up from packs, unable to wear them on their hips due to the backpack straps, all bundled in so many layers they looked like colorful marshmallows.

Packs stuffed with gear, water, and dehydrated food, they huddled in a circle while Xander dribbled some of his blood from a vial onto the Clovis point. It thrummed with blue light, then swiveled in his hand, pointing westward, along the frozen stream.

Ina took a deep breath as she looked at the mountain-framed horizon, and on her exhale said, "Off we go."

The group fell into step behind her, fanning out like a flock of geese, with Ina in the lead. Gwen was used to hiking, but not backpacking, and within the first mile, the weight of the pack wore into her shoulders and hips. Despite the low temperatures, the physical exertion and insulated clothing caused sweat to trickle down her back and neck, making her hair freeze to her skin. Gwen glanced at the others to see how they were doing, and noticed frost particles in Xander's stubble. The Cradle, who traveled with suns in their hands, wove through the group, thawing out everyone's frozen eyelashes and bringing up their body temperatures.

No one spoke, the weeks of travel together wearing them down of all conversation. The only sounds as they tromped through the range were the crunch of the snowshoes compressing the snow, the rustling of shifting clothes, and their ever-harshening breaths.

They stopped every now and then to eat a snack, Ina shouting "water!" intermittently to remind people to drink. Gwen's thoughts spun out, wondering how Farrell and the others would fare in their cabins, where her sisters and not-Tyee were, how Nikki was doing. Had Nikki made any progress in locating the Scythians? Had the Scythians found this ring? Gwen wondered if the ring she found at Nikki's place was the one they were looking for, but considering it amplified her magic rather than take it away, she discarded the thought.

Gwen watched Xander's back, the hilt of the reforged legendary sword peeking out from his pack, slung diagonally across his back. She wondered what he was thinking, if Terrance had knocked some sense into him, or if he was committed to his suicide mission. She wanted to talk to him, to convince him he wasn't alone and that he still mattered, but she worried they weren't close enough for her to do so. She resigned herself to sending him good vibes and hoped they wound their way into him.

Ina called to make camp when the sun was well below the mountain range, sparse rays still illuminating the western sky, the east just beginning to darken. Gwen heaved her pack off her shoulders, dropping it into the snow and collapsing with a sigh, her legs wobbly with fatigue.

"Don't get comfortable yet, Gwen," Ina said, putting down her pack with more grace. "We need to set up camp. It requires all hands on deck."

"Uuuggghhh," Gwen groaned as Theo offered her a hand, pulling her back to her unsteady feet. "Here's your chance to boss me around without me getting upset," Gwen said to Theo.

Theo grinned. "I better not let this opportunity go to waste, then."

Gwen returned Theo's smile and kissed her.

"Later!" Ina yelled, unbundling her tent.

Gwen made a face, and Theo chuckled, then directed Gwen on how to set up the tent. When all tents were set up in a close circle, they cleared away some snow and made a ring for a fire, using a fire starter for kindling and the Cradle's magical suns to start it. Gwen created a barrier around the camp, condensing the air in a tight, shielded dome. If they encountered their ex-coven leader and her sisters, at least they would have a little protection from them.

Over the fire, they boiled water and poured it into the bags of dehydrated meals. Waiting for the food to "cook," Gwen asked, "So, how long are we doing this?"

"Until we get there," Ina replied. Gwen's mouth popped open, but before she could speak, Ina continued. "And we won't know that until the point indicates. It could be tomorrow. It could be weeks."

"Do we even have enough supplies for weeks?"

"We'll make do."

"That doesn't fill me with confidence."

"I am capable in this regard, Gwen. I've done lots of backpacking and fieldwork."

"Yeah, yeah," Gwen said, wrapping her arms around her legs and resting her chin on her knees, staring into the flames. The light of the campfire flickered against the silhouettes of her companions.

"We had an easy day today –"

"Easy?"

"Yes, easy. All we did was walk. I want everyone to continue their sparring tomorrow."

"But our teachers aren't with us."

"No, but you can still practice the forms they taught you. We will start and end the day with these exercises."

Gwen groaned, but none of her comrades did. It seemed she was the only one who had issues with this. She guessed that meant she was the least physically fit. But she had magic, so did that really matter?

They ate their rehydrated food quietly, each one spacing out as they looked into the dancing flames, the Cradle infusing it with additional fire as it faded. Ina, Alessa, Julian, and Elena took turns staying awake to keep watch and keep the fire going, ensuring the group stayed warm overnight. With aching muscles and tired bones, Gwen and Theo crawled into their tent, changed into their fleece pajamas, and curled into their sleeping bags.

"Having fun yet?" Theo teased, snuggling close enough to Gwen that their noses touched. Gwen barked a laugh. "The time of my life. I love the cold. I love dehydrated food. Oh, and don't forget about the exciting cat and mouse game with ancient vampires. Very exciting."

Theo chuckled, but it was halfhearted. "Maybe you'll find something new to use in your spells and potions, at least."

"Maybe," Gwen replied, voice drifting as her eyelids closed, sleep quickly overtaking her mind and pulling her into darkness.

True to her word, Ina woke them up at the crack of dawn. Not kindly, either. She didn't beckon them awake with false birdsong, or the smell of coffee, but with clapping her hands as hard as she could and yelling, "Everybody up! Everybody up!" Until, indeed, everyone was up, and perhaps pondering how to silence her.

While water boiled for instant coffee, the Peruvians led them through various fighting stances and exercises, making Xander, Gwen, and Terrance wield their weapons while doing so. Gwen should have stolen Theo's idea and practiced with guns, as much as they made her uncomfortable. If that were the case, she wouldn't have to hold a sword in her tired arms this early in the morning.

While they practiced, the others prepped coffee and more dehydrated food. Once they ate and packed up camp, they turned their backs to the sun and continued on their quest to find Aclima despite their already tired limbs.

Chapter Sixty-Six

Nikki spread her consciousness throughout the forest surrounding the Scythians, following their light footsteps in the dense vegetation. She relished the sense of connectedness while she could, before having to inevitably return to herself in the Tree. Birds and small mammals rested in the midnight-dappled leaves and underbrush, worms wriggling in the soil, the trees breathing in and out like a soothing lullaby.

Several hours earlier, the Scythians checked their GPS location and compared it to a paper map. Vadasz announced, "Lilith lost track of it somewhere southwest of here. We're getting close."

Aella dropped to the ground, shoving away low-growing ferns to plunge her hands below the soil surface. Nikki felt Aella wind herself through the earth, and Nikki recoiled, reducing the number of trees she spied out of, afraid that Aella would sense her watching. But Aella's magic crawled deeper into the earth, rather than up into the vegetation, and then spread out.

Many minutes passed, Aella stretching her magic while Vadasz and Uase waited more patiently than Nikki, eager to discover what she was looking for, what she would find.

Finally, Aella's magic receded into herself, and she stood. "There are many bones in this forest."

"Unsurprising," Vadasz said. "Any burial sites?"

"Nothing so formal as burial sites. Rather, sites where the forest has reclaimed the dead. Concentrations of bones and metal are just to the south."

"Lead the way, then," Vadasz said, sweeping his arm out for Aella to step in front of him.

"It will take much time to sort through all the bones to find the one we are looking for," Aella said, stepping forward and walking south.

"Well, we don't have much choice in the matter, do we?"

Uase grunted, arms folding across his broad chest.

Nikki followed them, trying to identify where they were, looking at the mix of ferns, shrubs, and broadleaf trees. They were all plants she hadn't seen before. The birds the Scythians ate were all unfamiliar to her as well. Nikki followed them until she sensed her body in the Tree jolt, a spike of adrenaline tugging at her consciousness to return.

Reluctant, Nikki unwove herself from the forest, leaving the Scythians to their quest of looking for old bones.

She funneled through the roots of the world and collided with her body, the weight of physical sensations heavy, despite the suspension.

Cat fussed on the outside of the tree, muttering and puttering. At first, Nikki thought she was talking to herself, but other voices came through.

"...go, I'm the better sailor," Marcus said.

"And what? I'm supposed to sit here playing babysitter while you get your glory?" Titania spat.

"I don't need babysitting," Cat snapped. "My daughter, my husband, are here. I'm not leaving."

Marcus and Titania ignored her. Marcus said, "You read the letter from Mannus – one of us needs to watch the waters."

"I don't see why that has to be you. I have sailed the seas of the world just as much as you."

"We can't leave her unattended. Even if she is relatively complacent now, she could be biding her time."

"Biding my time for what? Finding a chainsaw and cutting my daughter out of this abominable tree? Yes, quite likely."

Io flickered in the dark.

"What's going on?" Nikki asked.

"Do you recall the sirens protecting the island?"

"The aquatic cousins of vampires? How could I forget?" Nikki thought with a shiver, remembering her encounter with them that night on the boat with Hormin. How eerie their song was. How viciously they ate the meat Hormin threw to them.

"Marcus and Titania have been summoned to support the sirens in protecting the island. And in providing other vampires safe passage over."

"Other vampires? Why?" Nikki asked, dread coiling in her stomach.

Io remained silent, but the flickers twitched with anxiety.

"We could both go if we took care of her," Titania said.

"What?" Cat whispered.

Cold fear swept through Nikki's body.

She couldn't lose her mom, too.

"The Mother wouldn't like that."

"She doesn't have to know, brother."

"I'll behave, I promise. I just want to be near my daughter –"

A hard smack rippled through the air, and a body crumpled to the ground.

"Would you be quiet?" Titania yelled. "No one cares what you think."

Marcus sighed.

"We could just tie her up. The Mother didn't give us permission to kill her, but we could leave her tied up in the house."

"No, please –"

"How would she eat?" Marcus asked.

"She wouldn't. But who cares? Not like she'd die for a long, long time. We'd be back before that happens."

Marcus sucked on his teeth and the uncomfortable quiet stretched out around them, undercut by Cat's crying to please not be tied up. Nikki's dry eyes burned, wishing she could move, that she could do anything. She was so close, yet impossibly far.

"Fine," Marcus eventually replied. "I'd rather ask the Mother's forgiveness later than fight with you now. I'm eager to return to the seas."

"As am I," Titania replied, and Nikki could hear the smile in her voice.

Nikki heard rustles of fabric and feet scuffling. Her mother cried, fighting against Marcus and Titania as they dragged her back to the house. Nikki squeezed her eyes shut and grit her teeth, trying to block out the sound.

When the sound of her mother's cries died, a bitter flame shot through Nikki's veins.

"You see the pain Lilith is causing to so many people everywhere. The Cradle, my family, all your beloved creations, and yet you still won't help us? Help me?"

Io flickered slowly, sorrow and uncertainty filling the air around her. *"I do not know how."*

Nikki bit back a harsh laugh. *"You could do anything, say anything, and it would be helpful. You don't want to help us stop Lilith? Fine, whatever, we can figure it out. But how about helping us not get hurt anymore? Give us warning when something bad is about to happen to us? The Scythians are hunting for an item that may erase Adam's magic entirely, your first special creation. Your first love, if you can even feel such a thing. You won't even tell us if such an item exists. How close the Scythians are to finding it or where they are, so we know how much time we have to hide Xander once they find it."*

Glitters of gold twitched, a hitch like fleeting irritation settling back into shame. *"I cannot keep track of every artifact in the world. But yes, the Ring of Dispel exists."*

"Great," Nikki thought bitterly. *"And where are the Scythians? Are they close to Xander?"*

"Yes and no."

Nikki bit back a frustrated scream. *"What does that mean?"*

"They could be farther away, but it would take many days for them to find Alexander and the rest. They are in New Zealand."

Now, Nikki did laugh, and the roots crawled into her mouth. She bit them off and spit them out.

"What is funny?"

"They're looking for a magical ring in New Zealand?"

"Yes, why is that amusing?"

"I suppose you've never read a book or watched a movie."

"No. Such mortal amusements are of no interest to me."

"Of course not," Nikki replied, processing the news. At least the Scythians were across an ocean from her friends. There would be time to warn them if, or when, the ring was found.

Chapter Sixty-Seven

Gwen peeled sweat-slicked clothes from her body each night, relishing the brisk chill against the moisture before it became too cold and she wrapped herself in her sleeping clothes. Everyone, everything, was starting to smell. Xander still would not talk to his mom. He would barely look at her, or anyone else.

Nikki checked in on the third day to tell her that the Scythians were in New Zealand and that the Ring of Dispel was real, news that settled strangely on the group. Like Nikki had said, it was comforting to know they were across an ocean, but it was concerning that they were close to finding this ring. Nikki also told her that something was changing, that Marcus and Titania had left to guard the island, tying Cat up in the house near the Tree. But she didn't know what they were planning.

What were they up to?

What was Lilith plotting?

Xander's jaw ticked when he heard the news, but he turned away and kept walking.

Gwen sensed Theo's thrum of worry, a jitteriness in her movements, but wearing gloves prevented her from biting her nails, so that was something, at least.

On the fourth day, Gwen's muscles were so painful that she tried to heal them with her magic. She knew the discomfort meant she was getting stronger, but she worried she would collapse and slow the group down. That was if they didn't just leave her behind. While magicking her muscles relieved the ache, it made her more fatigued to expend her energy in that way. She'd just have to deal with the pain.

The moon and sun chased each other across the sky as the group wound their way through the mountain range, following the river westward. The Clovis point did not waver. Gwen wondered why, in all the adventure books and movies, no one mentioned how boring adventuring was. You ran out of things to talk about, your body hurt, the days blended into each other, and yet the scenery didn't change. She wasn't even able to forage for plants like Theo suggested, the temperature still too cold for them to germinate, grow, and bloom. The only thing she had to occupy herself were her own horrid thoughts, circling over everything that went wrong, going over every potential outcome, hyperfixated on the worst ones.

The more she thought about it, the more she realized that what they were doing was ridiculous. Traveling in the middle of nowhere in winter, using a magical arrow to guide them to a mythical woman no one had seen or heard from in centuries, if not millennia, and who may or may not want to help them at all.

As they neared a week into their journey, sloughing packs off their backs like a hated second skin, Ina beckoned Xander to do his nightly blood test on the Clovis point. Theo set up their tent while Gwen crafted the barrier before they went through their nightly exercises. Ina boiled water, Gwen fantasizing about veggie burgers and French fries and ice cream.

"What does that mean?" Xander asked, and the hesitation in his voice made Gwen pause. Gwen looked over to Xander and Ina, who stared at his palm with open mouths and furrowed brows.

"What's up?" Gwen asked, as everyone walked over to them.

"I'm not sure," Ina replied.

Gwen glanced at the point in Xander's palm, and although it gave off the same faint blue glow, it no longer pointed westward. Instead, it spun in a steady circle, as if it couldn't decide which way to point.

"Does that mean we're close?" Gwen asked.

"You'd think it would still point in her general direction. She is only one person," Theo said. "Unless we're above or below her."

They looked at their feet, at the compacted layer of snow and ice below.

"How could she be below us?"

Theo shrugged. "I don't know. I'm just throwing out ideas."

"Maybe whatever her magic is throws off the point," Terrance added.

"Perhaps," Ina replied, contemplative. She furrowed her brow deeper, and they all watched the point continue to spin until the blue glow faded, the spell ended. "Tomorrow, instead of continuing our hike, let's scout the area. Maybe we can find her or her dwelling. Or whatever it is that is interfering with the point."

Chapter Sixty-Eight

THEY SPLIT into pairs the next day to scour the area for any sign of hidden habitations. The landscape had changed without Gwen realizing it, with pine trees thinning out, giving way to rocky ledges peeking out beneath the snow. She and Theo walked north, up one of the ridges that closed them in, looking for any openings. They brought lunch with them, and at midday, they dropped into the snow to eat, ignoring the cold that pressed against their legs.

They ate in silence, staring downslope at their camp, bright sunlight glittering on the blanket of white, casting the mountains into pearlescent diamonds. In the distance, they saw the rest of the group wandering, with Xander and Alessa walking west toward a small lake they could not see from camp. From the ridge where Gwen and Theo sat, it was a blue haven amidst so much gray and white, eager herbs and trees crowding the edges. Theo wondered aloud if there were any fish in the lake, and if they might be able to catch some, while Gwen hoped at some point she could meander down there herself to see if there were any plant parts she could forage.

The rest of the day was spent in the same uneventful manner, but Gwen appreciated the quiet alone time with Theo while she could. They were so rarely alone these days, and even with the silence, being around Theo was so comfortable, so...peaceful. Like snuggling into blankets after a long day.

Before dusk, the group reconvened at camp, with sullen announcements that no one had found any sign of human or vampire life. Xander found that at the lake edge the Clovis point swung back to the east, pointing toward their camp. They agreed to rotate directions the next day so Xander could find the boundary where the point turned back again, narrowing the area of their search.

As night draped a dark blanket over them, diminishing their line of sight to just their immediate surroundings, the hairs on the back of Gwen's neck prickled, raising with the uneasy sense of being watched.

She turned her head to look behind her into the vast dark, but of course she could neither see nor hear anything.

"What is it?" Theo asked, following her gaze.

"I just had a strange feeling that someone is out there."

"Hmmm," Theo hummed, chewing her lip. Without being able to bite her nails, her nipping habit had shifted to her mouth, the cold and teeth tearing at the sensitive skin there.

Gwen's heartbeat settled from its anxious, raised state, turning into nauseous foreboding. It could just be an animal. But what animals were out at this time of year?

It could be Aclima, but why wouldn't she introduce herself?

Worst of all, it could be not-Tyee and her sisters, waiting for an opportune moment to strike.

Gwen did not sleep that night. Even with the protection of her shield and the shelter of the tent, she could not shake the feeling of eyes watching them.

Chapter Sixty-Nine

THE FOLLOWING day passed in much the same way. As did the next. They scoured the area, looking for signs of life. Xander marked the boundaries of where the Clovis point directed them toward camp, and where it spun in confused circles. Stumped, the Cradle summoned suns in their hands and melted away the snow around their camp, hoping it would expedite their search for any openings in the ground where someone might hide. Or any object that would interfere with the Clovis point's magic.

By the end of the third day, they had not found anything. And still, in the dark and twilight hours, Gwen sensed something, or someone, watching them. Circling them. Nikki checked up on them, and Gwen asked her to help with their search. Nikki tried to spread herself throughout the forest, but the vegetation wasn't dense enough. Even unable to help them, Nikki lingered with Gwen, bringing with her a heaviness that wore at Gwen's mind. Nikki's sadness at being trapped, at being unable to walk in the sun, followed her, but she couldn't bring herself to push her friend out, despite how heavy her own thoughts were. Nikki always left on her own anyway, so Gwen let her linger out in the world while she could.

That night, shouts and blinding flashes of light woke her from a dead sleep. Gasping as she bolted upright, adrenaline shooting through her veins, she blinked against the sudden change from dark to light, light to dark. Theo woke with a start beside her, and they wrapped themselves in clothes as quickly as possible, strapping their weapons close to their hips before running out into the night.

"Have you found her?" a familiar voice whispered from the darkness as Gwen and Theo stood beside Julian and Alessa, who had been on guard, while everyone else clambered from their tents.

Ina stepped forward, casting a ball of sunlight in her palm. "Show yourself. You and your companions."

"And burn in your light? No, I do not think so. I may tolerate the sun more than most vampires, but I am not foolish enough to test the limits of my resistance," not-Tyee said from the darkness.

Gwen twisted, looking around, but despite the miniature suns illuminating their immediate area, it was quickly swallowed by the dark, and if her sisters were indeed with Tyee, they moved too quietly to be heard.

"I ask again," not-Tyee said, "have you found her?"

"What business is that of yours?" Ina asked the dark.

"It is my entire business," not-Tyee said, voice coming from Gwen's left instead of in front of her.

The group swiveled to the new direction, empty hands flying to their hilts and handles.

"What do you want with her?" Ina asked.

Silence.

Ina stepped in a circle around them. "Have *you* found her?"

"If we had, she'd be dead," said the sneering voice of Bridget from the opposite side of the dark. "But to keep the Mother's secrets safe, it seems we must kill you first."

The ground rumbled beneath their feet, and the group stepped away, their tight circle widening as they tried to see where the earth shifted.

The lights of the Cradle flickered like dying stars.

With a loud crack and grumbling of the ground, the vampires popped up from the earth in the center of their camp in an explosion of rock, dirt, and snow. Gwen had never considered creating a barrier like a bubble that extended into the earth, and regret flooded her system at this realization.

The lights of the Cradle went out as each one lifted their arms to shield their faces from the hail of rock raining down on them.

And in that split second of darkness, the vampires attacked.

Theo, Terrance, Xander, and Gwen stood in a tight circle, backs to each other, watching the struggle, unsure how to help without harming their allies. Gwen's palm turned slick on the handle of her sickle sword. Theo had her guns raised, Terrance and Xander held their weapons, watching as the suns flashed in the dark like strobe lights. Not-Tyee held Alessa on the ground, who held a sun above their head that melted the snow and burned layers from not-Tyee's face.

Ina, slamming a burning palm into Brienne's cheek, wrenched free from her grasp and threw an orb at not-Tyee, catching her on her side and causing her to roll off Alessa with the pain. As the sun burned through her clothes and skin, it left a mess of blood and exposed ribs behind.

Julian and Elena wrestled with Bridget, who clawed and snapped and writhed like a feral cat. She dodged their burning fists so only the top layers of her skin peeled away beneath the light, her bloodlust grin turning into a horrid visage of mottled flesh and muscle. Brienne joined her sister, leaping onto Elena's back and digging her claws into her neck, blood spurting out across the snow.

"No!"

"Elena!"

Julian and Alessa screamed as Elena's eyes widened and she coughed out blood that pooled and caught in her ravaged throat, then fell to the ground, the sun that burned in her veins bleeding into the snow, sizzling as it melted away.

Bridget and Brienne leapt at Julian, who barely dodged beneath them and lifted his light, bringing palms together to make the sun as large as possible, while not-Tyee jumped around the orbs that Ina and Alessa threw at her.

"There's too much movement, I can't shoot," Theo said, voice shaking.

"And it's too dark for me to swing," Terrance added, shifting his grip on the handle of his hammer.

Bridget and Brienne circled Julian, their sunburned faces twisted into ugly sneers. They leapt toward him at the same time, and Alessa veered to knock Brienne out of her lunge, making her stumble, too strong to be knocked to the ground. But it was enough to make her miss, and in the moment of distraction, Alessa held high a blazing sun before pushing it into Brienne's chest. Gwen's sister let out a piercing screech as the light melted through her clothes, chest, and ribs.

When she fell to the ground, Alessa followed, burying their glowing fist deeper into Brienne's torso, until the only light in Brienne's eyes was the one reflected from Alessa's sun.

Something twisted inside Gwen, a feeling she could not name but made her want to scream, to vomit, to run into the woods, as she stared at the gaping cavity of a corpse that had been her terrible sister.

But in her distraction, she had missed Bridget ripping open Julian's guts, his scream eclipsed by Brienne's. He lay in a puddle of his own gore, Bridget's hands sizzling where his blood had burned away at her flesh. Bridget's face was a terrifying expression of pain and anger as she took in her dead sister and then the one who had ended Brienne's life. Bridget threw herself at Alessa with a strangled scream just as not-Tyee crashed into Ina, who had averted her gaze briefly to see who had been screaming.

"No!" Xander yelled as not-Tyee pushed Ina to the ground with a hard crunch. Xander broke from the circle, rushing toward them with his sword held out before him.

With a quick succession of suns thrown at Bridget, Alessa twisted to chase after Xander. Not-Tyee held Ina at the wrists, restricting her blood flow, preventing her from summoning suns. Only faint flickers of light illuminated her palms as she struggled.

Xander lifted his sword high and shouted, "Let her go!" As he swung his weapon down, it brightened, casting sunrays from the blade that stretched farther than the Cradle's magic, and Gwen squinted against the light.

Not-Tyee flinched and rolled out of the path of the sword's arc but not with enough time to avoid getting cut on the arm. She let out a hiss as it sliced like butter through her skin.

Ina scrambled back to Alessa, and Bridget ran to not-Tyee's side. Finally seeing a dividing line between their sides, Gwen ran forward, gathering as much magic within her body as she could, pooling air around her skin. Skin aglow, she shot her hands forward, sending the strongest wind she could at their enemies. With a howl, the air tore through the night, tossing the vampires up and back outside the boundary.

Gwen collapsed to her knees, sweat trickling down her face, all her muscles weak.

Gasping for breath, she lifted her head to look at her sister and ex-coven leader, who panted on the other side of the barrier. Bridget's skin was barely on her body, burned away from the Cradle's blood. Not-Tyee clutched her exposed side with her good arm. Their wounds slowly stitched back together, muscle weaving with muscle, and flesh forming over it, except for not-Tyee's arm that Xander had slashed. It hung limp at her side, not repairing.

"We can't beat them like this," Ina said, "they can always retreat and heal."

Dread sank in Gwen's stomach. They'd all die here. Even with Xander's newfound magical sword, they weren't experienced enough to beat them.

The vampires caught their breath, and when their wounds were healed enough, they took a step forward. Not-Tyee raised one hand to manipulate the earth. Gwen didn't move, a cold acceptance combining with her fatigue. She didn't have any more fight. She used all she could to get them out, and had hoped they'd be too weak to get back in.

Tears burned in her eyes. They had tried so hard. And it wasn't good enough.

Maybe the rest of the Cradle could rally and fight back.

She looked over her shoulder and saw her feelings written on the faces of everyone else. She met Theo's eyes and mouthed, "I love you."

In the light of Xander's still glowing sword, Theo's eyes glistened, and she mouthed, "I love you, too."

Staring into Theo's beautiful face, the ground rumbled again, and she braced herself for her end.

364

Chapter Seventy

THE ABSENCE of her mom hit Nikki harder than she expected. She didn't realize how much she depended on Cat's muttering and puttering around the Tree for some semblance of company. Now, surrounded by silence both within and without the Tree, she felt as if she were plunged into an empty void, entirely alone.

Every now and then, footsteps moved up the hill and across the grass to the house. Probably a villager checking that she and Cat were still tucked away as Lilith wanted. Marcus and Titania left not long after tying up Cat, excitedly chatting about being on the sea again. Which sea, she still did not know. But they didn't say ocean, so that narrowed it down. A little. Why they had been summoned to patrol the water, they did not say. Nikki knew that Gwen was still in Alaska, but she hoped it meant that some other faction of the Cradle was on their way to at least save her mom. Why else would they need to protect the island, if not for the Cradle invading? That meant someone, somewhere, knew where she was. And once she found out, she could tell Gwen. If they didn't already figure it out from Aclima.

Nikki reached out to Io, *"How is she? My mom."*

Io pulled into her awareness in a cascade of glitter. The flickers paused, musing, and Io said, *"She suffers, but no more than she has been.*

Cat no longer cares for her physical form, and so the starvation does not phase her. Instead, she continues to replay the worst of recent events over and over in her mind. As she has been the past weeks."

Nikki's heart sank, and she hung her head, wishing she could wrap her arms around her mom, wishing they could hug and cry and mourn in the ways mothers and daughters should, rather than being trapped in their own hells.

With a sigh through her nose, Nikki plunged down into the earth to check on the Scythians. She followed their purple and teal threads and crept through the forest around them, the skittering of insects and rustle of brushing leaves alleviating the loneliness that yawned inside her chest.

The last time Nikki had checked, the Scythians were still digging. They stood chest deep in a wide pit, thrusting soil and plant debris over their shoulders while they searched for the mass of bones Aella sensed buried beneath the earth.

Now, they had dug far enough into the earth and sifted through the mass grave, tossing the small bones of phalanges, long femurs, and skulls out of the excavation while they searched for the ring. Despite their relentlessness, they didn't break a sweat, their ancient vampiric strength lending them incredible endurance.

Nikki watched them for hours, the pile of dirt and bone growing on the ground, wondering just how many people were buried here. Who were they? How did they come to be buried in an unmarked grave? There was something so sad about it, to be reduced to nothing more than unknown bones. Mixed with others and picked apart by vampires who cared nothing for what you once were.

"Is this it?" Uase grumbled, snapping Nikki out of her morose musings.

Uase picked up a damp, moldy cloth so thin and frayed it was barely there. Its edges unfolded, revealing a small, white item in the middle.

"Be careful with that," Aella warned, as she and Vadasz traipsed through the bones, cracking under their feet, and stood beside him.

"Why? Not like it could make me not a vampire."

"Perhaps, perhaps not. We do not know what it would do, however. Best be cautious. If that *is* the ring."

Nikki stretched her awareness to the forest canopy to look down at them as they peered at the object within the rotting cloth.

Within Uase's palm was a ring carved from bone, gleaming brighter than the other yellowing remains.

"It has to be," Vadasz murmured.

"It thrums with power," Aella added, eyes widening with greed.

Uase grunted and took out a bandana, wrapping it in fresh fabric.

"*Io?*" Nikki asked, her mental voice shaking with trepidation. "*Was that it? The ring that could erase people's power? Make Xander...edible?*"

The warmth of Io's presence suffused the forest around her, but the Scythians were too focused on their luck to notice.

"*Yes, that is the ring,*" Io said, dripping with reluctance.

"*I need to warn the others.*"

Nikki spent a few more moments with the Scythians, enough time to overhear them plan their next steps, like how to contact Lilith and where to begin their search for the rewards she promised they could claim.

The closer she got to her body as she propelled herself back through the earth, the heavier her sense of dread became. She should not have been surprised they found the ring. The Scythians had spent centuries, nigh on millennia, as hunters and scout. Whatever reward they would look for next, they'd surely find. And that would just as certainly spell bad news for all who stood against Lilith.

Chapter Seventy-One

Gwen clenched her eyes tight while the earth rumbled. She waited to be sucked in, to be crushed, to fall into nothingness at any moment.

Yet when the ground stopped grumbling, she could still breathe, could still feel, and had no more aches and pains than what she had carried the previous days. Tension released from her muscles, and she opened her eyes with caution.

In the faint glow of the Cradle's suns and Xander's dimming sword, Gwen saw not-Tyee and Bridget trapped in place. Large roots with a thick layer of ice twined up their bodies, squeezing tight enough that their extremities changed color, Tyee's hands frozen, unable to weave the earth to her command.

"You are not welcome here," a strong female voice said from the darkness.

The roots wove tighter, Bridget's face turning purple as not-Tyee snarled, veins in her forehead bulging.

"Leave or die here. Your choice."

Not-Tyee's nose twitched with anger and disgust, but she managed a minute nod despite the icy roots around her neck. After a moment, the plants loosened just enough for not-Tyee to move her hands. The ground below growled and cracked, then not-Tyee and Bridget disappeared in a puff of snow and a cascade of frosty soil, the plants that held them collapsing to the surface in their absence. Gwen took steadying breaths, counting the seconds in her head, waiting for not-Tyee and Bridget to reappear in her barrier and rip them all to shreds.

But as the seconds ticked by and the group still had all their blood on the inside, Gwen breathed a little easier.

"They are gone," the voice said, and Gwen swiveled her head to find the source.

Out of the darkness, a woman of average height, skin as dark as midnight and eyes as bright white as the moon, stepped forward. She held an intricately carved wooden staff as tall as she was, and she was draped in animal hides and fur.

"Aclima," Ina breathed, awed.

Aclima blinked in Ina's direction. She made eye contact with each of them, assessing. When her eyes met Gwen's, it was like being struck by lightning. Or chugging several espresso shots. Not only was her gaze intense, she had no iris, her eyes appearing larger with the complete whiteness. Without another word, Aclima turned on her heels and retreated into the darkness.

"Wait!" Ina shouted after her, running in her direction. "We need to speak with you."

Aclima paused, but did not turn around. Over her shoulder, she said, "Yet, I do not need to speak with you. I have protected your lives and my home. Our business is concluded." Aclima resumed her walk, steps soundless in the snow.

"No, it's not, because they won't leave you alone, not until Lilith is defeated. And we need your help to do that. She's free, did you know that?" Ina asked.

Aclima stiffened, and with an impatient tapping of her staff on the ground, she turned. Nothing but her eyes were visible in the night. "No, I did not know. How?"

"She found me," Xander said. Ina's mouth popped open, but she didn't interrupt, and Gwen was grateful to Xander for jumping into the conversation before Ina once again laid blame on Nikki for everything. "She found me, a descendant of –"

"Adam. I know. I can smell my kin." Aclima tapped her staff again on the ground. Silence spread between the group and the other woman, the tether to Aclima's attention fragile and liable to disappear. They had to pick their next words carefully or she would be lost to them.

Xander's fingers twitched, and Ina jumped in. "Please, we need your help. She wants to enslave humanity. End Adam's bloodline and kill all the Cradle. We think we can stop her if we remove her replacement in the Tree, as it is another vampire who now sustains it."

Gwen flinched, hearing Nikki spoken of so callously, as if she weren't a person. Just a pawn to be moved on the chessboard.

"You do know where the Tree is, don't you?" Ina asked, eyes wide and hands wringing.

Aclima did not respond, but instead stared at Xander, then Ina, with unblinking intensity. After several long moments, she said, "You assume this concerns me. Why do you think I would help? I am content here in my mountains."

"The fate of –" Ina started, voice rising with indignation and frustration, but Xander cut her off with a raised hand.

"We didn't know if you would care, or if you would help. We didn't even know if you were still alive. Maybe the world, maybe humanity, doesn't matter to you anymore. But it matters to us, and we had to try. Please, if you know where the Tree is, if you know how we can get Nikki – our...friend," Xander said, choking on the word, "please tell us. That's all we ask. Nothing more. Just the chance to save the world we love."

Aclima took a step into the light, a small smile curving one side of her face. "I could swear my father said those words once, long ago." Her smile faltered into a frown. "But Io did not listen, and the garden fell."

Aclima searched Xander's face, milky white eyes roving over him, and Gwen wondered what she actually saw as she looked at them through her blindness. Xander stood firm under her gaze, jaw ticking.

"Fine," Aclima said. "I make no promises, but I will speak with the son of Adam and Eve." Aclima's gaze roved over the group and landed on Gwen, her fierce stare piercing Gwen. "And the witch. No one else."

"What? Why?" Gwen asked.

"We just got him back from harm. I won't let him out of my sight," Ina retorted.

"I am no killer. Especially not of kin," Aclima responded, holding up a yielding hand. "And you would do well to remember that it is not only Adam that makes his bloodline unique. It is my mother's as well. I will not have her forgotten, in this battle between Adam and Lilith."

"I – of course," Ina stammered, "I'm sorry. I didn't mean to be disrespectful."

Gwen blinked with surprise at Ina's deference.

"Come along," Aclima demanded, turning her back on them and heading into the dark, still without answering Gwen's question.

Gwen leapt to her feet, gave Theo a quick peck on the cheek and squeeze of her hand.

"Be careful," Theo whispered as Gwen pulled back.

"I will," she said, then fell into step beside Xander and followed Aclima into the night.

Chapter Seventy-Two

Gwen stumbled through the snow, the ever-fading light from Xander's sword making it increasingly difficult to see the ground in front of her. Aclima, with her vampiric eyes, did not slow down for them.

"Can you light it up again?" Gwen asked Xander, nodding to the sword in his hand.

"I'm not sure how," he said with a frown, the blade giving off little more than a warm glow. He concentrated on it, brow furrowed as if his gaze alone could ignite it, but nothing happened.

Gwen tripped over her own feet, distracted as she was watching Xander. He caught her arm before she hit the ground.

"Can you slow down?" Gwen asked Aclima's back, steadying herself back on her feet.

"No," Aclima responded without hesitating, either in speech or stride.

Gwen huffed, but looped her arm through Xander's after a moment's hesitation. She wasn't sure if he was okay being touched yet, but he didn't flinch or shrug her off. They used each other as support to navigate through the dark, catching each other when they stumbled, huddling close for warmth, comfort, and stability.

Discomfort squirmed in Gwen's stomach, unsure if she should try to talk to him or not. Thanks to all the conversations she had with Nikki when she and Xander were dating, plus all the stories she heard from Theo about their childhood, she felt like she knew Xander well, but in reality she didn't. They had only been around each other twice before shit hit the fan, and had barely spoken since they got him back from Hormin and Lilith. Nikki should be the one here with her arm looped through his. She would know what to say, if anything at all. Xander seemed to sense her awkwardness, casting her sideways glances. Gwen decided to chill out and take the Nikki approach. Take a couple deep breaths and don't say anything. He can engage if he wants to.

They followed Aclima for what felt like miles, although it could have been much shorter. The silence seemed to stretch time, and Gwen grew tired of yet *more* walking. They walked up and down slopes, and although Gwen had tried to track their direction, she soon got so turned around, she had no idea where they were on the mountain relative to their camp. Eventually, Aclima paused before an exposed wall of stone and tapped her staff on the ground three times. With a tired grumble, the stone groaned and pulled away, opening to reveal an empty space darker than the night around them.

Aclima stepped into the void, Xander and Gwen hesitating as they watched the dark swallow her whole.

"Come along," Aclima commanded, and with nervous glances at each other and the cave, Xander and Gwen stepped forward.

One bright light flared in the dark, silhouetting Aclima as she turned to them.

"Here," Aclima said, handing the torch to Gwen and turning her back on them as soon as the light was in Gwen's hand.

Gwen stretched out her hand, trying to get a lay of the land, but the light from the torch wasn't even enough to illuminate the cave walls. Xander tugged her forward to resume following Aclima, the cave sloping downward in a gentle spiral. They barely had enough light to see their feet, the steps of which echoed against the cold stone. Gwen wondered how big this cavity was and how far it descended beneath the mountains.

Around a small curve, the path flattened, giving way to a large, open cavern. With a flick of her hand, Aclima ignited dozens of small tallow candles attached to the walls, set on the ground, and placed around stone furniture.

The space was filled with raised stone in the shape of a bed, a table, chairs, and a workbench, each piece was layered with furs, as was the ground they walked on. On the far side of the cave, a small body of water glittered under the candlelight, the soft trickle of flowing water in and out of the cavern a pleasant babble in the large space.

Gwen raised her head, the ceiling of the cavern far above them, and grinned. Theo had been right, after all. Aclima was underground, and that's why the Clovis point couldn't help them find her.

Aclima waved her hand over a hearth carved into the cave's side, a small fire catching. Gwen shivered, the cold damp of the cave washing over her as the warmth of the fire blazed against one side of her body. Aclima ushered them closer and bade them sit on the furs on the ground, then draped a bear coat over Gwen's shoulder. Gwen grimaced, but couldn't deny how nice its warmth was. Xander sat across from her and tugged another bear fur around his shoulders, gazing distantly into the fireplace.

"How long have you lived here?" Gwen asked, once the shiver left her bones.

Aclima sat on a chair beside them, bright white eyes a pale orange in the firelight.

"A long time," she responded. "I do not know the answer in years."

"How do you survive? I'd guess not many people come through here."

"There are creatures willing to donate their lives to me. They give me blood while they live, their pelts when they die. In return, they are free and safe to roam across this area."

"I thought the Made couldn't drink animal blood."

Aclima cringed, nose curling in a flicker of disgust. "I am not just what Lilith made me. Before all things, I am the daughter of Adam and Eve. The wilds, and its creatures, are part of me."

"What does that mean, exactly?" Gwen asked, perking up at the idea of a new type of magic.

Aclima raised her hand. "Child, I allowed you here to plead your argument. Not to interrogate me."

Gwen huffed, and Xander said, "I am curious about the answer to that question too. Everyone is fussing about me being a descendant of Adam. And Eve. But no one has told me why that is special, besides the fact that it helped free Lilith."

Aclima's milky eyes stared at Xander. "How does one explain the importance of the first tree that grows in the forest? The first deep snow of winter that sustains life through summer? That is what it means to be of Adam and Eve. To be not only the beginning, but what sustains life ever forward. The blessings of Eve, who knows the ways of nature, are different from Adam, who knows the ways of people. Whether through sowing life through the earth or igniting the flames that reside within each person, we spur life ever onward."

Xander's brow furrowed, fingers twitching with thought. "I don't understand. How do we – I – do this? I've never done something that sounds like that in my life."

"I doubt that. Only a short while ago, you convinced me that the spark of my parents is still alive, at least enough to bring you to my home. Which I have never shown anyone. I imagine you have encouraged life in more ways than you realize. The blessings of Adam and Eve are more subtle than the magics wielded by others."

"Is it because of them, their blessing, that I could light up the sword?"

"No, that is a trick of the Cradle."

"But I can't make suns. I've tried. How can I summon sunlight this way?"

"Few of our line have had such a strong blend of Adam and Eve's blood with the Cradle. I would assume that the previous owner of that sword was also of mixed heritage, and only those with the blessings of both in enough strength could summon the power in such a way."

The three stared at the sword, as if waiting for something else miraculous to happen. "Maybe it really was King Arthur's sword," Xander breathed.

"He was supposedly a great leader in his time. That seems to fit Aclima's description," Gwen replied. Gwen and Xander looked at Aclima, waiting for her confirmation.

But she stared blankly at the two of them and said, "I do not know who this King Arthur is, but it sounds likely he was of both bloods."

Gwen's mouth popped open. "You've never heard of King Arthur?"

"I am the second oldest creature on this earth, child. I stopped paying attention to human affairs a long time ago."

Gwen hummed, then looked at Xander, whose furrowed face indicated his mind was whirring too fast, trying to figure out what was special about him, how he fit into this image of what it was to be a descendant of Adam and Eve. After a minute, Gwen tapped him on the leg. "Dude, you're training to be a veterinarian. To save animals. I'd say that counts."

"I guess so," Xander replied, eyebrows flicking up with surprise.

"Yes, it would." Aclima smiled briefly before her face fell flat. "Now, tell me what has happened, how Lilith is unbound. And tell me why I have both the Cradle and servants of Lilith on my doorstep."

Xander launched into the tale of the past several months, cutting out the more personal corners. He told her of how he and Nikki met, of Nikki resisting the compelling. Gwen heard Xander's voice rise and shake with increasing distress as he spoke, so Gwen cut him off and took the lead on telling the story. When she told Aclima of Hormin and the Scythians, Aclima winced at the mention of Hormin's name and murmured her dislike. During the retelling, Gwen felt Nikki slide into the back of her mind, an anxious hum, but Nikki remained silent, listening, her presence growing heavier as Gwen got to the parts where she knew Nikki felt she had failed. Gwen skipped over where her flock had been killed, the fight between Xander and Nikki that caused them to separate, the betrayal of Nikki's mom. She glossed over both of their kidnappings, and told what she knew of Lilith's release, Nikki's placement in the Tree, what they knew of Lilith's movements since then. She told Aclima of the fight in Peru where Lilith had been reduced to little more than bones, concluding that they needed to get a vampire out of the Tree to make Lilith killable.

Aclima listened without interruption, so still and unblinking that Gwen felt she was talking to a piece of furniture. Almost. The intensity of Aclima's milky white gaze was the only indication there was a living being inside the statue-esque body.

Gwen's voice was hoarse when she finished, Nikki bouncing around her mind restlessly like a pollen-drunk bee. Aclima retrieved a cold cup of water for her, and it soothed her throat.

When Aclima sat back down, she stared between the two of them, Xander gazing into the fire, his face drawn and pale. Gwen fidgeted with the cup, heart pulling her chest into her stomach, remembering her lost flock, how her hands felt around those brittle, broken bones. The soft feathers and limp muscles.

"Children," Aclima said, her voice soft, "do not carry the weight so heavily upon your shoulders. Lilith's freedom was a matter of time. In truth, I am surprised it took this long."

"That doesn't comfort me when we are still the ones to blame. The ones who carry the scars," Xander said.

Nikki flinched in Gwen's mind and said, *"He has more bite than he used to."*

Gwen held her tongue, wanting to finish the conversation with Aclima before revealing Nikki was with her. The memory of Xander lashing out at his mom and offering himself as a martyr surfaced, and she squashed it, but not before Nikki sensed her worried state.

"What are you hiding, Gwen?" Nikki asked.

Again, Gwen did not respond, instead focusing her gaze back on Aclima.

"I understand," Aclima said to Xander, gaze roaming his body as if she could see where he had been beaten, bloodied, and bruised. "Still, this does not explain why both you and the vampires have hunted me."

"As far as we go, we think you're the only one who could tell us where the Tree is, and maybe how to get Nikki out. I guess that Lilith thinks the same, and wanted to either intercept us or get to you before we could get those answers," Gwen said.

"I see."

Silence settled around them, save for the echoing trickle of water through the cave, the flickering of fire.

"So," Gwen said, "are we right? Can you help us?"

Aclima hesitated. "Even if I could, why would I? I have not been embroiled in the affairs of humans, or vampires, in countless millennia. While I have no love for Lilith, for the monster she made me," Aclima paused, baring her shark-like teeth, "I am no fighter. I only confronted your coven leader to protect my home. Nothing more. I simply wish to live my life in peace."

"Too late for that," Gwen said. "If you don't help us, we'll leave you alone, but Lilith won't. She'll keep sending lackeys after you until you're on her side or dead."

"I will never be on her side," Aclima growled. "She destroyed my home, slaughtered my family, and tried to enslave me."

"Well, then, I guess you get to look forward to her killing you."

"Gwen, is this harshness the best approach?"

"Or maybe she'll enslave you and let you watch her end your parents' bloodline, massacre the Cradle, and treat humanity like cattle. Doesn't that sound fun?"

Nikki sighed in her mind, and Aclima stared at her with the weight of her long life. Gwen felt her body folding under the pressure, but she took a deep breath and kept her back straight, trying to project strength. She had learned well from her flock, from dealing with her family, that sometimes pretending to be strong was good enough to convince the opposing side to bend to your will.

Aclima tsked and grabbed the staff leaning against the stone table beside her. Using it to push herself to her feet, she said, "I will think on it and give you my answer tomorrow night. You will remain here for the day. It is too close to dawn to return you to your camp."

"How do you know what time it is down here?"

"Live through hundreds of thousands of days and the same amount of seasons, and you will know. I have no spare beds, but you may lay the furs before the fire to keep warm. I will maintain it."

Gwen didn't like the idea of staying in a cold cave all day, waiting for Aclima's answers, but sleep tugged at her eyelids, and she hoped she could sleep the day away to make time disappear. Nikki nudged her mind and said, *"I'm here for a reason. I have news."*

"Good news, I hope?" Gwen asked. Xander and Aclima looked at her, surprised by her non sequitur. Xander's face settled into understanding, but his stormy, oceanic eyes bored into her, eager and anxious.

"They've found it. The ring. Io confirmed it, too."

"Oh," Gwen said, limbs heavy with dread.

Seeing her fallen face, Xander asked, "What is it?"

"They found the ring."

"What ring?" Aclima asked.

"The Ring of Dispel."

Aclima shook her head, not understanding.

"It's a ring that can supposedly purge the magic from someone. Lilith wants to use it on Xander so she can drink him. Io confirmed it's the real deal."

Xander winced, then cast his gaze into the fire. Gwen felt Nikki stir in her mind, trying to analyze him through her eyes, wishing she could reach out to him. Gwen twitched her fingers, resisting Nikki's temptation to touch him, instead looking to Aclima.

Aclima's eyes widened. "Your friend truly does speak with the Infinite One, then."

"Yes, like I said she did."

"Many claim to speak to a higher power, few actually do." Aclima tapped her staff on the ground so hard it echoed through the chamber. "This is not good. The line of Adam and Eve cannot end."

"So that means you'll help us?"

"As I said, I will think on it, witch," Aclima responded, and for the first time in her life, 'witch' didn't sound like an insult. Aclima turned her back on them, but before she could disappear into the black of the cave, Gwen shouted after her.

"Wait!" Anxiety burbled in Gwen's gut, as the question burning on her tongue all night finally had time to escape. Aclima turned her head, but not her body, listening. "I get why you would talk to Xander, but why me?"

Aclima's milky moonlight eyes settled on her, shining. "There is a likeness, between you and me. We are both within and without. Inside and out. Both a part, and apart."

Aclima's words were like a clenched fist squeezing Gwen's heart, and she had to force air out of her lungs to speak through her tightened chest. "How would you know that after only just meeting me?"

Aclima gave her a sad smile, and without another word disappeared into the cave, not even her footsteps making a sound.

Gwen sighed, releasing the tension in her shoulders, but the weight in her heart remained. "Well, look at us," Gwen said to Xander, whose gaze shifted away from the flames and to her, "two doomed peas in a pod, at the far ends of the Earth."

Xander's mouth flickered with forced amusement. His gaze intensified, boring into her, and she tried not to fidget. It was weird having him look at her like that. In the way only Theo did.

"Is she still here?" he whispered.

Nikki swirled toward the forefront of her mind, and Gwen nodded. Xander's face twisted with hurt and longing, his gaze growing more searching as he looked for Nikki in her eyes, and Nikki pushed against Gwen's body, yearning to reach out to him, to cup his face and tell him how sorry she was, how she wished she could tell him everything would be okay.

Gwen felt like she was being crushed between two boulders, and she blurted, "Stop it, you two! Your heartbroken yearning is too much for me."

Xander blinked and broke her gaze. With an abrupt apology, Nikki swept away from Gwen's mind. Xander stood, and Gwen asked, "What are you doing?"

"Might as well try to sleep," he said without looking at her, gathering as many furs as he could find. "Nothing else to do but wait."

"Good point," Gwen said and stood, stomach grumbling with the movement. "Don't suppose she has anything we can eat?"

"Not likely, unless you've acquired a taste for blood."

"Ugh," Gwen gagged, then helped Xander gather all the pelts they could find, and piled them high near the fire. Even though she couldn't feel the cold from the stone floor, it was still a hard, uncomfortable spot to lie down. She didn't think she'd be able to sleep, but as she lay there thinking about how restless she was going to be all day, somewhere between the fatigue and the flickering flames, she fell into a fitful sleep.

Chapter Seventy-Three

WHEN GWEN WOKE FOR GOOD, after a day of frequent wakings due to stiff muscles and anxious thoughts, she groaned. Her whole body felt like it had undergone a beating, like a slab of meat being tenderized. Xander still slept beside her, an arm slung over his eyes.

When she sat up, her stomach clenched with hunger so fierce it made her dizzy.

"I can ask one of the forest animals if they would sacrifice themselves for your strength," Aclima said from behind her, and Gwen startled, hand flying to her chest as if that would settle her heart.

Gwen got up and stretched, then sat opposite Aclima at the stone table, wrapping herself in an extra layer of fur to eliminate the chill. Aclima wove grasses and sticks together, creating some sort of basket. Gwen brushed her fingers through her matted hair and said, "No, I don't eat meat. But thanks anyway."

Aclima's mouth twitched with approval. "Who taught you?"

"Taught me what? Magic?"

Aclima nodded.

"I'm self-taught, thank you very much."

"That explains it."

"Explains what?" Gwen said, trying to keep the bite out of her voice.

"You use your magic wrong."

Gwen took a deep breath before responding, tasting acid. "You know, that's the third time I've heard that, and yet somehow still no one has explained what that means."

"It means you use your magic like a vampire."

"Well, duh. Everyone in my family is a vampire. I have vampire blood. How else am I supposed to use it?"

"Like a witch."

"Ugh," Gwen groaned and dropped her head to the table, resting her forehead on the cool stone. "With both you and Ina, it's like talking in circles. Why can't anyone just be straightforward?"

Aclima didn't respond, and Gwen kept her head down, trying to let the cold stone cool the annoyance that burned in her body.

They sat like that for some time, Gwen trying to ignore the anger and hunger in her stomach while Aclima wove, Xander breathing deeply in his sleep. After some time, his breaths became shallow, and he stirred, rising with a sigh and stretch from the ground. He rolled his neck, and upon hearing Aclima's soft weaving, turned to look at them at the table. Gwen gave him a small smile, and he nodded in response, stomach gurgling.

"I will return you to your camp when the sun sets," Aclima said.

"How long is that?" Gwen asked.

"Not long now."

Gwen rolled her eyes at yet another non-answer.

Aclima retrieved water for them, and although it was icy cold, almost painfully so, it was clean and refreshing. Aclima, back at her seat, said, "I have come to my decision."

"And?"

"I will aid you to the best of my abilities." Gwen's heart lifted, but at the pleasure on her face, Aclima raised a palm to still her. "However, my help comes with caveats. One, I do not fight. I will not engage in any battles."

"But you interfered with not-Tyee and my sisters –" Gwen broke off, the word catching in her throat unexpectedly. "Sister."

"Yes. As I said, it was because they threatened my home. I would not have killed them, instead hoping that the intimidation was enough. Which it was. Second," Aclima continued before Gwen could interrupt again, "I do not know how to free your friend from the Tree. Not precisely. Blood curses are difficult to lift and often require blood for a counterspell. If we can find the Tree, then perhaps we can discover a solution."

"What do you mean 'if' we find the Tree? Don't you know where it is?" Gwen asked, Aclima's words disheartening her.

"I knew, once. I do not know how the world has shifted since that time. It was hidden in a sea of thousands of islands. The last time I felt its pull, I was in a city called Krekropia. I do not know if it still stands. Or if the name remains the same."

Gwen looked at Xander, and he shrugged, neither of them knowing where that city was.

Seeing the blank looks on their faces, Aclima said, "If you have a map, I may be able to deduce where it is located."

"We'd have to go back to the cabins," Xander said. "I don't think we have a global map on us or at camp."

Aclima nodded. "Very well. We will return to your camp when night falls, then you will take me to your cabins and consult your maps."

"Sounds good," Gwen replied. "Out of curiosity, besides it being the right thing to do, why did you decide to help us?"

Aclima's moon-white gaze grew distant. "I still remember the day Lilith and her brood infiltrated the garden. The slaughter..." Aclima's throat caught, and she looked at Xander, "I would not see that happen again. My family, all my siblings, lovers, and friends, perished that day. And I was left to wander the world alone. As this. Or so I thought. Yet here you are, and I feel there is hope to put Lilith to rest. To put this millennia-long story to bed. Finally. I knew her once, before the corruption overtook her. She was fierce," Aclima said, a small twitch to her mouth. "She was an angry woman, yet still a woman. She was strong, curious, and attuned to the natural world in a way not even my mother was. I cannot imagine that if even a fragment of her true, original self remains, she is content with what she has become."

"So, you want to save Lilith?" Gwen asked, incredulous.

Aclima was silent in thought for a moment, and then said, "I would not say it like so. I would put an end to what she has become in honor of her past self. I would see the innocent protected. The last vestiges of my family preserved. Then I can return to my quiet life, knowing my survival had purpose, and that I no longer need to fear her return."

Gwen did not respond, and neither did Xander, letting Aclima's words settle. Aclima raised a palm, and the fire behind Xander lifted, soft heat pulsing through the cave. She turned back to her weaving, leaving Gwen and Xander to idle away their time in boredom. Gwen moved back to the newly brightened fire across from Xander.

"How are you feeling?" she asked.

His brow furrowed, and he tucked an errant curl of hair behind his ear. "I don't know. Glad that this journey wasn't for nothing. But exhausted, mentally and physically. I still don't understand why there's all this fuss about my bloodline. It feels like Elena and Julian died for no reason. And Miguel. So many people have died for me, or because of me, and I don't understand why."

"It's not your fault. Lilith is cuckoo."

"But isn't it? Because of something out of my control, of the nature of my heritage. I still fail to see why it is so important. Maybe long ago it made sense, but why does it matter now?"

Gwen remained silent, not knowing why herself, and unsure how to comfort him. The image of Brienne, her chest nothing but a burned cavity in the snow, flashed through her mind. A tangled twist of conflicting emotions centered around how she should feel sadder than she was at the loss of a future where they could ever reconcile and be family.

"Adam and Eve provided the first utopia," Aclima said from the table. "The first guidance for weaving magic, for using it to better the world and those around you."

"Sure, but I don't do those things. Which is the point. Why does anyone still care so much? Why does it still matter?"

"The spirit of them still lives in you. Others sense it and are drawn to you. The peace. The greatness. The feeling that there is something more to this world. It gives them hope."

"This is what bothers me. I'm valued for what I am, not *who* I am. For something I have no control over rather than something I chose to do."

"No one can separate what we are from *who* we are," Aclima said with a snarl, her shark-like fangs glistening orange in the firelight. "Let me ask you this. Your vampire – do you love her because of, or in spite of, her vampirism?"

Xander flinched, offended. "Neither. She's just...Nikki."

"My point exactly," Aclima replied, satisfied. "Yet she would not be the same Nikki if she were not a vampire. As you would not be the same Xander if you were not of Adam and Eve, if you were not of the Cradle. These heritages and their blessings are a part of you. A part of what has made you the person who you have become. You are loved neither because of them nor in spite of them. While they have influenced who you are, the choices you make, ultimately it is you, the *who*, not the *what*, that is cherished."

Xander's furrowed brow deepened and he looked away from Aclima back into the fire. Aclima stared at him a moment longer, then returned to her weaving. Gwen fidgeted with the fabric of her clothing, ruminating on Aclima's speech. Not just how it related to Xander, and how she hoped it got through to him, but what it meant for her. She had always put so much of her self-worth into being a witch, into what that identity meant for her. Who would she be without it? She had thought her value relied on her power, that she would use her power one day to show her family she was worthy of their acceptance. But maybe there was value to her outside of her magic.

The broken and bloodied flock scattered around her studio flashed across her mind, crushing her chest so tightly she couldn't breathe. She hoped she had more worth than being a witch, since apparently she was bad at it. She couldn't protect her flock, and so many people told her she used her magic wrong anyway.

Gwen sat with her thoughts until they became too circular and made her restless. Her fidgeting must have annoyed Aclima, because she gave Gwen a torch to light in the fire and told her to take laps around the cave. Glad to finally have something to do, she wandered off, Xander joining her on the walk.

They moved slowly, taking in the odds and ends that Aclima had collected over the years, the shaping of the cave to smooth the walls and let in the stream. It was as homey as a virtually blind, isolated, reclusive vampire could make a cave.

They stopped at the stream and wiped the grime from their hands, faces, and hair, grateful for the biting refreshment of water on their bodies after days of being covered in sweat. Gwen couldn't wait for a real bath.

She lost count of the laps they did, small as the cave was, relighting the torch in the mantle every time they passed. Aclima puttered around her home, disappearing and reappearing from the dark corners. Eventually, she stopped their meandering and bid them follow her, night having descended.

Relief washed over Gwen, ready to see Theo, to move forward. But as soon as the thought struck her, she remembered the last night at the camp, and she wondered what had been done with the bodies. Did they bury them? Burn them? Or leave them and just move camp? Would Julian, Elena, and her sister be left to freeze under the Alaskan sky?

No, Gwen couldn't believe Ina would leave them sitting out like that, subject to the elements. Well, maybe not Julian and Elena. She might leave Brienne out to decay. Or be eaten.

They walked back up through the winding cavern, Aclima carrying a small pack on her back, the staff tapping light against the stone floor with each soft footstep.

"Gwen," Aclima said, bidding Gwen to step beside her as they walked. It was a narrow path, so Gwen walked as close to her as possible, but she still remained a step behind. "I do not know how long we will travel together, but I will teach you what I know as we do."

"You mean you'll tell me how to use my magic the 'right' way?"

"Yes."

Gwen sucked the insides of her cheek, swallowing her pride. The taste of it was acidic, and it burned her chest. "Fine."

Xander cleared his throat, and she shot him a look. He raised an eyebrow at her, the torch illuminating half of his face.

Gwen sighed and said to Aclima, "Thanks." She caught the flicker of a grin on Xander's face and said, "I would've thanked her on my own, you know. Eventually."

"I didn't say anything," he replied, still looking rather too smug.

Gwen leered at him jokingly and said, "You and Nikki really rubbed off on each other, didn't you? So proud to be proper and polite." Xander's face fell at her joke, and she sighed. "Both so sensitive, too," she mumbled, smothering the surge of guilt.

After a few quiet footsteps, the path forever angling upward, Gwen said to Aclima, "So, how do I use my magic correctly?"

"First, you must understand the source of your magic. You use what is within you, like a vampire does. This is what drains you. What limits your abilities."

"But that's where my magic is – inside of me. Why wouldn't I tap into that?"

"That is the vampire's way. In the days of the garden, magic was abundant, both within and without humanity. Lilith corrupted the magic within herself, turning her into the first vampire. That internal, corrupted magic is what has been passed down through the generations. It is what gives vampires their long life. Their strength. Their heightened senses. The same corrupted magic flows through your veins, yet you do not have those benefits. So, how does it manifest?"

"As free flowing magic that I can use?"

"Still, that is a vampire's way of thinking. The vampiric use of magic is selfish. It nourishes them and nothing, no one, else. What makes witches formidable is their ability to attune to the magic within them and to that which is outside of them."

"I've done that a little, with animals. I had a flock for a while," Gwen said, heart sinking. "But they were all killed and I didn't sense it. So, I guess I did that wrong, too."

"Do not blame yourself too harshly if no one taught you. I will teach you how to create proper bonds with other creatures of the earth. It is more than just giving a piece of yourself to them, or them to you. As I said, it is attunement. If you can learn to attune your internal magic to what is external, you can tap into the free roaming magic in the world. Instead of draining your own resources, you will take from the earth. More power will be yours to wield, at less cost to yourself. Witches who learn to do this are nigh unstoppable."

"I like the sound of that."

"Yes, I thought you would," Aclima replied. Several seconds of silence passed before she continued. "You appear well practiced at calling the magic within you. I do not think it will take you long to learn how to attune it to the magic without you. Sustaining it, however, will require practice. Witches have perished, accidentally switching from pulling threads from the earth to using that which is within themselves, using all their life force."

Gwen grimaced, "Yeah, I'd rather not accidentally kill myself."

"Once you're attuned, we will practice sustaining the draw. Extending the length little by little until you are accustomed to the feel of it, as well as the nuance of how it feels to use the different magics and know when you must cease."

"Sounds good to me," Gwen replied, excited at the prospect of near limitless power. "Then I can stop practicing with the stupid sickle."

"No, you should not," Aclima interjected, dashing Gwen's dreams of never wielding a weapon again. "If your magic is blocked, weakened, or drained, you will need something else to rely on to protect you. Or fight with. And in time, you may learn how to combine the use of magic and the sickle, an even more formidable combination than one could be on its own."

Gwen hummed, "I guess you're right." Aclima didn't respond, and Gwen spent the rest of the walk musing over her potential. She tugged at the pools of magic in her body, trying to put words to the sensations she felt when she used or touched magic. Nikki's ring thrummed as she practiced, amplifying the feelings of a hot summer wind or warm whiskey sliding down her throat.

"Good," Aclima said, "keep practicing."

Gwen grinned at the affirmation and exercised her magic the whole walk home, barely noticing when the dark of the cave shifted to the black of night, only evidenced by the change from damp air to a fresh breeze, the weight of stone overhead lifting from her shoulders.

"Not to sound rude, but I've been wondering, how do you see?"

Xander asked as he tripped over another errant root that Aclima had avoided.

"My eyes no longer respond to light, it is true. But I can sense shapes in the earth, feel the essence of others in the air around me."

"Like, you see our auras?" Gwen asked. "What's mine?"

"I do not remember what colors look like, or what they are called. But do not worry, I can see the world well, in my own way. I will not be a hindrance." Aclima relit the torch in Xander's hands, and continued to do so periodically as the chilly wind blew it out. Gwen barely even noticed the cold, warmed as she was by the push and pull of power in her body and the excitement of being greater than she already was.

The bright light of a small fire soon poured through the dark, and they followed it, the flames growing brighter as they approached. Everyone in camp was awake, huddled around the fire, unspeaking. Theo and Ina leapt to their feet when they saw the trio, Theo running to Gwen and wrapping her in a tight hug, Ina doing the same for Xander. Gwen drank in Theo's affection and scent, rich yet chemically from disinfectant wipes.

"I was worried about you," Theo said, pulling back.

"I was worried about you, too. Out here and not knowing where not-Tyee and Bridget went."

"They haven't reappeared, so we're hoping it means they've left the area."

"Fingers crossed," Gwen replied, winding her fingers through Theo's and heading towards the fire, where Alessa stared into the flames with unseeing eyes and Terrance rubbed his hands together, anxious.

"Thank you for returning them safe," Ina said to Aclima, everyone repositioning around the fire.

"You thought I would do otherwise?"

"No, of course not," Ina stammered, "but I worried you might encounter more unpleasant company."

"I see," Aclima replied, pale gaze piercing Ina. Xander's stomach produced a loud growl, and Gwen's clenched in hungry response. Ina winced in disapproval but did not berate Aclima for failing to feed them, instead starting water to boil to rehydrate some food for them, tossing them snack bars to eat in the meantime. Gwen's stomach knotted painfully as the promise of food became reality, and she ate the bar with barely a chew and swallow. In those brief moments, Gwen peered around the group where she had seen Julian, Elena, and Brienne fall. No bodies, or mounds, were in sight. What had they done with them?

Before Gwen could ask, Aclima and Ina were in conversation, Aclima explaining her agreements and caveats to the group for her help. When Aclima told her of how she last got to the Tree, Ina blinked, thinking.

"Krekopia..." Ina rolled the name around her tongue, handing Xander and Gwen their own packs of prepared food which they both dove into, Gwen not caring how it scalded the roof of her mouth. "I believe that is now what is called Athens."

"Damn, Ina, do you know everything?" Gwen asked, surprised.

Ina smirked. "No, but I am good with my geography and history. I have to be." Ina pursed her mouth, thinking. "Perhaps we can approach by the other side. If we return to John, he can open the portal to the Cradle in Egypt. Then we can sail from Alexandria. Would you be able to guide us from a different side of the sea?"

Aclima nodded. "I should. The Tree is a constant pull on my spirit. One that strengthens the closer I am. It was one of the reasons I traveled so far. To detach myself from it."

A small knot of guilt curled in Gwen, at dragging Aclima out of her home, her normalcy, to a situation she had tried so hard and long to avoid. But they had no other choice.

One of Aclima's gifts as a descendant from Adam was that of language, so she could understand all languages ever spoken, and she fell into easy conversation with Alessa. The group spoke of logistics, of timelines and methods for getting back to John. Satiated, the excitement of the last twenty-four hours caught up to her, and her eyelids grew heavy, the firelight dimming in her fading vision. Aclima assured them that she would be able to hide from the sun during the day, though they would now have to travel at night. With the promise to begin their return journey the following evening, everyone said goodnight. Aclima took a firm stance and slammed her staff into the ground. The earth grumbled, and walls of frost-covered soil erupted upward, spraying dirt and buried debris over the campsite. Everyone except Alessa, who was too lost in thought to respond, looked in awe as Aclima bent the world to her will in a way none of them had seen, not even by not-Tyee. Aclima waved her arm and the earth-risen home opened for her. She turned to look at them, sensing their stares, but Aclima did not grin with pride, this display of power clearly a normal activity for her. With a flick of her staff, the mound closed, sealing her away for the day.

Chapter Seventy-Four

Gwen slept terribly, interrupted as it was by the bright of day and the anxiety of the impending end. Of having to return to the excruciatingly long car ride, once again. Outside the tent, it seemed everyone else had slept just as poorly, with heavy bags under their eyes, the whites of Alessa's red with sorrow.

They started taking down camp, repacking so that they were ready to go when Aclima was able to leave. In the last dregs of sunset, hazy light framing the mountains, Ina approached Gwen with a serious look on her face, hands clasped tight in front of her sternum.

"What's up?" Gwen asked, flicking her fingers with anxiety at Ina's expression.

Ina opened her mouth, then closed it again, pulling a flask from her jacket pocket. Gwen took it, but when she jostled it, it didn't slosh with liquid. Instead, it sifted like dirt and small rocks. Her body went cold, and she whispered, "What is this?"

"We didn't know what to do with her – your sister," Ina said, hands tightening, and the acid in Gwen's stomach churned. "We didn't know what to do with any of them, so we burned them. It's not all of her, but... we did the best we could and gathered the ashes that didn't float away. Alessa has Julian and Elena to return to their families. It didn't seem right to leave your sister behind. I thought you might want her. Or to return her to your parents." Ina twisted her hands again, but Gwen's gaze was fixed on the flask filled with her sister's remains. "I'm sorry," Ina whispered, then put a hand on Gwen's arm and squeezed, before leaving her to her thoughts.

Gwen didn't know how long she stood there, looking at the flask, sometimes shaking it to hear the bits of bone hit the metal, the ash slide. It was surreal, knowing that this was all that remained of her sister. There was no future for Brienne.

A delicate hand dropped onto her shoulder, startling her.

"I'm so sorry," Theo said.

Gwen shook her head, as if it would sort out her feelings. "I don't know whether to say 'don't be' or 'thanks.' We weren't close. We didn't even like each other, and yet...for some reason, I feel worse about this, about her dying, than I did for actually killing someone. When I killed Atoc, I was disturbed so briefly, and then I realized I was more bothered by how I wasn't as disturbed as much as I thought I should be. But now I don't know how to feel. It's one less enemy, but she was still my sister. Maybe I never realized that until now. And I don't know why it matters. We were practically strangers."

Theo was silent for several seconds. "She was still your sister. Atoc was a stranger threatening to kill you and people you care about. You killed him in self-defense, so I understand why you don't feel guilty. But Brienne was still family, despite everything."

"I didn't think about how choosing this side of things would mean watching my family die. I knew we would have to fight, and oppose each other, but we've been doing it for so long, I didn't realize it would turn from spats and name-calling and the occasional slap to actually trying to kill each other." Gwen sucked in a breath despite the fact that it felt as if her airways were closing. With another long look at the flask, she put it in her jacket pocket and then turned into Theo, who wrapped her in strong arms.

"I'm so sorry, Gwen," Theo whispered into her hair and kissed the top of her head.

"Me too," she replied, squeezing Theo and closing her eyes, hiding herself in the embrace while she could.

Alessa called them over, and in the last minutes of the day made everyone except Ina rotate through exercises with their weapons. With the sickle in her hand, Gwen wondered at what she might be able to do, combining it with her magic. Could she make it like a boomerang, guiding it out and then back with the wind? Could she sharpen the edges with the bite of a cold breeze?

Aclima emerged from her mound just as dark fell, easing her hideout back into the earth with a gentle settling motion of her free hand. With little more than head nods between Aclima and Ina, the group set off back west, back toward civilization.

Aclima stepped beside Gwen and told her to keep practicing as she had yesterday, teasing at the magic within her, bringing it to the edges of her body, and seeing if she could sense a matching energy on the outside of her as well. She nodded and did as she was told, and although the push and pull of magic kept her warm, she could not do anything different than what she already had. Gwen brought it to her fingertips, let some of it slip from within herself to the outside, seeing if that would beckon to whatever existed outside of her that she was supposed to tap into. Aclima chided her for expelling the magic, saying that was how she would exhaust herself. She needed to keep it at the boundary of herself to maintain her own energy, and pull matching magic to herself like a magnet.

Besides to chastise her, Aclima stayed far back from the group so that Alessa and Ina could light their way, shifting positions to make sure every human could use their suns to stay warm. Aclima lit the torch, and Xander, Terrance, and Theo took turns holding it, leaving Gwen to do her magic exercises. Despite the hours upon hours of feeling her magic, of trying to call out to a matching energy in the space around her, she felt nothing. No return call, no warm swarm of power drawing itself toward her. With each failed minute, Gwen grew more frustrated, wanting to lash out at Aclima for not giving her more direction, at Ina for pulling her into this stupid quest, and at herself for not just being able to do what Aclima could with nothing more than a simple tap of her staff.

It was stupid. All of it.

But Gwen trudged on, stomping her feet heavier and heavier into the snow, until Ina called it a night. And so continued the same cycle of camp setup, eating, sleeping, breakdown, walking, and failing to sense any magic outside of her.

Chapter Seventy-Five

Nikki checked in on Gwen once a day, but Gwen was such a torrent of emotions she couldn't stay there long. Swathed in anger, she grieved and hated herself for doing so, amplified by her inability to grasp how she was supposed to use her magic. As a result, Nikki left her to stomp back to Wiseman, only checking in to calm her own nerves, to ensure everyone else was still okay.

The rest of her time was spent amongst the forests of the world or watching the Scythians. Her mom was still lost to her, despite her proximity. Individuals from the village continued to check on Cat, but otherwise all else was quiet and boring in her trapped body.

To ease her spiraling, she breathed through the forests of the Amazon, the Taiga, the Xishuangbanna. She lost her consciousness when she was the forest, instead becoming something greater, something freer, something more whole than she had ever been. When she had lost herself too much, Io would nudge her, insisting she return to her body so she wouldn't lose herself entirely.

Each time, she left the forests with a heavy heart, having to return to her singular, stuck self. She followed the Scythians through the western forests of New Zealand, but now that they had found the ring, they were rather boring. They meandered without speaking much, focused as they were on returning to a city to contact Lilith, somehow.

The trees thinned as the Scythians approached the edge of the forest, signs of human development bleeding into nature. Nikki shifted her awareness as the vegetation was lost, jumping from tree to tree along sidewalks rather than spreading out over many individuals as one being.

They found a city park to rest, dropping their packs and bodies to the grass. Vadasz retrieved a cell phone from his bag and turned it on, grunting with annoyance as it lit up with notification after notification. They tried calling Hormin with no luck, then decided to eat while waiting for an answer. Nikki followed them through the park, hoping Hormin would call them back before they were in their hotel room and out of her sight and hearing.

The Scythians spotted a young couple resting near a manmade pond in the park, faces bent close together. The Scythians circled around, giving the couple a wide berth, and hid behind the trees and vegetation at the couple's backs, not making a sound as they laid their trap, spread out so the humans had nowhere to run.

The moment before they could leap at their prey, the phone in Vadasz's pocket lit up. His nose crinkled at the interruption of his hunt. He moved deeper into the park as he answered, "Yes?"

Nikki could hear the sound of another voice coming through the speaker, but could not make out what it said.

Vadasz's face fell, then turned to stone, as he listened. "No, we were promised –"

But whatever he was going to say was cut off, and the murderous expression on his face worsened.

"Fine, but if the plan changes again, we won't follow it. A promise is a promise, Hormin."

He rolled his eyes at whatever Hormin said, then hung up. Aella and Uase had crept close to him during the call, and Aella asked, "What is it?"

"A change in plans. Seems our favorite witch and her deceiver friends know the Mother's secret. We are commanded to intercept them before they reach the Tree."

Aella clenched her jaw. "But we were promised – "

"I know. I reminded Hormin. He vowed that once this little problem is corrected, and once the ring is safely in the Mother's grasp, the promise will be fulfilled."

A disapproving growl rumbled in Uase's throat.

"I know, my friend," Vadasz sighed. "Let's try to not let it spoil our dinner."

The three grinned at each other, wicked and hungry, then spread out again around the couple, who still had not heard or sensed their presence.

Vadasz leapt out from the shrubbery, fangs sinking into the man's neck, cutting off his yell of surprise. Blood spurt from his neck before Vadasz closed the seal, splattering his girlfriend's face. At first, she froze, blinking in terror, then she shrieked and leapt to her feet, running into Uase's broad chest. He smiled at her horror, then snapped her neck with a quick twist of his massive hands.

Nikki peeled herself away from the trees after that, unable to stomach more.

Chapter Seventy-Six

Back in the Tree, Nikki gritted her teeth to ignore the swirl of sensation that sickened her body as she watched the Scythians kill the couple. She took several deep breaths through her nose, calming her body, processing the information she had gleaned.

Not only did they have the Ring of Dispel, but they also knew Gwen and the others were on their way to free her. Which must mean that not-Tyee and Bridget somehow got into contact with Lilith, told her of their confrontation, and assumed Aclima would help them. Unless they had stayed and watched the group, listening to their conversation?

But no, when she had checked on Gwen, when she had filtered herself through the Alaskan forest, she hadn't felt their presence.

So where were they?

Where was Lilith?

"Io?" Nikki thought to the faint glimmers in the darkness. Io never truly left her these days, keeping some of Their presence with her while They did whatever else They did.

"Yes, child?" Io replied, pulling themselves into the Tree, the pressure of Their presence filling the space around Nikki as the density of glitter grew.

"Where's Lilith?"

Io hesitated, and a flame burned in Nikki's chest.

"I can't believe you still refuse to help us at all. Even after you've seen the way Lilith has massacred people. We are completely in the dark compared to her and her allies. They know of the artifacts that can be used against us. They have so many more magical capabilities and strengths to use against us. You won't even level the playing field by telling us where she is? Or where not-Tyee and Bridget are? How are we supposed to have a fighting chance of saving not just ourselves, but humanity, without your help?"

Io's presence grew heavy, like a long-held sigh. *"You do not need to repeat your same arguments to me, child. I do not hesitate from an unwillingness to help you. I hesitate with not knowing how. What is fair? What is helpful? These questions I ponder perpetually."*

"Well, while you're philosophizing, Lilith gets closer to world domination. Soon, your pondering won't matter."

"I am aware. If you would still your thoughts and finish listening to me, you would hear my conclusions."

Nikki recoiled, like she'd been slapped. She let her emotions run away from her, but she could not help that the kindle of irritation remained white-hot in her chest at how long it had taken Io to reach Their decision.

"The covens of the earth stir. Even those so ancient the forests have no memories of them."

"What does that mean?"

"I am not certain. But they heard a call and are responding. Whether they accept or reject it has yet to be determined."

"A call to what, exactly?"

"Exactly? I do not know. I cannot tell you where Lilith resides. Nor where Bridget and the vampire formerly known as Tyee are located. The same magic she employed to hide her corrupting spirit all those millennia ago must be utilized now. Wherever she is, the former Tyee and Bridget are with her. With her hidden from me, I cannot know the commands she has imposed upon her children."

"This sounds bad."

"It does not bode well."

"So, Lilith is hiding, and the vampires of the earth are mobilizing, while we don't even know how to get me out of here and make her killable. How do we stand a chance?"

Io's flickers twitched, anxious. *"I do not know how to unweave Lilith's curse on you, but if your friends find a way, I may have a solution for how to sustain the Tree without another's sacrifice."*

"Really?" Nikki asked, heart lifting at finally, *finally* having some good news.

"Yes. However, my help comes on one condition."

"Anything."

"You cannot kill Lilith. Not without first giving her a chance to choose life."

Chapter Seventy-Seven

When they reached the cabins in Wiseman, Gwen still could not sense a kindred magic outside of herself. One morning, just before Aclima hid from the sunrise, Gwen snapped at her, complaining that she was led to believe it would be easy.

Aclima responded with annoying calm, unfazed by Gwen's attitude, and said that when she meant Gwen would pick it up quickly, she meant weeks or months, not days. Theo put a calming hand on Gwen's forearm before she could reply, which she later realized was for the best. Fighting with Aclima would serve no purpose. It would not make her any better at learning to do something she didn't know how to do.

Nikki's news was also met with mixed feelings. It was a relief to know Io didn't want Lilith to succeed, that They'd help humanity in whatever way They saw fit.

But how were they supposed to stop Lilith without killing her?

Nikki said she had posed that same question to Io and received little guidance. Nothing more than Io's suggestion that they, and everyone else, think on their options.

The knowledge that the Scythians knew where they were headed and planned to intercept them was even worse news. Gwen remembered their last encounter when they showed up at her studio on Nikki's birthday. How Vadasz pushed through Gwen's barrier, his flesh sloughing off his skeleton, and Aella healed him as if it were nothing. She shivered with dread.

Once the lights of the cabin were in sight, Gwen couldn't take her eyes off them. The promise of heat, a bed, and real food pulled her weary bones forward. She kept her magic close, the feel of it constantly swirling in her body, almost second nature. Now, it was a part of her just like her blood, rather than how she treated it before, like a tool to be called upon.

The rush of indoor heating slammed against her skin when she walked into the cabin, the cold on her face washed away in the pleasant blast. Terrance barely had a chance to take his pack off before Rachel leapt into his arms, wrapping her legs around his hips and holding him tight like a little spider monkey. He held her in return, and Gwen averted her gaze, giving them a moment of privacy.

Cora and the Lius greeted Ina, Xander, and Alessa, who introduced them to Aclima and filled her in on what had happened.

Farrell approached Gwen, giving Alessa a searching look as he passed by them. They returned his gaze, and the hollowness of the last few days briefly twinkled out, replaced by a strange spark, before their face crumpled into sadness again. Farrell's expression did not change as their gazes broke and he turned his focus to Gwen.

With a squeeze of her shoulder, Theo left to give Gwen and her brother some time alone, joining Ina and the others.

Farrell stopped a respectable distance in front of her and clasped his hands behind his back, as if unsure of the appropriate way to greet her. "I'm glad you have returned in one piece," he said with a soft smile. "It seems not everyone was so fortunate."

"No, they weren't," Gwen murmured, breaking his gaze to look at the ground. Gwen couldn't bring herself to store Brienne's remains in her pack, as if it were another casual, everyday item. The whole trek back, the weight of her sister's ashes sat heavy in her jacket pocket. Now, she pulled the flask out and handed it to Farrell, still unable to look him in the face. "Including our sister. This is Brienne. Or what's left of her."

Farrell took the flask from her hand and when she summoned the courage to look at his face, it was unreadable.

"I wondered which one of us would be the first to fall," he mused, gaze a million miles away. "I remember when she was born. Such a quiet baby. Not as quiet as Bronwen, but nowhere near as loud as Bridget. Or you."

Gwen soured at the comparison between her and Bridget. Farrell held the flask out as if to return it to her, and Gwen shook her head. "I don't want it."

Farrell blinked, the distant look in his eyes fading, and he slipped the flask into a large pants pocket. "Come. You must be famished. Let's get you something to eat."

She followed him to the kitchen, where Cora and the Lius were already cooking, the whole group crammed into the small space, telling and retelling bits of the story until everyone was up to speed. Aclima, draped in her furs and pelts, stood in the corner with a white-knuckled fist around her staff.

Gwen sidled up beside her and asked, "Are you okay?"

Aclima's filmy gaze roved over the people in the room before she responded, "I have not been around people, let alone this many of them in...I do not know how long. I find myself uncomfortable. I do not know what to say. And worry that anything I say will be wrong, ill-received, or inappropriate."

"Good old social anxiety."

"Is that what they call it?"

Gwen nodded. "But don't worry, this is one of the least judgmental groups ever. Well, except for Ina. If you get along with her, then you're gold. Everyone else is easy in comparison."

Ina squinted at Gwen as if she had heard her, and Gwen shot her a winning smile.

Aclima said, "I will do my best not to worry about it so much, then. Though that is easier said than done."

"As is trying to feel magic outside of me, like a sixth sense."

Aclima stared at her in a way Gwen couldn't read, somehow both appraising and curious. "Yes. Quite."

The rest of the evening passed in a blink, a mix of conversation and shoving their faces full of pasta, salad, and pie. Nothing of note had happened to those who'd stayed behind. They debated if there was any faster way to return to John, if some could fly while others drove, but there was no way around the time delay, so they decided to stick together. Groans erupted around the table at having to be in those vehicles for days on end again. They spoke of Io's request, of ways to stop Lilith, of how to deal with the Scythians if they were successful in intercepting them, of how best to get to the Tree. But with a full belly, Gwen didn't register much of what they were saying, the comfort of shelter and warm food making her sleepy. Everyone who had traveled with Gwen must have felt the same way, eyelids drooping in the middle of conversations. Those who stayed behind let them rest while they cleaned and packed the cabins, preparing to leave the following evening, and Gwen fell into the deep black sleep of satiation.

Chapter Seventy-Eight

ACLIMA DID NOT LIKE CARS.

Gwen shouldn't have been surprised to hear that she had never seen one, let alone ridden in one, yet she kept forgetting just how removed Aclima had been from humanity and for how long.

Aclima, Gwen, and Theo rode with Farrell that first evening, Aclima grimacing every time she looked outside, at the blur of the world passing by. "This makes me ill," she said, frowning. "I prefer having my feet on the ground."

"Just hope you don't have to ride in a plane," Gwen said.

"Plane?"

"Big flying thing in the sky."

"Ah." Aclima put a hand to her mouth as if suppressing bile. "I have seen and heard those. Did not know what they were called."

Thankfully, despite the nausea on her face, Aclima did not throw up. Gwen did not want to discover what a made vampire's vomit looked like, as their bellies were only filled with blood.

While Aclima tried to get a handle on her sickness, she made Gwen continue trying to sense the magic outside of her. Gwen huffed, since everyone else who wasn't driving got to just relax. Aclima kept telling her she would feel it eventually. Gwen was starting to believe her words were a lie, but it wasn't like she had another choice if she wanted to be more powerful.

The nights rolled into each other, just as they had on the trip up. The vampires hid in the trunks during the day while the humans rotated driving and sleeping shifts, taking periodic restroom and stretching breaks. Alessa made them practice their forms during those stretching breaks, the void of Julian and Elena yawning beside them, so tangible Gwen felt like their ghosts were standing nearby.

They passed over the Canadian border with as little fuss as they had crossing it into the United States, though both Aclima and Gwen had to hide away this time. Aclima liked being stuck in trunks even less than riding in a seat.

Soon, it felt as if they had never stopped their limbo of car travel. The Alaskan excursion faded like a dream. Only the presence of Aclima, and the absence of Elena and Julian, reminded Gwen that it had been real, that she hadn't been in these cars for eternity.

Aclima was a patient, albeit reserved, teacher. One evening, in Gwen's continued frustration that she couldn't feel a shared magic outside of herself, she snapped at Aclima again, demanding more direction.

Aclima didn't even blink at her attitude. "I cannot tell you what I do not know. I know how my magic feels. I know how your magic feels to me. I do not know how your magic feels to you. Or how it is echoed in the world. It is something you need to discover on your own."

"Isn't there anything you can do to, I don't know, hasten the process?"

"I will think on it."

Gwen sighed, but didn't argue further. Later that night, in the witching hours of early morning, Gwen pushed the magic out of her hand, certain that if it was outside of herself, she would be better able to feel an answering reply.

Aclima rapped Gwen's knuckles with the strength of an ancient vampire.

"Ow!" Gwen said, the magic in her palm dissipating. Rubbing her knuckles, she said, "Why won't you let me do that? How am I supposed to sense it outside of me without knowing how it feels outside of me? Without providing the magnet?"

"It is a bad habit," Aclima chided. "If you confuse sensing that which is outside of you with that pulled from inside yourself, you risk not being able to identify which one is which. That increases the risk of overdrawing from yourself. You need to learn how to distinguish between the two. How to draw on them separately. Not mixed."

Gwen grumbled, disagreeing, but did not push the argument. She didn't have time to try to learn this the way Aclima wanted. They were traveling toward a potential confrontation with the Scythians, and who knew what else waited for them.

Still, she practiced the way Aclima wanted. When Aclima was awake, at least. Then she practiced the way she wanted to when Aclima was hidden away for the day. Even if she learned how to summon it mixed, it would still be an improvement over how she currently used it. She could figure out the differences later when their circumstances weren't so dire.

By good fortune for them, or perhaps ill fortune for the border patrol, they passed back into the American border at the same place with the same security as on their way through. All it took was for Feng to flash his silver, sharklike teeth for the guards to quake, their voices shaking and sweat forming at their temples, ushering them through as quickly as someone tries to shake a bad dream upon waking.

The following day, sitting in the passenger seat of Farrell's car beside Theo, who drove, Gwen felt a tug at the magic in her palm. From something outside of her.

Her heart jolted into her throat, the sense of the warm power in her palm being gently pulled away from her.

She gasped when she jumped. Theo startled and asked, "What? What is it?"

"I felt it. Something tugged at my magic."

Theo hummed, tapping her fingers on the steering wheel. Theo disagreed with Gwen's decision to go against Aclima's teachings.

The window was slightly rolled down, the car stuffy after days of marinating bodies. Gwen looked out the window. It felt as if whatever had grabbed at her had come through the gust of wind and tried to pull it away from her, back into the air.

Rolling down the window another inch, Gwen re-summoned the magic into her palm, her hand growing warm and tingly. She focused on that fleeting feeling, of the pull on the power in her hand.

Several minutes later, staring at the glowing threads that wove around her fingers, she felt it at the same time she saw it. Not the magic itself, but the movement of her magic, lifting from the weave around her hands into strands that straightened and dissipated into the air, disappearing out the window.

A bead of sweat formed on her forehead, realizing that as the magic left her hand, more was pulled from her body. Gwen shifted her focus to follow the pull of the threads, trying to clasp whatever it was that tugged at her magic and bring it toward herself.

But as her senses followed it, she became lost.

While her power started and ended with her, the other side had no source. It was hot and cold with all the layers of the atmosphere. It was dry like desert heat and humid like a swamp. It was the brittle, freezing rain of winter, the breath of trees from the forest, the whirl of wind from hurricanes, the churn of air from the world spinning.

It was everything.

It was everywhere.

Gwen's body heaved with air like it had been filled with a black-smith's bellows, and she snapped back to herself, lungs so full her chest felt near to bursting. She was filled with so much power, she thought she'd suffocate on it. Her pulse rose with panic, beating loud in her ears, in her fingertips. Her temperature rose with the buildup of power within herself, and she choked out a heaving breath to expel it. As she forced out all the air and magic in her being, a roiling gust exploded from her body, cracking the windshield and pushing the steering wheel. Theo yelped as she slammed to the side despite her seatbelt, and she tried to straighten the car that had veered to the side of the road, hair whipping around her face.

In a blink, all within the car was still, and Gwen could breathe again, feverish chills winding up her body, cold sweat down her face.

"What the hell was that?" Theo yelled, hands shaking on the wheel.

"I'm sorry," Gwen gasped between breaths, terrified she'd never be able to breathe normally again. "I felt it, the magic on the outside. When I tried to follow it, to find how to grasp it, it...consumed me. I didn't realize I was absorbing it, and it was too much for me to handle."

"Damnit, Gwen! This is why you should listen to Aclima. What if there was a car on the other side of the road? We could have died."

"I'm sorry, okay? I really am. I didn't know that would, or could, happen." Gwen put a hand on Theo's leg and squeezed it, trying to comfort her. Gwen looked at the spider-webbed crack in the windshield, and could not deny the pride that swelled within her at the awesome power she had both harbored in her body and unleashed into the world. Now that she knew what it felt like, she could practice controlling it. Now that she knew it was sourceless, she knew not to follow it too far, but to grab just at the ends that wound with her magic. Perhaps soon she'd be able to see the threads, too. If she could see them, that would make it even easier to call upon.

Gwen grinned.

She'd be limitless.

Unstoppable.

Chapter Seventy-Nine

GWEN CONTINUED to defy Aclima's guidance and Theo's anxious humming, practicing her way during the day when Aclima was asleep and in another vehicle, hopefully unable to sense Gwen's disobedience. When Gwen and Aclima were awake at the same time, Gwen practiced Aclima's way, swarming the magic in streaming veins through her hands, illuminating her skin from underneath it. Sometimes, she thought she could feel the resonant strands of magic from the air brush against the outer layer of skin, but she couldn't grasp it. The magic within her was like water, the magic outside like oil. No matter how hard she tried to hold the oil, it slipped through and around her body, slick and thin.

When she could practice her way, it was like...cold and warm air meeting. They interacted to create a new cloud, a new thunderhead, rather than canceling each other out.

Each time she was able to hold magic in this way, adrenaline surged through her body, amplified by the power from without that she welcomed in, filling her with strength and vigor. She couldn't see the threads of the world's magic, but she could feel when it attached, like a jolt of lightning. Or the pressure from an incoming storm. She practiced holding it, forming it, and releasing it slow so it didn't burst like it had the first time.

Sometimes Aclima looked at her with squinted eyes, as if she could sense something wasn't right, but she had no proof of Gwen's defiance. On those days, Gwen made sure to act frustrated and disappointed, hoping it would make Aclima think she was doing her best to learn the other way.

Overall, the ride back to John was uneventful, just another limbo of travel with everyone's stress and anxiety rising as they became increasingly restless and stressed about the conflict ahead of them. At least this time Gwen had something to distract herself with, and the time flew by faster than it did before, made even quicker by the thawing roads and improved weather as the world crawled toward spring.

Nikki checked in with her every now and then, having lost the Scythians. She thought they might be at sea or in the air, and therefore she couldn't find them. They discussed how they could possibly meet Io's condition, stopping Lilith without killing her, but they were clueless. Nikki vowed she would keep picking away at Io until They gave them some hint, but Io was as stubborn as the rest of them and even more cryptic.

By the time they reached Epps, Gwen could call upon the magic outside of her with ease, as long as she pushed her own magic through the pores of her skin to magnetize it. She still couldn't pull it into herself without extending part of herself out, but she'd keep trying. For now, this was enough for her. It still exhausted her if she did it too long, as it required some expenditure of her own resources, but it extended the duration and strength, with which she could wield the air and wind before she was too tired to carry on.

They pulled into John's house just after 3 am, cars bouncing on the gravel, the grass only slightly less frost-crusted than it had been a couple weeks ago. Frigid dew still clung to the edges of the blades, shining from the light that bled from the inside of the house.

Three more cars were parked in his driveway, and as the incoming group parked awkwardly around them, they heard Sunny barking from inside. The curtains parted, and Gwen saw Sunny's happily yapping face pressed almost at the glass, tail wagging. A figure moved behind him, looking out.

With stretches, sighs, and groans, they all exited the cars, leaving their belongings as they were too eager to stand, to be in a real house again. Gwen released the magic she had been pooling in her palm under Aclima's watchful gaze, letting it disperse back into her body, no longer looking like a human nightlight.

The door swung open before they could knock. At first, Gwen thought it was John, as the silhouette had a similar frame. But as the figure stepped back and the light of the house illuminated his face, she realized it wasn't. His features were similar, but softer, kinder. He had more laugh lines around his mouth, shorter hair, and a slightly crooked nose. He gave them a lopsided grin as they stepped by him into the warmth of the house, the smirk only faltering into discomfort as the vampires passed him. But he covered the grimace quickly, and shut the door behind them, keeping out the chill.

Sunny danced around all the humans, jumping and spinning in circles in the excitement of seeing them again.

"John!" the man who opened the door yelled. "They're here!"

Gwen turned to look back at him and he smiled at them again. "I'm Joseph, his brother," he said, extending his arm to shake everyone's hand. Aclima just stared at the offered hand in confusion, and even though she had watched everyone else shake it, she didn't take it, not understanding the custom. Joseph dropped his hand and swiped it against his pant leg with an awkward laugh.

"Welcome back, my friends!" John said, coming around the corner from his bedroom. His eyes widened when they landed on Aclima, and he asked, "Is this who I think it is?"

"Depends on who you think I am," Aclima replied, hand wringing the staff.

"The long lost Aclima."

Aclima's mouth twitched, but Gwen couldn't tell if it was in amusement or annoyance. "I was not lost. I knew where I was."

"Well, lost to humanity then," John replied. Aclima hmphed, and he continued, "I see you've met my brother, but there are others for you to still meet. Come." John crooked a hand to beckon them deeper into the house. Over his shoulder, he said, "In your absence, I summoned the rest of the Council. We are all eager to hear of your journey. What you've learned, and to discuss what our next steps should be. We've discussed it some, with our limited knowledge."

"Did they punish you for helping us?" Ina asked.

"I got a stern talking to for allowing a vampire through the portal, but considering the success you all had, and how dire the situation is, there will be no other punishment," he replied with a grin.

John led them to a closed door at the back of the house. The door opened, revealing silhouettes of several bodies, but Gwen was toward the back of the group and couldn't see far into the room. John ushered in Ina, Xander, and Alessa, but when Feng's foot stepped over the threshold, a voice called, "Hold."

Over Daiyu and Feng's shoulders, Gwen saw a woman of average height but extraordinarily long white hair with thick black streaks rise from a table.

"Cradle business only," she said, her tone brooking no argument.

Feng stiffened, but stepped back out of the doorway. John gave them an awkward, embarrassed grin, and as he closed the door in their faces said, "Sorry."

Gwen stared at the knots of wood in the door, the rest of the group moving to look at each other. But the door did not open, despite how much she glared at it, and no matter how bitter the taste in her mouth.

"Rude," she said.

Terrance shrugged. "They can make the plan if they want to. At least this way we can get some real rest. "

"Oh, yes please," Rachel replied. Terrance wrapped an arm around her shoulders as they walked away.

"Good idea," Cora said, and followed them out of the hall.

Feng glanced at his wife, then Farrell. "How about a hunt?"

"I do not think the Cradle would be happy with us, dear, if they found out," Daiyu said.

"They do not have to know," Feng replied, "but I tire of old blood."

"I must admit, I do, too."

"As do I," Farrell added.

Feng lifted a brow at Aclima. "Would you like to join us?"

Aclima grimaced. "No. Pseudo-cannibalism does not entice me."

"Suit yourself," Feng replied, nonplussed by the insult.

"Be back later," Farrell said to Gwen, leaving her, Aclima, and Theo alone.

Aclima fixed her moonlight eyes on Gwen and tapped her staff on the hardwood floor. "Come with me."

Aclima turned on her heel without waiting for Gwen's response. Gwen watched her rigid back disappear, the back door creaking open and closed.

Gwen looked at Theo, who said, "It's fine, I'll get some rest, too. Have fun with whatever that's all about."

"Thanks," Gwen said, huffing a laugh and giving Theo a quick kiss. "Have fun with your rest."

With a tired smile, Theo retreated to the guesthouse. Gwen wound her way outside, finding Aclima standing in the backyard, gaze fixed to the heavens. The night was clear and sprinkled with stars, the Milky Way a faint brushstroke across the sky.

"So, what's up, boss?" Gwen asked, stopping beside Aclima and following her gaze to the stars.

Aclima leveled her head and tapped her staff on the ground, closing her eyes as if listening to the reverberations of the thud through the earth.

"A promise fulfilled," Aclima responded.

"Mysterious." Gwen placed her hands on her hips, repressing the anxious urge to press Aclima to hurry so that she could go to sleep. She knew by now it was pointless to rush Aclima.

Silent seconds that seemed to stretch into hours passed until a faint wingbeat broke the quiet. Gwen turned to the sound, but amidst the dark, she couldn't decipher the shape of the bird, the wings growing louder as it approached. Then, in a rush of wings, a barred owl landed on top of Aclima's staff.

With her free hand, Aclima wove her hand in the air, silvery threads forming from her forearm and the space outside it. "Do as I do," Aclima commanded, "summon your magic, infusing it with the request to share a bond."

Gwen's heart gave a sudden kick in her chest, while her stomach plummeted at the same time, flashes of her old flock lying broken and bloodied.

She did as Aclima said, and as she pulled the request from within and without herself, Aclima added, "You must ask for an exchange. You cannot just give of yourself, or take of them, if you wish for a true connection."

Gwen nodded and poured her thoughts into the weave around her arm, keeping her gaze on the bird, which stared back at her with a cocked head.

"Now, ask him."

Sick with the anxiety of rejection, Gwen stretched her arm to the owl. "Would you... would you like to bond with me?"

The owl's cocked head straightened and bobbed, assessing her and the pulsing light that emanated from her. It hopped from the staff to Gwen's forearm, but Gwen didn't flinch as the claws dug into her skin. The owl and she maintained eye contact, and while hope bloomed in her chest, she also thought she might barf.

But the threads of her magic wove around the owl and into it, and just as the light faded, it flashed with a quick burst of silvery-blue, reversing the flow back into Gwen with a zap like lightning. Gwen jolted, and the bird launched into the air, returning to the forest.

As it retreated, she felt something...*other* settle into her chest. Something faint like the rush of wind under wings, the hush of rodents scuttling in the understory, the comfort of a dense canopy.

Then the sensations faded and a warmth filled her veins.

"Thank you," Gwen whispered, eyes glassing as she turned to Aclima. "That's what I did wrong before. I bound them to me, but I didn't bind myself to them. That meant I didn't know when something was wrong."

"Do not shame yourself too much, Gwen. How were you to know the way, without anyone to show you?"

Aclima's words were a brief tonic to Gwen's pain, assuaging the edges of her grief. Yet still, she could not shake the sense of failure. Not wanting to say this aloud, she remained silent. If only she had known this before she went to Peru, she could have bonded with the terns the right way. Started a new international flock with any birds that would trust her. She would never fail her flock. Ever again.

"This is the only magic you should give of yourself. You send a piece away to maintain the connection, nothing else. Therefore, you will not be drained. Do you understand?"

Guilt curdled in her stomach at how easy it was for her to summon the power outside of her by magnetizing it to her own, against Aclima's teachings.

"Do you understand?" Aclima repeated.

"Yeah, yeah. I understand."

Aclima gave her a hard look, then exhaled. She put a hand on Gwen's shoulder and said, "Get some rest."

"Thanks, you too," Gwen mumbled. Aclima's hand slipped away as she retreated to the house, leaving Gwen standing alone in the dark, gaze fixed on the dark silhouette of the forest on the horizon.

Chapter Eighty

Once the vampires awoke the following evening, Ina called a group meeting. The council John had called was gone already, and Gwen commented on how rude it was that they didn't stay to meet the rest of them. Ina snapped that they had more important things to do than wait for everyone to wake up.

"Introductions can be made later," Ina said, "when the survival of humanity is no longer under threat."

Gwen rolled her eyes, although Ina did have a point.

So, it was just their main group plus John and Joseph cluttered in the living room to review what the council had planned the night before.

"We need to get to Nikki before the Scythians do," Ina began. "And plans with the rest of the Cradle need to be made to neutralize the threat. That's where the rest of the council went. Except to the Egyptian cradle, as that's where we're going. John and Joseph will open the portal for us, then stay here to rally the known Cradle members in North America. From the Egyptian Cradle, we will make our way to Alexandria, where a ship awaits us to sail to the island, following Aclima's guidance. Any questions?"

"Several, actually," Gwen said. "Where's the Egyptian Cradle? What are we going to do if we run into the Scythians? Or if they get to Nikki first? What if we can't find the island? Are we only traveling at night? If not, how are we transporting the v –"

"Stop," Ina quipped, holding up a hand to stop Gwen's tirade. "Some things we will have to figure out as we go, since time is of the essence, such as the travel logistics from Faiyum to Alexandria."

"Faiyum? Never heard of it."

"Well, now you have."

Gwen and Ina stared at each other for an awkward second before Feng cleared his throat. "Gwen has a good point. What is our contingency plan for encountering the Scythians? Or if they get to the Tree first?"

Ina grimaced and wrung her hands together. "There is no contingency plan. Except to fight and try to survive."

Expressions of worry and wariness wavered over the faces of the mortals, while the vampires' facial expressions hardened.

"Well, I'm filled with confidence," Gwen said.

"This is an inappropriate time for your sarcasm."

Gwen shrugged. "Someone has to counter your solemnity."

Ina sighed. "But do they, really?"

"Yes, or we'll all die from concern before we get anywhere," Gwen replied, getting to her feet. "Now, let's get going while we still think there's hope and before we realize we're all probably going to die. Well, those of us who are mortal, at least."

Ina sighed again and pinched the bridge of her nose, while Xander, Terrance, Rachel, and Theo produced stilted laughs. Even so, they stood. One by one, everyone else got to their sluggish feet, packing clothes and weapons, hoping they wouldn't have to use the latter sooner rather than later.

The car rides to Poverty Point were heavy with silence and foreboding. Gwen tried reaching out to Nikki to see if she could give them an update on where the Scythians were, or if Io had given her any more information on how They would sustain the Tree without Nikki in it. But Nikki was unreachable, forcing Gwen to bathe in the painful anxiety that hummed within the group.

Once parked and unpacked, all stood in a circle, feet shifting, weapons and bags slung across shoulders, backs, and hips.

"My car isn't going to sit here the whole time, is it?" Terrance asked.

"We'll shuttle back and forth until they're all back at my place," John replied. "Don't worry, we'll keep them maintained until your return."

"If we return," Gwen murmured, and Ina shot her a sharp look. "Sorry, didn't mean to say that out loud."

"Seems to be the case with most of your thoughts."

"I could say the same about you."

"Excuse me?" Ina's brows shot up.

"I'm just sayin', most people wouldn't say that to some –"

"Enough," Aclima said, smacking her staff with a hard crack on the ground. "Let's go."

Ina set her jaw and nodded, biting back whatever words bubbled in her throat. Theo put a hand on Gwen's shoulder, coaxing her to relax her hackles. With an exhale, she tried to release the tension in her body, falling into step behind John and the rest of the group. But the unknown road before them, the threat of confrontation looming overhead, pressed the stress deep into her bones.

Inside the mound, Cora and Farrell looked with ill-hidden awe at the interior, the detailed archways where portals could be opened, the glow of magic twining through the earth above them.

John blessed Farrell with the same language spell he had performed on the rest of them, then opened a portal. As John's blood moved up the twining pillars, glowing magic whirled together, creating the swirling circle that shone in golds, whites, silvers, and bright jewel tones. Warmth emanated from it, a slow infusion into the chill air.

"It's ready," John said, stepping back. "Who first?"

"I'll go," Ina said.

One by one, they stepped through the portal.

"See you on the other side," Theo said with a grin over her shoulder, then disappeared into the whirl. Gwen allowed herself a half-second to brace herself for whatever awaited her across the world before letting the calm and bright magic sweep her away.

Chapter Eighty-One

Screams rang through the air, piercing Gwen's ears.

Adrenaline shot through her veins, blinded as she was by the portal's light, images of the decimated Mexican cradle flooding her mind.

She raised her hands, pooling the magic from within herself into her hands, not caring that she wasn't doing it right, just preparing herself to fight. She blinked, trying to find the source of the screams, and – no, those weren't screams. They were shrieks.

Shrieks of delight.

Two children rushed from an entryway and charged Xander, shouting his name as they threw themselves at him.

A sudden and hard THWAP smacked Gwen's hands, and she yelled, "Ow!"

Shaking the pain out of her hands, she looked at Aclima, staff retracting from hitting Gwen.

"Wrong," Aclima said.

"Okay, sure, but was it really necessary to hit me?"

"I will beat your bad instincts out of you if I have to. Better bruised hands than death."

"Death? Don't you think you're being a little dramatic?"

"No." Aclima looked at her, impassive as stone.

Gwen sighed. "Fine."

With a stiff nod, Aclima turned away from her to regroup with the others.

Rubbing her hand, the yells faded into the sound of soft, rushing water. Gwen tilted her head back and took in their surroundings. They were in a large pyramidal room, the ceiling disappearing into black, open space. Eleven portals circled the room, each one on a pedestal surrounded by sapphire water. Waterfalls flowed from the walls and down into the pools surrounding the portals, adjacent walkways, and circular stage in the center of the room. Broadleaf plants she didn't know the names of stretched from the floor and sprouted from the walls, the combination of plants and water making the room not only pleasantly humid, but a dazzling array of color.

"This is amazing," Gwen breathed as she joined the others around Xander, the kids, and a tall man with Xander's hair, who she assumed was his dad. The boy prattled on about all the interesting things he had seen, swinging Xander's hands, and he spoke so fast Gwen tuned him out.

Apparently Xander did too, because mid-sentence he turned to his mom and asked, "Why didn't you tell me they were here?"

Ina had the grace to look ashamed, but she tucked a strand of hair behind her ear and recovered. "The fewer people who knew where they were, the safer they were."

"You think I would've told anyone?" Xander's face twisted, words like venom.

"Of course not. But someone could have overheard. Or if, Io forbid, you got captured again –"

"Right." Xander turned his back on Ina and pulled his hands from the boy, opening his arms to hug his dad.

"It's good to see you, son," the man said from within the embrace, leaving a hand on his shoulder as they pulled apart. Gwen's heart twisted, wondering what it must feel like to be hugged by a parent.

His dad said, "Quite an adventure we've had. I mean, I knew we were special, but this special? I had no idea."

"Yeah. Me neither," Xander spat with a poorly hidden glare at his mom.

Ina's cheeks burned crimson. "You can chastise me later. We have more important matters to deal with." She spun on her heel and took a sand-colored stone path to an open archway.

Gwen and everyone else fell into step behind Ina, making awkward introductions on the narrow path. The boy, Ishaq, was mystified by everything, and interrogated the vampires on all things vampiric, though Feng and Daiyu were the only ones who had the patience for his haranguing.

A tall, dark-skinned man with muscles the size of hams greeted them in the next room. He introduced himself as Essam and led them through a maze of rooms and hallways, channels of water glistening beneath lanterns and torchlight. The divine blue and white glow of magic weaved through the stone, thicker in some places than others. It thrummed a chord at the magic within Gwen, awakening the power within her. The longer they walked around this place, the more powerful she felt, as if the very stone was infusing her with magic, amplifying what was within her.

"I could get used to this," she said, looking at her hands. They felt like they were shaking yet remained still, the buzz of power like adrenaline rushing through her veins.

"I do not think you could," Aclima responded. "You can barely handle it now. But perhaps someday."

Gwen grumbled, and Theo twined their fingers together, Gwen's bruised hand brushing against the guns at Theo's hips.

The pathway transformed into stairs, winding higher and higher, the voices of the Cradle echoing around the halls. Halfway up the climb, Arthur and the kids left them with woeful expressions, forbidden from joining in on the planning. An ache built in Gwen's new leg muscles, a sweat breaking out on her forehead by the time their guide veered out of the stairwell, bringing them to a brightly lit room.

Nearly a dozen acolytes peppered the chamber, and introductions whirred between them and her group too quickly for Gwen to remember any names, just a blur of faces as they were sorted, some beckoned to the table and others ushered through another door. Ina, Xander, Alessa, and Aclima were allowed to stay with the Cradle, while everyone else was encouraged in a polite yet unquestionable way to continue forward.

When they were dumped into a dining room with a long table decorated with filled carafes, fruits, vegetables, and baked goods, Gwen's head spun from the winding stairs, the whirl of faces, the bombardment of names.

She liked chaos, but this was too much. She couldn't keep her head straight.

The surge of magic from her surroundings seeping into her skin probably didn't help, either.

Theo loaded a plate with food, muttering something about how maybe Gwen's blood pressure was low and that's why she was so jittery. Gwen didn't argue, just picked and nibbled at whatever Theo put in front of her, trying to still the tempest in her mind.

Feng asked the acolyte for blood, the answer to which was a harsh, "You're lucky to be allowed here at all, devil."

Feng scowled but bit his tongue. Farrell gave the Lius pitying looks since he could eat some of the human food, although he griped at the absence of meat.

Rachel asked Cora, "Why didn't they let you stay with the Cradle? You're, like, special too, right?"

Cora grinned. "Thank you. Yes, I suppose I have some abilities. But I am not of the Cradle."

"Aclima isn't either."

"No, she is before it. Beyond it. And needed to find the Tree, so more important for planning."

Rachel hummed in understanding, and a hush fell over the room, disturbed only by crunching, chewing, and slurping. Eating didn't help Gwen's nerves, and she stood to explore the structure, but upon opening the door opposite where they came in, she found someone standing guard outside it.

"Sorry, but I can't let you leave the room." The man stepped into her path, face impassive.

"Really? Why?" The man's fine brow arched, and Gwen said, "Fine. I get it."

She returned to the room and went to the door they had entered, feeling as if energy were about to burst from her body.

Outside this door was another guard, who said the same thing. At least this one had the grace to look embarrassed.

Gwen groaned and rolled her eyes.

"We're stuck here," she announced, rapping her fingers on the table.

"You're surprised by this?" Farrell asked.

"I mean, no, but I didn't expect to be trapped. Maybe just under watch."

Feng sneered. "Wouldn't want to let devils stray into their home. Regardless if they turned against their own kind, fought alongside your friends, and saved their lives countless times."

"Yeah, it's bullshit," Gwen spat, skin crawling.

"Patience," Cora chided. "They will speak with us when necessary. Why don't you do some jumping jacks?"

Gwen barked a laugh. "I just walked up a million stairs. More exercise isn't going to help."

"Are you sure about that?"

Something in Cora's tone made Gwen pause. When a clairvoyant spoke with implications, one was forced to stop and think. But there was no way Gwen's anxious energy was important enough to warrant a vision, or whatever Cora had. Cora just knew her influence and was trying to get Gwen to settle. Gwen gave her a suspicious squint at the manipulation, but plopped back into her chair beside Theo.

"I just hate this 'hurry up and wait' shit. Like, hello, the future of humanity is hanging in the balance."

"You're not alone in that, Gwen," Feng said. "But displeasure doesn't change anything."

Gwen hmphed and slinked down into her seat. If no one else was going to complain, she guessed she wouldn't, either.

To pass the time, and ease the energy, she made little tornadoes in her hands, growing and shrinking them. Annoyed glances were thrown her way, but no one said anything, and Gwen supposed they'd prefer the gusts of her wind rather than the sound of her voice.

When heads slumped and eyes closed in slumber, the remainder of their group finally rejoined them, jolting everyone awake.

Bags hung under the mortals' eyes, dark curls falling from Xander's ponytail, Aclima's jaw clenched, staff tap-tap-tapping on the tile.

"Why do I sense bad news?" Gwen asked.

Ina sucked in a deep breath. "We won't be receiving as much help as we'd hoped. At least, not as far as having warriors help us in a potential confrontation with Vadasz and his crew."

"Why not?"

"They're staying to protect Dad," Xander replied, sidling into an empty chair and pecking at the old food before him. "And to prepare the Cradle for the inevitable battle with Lilith."

"Oh," Gwen said, dread sinking heavy in her stomach.

"We're not entirely resourceless, however. We'll be joined shortly by Captain Amira, who will transport us to Alexandria, then sail the ship to find the island and the Tree."

"And Nikki," Xander muttered.

Ina's gaze slid to him, jaw ticking, but she didn't correct herself. "We need to leave immediately," Ina said instead, looking over the group. "If we're lucky, we can make it to the boat before the Scythians arrive, and avoid a confrontation."

"And what do we do if we encounter them?" Feng asked, rising.

"Fight," Ina said. "The vampires and Cradle will try to hold them off, allowing Xander, Gwen, Theo, Terrance, and Rachel a chance to escape and hide until daylight. Then they can meet with Amira at the docks during the day, and whoever has survived will figure out what to do next."

"Did you really have to say that in the bleakest way possible?" Gwen asked.

"I'm only being realistic."

"Still."

Ina sighed. "Come on. Everyone besides Cora, let's go. You can sleep in the van. Our gear has already been loaded."

"You're not coming?" Rachel asked Cora.

"No, I'll be here as a lifeline. And...to negotiate resources." Cora smiled, a mischievous thing.

"Ooooohhh, I see," Rachel responded, not seeing at all. But Gwen didn't either. She wasn't sure if anyone was supposed to.

Chapter Eighty-Two

Nikki floated through the forests of the world, searching. She wasn't sure for what. She was simply looking, hoping to find…anything. Any observations that might help them. Maybe she'd find the Scythians. Hormin. Lilith. Anyone.

Io had acquiesced, stating that They would provide help where they deemed appropriate and necessary, but that, ultimately, this was a conflict for humans and vampires to solve.

With little conversation between her and Io, Gwen distracted with her adventure, and her mom quarantined, life within the Tree became even more boring for Nikki. She hadn't thought that was possible, yet here she was. But traversing the forests of Earth, from the tropics to the temperate and even the arctic, Nikki felt each breath and pulse of life within herself, and it didn't just fill her time, but her spirit. To be so many pieces, and yet only one…it made being back in her normal body feel strange.

Wrong.

"Nikki," Io whispered as Nikki swept through the foggy redwoods of California. *"Return."*

Anxiety rippled from her body to her consciousness, pulling her back to the Tree.

"What is it?" Nikki asked, trying to settle her mind back into the singular entity that was herself.

"Wait. Listen."

Nikki's gaze followed the flickers of Io's light in the Tree, ears straining to hear what was happening outside of it. There was movement, the rustling of feet over grass.

Then voices. Arguing. They were distant, muffled. From the direction of the building where her mom was held captive. Was it a villager antagonizing her mom?

No, Io wouldn't have bothered her with something like that. It must be someone from off-island who was here now. But who? And why? Why were they arguing with her mom?

The voices suddenly stopped.

A creeping sense of danger pricked at the back of her neck and crawled along her spine. She tried to twist against the Tree, but her limbs were long numb, and she couldn't move at all.

The drum of footsteps moved across the ground, accompanied by a shushing sound, like something being dragged across grass. The sounds grew louder and louder, until the steps stopped just before the Tree.

A heavy thud.

Like a body being dropped to the ground.

Nikki's stomach tightened, and if she had any food within her, she might have thrown it up.

"Hello, little duck."

Chapter Eighty-Three

Nikki crashed into Gwen's mind with the fury of a thousand crumbling bell towers, startling Gwen out of her half-dream state.

"It's Hormin."

"Huh?" Gwen rubbed her eyes, then blinked, trying to make sure she was actually awake. "What's Hormin?"

Everyone else in the van, except Amira, was asleep. The vampires traveled in their own van, the Cradle too wary of them to allow them within the same vehicle, despite the weeks they had already been on the road together.

Theo stirred on her lap, the hand in hers twitching, but she did not rise.

"The vampire sent to guard me – the Tree – from you freeing me. It's Hormin."

Cold crept over Gwen's skin, and denial wrapped around the fog in her mind. "What are you saying, Nik?"

"He's here, Gwen. So close I can hear him walking on the grass."

"That's really, really bad news."

Someone in the back row of the van moved, waking at the sound of Gwen's voice, but she was too frozen to move.

"You need to get more help before coming here. More people to fight."

"It's too late, Nik. We've left the Cradle already and are on the way to Alexandria."

Nikki's paralyzing fear wrapped around Gwen's own. She looked out the window, at the dark world and scattered lights whipping past them, mind whirring, working to think if there was anything they could do to avoid fighting him, too.

But she came up short.

If they were to free Nikki, they now had to face Hormin. If they could avoid fighting the Scythians, if they could all travel together, then maybe they had a chance at winning.

"Gwen, what's she saying?" Xander asked from the back seat. She turned to look at him, a dark silhouette with the occasional spark of light flashing across his glasses as they passed under street lamps.

Gwen gulped and turned away from him, stretching to the row in front of her and nudging Ina's shoulder. "Ina," she hissed. "Ina, wake up!"

Gwen shook Ina's shoulder hard enough to make Ina's head bob down, jolting her awake.

"Damn it, Gwen, you scared me!" Ina spat. "What do you want?"

"To scare you even more. Hormin's at the Tree."

A pause. "I hope this is a cruel joke."

"It's not. Nikki just told me."

"Well. Shit."

"Yeah."

"What do we do?" Rachel asked, voice thick with fatigue.

"I don't know if there's anything we can do." Ina pinched the bridge of her nose. "But let me think."

"Sorry I couldn't give you more warning," Nikki said as dreadful quiet descended over the van, as dark as the night.

"It's not your fault, Nik. Is he at least saying anything useful? Like where Lilith is?"

"No, just the usual rambles. How he's going to kill everyone and I'll be stuck in here forever watching Lilith rule the world."

"Lovely." Gwen sighed.

"On the plus side, Io has agreed to blow Marcus and Titania off course so you don't have to fight them."

"Well, that's something, at least. I'm glad They're coming around." Nikki's presence started to fade from her mind. "Just stay sane. We're on our way, and we'll get you out, I promise."

Appreciation and doubt flickered down their bond. "*Thank you,*" Nikki whispered, fully disengaging.

Gwen wound her fingers through Theo's, everyone except Ina too tense to speak. As they barreled closer to Alexandria, to Nikki, to Hormin, Ina made a series of phone calls. First to Feng, to let them know what awaited them. She tried calling different Cradles, first the one in Faiyum, then reaching out to other contacts of the closest primary and secondary Cradles.

No one answered her dozen calls, placed over the remaining hours of their drive.

They were in this alone.

Chapter Eighty-Four

The vehicles weaved through the dark streets of Alexandria, the nausea of fear climbing in Gwen's throat. As they wound through the city, she tried to ignore the dread in her gut by looking at the new surroundings, a distant part of her wanting to appreciate a place she might never see again.

Before she knew it, lights in the distance gave way to the abyssal black of the ocean, the dark of it yawning wider as they approached.

Honking blared from the vampire van – the *van*pire, Gwen thought with an insane cackle, drawing confused looks from Theo – and Ina's phone shouted its ring. The vanpire screeched to a halt behind them, pulling to the curb.

"What is it?" Ina asked, waving for Amira to pull over. After a pause, she said, "Shit."

And the pit in Gwen's stomach widened.

"What? What did he say?" she asked as Ina hung up. Instead of answering, Ina hopped out of the car, everyone scrambling after her, meeting up with the vampires. Feng and Daiyu's shoulders were rigid, Aclima tapped her staff on the ground, and Farrell shifted from hip to hip. Gwen had never seen him so restless, and her magic rose to her skin.

"What do we want to do?" Feng asked Ina, who chewed on the inside of her lip.

"How about tell us what's going on?" Gwen suggested, skin aglow.

"Stop that," Aclima chided, "you will reveal our location."

"Huh?" Gwen responded without thinking, a part of her knowing what must be happening, but denying it.

"They're here," Farrell said. "The Scythians. We can feel them ahead."

In unison, the faces of the vampires fell, and they looked over their shoulders in the direction they came. Farrell cleared his throat and said, "And behind us."

"Oh." Her magic flared with the fight or flight response, but with a few deep breaths, she managed to rein it in, shoving it deep down inside her belly, extinguishing the light.

"So – what do we do?" Feng repeated.

Rachel gulped. "Can't we just, like, hit them with the cars?"

"The vehicles will likely take more damage than they will," Ina answered. "Then we'll be without an escape."

"We are without one now," Feng replied. "They'll chase us until sunrise. And we can't wait for then. There's nowhere for us to hide from the sun, and you need Aclima on that boat."

A breeze whipped through Gwen's hair, carrying nothing but city sounds.

Only Alessa could voice what they all knew. "We fight, then."

Ina nodded. "We have to split up. Some stay to distract them so others can get on the ship. Aclima, Gwen, the Lius, Xander, and I will go."

"No!" Xander shouted, then brushed a hand through his hair, shaking away his outburst. "I'm not – I don't want to see Hormin again. Not yet."

"But you need to stay with me, you need the protection of the Cradle –"

"I will stay with him, Ina." Alessa placed a hand on their heart. "I will give him my life if needed."

Xander's face dropped like he had been punched in the gut. "Please don't."

Ina and Alessa shared a long glance, Alessa adding, "I am no longer needed as a sacrifice for the Tree, so I will keep him safe on this side of the water. If we cannot follow, I will see him safely returned to Faiyum."

Ina tensed her jaw, but nodded.

"In addition, I do not think Farrell, Alessa, and the children are enough to take on Vadasz, Aella, and Uase." Feng's gaze slid to them. "No offense."

"None taken," Terrance answered, Rachel wrapping an arm around his forearm and leaning against him.

Ina sighed, thinking. "Alessa, Xander, Farrell, and the Lius will distract the Scythians and either join us later or return to Faiyum. The rest of us will travel to the Tree."

"Do you really think the six of us are enough to beat Hormin?" Rachel asked, voice trembling.

"Six?" Aclima asked. "If you are counting me as a fighter, adjust your calculation. I am no such thing. I am a protector, a teacher, a guide. I will not fight. I will guide you to the Tree then return with the captain to pick up the others."

"But –" Gwen started, but Aclima threw up a hand to stop her.

"I am also a mender. I can aid with wounds received. Do not ask aught else of me."

"It's settled then." Ina looked at each of them in turn. "Draw their attention, lure them away. Return here each night to be picked up, if possible. Otherwise, return to Faiyum." Her gaze flicked to Alessa, then her son. "Be safe."

Car keys were exchanged with those staying behind, then weapons equipped. Their footsteps clacked on the concrete, hands twitching or placed on weapon handles, ready to wield. Following Amira, they approached the docks, the salt spray wafting off the sea, chilling Gwen's skin. On one side were industrial buildings, with dim lights and low walls. On the other side, shipping containers that bordered the port.

Ina and Amira led the charge, suns like small bombs in their hands. The vampires brought up the rear, staying as far away from the Cradle's light as possible. The rest of them were sandwiched between, anxiety rippling through the air, Gwen's power rising from her core to her fingertips, setting her alight. The magic in the wind responded, shimmers forming around her, meeting with her being, a whirlwind of magic waiting to be unleashed.

The silhouettes of two figures stood far ahead of them, stances casual yet alert. Gwen squinted, trying to make them out.

Vadasz and Aella.

"Can you sense who's behind us?" Gwen whispered to Farrell.

"Someone big," he responded, confirming Gwen's suspicion that Uase was closing them in.

Theo's hands twitched at her holster.

The white noise of the rolling ocean couldn't drown out the beat of her pulse in her head, a drum of war that made her want to vomit. Or run.

They paused a respectable distance away from Vadasz and Aella, where their voices were able to carry on the breeze.

"Let us pass," Ina declared, inflaming the fire in her hand, "or burn. This is your only warning."

"Turn back," Vadasz responded with a smirk, twirling the scimitar in his hand, "or be cut down. Though the latter is inevitable. It is only a matter of when."

Xander unsheathed his sword, and despite the trembling of his hands, the blade lit with sunlight, casting his honey skin in gold.

"Interesting trick," Vadasz said, a flicker of surprise and concern flashing across his face so fast Gwen would have missed it if she wasn't watching him so closely.

Aella drew the arrow in her bow back, still pointing it at the ground.

Vadasz looked past them and yelled to the vampires, "The era of humanity is over. You know this. Join us and be forgiven."

"We do not need forgiveness for doing what is right," Feng replied.

"Aren't you tired of hiding? A new age is upon us where we don't have to be stuck in the shadows."

"That is what it is to be a vampire – shadow, darkness, night. Enslaving mankind won't bring light back into your lives."

"Who said anything about light?" Vadasz's smirk widened. "All we want is glory."

A strangled scream split the air, and Gwen's body hit the ground, skin scraping on the cobbles and cement, as Farrell landed on top of her.

He leapt to his feet and pulled her back up with him as bullets rang from Theo's guns and an arrow whizzed past her face, chaos breaking loose. Farrell's shirt was cut and chest bled from where the arrow grazed him, one that would have pierced Gwen through the heart.

Bile rose to her throat, and she called the wind, condensing it into a shield around herself, watching several things happen at once.

Aclima tore a thrown hand axe from her shoulder and the ground erupted in a thunderous crack as she raised the earth to shield her from Uase, charging toward her, tattoos glowing in changing hues of purple and red.

He crashed into the wall, sending cement, rock, and dirt exploding into the air with the force of his collision.

Farrell, Feng, and Daiyu dashed to Aclima's aid, and Gwen whipped around just as another arrow flew by her head where Farrell had just stood. Amira and Ina threw orbs and flares of sun at Vadasz and Aella, whose tattoos also glowed, trying to press them back, but Vadasz and Aella did not give ground, instead trying to close quarters, forcing Ina and Amira to retreat farther from the boat.

Xander and Terrance charged forward to help Ina, Alessa, and Amira, blade and hammer swinging.

"No!" Ina screamed at her son. "Get out of here!"

Xander ignored her, lunging recklessly at Vadasz, who sidestepped the swing and swept his legs beneath Xander. He landed on his back with a thud and lost his grip on the sword. Terrance continued swinging his hammer at Aella, who danced away like a leaf in a breeze.

Even without a cut, Vadasz's skin sizzled with the singe of daylight.

Vadasz leapt forward to kick the sword out of the way, but Gwen funneled the wind whirling around her and pushed him back. It wasn't forceful enough to knock him off his feet, but just enough to change his trajectory and allow Ina to grab the sword.

"Get him out of here!" she screamed at Alessa, who grabbed Xander by his wrist and yanked him to his feet, dragging him down the nearest alley.

One of Aella's tattoos glowed bright and she leapt over Terrance, dashing after Xander and Alessa. Gwen's jaw popped open at the impressive jump.

Vadasz shouted, "No! Don't let them distract you. Let them go – we need to stop the rest from getting on the boat." Vadasz's gaze slid to Gwen, and he said to Aella, "Take down the witch."

"Ah, shit," Gwen breathed as Aella's hawkish features focused on her, making her feel as vulnerable as a rabbit. Gwen's trembling, magic-infused hands swept through the air, calling the wind toward herself, taking a step back for each step forward Aella took.

In the few seconds she had before Aella pulled an arrow from her quiver and brought it to her bow, she saw Ina, Terrance, and Amira press on Vadasz, but he dodged and slashed with millennia of experience, not taking any direct hits from their sunrays. Yet still, his skin bubbled and hissed with the shine, but it seemed to enrage him rather than weaken him. He tossed his sword to his other hand and pulled a strap from his back, unfolding a long leather whip.

He cracked it out, wrapping around the hammer's shaft and yanking it from Terrance's grip, pulling Terrance forward along with it.

Shots rang out, followed by arrows from above, and Gwen followed their trajectory, finding Theo and Rachel atop shipping containers shooting at Vadasz, providing Terrance cover to retreat.

On the other side, the vampires still battled Uase, Aclima raising pieces of earth for protection as he swung his hand axes in a whirlwind around himself. Feng, Daiyu, and Farrell danced around him, slashing and clawing, yet Uase's glowing skin did more damage to their weapons than they did to him, blades breaking yet giving him no more than shallow cuts.

Gwen's hair whipped around her face with the wind, and she slowed it into a hard bubble around herself while Aella drew closer, lifting the bow, pulling an arrow back, and pointing it at her.

Gwen gulped and took a deep breath, surprised to find that Aella's face did not hold the same vicious pleasure as Vadasz's. It was blank and dutiful, but held no malice.

Gwen rose the wind just as Aella unleashed her arrow, making it veer off course. Aella sneered, and Gwen wound the air as tight as she could and threw it toward Aella, but she jumped out of the way, the spear of wind exploding into the building behind her.

Aella slung her bow to her back, Gwen noticing a glowing gazelle tattoo fading, and a lion one shining. Aella shoved her fists to her sides, where she equipped claws and sprinted in a straight line to Gwen. She slashed gust after gust of wind at her, but Aella either dodged or braced, throwing her hands in front of her and crouching, maintaining her balance. Aella continued to push, Gwen stepping back and back and back, whipping gust after gust of air out in front of her, until the ocean breeze pushed at her back, and there was nowhere else to retreat.

Aella jumped, claws out, and Gwen pushed all she had into her shield, sweat forming on her brow as she pulled from within and without herself, Nikki's ring on her finger burning, while she pushed against Aella's strength, trying to not fall into the ocean.

To not have her face clawed off.

Shots rang out, and Aella stuttered in her tracks, slumping forward and grabbing her shoulder.

She whipped around just as Terrance swung his hammer, colliding with Aella's head, sending her cascading to the side. Blood seeped from her back where Theo shot her, one of Rachel's arrows protruding from her shoulder. Gwen shifted out of the way so her back was no longer to the ocean, caging Aella between her and the water.

Aella groaned, peeling herself from the ground, blood sticking to where she fell. Gwen recoiled when Aella turned, half of her face smashed in. Bones slid back into place, teeth regrowing, muscle and flesh knitting itself over the mess of her blood-matted head.

Aella roared as she stood, the newly forming muscles of her face pulling wide.

Gwen was sure now that when this was over, she would definitely vomit.

Shots echoed again, puncturing Aella's chest, stopping her scream short.

Aella looked down at her bleeding chest, and before she could recover, Gwen rolled out a blast of air, sending Aella careening into the abyssal ocean behind her.

"Thanks," Gwen panted to Terrance, who nodded, and they looked behind them.

Aclima had separated from the vampires to help the push past

Vadasz. The Lius and Farrell still fought Uase, who raged with the force of a stampede of rhinos.

Theo and Rachel jumped ahead on shipping containers, following the advance forward from the high ground. With one last glance at the ocean where Aella fell, Gwen and Terrance dashed forward to Ina and Amira.

Upon their approach, Ina sent an orb of light at Vadasz and yelled to Amira, "Don't wait for me, just take them and go!"

Amira nodded, and with a solar flare at Vadasz, who had a falcon tattoo blazing on his bicep, broke away from the fight and shouted, "This way!" waving for Gwen and Terrance to follow.

Gwen broke into a sprint, but after a few steps, a whip lashed around her ankle and she crashed to the concrete, her shield buffeting her fall, then dissipating as her surprise made her lose focus.

Vadasz yanked on the whip, pulling her toward him, and she screamed as her skin scraped on the rough road. Amira shot a flare at the whip, but it did not burn. Terrance ran back to grab it, playing a losing game of tug of war with Vadasz as the whip hissed through his hands.

A boom sounded behind Vadasz and Ina, followed by a strangled, gargled sound of pain. Everyone turned to see shrapnel and concrete embedded in Feng and Uase's skin, Farrell and Daiyu having stepped aside to give space for the grenade. Uase was shocked whereas Feng was not, and in Uase's scream, the Lius and Farrell ran forward, biting and cutting and slashing at the cuts on his skin until the glowing tattoos faded. As the magic left him, his skin weakened, the cuts and stabs going deeper until he dropped to his knees, covered in blood. With one last attempt to live, he lashed out, throwing Farrell off his body and sending him crashing through the nearby building.

"Farrell!" Gwen screamed, rising to her feet.

"No, Gwen, there's no time!" Ina snatched Gwen's forearm and yanked her to her feet, pulling her away from the gore, from her brother.

Gwen looked over her shoulder, stumbling over her feet. The Lius retained their hold on Uase, stabbing him over and over, until he collapsed in a red heap on the ground, unmoving.

"No!" Vadasz shouted, running toward his friend, just as his body hit the concrete. Vadasz looked back at Gwen, fists clenched. The tension in his body rose until he screeched, then with an assessing look at the ocean, at Uase's limp body, he jumped into the water after Aella.

Looking forward, the patter of their running feet synchronizing with the rhythm of the approaching emergency vehicles, the ocean breeze whisked tears off Gwen's cheeks as they ran toward their cabin cruiser. They piled in with few words, Ina and Amira removing the ropes that held it to the dock, and the engine roared to life, speeding off into the pitch-black horizon.

Chapter Eighty-Five

A FULL DAY passed before they made it to the right island. When they left Alexandria, Aclima stood at the bow, wind and salt spray whipping her face. She pointed Amira in the right direction, unable to speak over the roar of the engine and slice of the boat through the water. After, Aclima and Ina tended to Gwen and Terrance's wounds, soothing the burning cuts on Gwen's back from where Vadasz had pulled her along the road.

But the sting of those injuries was nothing compared to the ache in her heart, Farrell's limp body stuck in her mind. She hoped he had just been knocked unconscious, but didn't want to count on it. True, he was a vampire and could heal better than humans, but there was no telling just how much damage he had received from crashing through the building. She didn't get a chance to find him, let alone check for a pulse.

One sister, and maybe one brother, down.

The only one who didn't suck.

Did he still have Brienne with him? Would their ashes mix when the sun rose?

She hung her head and hissed as the skin on her back stretched, Aclima chiding her to be still.

Theo held her hand but reserved her words, knowing none would be good enough. Once mended, Aclima returned topside to aid Amira, who blasted through the sea at top speed.

Rest was elusive with the rocking and jolting of the boat, five of them crammed in the cabin below. But they winked in and out of slumber, too exhausted to stay awake. The night turned to day, and Aclima joined them in the cabin, explaining that Amira had been rapidly consuming energy drinks to stay up. They continued in the general direction of the Tree, but at a reduced speed so as not to take them too far and pass the island while Aclima hid from the sun.

Day turned to night, and again into day. Gwen woke just before dawn broke. She unwound her fingers from Theo's and went topside, where Aclima was once again with Amira, body rigid and eyes fixated on the distance. The sun was still below the horizon, but brightened the eastern sky. Patches of land littered the sea, leaving Gwen breathless at the beauty.

As Gwen gazed at the stars in the pre-dawn sky, she heard a melancholy singing from several voices. But Aclima and Amira had their mouths closed, and she knew it wasn't anyone below deck.

"Are those the sirens?" she asked. "Nikki told me about them."

"Yes, it means we're close," Aclima answered. "Remain alert. If you feel compelled to jump in the water after them, return below and plug your ears. I do not want to dive in after you."

"Rachel is going to be so jealous she missed out on hearing them."

Aclima hummed in agreement.

"You need to go below deck soon." Gwen sat on a bench near the bow, holding her arms tight around herself against the morning chill.

Aclima straightened and turned her head to the east, as if listening. "We'll be there before then."

Gwen hummed with anxiety, but Aclima was right. Amira steered the boat ashore a wide island that rose to a tall hill in the distance, covered in lush greenery Gwen had never seen before. The landing on wet sand woke the others, who climbed out from the cabin and gazed at where they came from and then where they were going with wide eyes and tense shoulders.

Aclima took Gwen's hands. "I must return with Amira to guide the others here. You fought well, but used much of yourself. To beat

Hormin, you must rely on the powers of the earth, not what resides in yourself. Doing so will drain you before he can be stopped." Aclima lifted a hand to Gwen's cheek. "Live."

Gwen swallowed, wanting to argue with Aclima, wanting to beg her to stay. Instead, she nodded and said, "I will."

Aclima smoothed a hand over Gwen's salt- and wind-messed hair, a small grin flickering over her mouth. Something fond and sad twisted in Gwen's heart as she watched Aclima disappear below deck. The one person who believed in her and helped her when others wouldn't was walking away. She hoped she'd live to see her again. To learn more from her. To show her more of the world's modern wonders.

With a deep breath, she turned to Ina, Theo, Terrance, and Rachel, weapons clasped in white-knuckled fingers. They nodded to one another, and with swift goodbyes to Amira, jumped off the boat into the wet sand, starting their trek upward through the jungle.

Chapter Eighty-Six

BY LUCK OR COINCIDENCE, they found a narrow trail that wound its way through the tangle of vegetation. The canopy trapped the moisture in the air, the humidity suffocating. Before this adventure, she would have been panting with discomfort, but the recent exercise and excursion through Alaska had strengthened her, increased her endurance.

No one spoke during their ascent, instead focusing on taking another step forward, trying not to think of what, or rather who, awaited them. It was impossible to tell how much time passed through the dense canopy, broad leaves and twining branches cloaking the sun's movement across the sky. Every couple minutes, the hair on her neck rose, the creeping sense of being watched sending her on high alert.

Each rustle of the wind through the trees made her search for hidden vampires, for Hormin, although she knew it was ridiculous since it was daylight. But she couldn't shake the feeling, the forest weighing heavier on her shoulders with each step she took.

Eventually, the forest opened into dirt paths and stone houses atop a hill.

A breeze pushed through, rattling shutters and creaking doors.

There was no sight or sign of a person or vampire. Gwen tensed, and the weave of magic responded, flaring into her fingertips.

"Where is everybody?" Rachel breathed, just above a whisper.

Hesitant, Ina ushered them forward, and they walked up the main path with hands on their weapons. Their gazes darted back and forth, front and back, and Gwen thought that maybe everyone had left, perhaps for some obscure or perverse task for Lilith, and that they wouldn't have an additional conflict.

Then the ground gave out from underneath them, and with shrieks, they fell through the ground. The trap, a mix of netting and compacted dirt, rained around them.

Gwen landed hard on her feet, the shock radiating up through her shins, knees, and hips, and she buckled forward with the impact, hands scraping against hard earth. She stood, wiping dirt and blood on her pants, looking up at the hole they fell into, the clear blue sky taunting them.

Terrance helped Rachel, who'd landed on her tailbone, to her feet, tears of pain rolling down her face. Theo stared up at the sky, and Ina circled the cramped space, running her fingers along the smooth sides.

"Well, shit." Gwen slumped against the wall and slid to the ground.

"It's too soon to give up," Ina said, smudging the soil between her fingers. "We do not know if this hole was for us, or if we fell in accidentally. Someone may yet come."

Theo chewed on a nail then said, "Terr Bear, give me a lift."

Terrance appraised the height of the hole then nodded, knelt, and cupped his hands to boost Theo. With catlike grace, she moved from his hands to shoulders then back to his hands, Terrane stretching his arms up as high as he could.

"Give me a jump," Theo called, and Gwen readied a bed of air in case she fell.

Terrance flexed, bent, and extended his arms, tossing Theo a few inches into the air. Her fingers grasped the edge of the hole, and she scrambled over the edge.

Theo's head popped over the side, and she said, "I'll see if I can find a rope or ladder," before disappearing into the day.

Ina rationed snacks and water while they waited, and as each second ticked by, Gwen became more certain Theo had walked into another trap and they would all rot in this pit, and the world as they knew it, as they loved it, would come to a blistering, bloody end.

"Gwen," Ina snapped to attention. "Could you push us out of here with gusts of wind?"

"Maybe?" Gwen responded, mind whirling. If she could summon enough to make a dense bed of it, if she could condense the pressure enough and then erupt it. If they were lucky, it might just shoot everyone upward –

"Um, guys?" Theo asked, voice shaking, stopping Gwen's train of thought.

She looked up, Theo's face peering over the edge, with the head of a spear pointing at her long neck.

"What's going on?" Gwen called. "Are you okay?"

Several other figures appeared, holding spears and axes, their shapes framing the hole above them. A young man, tanned from the sun with auburn hair, barely out of adolescence, called down to them in a choked voice, unable to conceal his fear. "We have instructions to keep you until midnight. A ladder will be sent down for ten minutes at that time." He gulped and cleared his throat. "If you escape before then, we are meant to fight you. To the death. We will hold this one above ground, and if you come out to fight us, we will cut her throat."

"Don't you dare harm a hair on her head!" Terrance yelled.

"Where are your masters?" Ina asked.

Fear rippled off the people around the hole, and after several seconds, the boy said, "I'm not allowed to tell you."

"We don't have to fight. You could let us up and let us go. We can free you from them." The humans gave each other knowing looks. "We cannot."

"What does that mean?"

The boy gulped again, and his voice trembled. "We – we cannot."

"They're probably being manipulated in a similar way the Lius did to the border patrol," Rachel whispered. "If they break the promise, their masters will know and will harm them and their loved ones. They don't have a choice."

"Damn," Ina breathed and pinched her nose. With a sigh, she said, "I understand your position. Please, do not hurt our friend."

"We won't, as long as you remain where you are."

One by one, the figures receded into daylight, and with a last, longing look, Theo was pulled away.

A surge of power, of anger, inflamed Gwen, magnified from the rage rolling off Terrance. "We can fight them, Ina. They're just normal humans. I'll lift us out of here and –"

"No." Ina's voice was flat.

"Think about it, won't you? They are only releasing us at night because they think we can't beat Hormin. Maybe they're right. Maybe we should engage in the fight we know we can win, then we can save Nikki and not fight Hormin at all."

Ina's gaze burned. "You would have us kill slaves."

"Well, I mean, I don't like the idea either, but it's for the greater good. Get past them to save all humanity. Are you confident we can beat Hormin?"

"No," Ina said, "but I will not harm innocents."

"You don't know they're innocent. How do you know they didn't enter into service to these vampires willingly?"

"How do you know they weren't forced into it?"

Gwen couldn't answer, and she looked at Terrance and Rachel for backup, but they avoided her gaze.

"Well, I guess you all think I'm the bad guy for suggesting this."

"It is important to consider all options, but harming those poor people is not one of them. No, we wait to fight Hormin."

"You're so confident we can beat him, but I'm telling you he is insane."

"All the more reason I am confident in us. We are not insane."

"But aren't we? For going on this whole adventure to begin with?"

Terrance huffed a laugh and rubbed a hand over his head.

"I know we will beat him, because we have to."

"That sounds ignorant and arrogant to me, Ina, but whatever. If we die and the world ends because of your morals, I will pester you forever in the afterlife."

"I would expect nothing less."

Gwen sighed and leaned her head back against the wall. She spaced out, watching the shadows move across the hole as the sun moved across the sky.

Chapter Eighty-Seven

TRUE TO THEIR WORD, a rope ladder unfurled in the dead of night. The clatter of wood against the side of the hole startled Gwen awake, and she blinked against the dark as her eyes adjusted. Ina produced a sun, momentarily blinding her. Rachel shook Terrance awake, stuck in a deep sleep.

Every muscle in Gwen's body ached.

What a terrible state to be in to confront one of the oldest vampires in existence.

They climbed out of the hole, Gwen's arms shaking with the effort. She really needed food and more rest.

Theo waited outside, no one else in sight. She extended a hand to Gwen, helping her to her feet.

"How was your day?" Gwen asked, leaning into Theo's embrace.

"Not bad, actually. They kept me in a room with a bed and brought me food."

"Ugh, lucky."

"Yes, well, you are too." Theo pulled out loaves of bread, olives, and cheese from her pack, and Gwen's mouth filled with saliva, stomach gurgling. "Either they thought I was really hungry or they didn't care I took it."

"You're a saint," Gwen said, filling her hands with the bounty.

"I know," Theo replied with a smile, then divvied out the food to Ina, Terrance, and Rachel. "They told me to tell you if we linger until sunrise, they'll fight us and put us back in the hole. They also showed me the path forward. It's just up ahead."

Ina sighed and nodded, then bade them to eat slowly so as not to upset their stomachs. Once satisfied, they began the climb, again absorbed by the jungle.

Gwen took Theo's elbow and fell back from the group. "I need you to promise me something."

Theo glanced at her sideways. "Maybe."

"If it looks like things are going bad, promise me you'll run and hide until daytime. Then wait until the others come or go back with Amira to the mainland and get reinforcements."

"I'm not leaving you behind."

"Please, Theo. You know if I had it my way, you wouldn't be here at all. But I promised not to fight you about coming, so I didn't. Please don't fight me over leaving if it looks bad." Gwen chewed her lip. "Maybe I should have made that a stipulation from the beginning."

"I won't – I *can't* – make that promise."

"Look, if things go south, the best hope we have is to get more help. The fastest way that will happen is if there's someone who can not only communicate that but explain the help that's needed. Like how he fights, any potential weaknesses observed. I promise I won't sacrifice myself needlessly, and I will try to get away too, if you promise me the same. That's all I'm asking."

Theo sucked in her cheeks, thinking. With a heavy exhale, she said, "Fine. But I don't like it."

"Me neither. I don't like any of this. But thank you."

Theo nodded and wound her fingers through Gwen's, squeezing tight. They walked side by side until the path narrowed into single file, following Ina's light through the dark and dank jungle. With each step forward, Gwen's pulse ratcheted higher in her throat until she felt she would choke on it.

Eventually the path flattened, opening to another clearing that revealed the largest tree she had ever seen, with thick, swirling bark and leaves that cloaked the star-bright sky. Plump mangoes dangled from the branches. It thrummed with power and timelessness, and suddenly Gwen felt small and vulnerable.

"Nikki," Gwen breathed, and Theo put a steadying hand on her shoulder.

Fruit littered the ground, and a small stone building sat to the side. The group took tentative steps forward, Ina casting her light higher to illuminate their surroundings, shining off the skin of the mangoes, the ground mirroring the sky in how it twinkled.

Gwen's skin crawled, and from around the back of the Tree, a figure emerged, dragging a body along with it.

"Took you long enough," Hormin sneered, tossing a limp Cat to the ground in front of him. Gwen moved to run to Cat's side to see if she was still alive, but Theo put a hand on her shoulder, stopping her in her tracks. Fists clenching, the blues and silvers of her magic rose to the surface of her skin, calling to the same forces outside of her until her hands were wrapped in the warm glow of power. She sensed the tension in her companions, Terrance gripping the shaft of his hammer tight, Rachel knocking an arrow in her bow, and Theo's hands resting on her holster.

Hormin pulled a greatsword from his back, and it lit with flames as soon as it met the air, fighting the sunlight cast from Ina. He stepped forward just enough to remain out of Ina's light, but the glow of it still burned like the fires of Hell in his eyes.

Resting the tip of the sword downward, the blade hissed in the grass. "I'm surprised and impressed you made it past Vadasz, Aella, and Uase. But you will not make it past me. Turn back, or die."

"No," Ina said, stepping forward.

The sun brushed against the exposed skin on Hormin's face, but his cheek did little more than turn a darker tan.

He grinned and walked into the light, the tan becoming an angry red. "You forget that I am of the first brood. I may have much of Mother's power, but I also have much of what makes humans so...resilient. Not the dull, faint traces of humanity that reside in the contemporary vampires, like your poor friend behind me. It will take much more than your weak rays to destroy me."

Ina sucked in a breath, tensing her shoulders, and seethed, "We'll see about that."

She launched forward, summoning and throwing an orb of sunlight from both hands. Hormin danced out of the way, as if the sword weighed nothing, and Ina's suns dissipated in the night. The group broke apart, spreading out to surround Hormin as Ina bombarded him with a barrage of suns, and Terrance charged with a scream, hammer held high.

Rachel dashed into the jungle behind them, climbing a tree to shoot at Hormin from above. Theo whipped out her pistols, shooting at Hormin when the dance of combat brought space between Hormin and Terrance, giving her an opening. Gwen pulled a shield around herself and used it to propel spears of wind at their opponent.

Hormin weaved through the suns, swings, arrows, bullets, and wind like a leaf on the breeze. The barrage kept him occupied, unable to lunge back at any of them with his sword, an evenly matched dance.

Gwen paused, a trail of sweat sliding down her temple. She needed to assess, to find a different tactic, or she'd burn out. Maybe that's what Hormin was trying to do – wear them down until they could be picked off one by one.

Theo seemed to have the same realization, and changed tack, slinging her pistols and removing a satchel of explosive powder from her belt.

"Move!" she screamed, and with quick glances at her, Terrance and Ina created space between them and Hormin. Theo tossed the powder into the air, Gwen pushed it close to Hormin with a gust as Ina lashed an orb at the powder just as it reached Hormin, exploding against his chest.

Hormin yelled, but once Gwen's sight adjusted to the light of the bang, she saw it barely ripped apart his shirt. His chest was scarred and red, but there was no blood. Hormin ran a hand over his skin, checking his injuries, and in the half-second of distraction, the clack of bullets and zing of arrows split the air, pummeling into Hormin.

The arrows scraped his skin and bounced off, the bullets embedding in the first layer of his flesh, little more than a surface wound.

But it was enough to draw blood, red streaks glistening down his bare chest.

Hormin snarled, baring his fangs and growling. A shadow of rage passed over his face, and Gwen's heart raced at the monster that revealed itself.

Terrance lunged forward in the time Gwen watched Hormin's demeanor change from toying with them to that of a predator, and she screamed, "No, wait!" sending a gust forward to try to stop him, to shield him, but she wasn't quite fast enough, and in a blink, Hormin's leg kicked out, catching Terrance in the chest with a crash and crack.

Terrance flew backward, the hammer falling to the ground, and landed against a tree with a sickening crack. When Terrance collided with the earth again, he did not get back up.

"Terrance!" both Theo and Rachel screamed, Rachel leaping down from her spot in the jungle to check him.

Ina roared and ran at Hormin, orbs of sun in her hands growing until they consumed most of her forearms and brightened the space so much it was almost daylight. Instead of dancing away, Hormin held his ground, letting her draw closer, Theo's bullets bruising and pinching his skin, bracing himself against the gusts of Gwen's wind. A hiss caught Gwen's attention and she glanced at Cat, her skin sizzling beneath Ina's light, and Gwen dashed in front of her. She hoped her shadow would prevent some of the damage, and that Cat had enough human in her to survive the onslaught of sunlight.

Gwen watched the skin on Hormin's face simmer, boil, then melt away as Ina closed the distance between them and raised her hands, ready to clasp them against his head. But just as her palms were about to enclose his skull, he jumped backward then swept the greatsword down in a fiery arc, the light extinguishing in the blink of an eye as the sword cleaved through Ina's forearms, her hands falling to the ground with a horrible thud.

Ina screamed, staring at the cauterized stubs of her arms, and as she fell to her knees with the pain, Hormin hit her in the head with the hilt of his sword. Ina's screams cut off, the silence ringing in Gwen's ears, and Ina crumpled to the ground, still.

"No!" Gwen shouted, but as she raised the wind to slash him,

Rachel released arrow after arrow, stopping Gwen from releasing her magic, despite how useless they were.

Hormin's gaze slid to Rachel. "These are as annoying as mosquito bites." He sprinted to Rachel, whose eyes widened as she stepped backward, releasing arrow after pointless arrow. Gwen shot forward a wall of wind, trying to create a shield for Rachel, but Hormin pushed through it like a knife through butter, and he grabbed the bow out of her hands then pulled her close, burying his fangs in her neck.

Hormin released Rachel, and she slumped to the ground, blood pouring from her neck. Hormin wiped the red from his mouth and flung the moisture to the side, gaze rounding on Gwen and Theo.

Theo shot at him, but her guns produced only a dull click.

Empty.

Theo checked her belt, but there were no more rounds.

Gwen and Theo locked eyes, Gwen putting all her pleading and love into her gaze as she could.

"Please," Gwen begged, a sob choking in her throat. "Get out of here."

Theo glanced at her brother's limp body then back at Gwen. Theo's hands fidgeted at her belt, seeming to look for anything she could weaponize.

But she had nothing left, and they both knew it.

"Please, Theo. Don't let this be for nothing."

Theo's eyes glassed, and her face contorted with pain and rage before she said, "I love you."

"I love you, too."

Gwen's vision blurred, and Theo dashed away, disappearing into the dark of the jungle. Gwen sniffed and blinked away her tears, focusing on Hormin, who stood staring in the direction Theo went.

"Truly heartwarming," Hormin said with a sarcastic sneer, turning his gaze to Gwen. He dropped the sword, the fire going out. "It's just you and me now, witch. Let's see what you can do."

He charged at her, and with a yelp, Gwen pulled power from within and without herself, condensing the air as much as she could into a thick shield in front of her. Hormin collided with it, and she crossed her arms, holding the power tight, pushing against him.

She pulled up all the dregs of her magic that she could find and called to the matching power in the atmosphere. The wind whipped around them as she pulled it in. It rose in ever-cascading swirls until it built into a storm that encompassed them, their hair flipping wildly in the wind. Sweat beaded on Gwen's face, and her finger burned where it met Nikki's ring, but she could not falter.

Hormin laughed in the storm, barely audible in the howling. "You've learned some new tricks." He jumped back from the shield, and they circled each other, assessing. Gwen grew the eye of the storm, folding them in a tornado, hoping to keep Hormin caged, hoping to give Theo a chance to escape.

The rags of Hormin's clothes whipped around him, the mess of his hair swirling around his face, and Gwen raised her hands, ready to unleash the storm on him. She'd spend herself if she had to, if it meant holding him back. She had no hope of beating him, but maybe she could delay him. At best, wound him.

"You could join us," he called over the storm. "The Mother does love an angry, powerful woman."

"I'm only angry because of what you and she have done!"

"We both know that's not true." He gave a slow smile. "You've been angry your whole life, little witch. Being different from your family, unloved by them. But my Mother could be your Mother, too."

Hormin's words stung, and flashes of every abuse and neglect she suffered from her family flittered through her head. How her sisters picked on her, tugged at her hair and called her ugly, tried to see if she'd drown, dumping her in the Columbia and leaving Farrell to come find her. The complete disinterest her family had for her, the blank looks from her mom and dad at each failed attempt to show them a new magic trick. The utter contempt Connell had for her.

"You'd have a place of power and appreciation you never had before."

A vision of her parents, her brother and sisters looking up at her while she sat on a throne of thorns and vines, surrounded by owls and eagles, bloomed in her mind. She would make them bend beneath her power, the wind forcing them to their knees, each vengeful desire blessed by Lilith, who cherished Gwen's abilities and taught her how to grow them, loving like a garden.

But then there were her friends, battered, broken, beaten. Nikki stuck in the Tree forever. Theo, Terrance, and Rachel enslaved with the rest of humanity. If Lilith let them live. Ina, Xander, and everyone else of the Cradle would be killed. She would be little more than a pawn to turn the tide. Hormin's words offered an illusion, a false promise. There would be no power for her, only a different kind of abuse. Despite how good revenge on her family would feel, it wouldn't feel as good as seeing Nikki's face again, as lying in Theo's arms.

"Nah," Gwen said.

"So be it."

He rushed her, dodging her sharp lashes of wind and bracing against the gusts, pushing against her shield with his brute strength. He shouldered and charged, kicked and punched, and his ancient strength vibrated through the shield, shocking Gwen's nerves. She absorbed more and more from the storm around them in order to amplify the shield's strength.

Sweat dripped down her face, and her clothes clung to her skin. Aclima's voice rang in her ears. *"To beat Hormin, you must rely on the powers of the earth, not what resides in yourself. Doing so will drain you before he can be stopped. Live."*

But the only way to keep him at bay was to use what was in herself. To accept her own death.

She panted, the storm around them a small breeze as her strength waned. Hormin clenched his fists together and raised them over his head, bashing them against her shield. The dense air broke like shattering glass, and there was nothing between her and Hormin as he loomed over her.

Hormin grabbed her by the throat, and Gwen called upon the last sliver of her own magic to push air between his hand and her neck. She wrapped her fingers on his forearm and hand, trying to peel off his grasp.

"Such a pity," Hormin said, lifting her off the ground to his eye level. "You could have been great. Instead, you, and those who hold you in their memories, will be swept away to nothing by the sands of time."

Hormin squeezed, and Gwen forced as much air as she could between his hand and her neck, choking, fighting, resisting.

Her mind reeled over the events of the past several months, from Vadasz on her doorstep to her dead flock to Lilith incinerated in Peru. Gwen chopping off Atoc's head, Brienne dying in Alaska and her vial of ashes, Ina's face somber as she handed them over, then finally to Farrell, who she'd left behind, likely dead, on the streets of Alexandria after they tried to end Uase.

Then there was Nikki, her pale and sad face as she grappled with her vampirism.

And finally, her mind filled with Theo. Lovely, loving Theo. Her winning smile, sleek hair, gloriously toned body. Her warm hands and strong arms and gentle voice.

As the edges of her vision went black, an idea clicked in her mind. She grasped Hormin's head with her hands and sacrificed the last of the magic that protected her neck to call to the wind around them.

It swirled to her hands and around Hormin's head. He furrowed a brow. "What are you doing?"

She couldn't answer as his fingers pressed harder, and finally something broke in her throat, blood bubbling up to her mouth and breaths coming in harsher wheezes.

Gwen ignored the pain, the salt and iron on her tongue, and disregarded the dimming of the world around her. She focused on Hormin, on draining every last morsel of energy in her body to funnel as much wind as she could through her hands.

The wind whistled as it moved through the air into fine tunnels and into Hormin's ears, his eyes bulging with the air she forced into his skull. His wide-set gaze grew larger as he understood what she was trying to do, and he shoved her to the ground, kneeling on top of her, wrapping both hands around her throat, squeezing tighter while his eyes bulged from his skull, a wild mania setting in his expression as the milliseconds ticked down to determine who would be the last one breathing.

The moment before blackness overtook her vision, the ring on her finger shattered and surged one last burst of power through her body. Gwen grabbed at that magic and poured it into Hormin's ears, nose, and mouth, the veins in his face and throat throbbing, spittle flying from his lips, vessels in his eyes red and eyeballs nearly popping out of their sockets. In that last push of hope, to see Nikki's face and to feel Theo's lips one more time, the air inside of Hormin's head released, and his skull exploded.

Hair, brain, bone, and blood rained down on Gwen, and his body fell on top of her.

With a wheezing gasp, she tried to suck in air past her broken windpipe, but there was little hope. The black abated to the edges of her vision, but crept back as she lost more and more breath. Gwen pushed his corpse off her, the Tree's leaves swaying overhead. Gasping for air, throat burning, and body drained, she crawled to the Tree, where Cat's body lay limp, blood matted in her hair from where Hormin had knocked her out.

Gwen smeared her hand in Cat's hair, taking some of the coagulated blood. Crawling to the Tree, she wiped her hands, bloodied from both Hormin and Cat, on the Tree.

"Blood of the enemy's son,

Blood of the prisoner's mother,

Please let that make the spell undone.

Please don't require the blood of another."

With each rasped word, the world darkened, and Gwen thought, *"Oh, that rhymed..."* before collapsing into nothingness.

Chapter Eighty-Eight

Nikki felt the moment Hormin died.

She watched the confrontation outside through Gwen's mind, staying to the back of it so as not to distract her. The sound that made it within the Tree was too dim and left too much to her imagination. Once Hormin had dropped her mom's body against her roots, Cat's blood seeping into the ground, she tasted her mom's blood and knew she was still alive. Just barely.

When Hormin exploded, so did his power. The ancient magic within him erupted like a supernova, pushing through the ethers of the world and into the Tree, snapping Nikki back into her body. It was old, angry, hungry power that looked for where to go now that it was no longer contained. It pushed itself through Nikki and down into the roots of the world, pulling Nikki along with it, tumbling down, down, down through the earth on its orange and red veins like fire, until it found its origin.

Lilith.

Nikki blasted into Lilith along with Hormin's essence, and Lilith rocked on her feet with the sudden force of it.

"No," Lilith breathed, clutching her chest and gasping for stolen breath. Lilith's chest drowned with sorrow, then erupted with fury, heart ablaze with newfound power and loss. The last of her first brood. Her most glorious son.

Gone.

Forever.

"No!" Lilith screamed, unleashing her rage in a physical blast that pushed all vegetation around her backward, bending as if in a hurricane. Lilith released another bloodcurdling cry, her denial and resistance shoving Nikki from her body, sending her careening back to the Tree.

Nikki gasped for air, body trembling.

Lilith knew Hormin was dead.

Retribution would be painful, if not swift.

A heap of another body collapsed against her trunk, then slid to the ground, just as a crack of light split through the wood.

Nikki blinked against the harsh brightness, the light of night too much against the ultimate black she was accustomed to.

The fissure widened, wood creaking and vines that bound her limbs loosening. Her eyes adjusted before she was released, and when the Tree dropped her, she stumbled out, flat on her stomach, her feet and hands too numb to catch her.

Blood rushed back into her arms and legs, and she brought herself to a sitting position, sucking in a deep breath of fresh air and taking in her surroundings, the handless body of Ina, the crumpled forms of Terrance and Rachel, the spattered bits of Hormin scattered on the grass.

Gwen, lying motionless beside her, covered in gore.

"No," Nikki rasped, voice hoarse and dry after months of disuse. She took Gwen's head in her lap and patted her cheeks. "Gwen, wake up."

Gwen's head lolled to the side.

"No, Gwen, you're not allowed to leave me. Not now," Nikki cried, tears blurring her vision.

Nikki bit into her skeletal wrist, dusty blood pooling on her pale skin. She opened Gwen's mouth and set her wrist to Gwen's lips, praying to Io that this would work, that even though Gwen was a vampire genetically, whatever made her mortal would sing at the presence of Nikki's blood and bring Gwen back to her.

A sudden pang of hunger clenched Nikki's stomach in an iron fist, and her lips cracked with dehydration. She watched her limbs grow thinner as the needs of a physical body caught up with her, no longer sustained by the Tree.

Her body caved into hunger and thirst, so deep it felt as if her organs were aflame, eating her from the inside out. But even as her body gave in to starvation and dehydration, her vision growing dark and blurry, she kept her blood to Gwen's mouth.

When she collapsed, Gwen's head remained cradled in her arms.

Chapter Eighty-Nine

N ikki woke with a start, wincing as white light blinded her.

Arms wrapped around her, and blackness overtook her vision once again, but it was soft and silky.

"Oh, my darling," Cat sobbed against Nikki, her mom's tears streaking down both their cheeks. "I was so worried you would not wake."

The black of Cat's hair retreated as her mom pulled back, unveiling the world. She lay on a bed in a small, undecorated room. Cat sat on a chair beside her, blocking her view of the room. When Nikki met her mom's eyes, all she could see was her dad's heart crushed in Lilith's hand, the love in his eyes the moment before he turned to dust.

Nikki swallowed the lump in her throat, flashes of falling out of the Tree, of Gwen's limp form, of giving her blood before collapsing. "What happened?" Nikki croaked. "Where's Gwen?"

Cat frowned and stood, pulling aside the blanket that hung by thumb tacks to the ceiling. "We didn't want you two to see each other without warning. And we didn't know who would wake first."

Nikki turned her head. On another bed on the opposite side of the room lay Gwen. She was clean, and Ina sat at the foot of the bed, one stump of a wrist lying in Gwen's open hand.

"Is she alive?" Nikki asked, choking on her heart in her throat.

"She is," Cat said, "but she's in a coma."

"Her wounds seem to be healed," Ina added, voice trembling. "However, we don't know how long her brain was without oxygen."

Nikki swallowed. "Will she wake up?"

"I don't know." Ina used a wrist to smooth Gwen's hair, and took a shaky breath. "I'd give anything to hear her tell me how stupid I've been."

Nikki watched Gwen's chest rise and fall, then turned her head to the ceiling, throwing an arm over her stinging eyes.

Cat rattled out the events of the last few days, her hands roving over Nikki's free hand, through her hair, winding through her fingers, as if she couldn't believe she was real.

Terrance had regained consciousness first, then checked on the others. Rachel was alive, but barely. He got her inside and dressed her wounds, then went out to rouse Ina, who was in shock at the sudden loss of her hands, but otherwise okay, thanks to the cauterized wounds. They moved Gwen, Nikki, and Cat inside, then opened the mangoes to find half were actually fruit, and the other half filled with blood. They fed the blood fruit to Nikki and Cat while feeding themselves and Gwen the real fruit. After a couple days of recovery, Amira, Aclima, Theo, the Lius, and Farrell arrived. Even Alessa and Xander had found their way back to the island.

A brief burst of hope and excitement bloomed in Nikki at the thought of Xander so close, but it popped like a balloon as memories flooded her, from her secrets and lies, to the torture he endured because of her.

There would be no salvaging what they had.

Nikki tried to let go of that pain as Cat told her Farrell was good as new, having fed and healed in Alexandria before meeting with Amira and Aclima.

Uase was dead.

But as they rose from massacring Uase, they saw Vadasz pull Aella from the water and disappear into the night.

As her mom spoke, feeling returned to Nikki's body, and she wriggled her toes, her fingers, senses once again sharpening.

Everything was too bright, her mom's voice too loud, hearing every shake and inhalation of breath. So uneven, and disruptive, compared to the breath of the world. Of the forests. The cotton bedding and clothes scratched at her skin, whereas the rustle of leaves and brush of the wind had been gentle and soothing.

Though she knew her body was made of countless bacteria and microbes, it was nothing compared to the wealth of life she'd felt when she was the forest, floating through the trees, through the breeze. When she heard the crawl of mammals and the call of the birds, the scuttle of insects, the lull of rain and touch of sunlight on leaves.

The sorrow in her throat broke, tears spilling down her face.

Everything was broken.

She was nothing, no one.

And so very, very small.

"No, you are not," Io whispered.

Nikki's heart lifted at Io's voice, at the warm presence of Them in her mind. She thought that once she was out of the Tree she wouldn't be able to talk to Io anymore. That the only thoughts she'd hear would be her own miserable ones. Knowing Io chose to stay connected with her made her feel loved, but that joy burst within the blink of an eye. Even though she was still connected to Io, she had lost her connection to everything else. And the echo of Io's voice reminded Nikki of what was missing. Of how lonely it was to be a singular entity.

The pain twisted in Nikki, rising from her core, burning in her chest and throat, turning her moan into a wail, and she cried for the hollowness within her. Not just the absence of the forest, but for her dad, Gwen, her mom, Xander, and Ina.

Cat folded into Nikki, her own sorrow spilling over. While they held each other and wept, Cat whispered soothing promises that Nikki did not believe.

Epilogue

X ANDER SAT at the top of the hill beneath the Tree, looking into the sunset.

Shame ate his guts, devouring him from the inside out. While his friends and mom fought, he had run. Yes, he'd run forward and tried to fight first, but when he realized how outmatched he was, he didn't hold his ground like the others did. He took advantage of Alessa's protection and did not fight them when they pulled him away.

He took the opportunity to run.

Like a coward.

Now his mom was maimed and Gwen in a coma, and Nikki...he didn't want to think about her yet. He hadn't gone to look at her, both terrified and excited at the thought of her looking at him again with her eyes as dark as the new moon.

He didn't know what he would say to her. Even worse, he didn't know what she would say to him.

And he hated himself for being so tied up in thoughts of her when humanity dangled at the edge of slavery.

"You worry about much, son of Adam," Senoy said from his left.

"We could ease the pain, if you let us." Sansenoy said from his right.

The angels stepped around the Tree beside him, having arrived earlier that day. They said Io commanded them not to seek retribution at the slaughter of their sibling, but with Lilith's violent advancements, they were released from that binding. While free to avenge their sibling, they were not to use their divine wrath on Lilith directly, but instead help humanity find their own path to survival.

"I'll be fine," Xander spat, harsher than he intended. "Thanks, though."

They walked in front of him, taking in the purpling sunset over the sea. They were at least six and a half feet tall, with marbled skin veined with streaks of white, silver, and blue. Their hair flowed in similar colors, ever-changing, fading into the air. Their wings were feathery, and tucked close to their bodies.

They stood like silent sentinels, and Xander's shoulders tensed, just wanting some peace and quiet, for people to, just this once, treat him like a person, and not hover around him like he was nothing more than a prized pet, or some precious antique.

"You wish to be alone," Sansenoy said, distinguishable from Senoy by the half-knot on top of his head, whereas Senoy's hair was unbound.

Before Xander could respond, the angels disappeared in a blink of gold, off to wherever angels spent their time.

Xander exhaled and ran a hand through his hair, wondering how his dad and siblings were doing, hoping they were safe and maybe even having fun. As the horizon devoured the sun and night draped over him, he tried not to think of what was ahead of them, instead pulling forward memories from when Ish and Zee were younger. Of the joyful nonsense they got up to.

Imagining Ish's wild, grinning face after he experienced his first roller coaster, Xander was startled when Hormin's hand grabbed his shoulder. He flinched, covering his head as he braced for the blow –

"I'm sorry," a quiet but firm voice said behind him. "I didn't mean to startle you."

Xander's rampaging heart settled and he sucked in a few deep breaths.

Hormin was dead.

He'd never see, hear, or feel him again.

Xander looked over his shoulder, and there she was, on her feet and appearing no different from the last time he saw her, except for the look in her eyes.

Distant. Sorrowful. Aged.

"Nikki," he breathed, and he hated how wounded he sounded.

The Tree behind them seemed to curve toward her, leaves bending down to touch her. With the Tree bowing to her and the billions of stars overhead, she looked every bit the goddess he once thought.

"May I join you?" she asked, and the doubt in her voice cracked his heart enough to nod.

She settled in beside him, legs crossed beneath her. He took in her profile, the soft curves of her moon-white face, the pink bow of her mouth, and he couldn't deny the lift in his being at sitting beside her again.

But his heart was still a tangle, and it burned when he thought of all the secrets and lies that led them to this moment, even if so much of it was out of her control.

He just felt so stupid for not seeing the truth sooner, for ignoring every single red flag.

It had led to him being used and abused. He knew she had not done those things, but her actions, and her lack of them, had led him down this path.

"Xander, I'm sorry–"

"I can't do this right now, Nikki." He pulled the hair tight away from his face, the sourness of self-loathing curdling in his stomach as he spoke with more acidity than he meant to. He calmed his voice and said, "I'm sorry, I just can't. I've missed you, and I want nothing more than to hold you, but I'm so goddamn mad at you, I can barely even look at you."

Nikki flinched and swallowed, turning her gaze from him to the dark sea beyond. "I understand."

He curled his fists, thinking, *That's it? That's all she has to say?* But really, what was she supposed to say when he just shut her down like that?

He groaned at the mess of their relationship. At the futility of trying to figure it out when they might not even live to have one. "I'm sorry, but I don't see the point of getting into it right now. Why should we, when I can't even see how we get out of this alive?"

"We've gotten this far."

"No, *we* haven't. Everyone around us has. But none of us are heroes. We're just the unlucky people who drew the short straw."

Nikki thought for a second. "That's not entirely true. You and me, maybe we're not heroes. But everyone else is. Gwen, your mom, Terrance, the Lius...all of them have shown so much bravery, strength, and sacrifice. You can't say they're not heroes. And we're not just pawns on the board, Xander. We're in play. By the end of this, by the time we go home, we'll be heroes, too."

Xander didn't believe her, but he wanted to, so he didn't argue. Instead, he looked at Nikki, missing the early days of the library, of holding her in his arms, while she stared into the night as if whatever she was missing could be found in the horizon.

Thank you for reading!

I hope you enjoyed reading *Blood of the Cradle* as much as I did writing it. If so, please hop online when you have a minute and leave an honest rating/review. It really helps us indie authors!

Keep reading for a sneak peek of book 3 in the series, *Cold of the Dawn.*

Cold of the Dawn

PROLOGUE

POWER SURGES across the ether as my son's life force scatters across the world, and grief rips through me like snow turns into a blizzard into an avalanche.

Woe is a spear of darkness, and I no longer know where vengeance ends and sorrow begins.

Gone is the last of those who first called me mother. And I—

I am the rupturing fault line.

The earthquake that will break the world.

My most treasured boy ... he shone brightest of his brood.

He sprinted where others crawled.

Relished his bloodlust where others cowered.

From the beginning, he loved what he was. What *we* were. And he understood what the world owed us.

What *They* owed us.

Hormin's loyalty put the ocean's tidal dependence on the moon to shame. Now he is gone, and I am unanchored. Unmoored.

His spirit is free, and gore will drown my enemies like a monsoon fueled landslide consumes forests.

They thought they could cripple me, defeat me.

But arrogance leads to blindness.

They will all suffer for what they took from me.

They do not yet know the true meaning of "scorched earth."

Through the cunning of my children, we will destroy Their creations.

Through the power of my children, we will shatter the era of humanity.

A new twilight will break, free of the deceivers, the shields, and the false saints who oppressed us.

The time for my progeny, for *me*, to create a blood-filled world is upon us.

No one will take from me ever again.

They forget — the world was *mine* first.

Cold of the Dawn

CHAPTER ONE

NIKKI TRAVERSED THE AMAZONIAN RAINFOREST. Or she pretended to. Eyes closed, she imagined the brush of air on her skin was the dapple of sunlight on overstory leaves. The shuffle of footsteps the scuttle of insects on the forest floor. The soft whispers nothing more than distant animal calls.

But her fleshy body could not recall these sensations.

There was the press of the bed on her spine, the pillow under her head. Worst of all, the gnawing hunger, yearning for blood satiation. All reminding her of her meaty form. Of what she no longer was. What she no longer had.

Heaving a defeated sigh and wishing it was the expelling of gas during photosynthesis rather than the squeeze of air from her lungs, she opened her eyes.

"How did Lilith give that up?" she asked Io, staring at the wooden slats in the ceiling.

"She never wanted it."

"I didn't either."

"You did not spend millennia dreaming of revenge, either. The peace within you, which does not exist in Lilith, let you attach to the beauty of the world."

Nikki hummed and sat up in bed, fighting against the anchor in her chest that begged her to stay down.

"You're awake!" her mother, Cat, exclaimed, rushing from the adjacent room to her bedside before Nikki had a second to blink. She wrapped one pale hand over Nikki's, the other tucking a loose strand of black hair behind her ear.

It was strange, the short hair that tickled her neck. She couldn't remember a time in her life when it wasn't long. But thanks to Lilith shearing her hair before shoving her in the Tree, it now fell in jagged curtains that did not reach her shoulders.

"What do you need, my darling?" Cat asked, dark eyes roving over Nikki's face.

Her skin crawled at the intensity of her mother's expression, the desperation in her voice, the neediness in her touch. It was too much, too soon. It couldn't have been more than a few days since she was released from the Tree, and she hadn't processed everything that had happened. The transition from being in the forests of the world to being back in a singular form. The loss of Gwen, comatose in the bed beside her.

The last thing she wanted was to be coddled, but the old-fashioned training her parents instilled in her told her to bite her tongue, to be tactful. To be respectful and let her elders take care of her.

But she was tired of hiding herself. Of keeping secrets. How much of her life had she spent keeping her thoughts and feelings suppressed? Then those months physically trapped in the Tree... No, she had been trapped long enough.

"Mom, please," Nikki breathed, pulling her hand out from under Cat's. "I need some space. I'm disoriented after the last couple months. I need time to think. To heal."

Cat leaned back, expression shuttering closed and fists tightening in her clothes. "You do not have to heal alone. I can help you. Take care of you. I am your mother, after all. I am competent in this regard. I am sure you must be hungry; you're still barely more than skin and bone. I will go get you some blood fruit."

"Mom, no, please just stop. I don't need to be fussed over. I'm not a baby anymore. I can take care of myself in my own way, in my own time."

"You may not be a baby but are you still *my* baby. I cannot help my compulsion to take care of you. Let me do so. Please. Tell me what you need."

Nikki heaved out a large sigh and said through gritted teeth, "I already told you, but you didn't listen. I need space. I don't need your hovering."

"Hovering? I am ensuring you are cared for." Tears sprang in her mom's eyes. "I was so worried for you. I thought you were lost to me forever."

The moisture in her mom's eyes made Nikki's stomach curdle. How was it fair that on top of everything else she needed to sort through, she now had to burden guilt? Irritation flared in her chest, and she blurted, "I can't take care of your feelings right now! I can't begin to tell you the depths of what I'm feeling, not to mention my best friend is literally in a coma right beside me!"

They glanced at Gwen's bed, where she still lay with eyes closed, her chest rising in shallow, steady breaths. Nikki noticed for the first time that Aclima was beside Gwen's bed, and her cheeks heated with shame at the outburst.

Aclima must have felt their eyes on her, because she turned her head and said, "Do not mind me."

Nikki pushed her knuckles against her eyes, begging the darkness to calm her.

She heard her mother stand, the bedside chair scratching against the floor. "Your whole life, you have pushed me away. What have I ever done to deserve your ire? All I've ever done was love you."

Nikki spat out a bitter laugh. "Oh, is that all? Was it love when you refused to listen to me? When I told you I didn't want this life? And instead of helping me find ways of acceptance, you forced your religion down my throat? Forced me to drink blood on your terms rather than mine? Forced me to participate in your ridiculous rituals. To drink blood and leaves and thank you for it? No, you never heard me. You just kept forcing down what you thought was right for me, regardless of what I said. And that's exactly what you're doing now. Instead of listening to me when I say I need space, when I say I cannot burden your feelings right now, you stand here and bury me deeper in them. All while adding in a guilt trip. You claim to be my mother, and yet here I am, giving you a lesson in how not to be so childish."

Cat's chin trembled, and Nikki looked away, fighting against the pit of shame in her stomach. How much of her life was spent feeling guilty? For being a bad friend, a bad daughter? For simply existing as a vampire? She couldn't take it anymore.

Io, she missed the trees.

"I see," her mom said. "If your father were here, he'd be ashamed of how you're speaking to me."

The air vacuumed out of Nikki's chest. "You're wrong. If he were here, he'd tell you to leave me alone." She swung her legs off the bed and stared at the floor. "In any case, he isn't here, so it doesn't matter."

Terrible silence settled over them as Nikki stared at her feet. She heard her mother sniffle and rummage in her pocket.

Cat laid an object on the bed beside her and said, "So much of him was carried away on the breeze. What I could salvage is split between us." She hesitated, waiting for Nikki to respond.

But Nikki kept her gaze fixed on her toes until her mom walked out of the room with a defeated sigh. She turned her head to the item Cat had placed on the sheets, and a lump formed in her throat. It was a small vial, half empty with ashes.

Her dad.

She clutched it tight in her hands and held it against her chest, eyes burning. Io's presence hummed in her mind, a gentle yet reprimanding tune.

What a mess her and her mom were without her dad. He was always the mediator. The one who knew how to bridge their differences and smooth out their similarities. She'd give anything to have him here. To tell her everything would be okay. To make her mom laugh again. And more than anything, she wished she could tell him she was sorry. That she didn't mean it when she said she was disappointed in him. She wished she could tell him about how she traveled the forest, he'd find it fascinating.

Nikki hoped that wherever he was now, if he was more than just the ashes in her fist, he experienced something as beautiful and unbelievable as she did, if not more so.

Plucking up her courage, she stumbled to stand next to Gwen's bed. Her legs still shook as if they had forgotten how to walk after all that time trapped. She hadn't spoken to Aclima much yet, nothing more than brief hellos when she entered the room. But Aclima came every night and channeled healing into Gwen's prone form as much as she could.

Aclima's magic was amazing to behold. When healing, she called power from the ground, soft tendrils of white and gold winding their way through the floorboards up her legs, around her torso, down her arms and into her hands, where she pooled it around Gwen's head.

"Any progress?" Nikki asked.

Aclima stared at her with milky white eyes, and Nikki fought to maintain her unnerving gaze. It was as if her pale eyes were a reflection of yourself, and the longer you stared, the more you saw your true self.

Nikki couldn't stomach it.

"No, yet she remains stable," Aclima responded, breaking her gaze. "Hope remains."

"Good," she said, placing a bracing hand on the headboard to keep herself upright. Gwen's hair fanned on the pillow, grease stains running through it from how many fingers had lovingly brushed her hair back.

So many people were lost without her.

The glow of Aclima's magic faded and she stood, leaning on her staff. Nikki felt Aclima's eyes on her and she met that cold gaze, summoning Gwen's spirit and lifting her chin. Aclima continued to stare, and Nikki's confidence wavered. Why was she looking at her like that?

"What?" she snapped, harsher than she meant to.

Aclima tilted her head like a curious crow. "I am merely examining the creature who led my nephew and protégé down this dark path."

"Led? I didn't mean for this to happen."

"Yet you let it. You let Xander walk into Lilith's trap. You let Gwen sacrifice herself for your freedom."

Nikki reeled. "First, I didn't know there was a trap. I tried to protect him. And second, if you knew Gwen at all, you'd know there's no letting her do anything. She does as she wants."

"And if you knew her at all," Aclima said, slamming her staff on the ground as she stepped into Nikki's face, "you would know she considers the words of others. You could have discussed a different path. One that would not have led to this."

"What could I have possibly done?" Nikki shouted. The hateful self-critic within her said same thing, but she couldn't swallow it as truth. She tried her best. She would have done anything to prevent this from happening. She just wasn't good enough. "How can you possibly blame me for this? It's Lilith's fault, not mine."

"Many paths led to this destination. Not only Lillith's." Aclima's gaze bore into Nikki, her moon white eyes shining like flashlights into her soul. "I see you, Nicoletta Neves Silva, born vampire of the Americas, and I find you lacking." She tapped her staff on the floor one last time as she turned her back on Nikki.

"Lacking what?" Nikki called after her.

Aclima did not pause, did not look back, as she left the room.

Nikki stared at the empty space where she had stood, then plopped into the chair besides Gwen's bed. With shaking hands, she took Gwen's limp arm and rested her cheek in her palm. Gwen's hand was still warm, her pulse a delicate bird in her veins.

"Please, wake up. I can't do this without you."

Gwen did not stir.

Cold of the Dawn

CHAPTER TWO

Xander sat at the edge of the grass that was burned in the shape of Hormin's body. Patches of charred spots scattered the clearing where his skull and brain matter landed when Gwen exploded his head. It took hours for him to disintegrate, a testament to not only the power he inherited from Lilith, but the humanity he had from whatever poor ancient man sired him.

From a distance, Xander had watched his corpse flake away, bit by bit, in the sun, waiting for Hormin to rise again. But he did not. The body he once weaponized turned to ash before his eyes. During the time it took for him to become no more than the dust of the earth, the others debated what to do with his body. But by the time they decided to move it, it was already gone, leaving the ground burned in the shape of his silhouette.

Now Xander brushed a hand over the line between growing grass and bare, scorched earth. Fingertips on the blades of grass, he caught glimmers in the green. He moved the blades, and with a sinking feeling, picked up the broken pieces of the ring he bought for Nikki on her birthday all those months ago. The metal fractured into three pieces, the once vibrant blue gem studded with gold and whirls of white, was now punctured and dull. What an apt metaphor for his relationship with her. He stared at the pieces in his palm, tempted to let them slip back to the ground and be forgotten with time, but he could not flip his hand. Instead, Xander wrapped his hand around the cold metal and, after a beat, put the pieces into his pocket, where the stone sat like a boulder.

Xander roved his hand over the incinerated ground, and as his skin moved to where Hormin once lay, a flash of Hormin's fist ramming into his stomach crossed his mind. The punch had struck him with such force he crashed against the tree behind him, smacking the back of his head on the gnarled bark. The breath left his body as if the hit just landed, sternum constricting from the sudden lack of oxygen. His lungs burned with such pain he was certain he would never breathe again, and he wheezed from the effort, but Hormin's footsteps approached and—

"Breathe, son of Adam," Senoy said. The angel loomed beside him, marbled skin with ever-shifting, glowing lines of white, silver, and blue illuminating the space around Xander.

He blinked, and the memory faded.

Right. Hormin was dead, killed by Gwen in some miracle. He would never hurt him or anyone else ever again.

Heart rate settling, Xander took a deep breath to brace him in this reality. Senoy and Sansenoy, distinguishable only by Sansenoy's top knot, stood on either side of him, his ever, overprotective guardians.

"You don't need to show up every time I feel something. I managed well enough on my own before."

"That was more than just a feeling, Alexander. You ceased breathing," Sansenoy replied.

"I was short of breath. It happens. I wouldn't have died," Xander said, standing and brushing the dirt from his hands on his pant leg. "Don't you two have anything better to do than hover over me? I get that enough from my mom and the Cradle."

The angels stared at him as if they were machines with commands that did not compute.

Xander groaned. "I'm fine. I release you from my side."

They nodded, and in a blazing comet of bright white light flecked with all colors, they disappeared into the sky.

He sighed, relieved of their presence. Whenever they showed up, it felt as if he was supposed to be doing something. Being a leader of man. A warrior against Lilith's armies. But he didn't feel anything special was within him, and the expectations simply felt like a burden. It took a few days for him to figure out how easy it was to dismiss them using that command, but it didn't stop them from showing up whenever they felt like it. He assumed they were never that far, waiting for his next order.

Why was he the one in charge of them? It didn't make sense. There were plenty of people around him who were much more qualified for that task. His mom, Aclima, hell, even Nikki, with how she was connected to Io. He was just a boy ripped from his life—and almost stripped of it—who wanted to go back to his world of long runs in the sun and curing animals of their ailments.

He turned his face toward the sky, the day bright and beautiful in a way it shouldn't be given the darkness of everything around them. On one side, there was Hormin's imprint, a reminder of death, pain, and horror. Off to the side lay Hormin's greatsword, dull and flameless. No one had been able to move it, despite trying. The strongest of them—Terrance, Farrell, and the Lius—had all tried to pick it up but described it as a block of concrete. They couldn't even lift it an inch. They assumed some enchantment was on it, but what it was eluded them. So there the sword lay, abandoned in the grass.

Behind him was the Tree, a prison, a reminder of Lilith and that terrible night when he had to watch the bark swallow Nikki whole, her screams dying as it trapped her moments after Lilith ripped her dad's heart from his chest.

There was the small, windowless house where Nikki rested and Gwen lay comatose. Where everyone else tended their mental and physical wounds. Where Theo was spinning out in a way he'd never seen before, seeming angry at everyone and everything. Her only respite was in training with the Lius until she was so exhausted she fell into a sleep almost as deep as Gwen's coma.

And before him, down the hill, was the village of human prisoners. No one had ventured down there since regrouping at the Tree, instead sidling down the other side of the island to gather resources. They didn't know what awaited them in the village, if their masters were back, if an ambush was planned. No one came to talk to them though, and they were in no mood to press their luck after fighting Hormin. When Amira, their boat captain from Faiyum, joined them once again, she traversed the island during the day and didn't see anyone. But that didn't mean the village was abandoned.

He looked at the tiny building everyone crammed themselves into, sleeping on blankets on the floor, packed liked sardines. There were only two beds, and Gwen and Nikki got them.

Every time he looked in that direction, he sensed Nikki like a magnet. A pull from his chest toward wherever she was, and it took all his effort not to follow the lure. They hadn't spoken since that night under the Tree when he shut down her attempts at talking. What was there to even say?

I love you? I miss you?

How could you look me in the eye and hide so many things from me?

Xander clenched his jaw and rejected the tug Nikki had on him, turning his back on the house and following a trail the Lius made down the back of the island to a rocky outcrop overlooking the sea and numerous islands beyond.

His mom sat at the outcrop, wisps of dark, curly hair loosening from her braid and catching in the gentle breeze. She pushed a wrist against a strand, trying to get it out of her face, but without fingers, she struggled to have it catch, and the hairs flew back in her face.

Ina spent most of her time alone now. When she was with others, Xander saw her try to put on a brave face but could see the pain and anger writhing underneath. All the anger he had held at his mom for keeping secrets from him, from Dad, when they only met because she was sent to guard him, dissipated the first moment he saw the singed wounds on her forearm where Hormin sliced off her hands. One look at the maimed arms that now missed the hands that fed him, cleaned his wounds, held him when he was scared, wiped away his tears, combed his hair ... the pain and anger didn't matter anymore. She was his mom, and of course she loved him and his dad. He never should have accused her of otherwise. Just because she was sent to watch Arthur didn't mean she had to marry him and have his kids. It was just a lucky circumstance for them.

Or unlucky, considering her current condition.

But why didn't the same logic apply to Nikki? If she was only trying to protect him, she could have friend zoned him. Or used Gwen's flock to spy on him. She didn't have to date him to keep an eye on him, so of course their relationship was real. Or had been. So why couldn't he get rid of his anger at Nikki for keeping secrets like he could his mom?

Parents were supposed to protect you. To keep the monsters under your bed at bay. But your partner shouldn't treat you like an inferior person. They should lift up the covers and face the dark with you, hand in hand.

Their second day on the island together, him and his mom went on a walk just the two of them, looking for a place to bury her hands. It was the first time since his rescue in Peru that being around his mom didn't feel strained. They finally had a real conversation, an honest one, about their past. Until that talk, the woman who had been next to him for months had seemed like a stranger, a war-bent hero.

It was good to have his mom back.

As Xander covered her severed hands with dirt, flashes of their significance in his life strobing in his mind, so too was his rage smothered. He sat with her while they mourned in silence until she was ready to say goodbye to herself.

"Hey, Mom," Xander said as he approached his mom on the outcrop, not wanting to startle her. He sat beside her on the ledge, legs dangling.

"Hi, sweetheart," Ina replied with a closed lipped smile that did not reach her eyes.

Xander plucked the loose hair billowing in her face and tucked it behind her ear.

"Thank you," she said, returning her gaze to the sea.

"Of course. What are you up to?"

"Practicing," Ina replied, lifting her arms so that her wrists pointed upward. Her brow furrowed, and faint traces of sunlight glowed in her arms, traveling upward, but the light faded as it reached the end of her body. "I don't understand why I cannot summon the sun outside of myself anymore. They were just hands. The principle of this should be the same. So why can't I do it?"

Ina lowered her arms and looked down at the steep drop below them.

"I'm sorry, Mom. But I'm sure you'll figure it out."

"I'm not, but thank you for saying that." Ina leaned her head against his shoulder.

He rested his cheek on top of hers, wanting to say something more encouraging. The Xander of last year was everyone's cheerleader, and he still had that urge to say they could do anything. That they'd win if they put their minds to it. That everything would turn out for the best. That they'd all make it out alive.

But his mouth wouldn't open for those thoughts. He was no longer that person. He no longer believed everything would be okay, and he was never a liar.

"What do we do now?" he asked instead.

"I don't know. I tried so hard over the last few months to keep our resistance organized and moving forward. Now that we're here, that we got Nikki out of the Tree and hopefully made Lilith mortal, I don't know what the next move is. As much as she got under my skin, I needed Gwen to bounce ideas off. She was the only one who'd push back." His mom's voice broke at the end, and he put a reassuring arm around her shoulders, giving it a squeeze. Ina sniffled and steadied her breath before continuing. "There's a leadership void, now. Half of the group looked to Gwen, and half looked to me. But Gwen is gone. And I'm so tired, sweetheart."

"I know, Mom," he whispered. He wanted to say "we'll figure it out" but again, the words wouldn't form.

"I suppose we all are. And we'll just have to find a way."

Xander nodded, and his mind spiraled into different pathways, all the outcomes he could fathom. His mom was right. They would have to find a way to rally themselves to fight again. To somehow move through their losses when the island offered a beautiful illusion of tranquility.

He wished this moment could stretch into eternity, with the sea breeze filling his nose, the sky and water the most dazzling blues he'd ever seen, the sun beating down warm daylight, peace between he and his mom, and the sense of safety around them.

But he knew the moment would end too soon, so instead he tried to bottle it as best he could to relive again in darker days.

* * *

Keep reading *Cold of the Dawn* on Amazon!

Also by Morgan Vayle

The Dust of the Earth Series

Dust of the Earth

Blood of the Cradle

Cold of the Dawn

The Withering Wood

About the Author

Morgan lives in the Pacific Northwest with her husband and two needy cats. She's been writing since she first learned how to hold a pencil and string words together. When not day dreaming of fantasy worlds, she can be found reading or frolicking among the wildflowers.